SIGN OF MISFORTUNE

PUBLISHED BY
ALLERTON PRESS, INC. / 150 FIFTH AVENUE / NEW YORK, NY 10011

SIGN OF MISFORTUNE

_____

VASIL BYKOV

Translated from the Russian by Alan Myers

Library of Congress Cataloging-in-Publication Data

Bykaŭ, Vasil', 1924–
   [Znak biady. English]
   Sign of misfortune / Vasil Bykov : translator, Alan Myers.
      p.   cm.
   Translation of: Znak biady.
   ISBN 0-89864-049-0
   I. Title.
PG2835.2.B9Z413 1990   89-18163
891.73'44--dc20   CIP

Introduction

Since the early 1960s leading Soviet prose writer Vasil' Bykaw (in Russian Bykov; born 1924) has been one of the most popular and widely respected authors not only of his native Byelorussia but throughout the Soviet Union. The high regard and affection in which he is held derive in part from the psychologically subtle and thematically absorbing nature of his fiction, but also from the immense consistency of his moral stance and his unwavering fight against the residual forces of Stalinist reaction and oppression. In the new conditions of *glasnost'* and *perestroika* Bykaw has played an increasingly publicist, even political, role, acting as a leader of the campaign to expose Stalin's war crimes and a leader of the Byelorussian Popular Front which, like similar movements in the Baltic and other parts of the Soviet Union, seeks to restore prestige and currency to a long neglected and repressed national language as well as to win for the country a greater measure of democratic independence. This stand has led to his being, on the one hand, denounced as an ambitious demagogue (a manifestly absurd charge in the eyes of anyone who has met this most modest of writers) and, on the other, acclaimed as the conscience of the Byelorussian people. Fortunately, he has managed to avoid the danger of writers who become entirely absorbed by public life, and his creative writing proceeds with undiminished vigour, as can be seen from such recent novels as *Sign of Misfortune* (*Znak biady* [in Russian *Znak bedy*], 1982) and *The Quarry*, (*Kar'er*, 1986).

From the very beginning of his career, and with few departures since, Bykaw has set his novels in wartime. However, rather than painting the broad and falsely heroic scenes so characteristic of much Soviet war fiction, he has instead concentrated on the depiction of the acute psychological and moral problems of young soldiers in situations of extreme tension, at moments of mental and physical crisis. Such features have led some observers, including the distinguished film director Larysa Shepit'ko, to perceive affinities between Bykaw and Dostoevskii; on the other hand, his moral fortitude provoked at least one perceptive commentator in the sixties to associate his name with that of Solzhenitsyn. A particular watershed was the novel *The Dead Feel No Pain* (*Miortvym ne balits'* [Russian *Mertvym ne bol'no*], 1965), for two decades suppressed on account of its unmistakable linking of Stalinist behavior in wartime with the mentality of bureaucrats and political apparatchiks in peacetime. It was also at this time that Bykaw, the only non-Party Byelorussian writer of any prominence in his generation, had the windows of his modest apartment in Hrodna broken by officially-inspired hooligans.

Bykaw has not, however, been bowed by such despicable attempts at intimidation, and after a somewhat subdued period at the height of Brezhnev's reign (a time when many major Soviet writers were driven to silence or emigration), he has found renewed creative strength, and in *Sign of Misfortune* produced a gripping and psychologically truthful story that not only recreates the horror of war through the eyes of small, insignificant peasant characters, but sets the Soviet wartime experience in its proper historical context; in the case of the old couple Piatrok and Stepanida, the trauma without which their situation and actions cannot be fully understood was Stalin's collectivization of agriculture in the early thirties, a topic never neglected by unscrupulous hack writers, but rarely, if ever, portrayed with such honest realism. It was precisely these parts of the book, presented as flashbacks, that made the otherwise rather unremarkable screen version of this novel into a widely discussed movie.

It would be wrong to overstress the political nature of Bykaw's writing, for as well as being a brave and outspoken citizen he is also a first-class story-teller whose concise, at times lapidary, narrative manner and relative lack of external drama or melodrama serve to intensify the acute tension that is a feature of almost all his fiction. In dialogue, characterization, lexical richness, syntax and plot control Byelorussia's leading living writer remains a master without peer.

Hitherto it has been a matter of some puzzlement to Bykaw's fellow-countrymen that his works have not found greater resonance in the West, but one obvious explanation is the lack of good translations into Western languages. Bykaw has not, in fact, been lucky with translators. In the early sixties novels like *The Third Flare* (*Tretsiaia raketa*, 1961) and *Alpine Ballad* (*Alpiiskaia balada*, 1963) were distorted and bowdlerized by the Soviet translators (particularly where Bykaw's heroes referred to their national identity) when putting the Byelorussian originals into Russian. To avoid such treatment Bykaw began before long to translate his own works into Russian soon after their first appearance in Byelorussian. Most Western translations have been made from the author's Russian versions and, regrettably, have more often than not failed to indicate the author's Byelorussian nationality; apart from this, the English-language translations have tended to be inaccurate. Thus, it gives cause for great satisfaction that in the present version of *Sign of Misfortune* Bykaw is served by a distinguished translator, well known for his sensitive versions of modern poetry. There is every reason to hope that this book will bring the name of Vasil' Bykaw before a new and appreciative audience.

Arnold McMillin
University of London

Translator's Note

The number of native Belorussian words in the Russian text presents a problem for anyone rendering the work into English. To fulfil his duty to both author and reader, the translator must be accurate without being pedantic; at the same time he must try to convey some of that sense of location which was Bykaw's aim in using the words in the first place.

To employ any definite dialect, however, whether English or American, would subvert Bykaw's manifest intentions. He is concerned, like Valentin Rasputin in his Siberian stories, to confer dignity and universality upon his humble characters, partly through the speech they employ. In addition, lacking Rasputin's mighty immemorial forest to act as a potent symbol of continuity and integrity, Bykaw emphasizes the passage of the seasons, and festivals, the recurrent farm tasks and, by constant repetition, the farm buildings themselves and their environs. Gradually, the reader becomes intensely aware of the peasant farmers' bond with the land, to which Bykaw adds a Christian sanction with the name Golgotha and the bitter symbol of the cross. The heart of the novel lies in the powerful tension between this link with the earth and the gross disruption of it by totalitarian forces from within and without.

Bykaw had the problem of seeing everything through the eyes of two uneducated illiterate peasants, but he avoids the seductive error of making them too embarrassingly articulate. Their speech is terse, restrained and oddly impressive. They are given an appropriately richer interior monologue on the other hand, to enable them to comment on events and to convey the author's views. This device does occasionally creak, however, and we encounter passages of strained repetition or an occasional slip into the wrong intellectual register. These internal monologues are couched in straightforward language, and so avoid the quaintness and marginalizing effect of dialect.

Intriguingly, this affects the content of the novel as well as the style. Stepanida is able to avoid confronting large-scale political events by accepting that others are cleverer than she is. When she does begin to question, it is on the personal level, where she feels she can cope. But it is this same 'ignorance' which enables her to escape the moral corruption which affects the more sophisticated and opportunist characters. The irony of the impressive scene where the mighty of the land are marooned in Stepanida's hut and forced to confront the results of their policies, with the pendant scene of Petroc's visit to Minsk, would be impossible to bring off without the saintly simplicity and moral constancy of the two main characters.

Alan Myers

SIGN OF MISFORTUNE

People and time had left little of what had once been an ample and
extensive farm estate. Remains could be seen here and there peeping out
on the surface; a foundation corner-stone, a sunken mound of bricks and
two stone steps close by the former entrance. These threshold blocks rested
in the same position as they had many years before and tiny ginger-colored
ants, electing to make their dwelling somewhere in the vicinity, went about
their business across the lower step, sunk deep in the earth. The alder
thickets from the gully now hemmed in the fields and came up tight against
the farmyard; where the boiler-house had been, a dense clump of wild roses
spread majestically amid the encircling docks, nettles and raspberry bushes.
Nothing was left of the well, the wooden framework had rotted away or
perhaps had been destroyed; the water, no longer needed, had dried up and
vanished into the bowels of the earth. Where a hut had once stood, a prickly
wild pear straggled above the weeds - an obscene offshoot from the pears
once cultivated here, or perhaps a chance self-seeding carried in by the
woodland birds.

From the main road there was little to indicate there had ever been a
farmstead here, apart from one of a pair of limes which had adorned the
gateway. There was no sign at all of the other tree, and even the survivor
presented a pitiable spectacle: scorched and lopsided, its stout ugly trunk
was rotted into a crooked gaping hollow. Somehow it managed to maintain
a number of mighty branches, but birds flying in from the forest never
alighted for some reason, preferring a mature alder nearby. Perhaps the
crows remembered something, or perhaps their ancient instinct sensed an
evil spirit in the deformed tree, a mark of some catastrophe long ago. This
fateful mark lay upon everything here: on the decayed remains of the
farmstead, on the abundant weeds and raspberries running wild, on the
eglantine, complacent in its thorn defenses, even on the twisted wild pear.
Only a slender young rowan sapling, just putting out its first few leaves amid
the rampant grasses of the farmyard appeared, in its daring vulnerability, to

be a visitor from another world, an incarnation of hope, of a life that was totally other.

It seemed everything else here belonged to a past that was subject to decay and oblivion.

Everything, that is, apart from human memory, all-encompassing and independent of time, endowed from everlasting with the capacity to turn the past into the present, and link the present with the future. . .

1

Patiently insatiable, the cow was cropping the dew-damp grass, moving leisurely as always along her accustomed route: down by the main road, then the ditch, overgrown with tall weeds, past the embankment, then across the hollow with its smooth boulder in the shape of a fattened pig and onwards to the skirts of the woodland which encircled the farm and its hillock in a wide arc. Stepanida knew that once it reached the trees the cow would turn in the direction of Sheep Valley; she'd have to keep an eye on it among the alders in case it slipped off somewhere out of sight. Bobovka was quick on her feet for a cow and although she was piebald, white on black, once she started straying, it meant a run after her through the thickets. For the moment, however, there was nowhere for her to go, just the low embankment and the bare potato field, Stepanida could sit in peace, resting her hip against the boulder's rounded flank. She settled her bare feet more firmly on the earth, glancing occasionally at Bobovka.

It wasn't cold, though it felt cool around her feet in the damp grass, and a breeze had got up. The sky was covered with clouds heavy with rain, the sun hadn't shown itself since morning; the drab, uninviting expanse was filled with the unceasing whispering of the wind across the fields. She couldn't help wanting to turn away from it and huddle tight inside her sheepskin jacket, unmoving. Close by, the main road was quiet and deserted, the usual thing these days, few people on foot and nobody driving now. If a rare passer-by did appear it was usually of a morning - some woman from the next village trotting rapidly through on her way to the township, not to be glimpsed again till evening. The desolation which had settled on the road depressed Stepanida, especially since the place had so recently been an uproar of vehicles, carts, horses, numberless columns of troops, day and night, stretching away towards the East. It had seemed that the mighty procession would never end and with it the tense hustle and bustle on the farm. It was understandable; the place was on everybody's main road, whatever was going on. Stepanida and Petroc had been rushed off their feet meeting and seeing off everyone who had driven by or dropped in to change his boots, have a drink, rest up under the limes in the sultry heat, feed the horses or himself and ask directions. Then the time came when the highway traffic had eased towards evening and seemed likely to dry up altogether. There were no more vehicles; instead, a formation of Red Army men turned off the road and spread out among the potatoes. Two officers had come onto the farm and studied a map for a long time; their groom asked for a bucket of water for the horses and said there would be a battle and that it would be dangerous to stay on the farm. Frightened, Stepanida threw a rope over the cow's horns and made her way to Sheep Valley. Petroc stayed on the farm, which couldn't be left to run itself. That night and half the next day, she sat out among the birch thickets in considerable trepidation. After midday, there came the droning of aircraft and the earth began shuddering; there was a thud then a clattering noise and a livid column of smoke rose into the sky beyond the valley. Gradually recovering from her fright, Stepanida realized that it had been a long way off along the highway, or even further, in the township perhaps. Soon, however, it grew as quiet as if nothing untoward had taken place at all. She waited for some time before gingerly making her way back to the farm with the cow in tow, not daring to hope that the place was still in one piece or Petroc still alive. But the farm was standing as before, placid under the limes set back from the road, and her Petroc, emerged from the cellar, was walking about with straw in his whiskers; the wind bore the familiar whiff of his hand-rolled tobacco from beyond the palings.

That night the Red Army soldiers abandoned a half-dug trench on the potato patch and moved off to positions on the flank; the highway became empty and silent. In the morning a few military vehicles turned back to detour via Kulbaki - beyond the pine woods aircraft had bombed the bridge across the marshy Derevyanka and it was impossible to get to the township along the main road.

A new life, terrible in its strangeness, now began as German rule began to establish itself with implacable insistence throughout the district. It began with the disbanding of the collective farm at the Settlement and the disposal of its small stock of assets, tools and horses. Stepanida dispatched Petroc for the old mare she had handed over to the farm at one time, but there was no sign of it at the collective when he got there. The day before the Germans arrived, they'd sent a youth down to the station with the horse and a cart and he just never came back. She gave Petroc a telling-off, because if that was the case, he should have taken any old horse - how could they run a farm with no horse? How could they make a living? Petroc was an old half-wit, you couldn't rely on him to do anything right. The only thing he was good at was puffing his smelly shag and saying nothing. He couldn't care less how they were going to survive. A good job they still had Bobovka, she was their only hope now, she was feeding the two of them. But what about later on?

Bobovka meanwhile had apparently got tired of grazing the rough roadside bank and had scrambled up higher onto the verge of the highway. Stepanida rose from her rock - why let the cow up over the bank, anything could happen if somebody caught sight of her. Of course, one thing she had learned in two months under the Germans was that you couldn't guard yourself against everything; however much you wanted to hide something, if they wanted to they could discover it. Especially now that they had found themselves assistants among the local population, polizei, who knew everybody and his business. Last week two communists had been hanged in the square, one the headmaster of the school her Fenka and Fedka had gone to. In the township the fences and houses were white with announcements threatening severe punishment for disobedience, insubordination and especially resistance to the German authorities.

Stepanida climbed up the embankment and brought her switch lightly down across Bobovka's hindquarters. The cow made no objection and obediently picked her way down towards the ditch. Of course the grass wasn't very edible there, just weeds and thistles, but it would do for today. Stepanida lingered on the road, gazing round at the farm fields she knew so intimately. Ten years had gone by since it had ceased to belong to her and Petroc and been collectivized. What was going to happen now? The Germans wouldn't give the land back to the peasants, that was for sure, they'd be well aware that once you let a thing go you never got it back again. Whatever it might be, this little patch of earth, this god-forsaken hillock called Golgotha, she ached for it, just as a mother would for her only child, ailing or not. How many miles had her aging legs walked here, how much labor done by her exhausted hands! How many years had she and Petroc plowed and sowed and harvested here, spread manure and broken down the clods, especially over there in the clay. In time Fedka had joined in the uncomplicated peasant labor. Fenya had wanted to study and went away to Minsk. Where were her children now? Fenya was alright, probably still alive if she'd been lucky enough to get away to the East in time. She'd be somewhere in Russia. What about Fedka? After joining up in the autumn, he'd sent three letters from Latvia through the winter. Just starting to train on tanks and the war comes! Where was he? Was he alive at least?

The sun cut through a narrow gap in the clouds and the earth shone unexpectedly in the cold light. The sad autumnal expanse at once lost its dismal aspect as it seemed to smile a welcome at the sun's caress. Lit by the slanting rays, the orchards, gardens and outbuildings of the Settlement were sharply outlined on the earth as they straggled in a long row on the low hill across the road. Beyond that rose the blue jagged rampart of the pine forest, while nearer at hand and to the right, the grove of young firs, divided by the narrow ribbon of road, cheerily nodded their curly tops on the slope. Beyond the field to one side of her, the farmstead beneath the crowns of its ancient lime trees cast long shadows. This was her own Yakimovschina. Stepanida peered more closely, trying to make out what Petroc was doing. As she drove the cow out that morning, she had given him some chores to do about the house but the main thing was to air the potato clamp* in the garden and cover it with soil. There was no sign of the old man out there and the sun soon hid behind the clouds, turning the field murky and cheerless. It was impossible to see anything going on in the farmyard.

Stepanida descended from the embankment - no need to hang about needlessly on the road - and wandered off after the cow.

She had gone a long way from the rock and had almost reached the fringes of the wood when she heard a voice from beyond the road. She raised her head and listened intently, but her alarm subsided as soon as frisky Rudka appeared on the bank. Leaping down onto the verge, the little dog at once stood stock-still as it in turn recognized the woman and joyously wagged its tail. Again the restrained guttural cry came borne on the wind and Stepanida knew that it was Yanka from the Settlement grazing his herd on yon side of the road, as she was doing with Bobovka on this. He did indeed appear behind Rudka on the embankment, a long-legged youth with his dark shirt tucked in his trousers and a whip in his hand. Stepanida quite often encountered him on this roadside field or in the thickets, always with the same four cows. And always her heart bled for him - he was so skinny and neglected-looking in his ancient pants tied round the middle with a bit of old rope. He never wore shoes. He gazed at her face in anxious bewilderment, as if trying vainly to comprehend. Now and again he would struggle to articulate something in an alien language of hands and abrupt guttural sounds which sometimes frightened her by their unexpectedness. On occasion she would try to communicate, but he only replied with the same throaty cries, and she never knew whether he had taken anything in. He would accept at once, however, any proffered potato or bit of bread and bacon-fat and hide himself away in the bushes and eat it to the last crumb. It seemed he did his rounds on an empty belly, and no wonder; he lived with some distant country relations, not with his own mother, and grazed their

---

*clamp - a mound in which potatoes and sometimes root crops are stored outdoors in winter when the cellars are full. They are earthed up in layers to protect them from the frost.

cattle from springtime onwards in exchange for scraps and a roof over his head at night.

The little herdsman meanwhile cast an eye over his few charges, cracked his whip in the air and came towards Stepanida before silently sitting down at the roadside. His legs were covered with sores and stuck out from his canvas shorts well above the knee; he hugged his shivering arms across his chest, elbows on knees, shuddering as he did so.

"Y-y-y, a-a-a!" He strove to say something. "A-e-e!"

Who could guess what thoughts were troubling him, why his unkempt head trembled under the broken peak of his little cap, what his eyes, wide and guileless, sought to convey? Stepanida would sometimes hand Bobovka over to him for a morning or so, if it was convenient, and on her way back would try to fetch him some sort of present - a fritter, some pork crackling, a handful of peas or at any rate a ripe apple from the tree. However, now she had nothing.

"Aren't you cold, Yanochka? Why didn't you put on something a bit warmer?" she reproached him as she looked up at him.

"A-a, e-e-e!" He mooed, waving his hands about.

"This wind'll go right through you, you'll catch your death of cold." She slapped herself across the chest. "Go and get something like this! Clothes, to keep warm!"

As if comprehending something of what she said, Yanka leapt down onto the road and inspected his sparse herd.

"A-a-a! U-a-a-a!"

"Go on, go on!" she said. "I'll keep an eye on them. I'll watch them!" she repeated loudly and pointed at his cows and Bobovka.

To her surprise, he understood something of this - easily, as if he had heard. Running off the road, he turned the lead black cow with a crack of his whip and took off for the pine woods where the highway turned towards the Settlement. Rudka ran after the boy at first, then seemed to recall his shepherding responsibilities and returned to sit by the roadside not far from Stepanida.

"Rudka, Rudka, here!" called Stepanida. Rudka, however, merely twitched his ears and kept a solicitous eye on the herd placidly grazing in the ditch and on the embankment. He was a grand dog really, full of tricks though. He never went near a human being unless he spotted something to eat in his hand.

To make her task easier, Stepanida drove Bobovka across the road and seated herself on the embankment. She could see all the cows from there and the dry roadside grass was easier on her feet. The wind blew harder up there though and she turned her back to it. Great piles of cloud passed swiftly across the sky and there was no sign of the sun or how soon it would be evening. She sensed that it was already well past noon and in another hour or two, twilight would be creeping across the fields. Formerly she had enjoyed and looked forward to just this time of day when she used to come back from the day's work to the farmhouse and the family would be together. She had never found household chores wearisome, even after tiring work in the fields. Now though, the onset of evening brought her little joy and there was no looking forward to cooking up things on the stove. The family wasn't there, were they? One by one the old folk had passed on to the next world, and the children had flown the nest as soon a they were a bit grown-up; all that was good and troublesome about bringing them up had passed unnoticed. Only Petroc was left and two old folk didn't need much. Something to eat, then lie down on your side, covered in a threadbare sheepskin, not bothering to keep the stove going through the night, they could get by without. Of course there were the animals: the cow, the piglet in the sty, a dozen hens. They had to be fed and watered and generally seen to. That about exhausted her simple domestic responsibilities.

A young red cow from the township herd began to lag behind the others and Stepanida quietly called out to her. The cow, however, clearly unaccustomed to the strange voice, was in no hurry to overtake the herd. Descending from the bank, Stepanida walked back to hurry her up. Regaining the road once more, she was surprised to see someone running from the direction of the pine wood at such a lick that his shirt was ballooning out behind him. Peering more closely, she made the runner out to be Yanka. But why had he come back, why hadn't he run to the township? Her eyes watered in the wind as she gazed at him and she felt a pang inside her - a subconscious alarm had conveyed itself to her from the youngster.

Stepanida stood stock-still on the highway, already aware that something bad had taken place, but not knowing yet what it could be. Later she would often recall this presentiment of hers and marvel how accurately it had hinted at the approach of what was to turn her life upside down. It was just a sensation akin to fear while Yanka ran towards her. Still a little way off, he rushed down from the embankment towards the lead cow and belabored her with his whip as he began furiously wheeling the whole group. The cows were at first reluctant but then, one after the other, began trotting along the ditch towards the edge of the wood, while Yanka gave out stentorian yells as he waved his whip in the air and pointed back the way they had come. His face was contorted with fear or amazement and Stepanida, a prey to indecision, turned Bobovka round too. Obviously some sort of danger had appeared in the pine wood and safety had to be sought, thus she interpreted Yanka's alarm and was ready to share it.

Fifteen minutes later they had driven the whole herd into the alders on the edge of the swamp, well away from the road, and she went over to Yanka. The young herdsman glanced at her in a new, unfamiliar way as he made anxious attempts to explain something with guttural shouts, all the while pointing towards the road.

"What's over there? What is it?" asked Stepanida, seeing only fear in his freckled weather-beaten face and burning ominously in his wide eyes. Yanka, however, explained only in gestures, constantly indicating the woods; his hands formed a rounded shape in the air and he pictured something with his fingers. She could make nothing of it.

'Lord did he have to be born such a dummy,' was her first thought, as she listened intently. It was quiet among the alders, apart from the wind in the branches and one of the cows snapping twigs among the brushwood some way off. From the road there came no sound and Stepanida resolved to take a trip over to the pines.

"You look after Bobovka for a bit. The cow, look after her! I'll just go over. Back soon."

Yanka waved his arms and gave out an inarticulate lowing sound of incomprehension or dissent. She waited for another minute, then began making her cautious way towards the road.

As before, there was no one on the road itself, or anywhere near the pine wood. She paused for a while in thought, then without going up onto the embankment, strode swiftly along by the ditch. She was completely baffled over what had happened to Yanka, though she kept her gaze fixed on the far end of the highway and halted three or four times to listen hard and ponder. In the Settlement everything was quiet too, as was her potato patch on the hillside next to the farm. A blustery wind met her head-on and she thought the sun would peep out at any moment from behind the clouds. But it never did. She was approaching the pine wood, a dense arm of which straddled the road, when for the first time, an odd sound reached her straining ear. Something like a heavy thud a long way beyond the trees was borne back to her on the chilly breeze; then realization came to her - the bridge! Yes, something was happening on the other side of the pines, not far off, beyond the bend in the road, where since summer, the remains of the bombed bridge had stuck up over the river.

Stepanida slackened her pace, ready to stop, but instead of doing so, ran up to the edge of the wood and turned off into the pines so as to avoid going on the road.

From here it was a stone's throw to the farm itself and after many a year of walking here, her feet knew every path and clearing. Almost at a run through the spiky branches, she skirted the low hillock of pine saplings and

cautiously peeped out from the edge of the trees at the wide sweep of
meadow where the unseen river elbow lay. Voices from the bridge carried
distinctly now and the sound of a log being dumped from a cart echoed
dully. She held a pine branch away from her face and froze. On the highway
near the bridge, down by the water's edge and on the embankment churned
up by the bombs, there were swarms of people: some were digging, others
were dumping logs from carts; while on the bluff by the twisted piles and
beams, several men in unfamiliar battledress were standing motionless with
weapons at their shoulders. One of these, in a high wide-peaked cap, was
pointing in various directions; the others listened in silence, gazing worried-
ly at the remains of the bridge. With an unexpected pang of terror, Stepanida
realized - these were Germans!

2

'What's going to happen now? What're the Germans going to think up? Where are our boys?' Petroc was wondering despondently. 'How are we going to go on now?'

There were a great number of tormenting questions like this, and unless you knew the answer to any one of them, the others remained a puzzle. No use worrying your head over it, there was nothing you could do, you just had to take what fate had in store.

You couldn't stop thinking though, nobody could do that: a persistent feeling of depression, like a boring-beetle, had been gnawing at his heart ever since the war began. It was impossible to suppress it.

Still, you couldn't say things on the farm were all that bad or that anything had changed under the new German order. On the contrary, practically everything here had stayed as it was: as always, they had got over the autumn worries about bread, there was the cow and the squalling piglet in the sty, the hens patrolling the farmyard. There was a little bit extra for the pot: beets, cabbage, potatoes in the kitchen garden, three stacks of corn in sheaves in the storeshed - Stepanida and he had harvested that on the abandoned collective field before autumn.

There was bread on the table, even more than there used to be, and you could dig extra potatoes if you wanted, over there on Golgotha behind the palings; used to be the collective farm's, now it was nobody's. Womenfolk from the settlement, a bit braver than the rest, used quietly to dig a few up from the road without waiting for permission. It wouldn't hurt to dig up a couple of sackfuls himself to put in this clamp he'd been busy on all week. Stepanida had told him to finish the job that day and she'd be fetching the cow in soon. There was no escaping a row. The trouble was Petroc's heart wasn't in his work; his head was crammed with preoccupations of a different sort. He was lethargic, forever smoking his home-grown weed and sitting out on the little bench by the door, like an invalid, or else wandering aimlessly around the yard. He couldn't concentrate on anything, every little thing around him was utterly familiar; it was like a part of himself. Not that

there was anything astonishing about that: he'd spent twenty years here, a
hard life of deprivation and worry, a life that was narrowing wedge-like down
to nothing, and he wouldn't have another one. Maybe he could have
finished his allotted span at least in comfort if not plenty. If it hadn't been
for the war. . .

After the rains, there had been a strong growth of grass lately by the porch
and under the palings. It was damp there and Petroc chose a dry path as he
walked round the soil parapet* and halted in the middle of the yard. He'd
been the master here for a good many years; well or ill, he'd run the farm,
but now he'd started to look at it as if through a stranger's eyes, as if he were
going away somewhere and would have to part from the place where he had
passed his life. Actually if you thought about it, what reason had he to regret?
The hut had seen better days, though the wood had been good quality,
matured resinous pine; the wall-logs had cracked a little bit, but not one
had rotted. The hut would stay upright, maybe come in for somebody. The
roof-ridge needed a patch; it had been leaking near the flue since spring,
same thing in the boiler-house, which connected with the hut through a
passage. It fairly poured through in there and after a heavy downpour there
was a pool on the floor. Stepanida had given him a telling off: all summer
and he hadn't managed to mend a hole. But it was no more than the truth,
he hadn't mended either of them, the main reason being that he didn't feel
much like dragging his bones up a tottering extension ladder to the roof.
When the rain stops, the pool will dry up, thought he. Otherwise you disturb
the rotted straw and make the hole worse, what do you expect with
something built a hundred odd years ago, when the Poles ruled round here
- and the boiler-house was even older. The roof on that, as far as Petroc
remembered, had always had a green mossy cap. In the single-pane window,
the glass was rainbowed with age.

Perhaps the sturdiest outhouse here was the new storage shed behind
the cowshed. It was the least noticeable in the yard as well; it had been cut
in a hurry from top growth and the walls were full of gaps, but that was all
right with a grain-shed. The drafts went through it and it never got damp.
Fedya and he had put it up; he'd thought it might do for his son if not for
him. He'd do his army service, get married and carry on the line. But where
was Fedya now?. . .The rye sheaves would dry out in the wind and bide their
time. From time to time, he would take off the top two or three, beat them
on the mat in the passage and grind them in the millstones. Stepanida would
bake a couple of loaves and that supplied them with bread for a week.

---

*parapet (zavalinka) - an earth rampart, heaped up all around the walls of peasant huts,
presumably for strength or to keep snow off the walls.

Morosely Petroc surveyed the drab autumnal expanse and the potato field stretching as far as the forest, then walked over to the well. Down in the dark pit a patch of water glistened - there was plenty there now, not like summer. The well-water was pleasant to the taste, always cold and clear as a teardrop. Even the Settlement didn't have water as good as that, not in any of its eight wells. The old men used to say that once upon a time a cheery spring used to bubble up from underground, and that was probably why the Polish Yakimovsky squires laid out their farmstead here on the hillock by the deep wooded gully. Whoever drank from this well always praised the water. Around eight years before, Petroc had fixed a wooden windlass on the frame instead of the clumsy old sweep and put up a narrow little roof to keep the rain out. He should really fit a lid on it to stop anything from the yard getting in, but it could manage without. What could get in anyway? The wind might carry in some leaves from the limes - they deposited plenty over the yard in autumn - but that was all. The limes had really grown over these last years and in the summer months they shaded almost half the vegetable garden. Stepanida was always on about lopping the branches, but he couldn't raise his hand against beauty like that. He hadn't planted them, someone else had. They'd grown here all his life, they could stay here after him.

After a while, Petroc looked over beyond the field towards the road where Stepanida had been visible with the cow a little time back. Now, however, neither Stepanida nor the cow were in evidence. Probably driven it into the thickets. It wasn't late yet, two hours grazing and his freedom would be over; he'd be set to work: draw water from the well, wash the potatoes for the pig, pound the barley in the mortar. After that, there'd be no time for thinking deep thoughts, Stepanida wouldn't let him loaf about.

Petroc rolled a cigarette as thick as his finger from a crumpled piece of newspaper and carefully did up his leather tobacco pouch; lighting up, however, meant going into the hut and finding a coal in the stove. There were a few matches left somewhere but Stepanida hid them and only used them in extreme emergencies. She was right too: where could you buy matches these days? There were no shops operating in the township, our own troops had carried off the stock of two stores back in the summer when the Germans looked like taking over; there was nothing left. He'd done a bit of foraging himself - Stepanida had driven him out - but he had hardly covered himself with glory. He'd drained out a sizeable bottle of kerosene with rusty sludge in the bottom from an overturned metal drum behind the store. It wasn't much of a haul, but it would come in handy when autumn and winter arrived. There was no salt though, that was worse, you couldn't get much down you without that. Still that wasn't the only thing they were short of.

Worst of all was having no horse.

Petroc turned away from the well and suddenly caught sight of the cow behind the palings. Bobovka was heading straight ahead across the potatoes from the direction of the woods for some reason, not along the road and through the gates as usual. Stepanida was running quickly along behind, quilted jacket open wide. His wife's whole appearance expressed alarm and fright: her kerchief was on the side of her head, and the wind was plucking at the grey lock of hair on her forehead. Petroc stared at her perspiring face in bewilderment - it was still early, Bobovka normally grazed till evening. Clearly something had happened. He went over to the wicket-gate and drew back the bar.

"Petroc, Germans!"

"What?"

"Germans, I said! Back there on the highway, they're repairing the bridge. . ."

"The bridge?"

This was something new. Petroc hadn't been ready for this. Perhaps it was only now he realized how well off they'd been here without the bridge and the danger that was moving towards them across that bridge from the township.

"Yes. That's bad."

"You're telling me it's bad! Our township folk are out there with carts unloading logs. We've got to do something! Otherwise they'll come here and take everything. Then what'll we do?"

"All right. Only what?" Petroc couldn't grasp the situation.

"Well, hide something for a start. The cow in the woods, if we tie it up. . .And the pig. . ."

Perhaps the cow might have been led off into the woods and tethered to a branch but you couldn't do that with a pig. A pig had to be fed. The hens as well. It wasn't exactly affluence, a dozen hens, but the farm would be lost without them. What could they do, where could they conceal it all?

"It's the pig that worries me," said Stepanida wearily, adjusting her kerchief. "They'll grab it. It's coming along fine as well."

"They're great ones for bacon-fat: missus - speck, missus - eggs!" said Petroc, having heard about Germans in the first war.

"Well, I think it'll have to be hid. You come here," she summoned her husband to the far end of the yard.

They went round the boiler-house past the low pile of logs by the wall and the old chopping-block on the ground, then through the railings into the kitchen garden. Here behind the drooping dock-leaves and tangled masses of nettles, an unsightly plank shed was jammed up under the overhanging roof of the boiler-house. This little shed had stood empty for ages without finding a use, a receptacle for all kinds of farm junk. They rarely looked in there, except to see if the birds had laid anything. Sometimes the hens would slip into the straw by the entrance; two old yellow eggs could be seen there now.

"What about in here?" said Stepanida, opening the lower hatch a bit wider. "He's a quiet little thing, he'll just sit still and let's hope they don't find him."

Whether they would or not, Lord alone knew, but Petroc was used to doing what his wife said; she was nobody's fool and in particular, always knew exactly what she wanted. So although the pig wasn't the greatest of Petroc's concerns at the moment, he obediently lent a hand in fixing up this new refuge. For a start he began carrying out the rubbish of many years, crammed in any old how. There were some dry sticks, an old trough gnawed by pigs, a broken wagon wheel, without spokes, an ancient plow dating back to his grandfather's time possibly, along with its rusted colter. Half an hour later, using a broken box and some palings, he had fenced off a kind of small pen. He fetched straw from the grain shed, untrimmed so as to attract less notice and stuffed it in the pen. Stepanida meanwhile was leading the piglet, which had put on weight over the summer, out of the sty, scratching him between the ears as she did so.

"Here now. . .Now this way. Good boy. . ."

"Like a bairn," mused Petroc, letting the piglet into the pen. After grunting, it sniffed the entrance and the straw trustingly and settled into its new quarters with every evidence of satisfaction, blissfully unaware of impending danger. He really was a placid, well-fed little pig and they certainly didn't want to lose him. Maybe he'd save his hide as well if he used his piggy brain, small as it was, and not squeal when strangers were around, Petroc thought.

"There then," said Stepanida, relaxing. "All nice and hidden. Let him sit in there."

They returned to the yard, where Bobovka awaited them with anxious expectation in her wistful eyes. Two hens wandered about by her feet.

"What about the hens?" Petroc inquired.

They had to be tucked away out of sight as well, but where could you stow a wretched hen? She wouldn't sit still and if she laid an egg she would cluck happily for the whole neighborhood to hear and so seal her fate. Still, the hens could wait, the cow was far more of a worry if she wasn't to be the first victim.

"Maybe we could take her over to Berestovka? To Manka's place? It's a bit further away from the township at any rate," suggested Petroc uncertainly. But Stepanida objected at once.

"No, no, I'm not handing Bobovka over to anybody else."

"Well what then?"

"Sheep Valley. On the tether or hobbled. Let her walk around a bit."

"What about at night?"

"Maybe they won't come at night. They usually go foraging during the day."

It sounded pretty weak, but having nothing better to offer, Petroc silently concurred.

The autumn day drew imperceptibly towards evening, getting a little darker; though in the yard and in the nearby fields, it was still light enough. Stepanida was in no hurry to milk Bobovka who stood sighing and in the absence of her mistress, began cropping the grass under the fence to make up for what she had missed in the fields. Petroc meanwhile kept glancing nervously through the gates and towards the highway, waiting for the Germans to put in an appearance. He listened too for any strange, suspicious sound in the evening quiet. But as always, the track and the road were deserted, the twilight calm lay all around on the dismal autumnal landscape. Only the tireless wind tormented the yellowing foliage of the limes, scattering it generously about the garden, the dirt track and the young grass in the yard. Petroc pulled up a bucket of water from the well and placed it in front of Bobovka. She, however, merely dipped her muzzle in and drank nothing, gazing out for some reason through the fence into the fields, as if expecting something from that direction. She should be herded into the cowshed, but Stepanida hung on inside the hut. Petroc called her:

"You hear? Milking time."

Stepanida made no reply and it came to him that something had really changed at Yakimovschina if the farmer's wife was late milking. Still, things had changed everywhere, so changes were to be expected on the farm, Petroc consoled himself philosophically. Without waiting for Stepanida to answer, he walked onto the flat doorstep and glanced into the passage. Stepanida was bent over the dark-blue trunk searching for something. She tossed a cardigan onto the baking bowl, then another; then she shook out a large kerchief, black with red flowers. Petroc was taken aback:

"What are you looking for?"

"There's that thing of Fenka's, hide it somewhere out of the way."

"Fenka's? Stop imagining things! Who would want that?"

"What d'you mean? The Germans!" snapped his wife, rummaging through the case. "And this? What do we do with this?"

She unrolled a thin paper tube. As he glanced at it, he recognized

Stepanida's old pride and joy - her diploma for flax processing. At the top was the coat of arms of White Russia in color, while below was the blue seal and sprawling signature of the executive committee president, Chervyakov. The diploma had hung on the wall between the windows at one time, but it had been taken down. They'd wanted to burn it, but Stepanida wouldn't give it up and put it away in her trunk.

"You put that in the stove!" cried Petroc, alarmed. "That's no joke you know."

"Ah, let it stay there. It's not for stealing other people's property, it's for my own hard work."

Stepanida rolled the diploma into a cylinder and secreted it among the clothes. From the rest of the contents she picked out mostly Fenka's things and wrapped them up in the black kerchief.

"Have to hide this. What about the potato clamp?"

"They'll rot. Anyway there's no point in this. The Germans are more interested in the food front. They don't touch clothes. I know."

"A fat lot you know!" cried his disbelieving wife. "You'd have no clothes left, you wouldn't."

"It's all right, we'll get by," said Petroc. "We've done nothing against them. If we treat them right, they'll maybe. . .they won't eat. . ."

He talked on, to keep his spirits up and calm his wife, though he was as dubious as she was: was what he had just said true? He just felt that they had to get through a testing period, keep their heads down, sit tight and better times would come along. This war wouldn't go on for ever, but to avoid trouble they had to be as careful and as quiet as possible. It was like confronting a savage dog inclined to bite; one had to walk on by without showing fear, pretending not to be afraid - but on no account getting involved with it. If he didn't get mixed up with the fascists, surely they wouldn't trouble him for no reason? He wasn't a boss, or a party member - or a Jew from the township. He was a local man, thank God, baptized into the Christian faith, a collective farm man, like everybody else in the region. If his son was in the Red Army, that didn't mean he was a volunteer. That was just the call-up, like under the Tsars and before. Plenty of people in the country had done military service, though Petroc hadn't - his health had let him down. He'd spent all his life here for everyone to see, why on earth should anybody pick on him?

3

With all the livestock bestowed after a fashion, they gulped down some of the soup which had gone cold on the stove and turned in for the night - he on the bed behind the cupboard and she behind the stove. For the time being, a deathly hush lay everywhere, and that silence and the routine of the evening chores somewhat diminished their anxiety. Petroc mumbled swiftly through "Our Father" in an indistinct monotone, something he hadn't done for long enough, and crossed himself with a sigh, hoping against hope that it would all blow over. They'd come and they'd go on by, what was there to keep them on the highway here? Maybe that was why they were repairing the bridge, so as to go on somewhere - what did they want with a farm standing by itself off the road? The front had rolled forward hell knew where, there were rumors that the Germans had taken Moscow, but it didn't look like that was the end of the fighting. It was going on some-where, this terrible war. Maybe in Siberia by now? Or maybe it was rubbish all that about Moscow, he wouldn't be surprised. They couldn't take Mos-cow. What if they had advanced a long way? So had Napoleon, but he got smashed. It wasn't so easy to swallow a huge chunk of Russia like that, even if you had a mouth like this Hitler. He'd get smashed as well sure enough.

Petroc tossed and turned on his straw mattress, sighing, and heard Stepanida doing the same behind the stove. He asked quietly:

"You asleep, woman?"

"Yes, why shouldn't I be?"

"Well, I was thinking, maybe we're getting scared over nothing. What are we to them? They'll go the same way as they came."

"If only! They're not getting out of the township though. That teacher and Podobed from the village shop are still swinging on the end of a rope."

"Ai, don't say things like that in the dark, God forbid." Petroc waved her words away, already sorry at starting the conversation.

They didn't talk any more and a shallow sleep, full of disquiet, overcame Petroc little by little, bringing him neither rest nor peace of mind. He dreamed for a long time about worms, a whole mass of tiny meat-maggots that crawled, stirred and seethed, twisting and knotting near his feet. Petroc felt disgust, even terror for some reason, and woke up. He realized at once that it was early yet, the cocks hadn't crowed over in the Settlement. In the silence of the hut, the ticking of the clocks was distinctly audible, but he had no desire to get up and look at the time. He stayed lying motionless, trying to go back to sleep or wait for the dawn. His thoughts were still on the same track: how to survive in a world where all the previous notions of order had collapsed so unexpectedly and totally; what was there to hold on to as a support in this hard and anxiety-ridden existence? He thought of his son Fyodor, probably no longer among the living by now - a war like this, so many people perishing. And Fenya as well. No news from her since spring and not home for the holidays either, disappeared in Minsk somewhere. Maybe she'd gone away East behind the lines, she'd been a medical student after all and people like that were in demand. That would be the best thing, as long as she hadn't been captured by the Germans. What if she hadn't managed to keep clear of them in the city or on the way home? Horrible to think what might have happened to the little girl.

Towards morning, he did manage to drop off for a while only to be wakened by the sound of Stepanida's footsteps round the hut. Another day full of tensions was beginning and a grey drizzly dawn lay behind the windows, steamed-up overnight. Stepanida, dressed in her quilted jacket, pulled back the curtain by the bed.

"You go and finish off the clamp. Otherwise we'll be left without potatoes. And feed the pig. I'm off. . . "

She went out into the yard and soon her steps could be heard rustling near the boiler-house, then came the stamp of cow's feet in the yard. Stepanida had obviously driven Bobovka into Sheep Valley, that made sense, further from the road, less chance of disturbance.

Petroc reluctantly started to get up. He dangled his drawer-clad legs and bare feet over the edge and sat there, debating whether to have a smoke or put his trousers on first. He'd wanted a smoke badly all night. It was chilly in the hut; Stepanida had been in a hurry to get Bobovka and hadn't lit the stove. He had farm chores to do on his own till noon. It was all right on his own, didn't have to hurry anywhere and the unfinished clamp at the end of the kitchen garden could wait for a bit probably: the weather was damp and didn't promise any sudden frost. Pulling on his pants, Petroc stuck his feet into his ancient shoes and slung his sheepskin over his shoulders. First priority was to retrieve a couple of home-grown leaves from the chimney and crumble them on the corner of the table. This was work dear to his heart - preparing his smokes for the day. The sharp knife-point readily sliced through the partly dried yellow leaf, producing an agreeable, nose-tickling smell. Petroc, anticipating the customary enjoyment to come, became briefly animated and glanced out of the window.

No, the track leading from farm to the high road was empty and there was no one to be seen near the pine woods; there did seem to be someone on the Settlement track, however. Knife in hand, Petroc approached the window and glanced upwards. Two distant human figures could be glimpsed through the sweating glass coming up to the farm turn-off at a smart pace.

He stood for a moment, peering, until a sudden surmise struck him - it was the Settlement polizei. Yes, it was Guzh and Kolondenok. This was the first time Petroc had seen them in their new police role, but he'd heard that they didn't confine themselves to snooping round the Settlement, the township and the surrounding villages and farms - they supported the German occupation too. Now they were on their way here, beefy broad-shouldered Guzh and baby-faced Kolondenok, both with rifles at the shoulder and white arm-bands. They were coming up to the fork and Petroc cherished a slim hope that they would turn towards the highway and go on their way. Of course, he was wrong. The polizei skirted a puddle at the fork and took the narrow, grass-grown track towards his farm.

Petroc hastily pulled on his jacket and flung open the passage door. Thereupon, not knowing what to do yet, but already sensing grim news, carefully closed it behind him and observed the polizei through the passage window. As they drew nearer, however, he grew calmer. Anyway, what was there to be afraid of, he didn't feel guilty of anything; Guzh was actually some sort of distant relative, through his granddad; Petroc had even drunk with him in company at the market in the township. Since the start of collectivization though, Petroc hadn't set eyes on him and had no desire to meet him.

The polizei soon passed through the gates under the limes and entered the yard. Guzh's avid glance swept across woodpile and cowshed before coming to rest on the passage door. Some sort of response seemed called for, however grudging, and Petroc went out into the passage and halted in indecision by the bench with the bucket. Only when the unfamiliar hand began rattling the latch did he open the door.

"A-ha! So this is where he hides himself!" boomed Guzh, seemingly in a jovial mood. He ducked his head and stepped across the threshold. "I look round the yard and no sign of him - good morning!"

"Good morning!" Petroc replied, faltering. "Like I was. . .I was waiting."

"Who for, visitors? Well, now we're here!"

"Aha, yes come along in," Petroc recovered himself and laid on the cordiality, opening the hut door wide. Rustling in his worn leather jacket, Guzh stepped inside, rifle in hand. The lanky Kolondenok, straps tight

across his greatcoat, followed him in. Then came Petroc, closing the door
and shifting the bench into the middle of the hut. The visitors didn't sit
down. Kolondenok leaned up by the door, as if on guard, while Guzh
unhurriedly tramped up to the table and back in his heavy boots, glancing
out of each window in turn.

"Like a holiday camp here!" came his bass voice. "Forest, river. Township
on your doorstep, right?"

"Not far," agreed Petroc, wondering cheerlessly what the hell had brought
them here at this hour. What were they after? He didn't ask them to sit down
a second time, maybe they'd come out with it and be gone.

But it appeared that they had no intention of going.

Having surveyed the dark corners and newspaper-covered walls of the
hut, Guzh stared long at the icons, as if counting them before undoing some
buttons on the chest of his tight-fitting russet jacket.

"Pretty warm in here."

"Well, it's. . .We haven't lit the stove yet."

"So it's a warm hut. That's good. Have to take this thing off, no objec-
tions?"

Petroc, naturally, did not object and Guzh grunted as he hauled the
second-hand jacket from his taut shoulders and hung it on a nail next to
Petroc's fiddle. He began pulling in his Red Army shirt, now worn yellow;
his belt had a big yellow buckle too.

"Still play?" he nodded towards the violin.

"Fat chance! No time for music", sighed Petroc. Actually, when had he had
time? For a long while now the music in his soul had been far from violin
solos. Still he wasn't going to start explaining, he just thought regretfully
he'd have to put the violin somewhere away from prying eyes.

"I remember we whooped it up at a wedding one time. In the township.
You on the fiddle and Yarmash on drums."

"That was then. . ."

"It did happen though!" said Guzh and slid behind the table into the
corner. He put his long rifle next to him on the bench. Kolondenok, who
hadn't taken his coat off, squatted down by the door. "Well now, how about
entertaining us, mine host!" Guzh stared at Petroc coldly from under his
bushy brows. "A half-liter. That's the way!"

"Ha, if I only had it." Petroc was almost glad. "There's a bite to eat, but
no vodka, so. . ."

"Life's hard is it, Bogatka? Didn't make your pile under the Soviets. . ."

"No, I didn't. . ."

"And under the Germans you don't want to. We're not like that. We've
got a little something."

Extending a thick booted leg under the table, Guzh extracted a shining bottle from his uniform trousers.

"Look at that, pure Moskovski!" With a loud preliminary rap, he set it on the table with ostentatious pride.

There was no spinning things out any longer, so, cursing everybody and everything, Petroc went to the dresser for the bread, remembering that the eggs were in the boiler-house along with a few gherkins in a barrel. And the bacon-fat, of course, in the tub. He bustled about trying to set the table as swiftly as he could so as to speed his guests' departure; he put out a loaf already cut into, but couldn't find the knife he'd just been holding. Where could it have got itself to? Without waiting for his host, Guzh pulled out one of his own from his boot - broad in the blade and raked back at the tip - and lightly cut off two thick slices.

"And where's your activist?" inquired the polizei, apparently casual, and his eyes narrowed as he waited for the reply. "Not digging over on the collective?"

"She's off with the cow, you know."

"You've got a cow? And making out you're poor."

"Oh, I get by. Like everybody else, you know. . ."

"And who's going to pick the potatoes?"

"What potatoes?"

"The collective's potatoes, over on Golgotha! The Soviet regime's conked out, but not the collective farms, oh no! Hitler's orders: keep the collective farms. So there'll be potato picking. And a quota, of course. Just like before the war, ha ha!" He laughed shortly.

Petroc had already heard that the Germans were going to keep the collective going, but had given small credence to the report. He'd thought the Germans might deal pretty roughly with the farm workers; now look at them. Because of the potatoes, probably. More convenient for them.

"Well, I've done my stint. Let some of the younger ones, they're. . .," Petroc made a weak attempt to get out of it, "they're stronger."

"Who's the weakling round here, then? You? Or is it that woman of yours? She was a real worker before the war, not half. Did the work of three and never a squeak about going sick. Made a speech at the assembly, so she did. Outstanding flax worker."

"What d'you mean, flax-worker?" said Petroc in a low voice, attempting somehow to deflect this heavy hinting as he placed a clean glass on the table. "There wasn't much flax grown in the last few years."

"However much they grew! She put the work in. People haven't forgotten. And now she's not very well. . ."

Petroc had to go to the boiler-house for the gherkins and bacon, but the blond Kolondenok was sitting across the threshold with his sour pimply face averted. This undermining of Stepanida worried Petroc a good deal: was that the reason they'd honored him with a visit?

"They told her to, so she made a speech. What else could she do?"

"Told her to, did they? And what if the German authorities say something different? What will you do then?"

"Us?" Petroc shrugged his shoulders. "We'll do what everybody else does."

Guzh settled himself more comfortably at the table, glanced out of the window and seized the bottle from the table with a proprietary gesture.

"Well, got any bacon-fat?"

"Surely, right away." Petroc turned for the door and at once bumped into Kolondenok, who hadn't budged.

"Let him through!" said Guzh evenly, at which the other finally shifted to let Petroc through the door.

Petroc left the passage and boiler-house doors wide open to give himself more light as he fished about in the tub for the bacon-fat in its layer of salt. He had already understood that this polizei visit was no chance matter; there was a definite purpose behind it which would no doubt emerge. Just so long as Stepanida didn't stick her head in here. How could he let her know what sort of visitors he had? He pondered feverishly, as he hurried into the hut with the bacon-fat.

"Now that's something else!" said Guzh with satisfaction. The polizei had already drunk off his vodka; the glass was empty and his puffy face was still twisted as it registered the spirit. He immediately began cutting into the bacon-fat. "Well. Now you. You're the master here after all. The Germans respect ownership. Not like under the Soviets. . ."

"Well, you know, I'm not exactly. . ."

"Now don't give me that!" Guzh raised his voice and waggling the bottle, poured out a good half-glass. "Drink up! To victory!"

"Well, hardly that," said Petroc gloomily, taking the glass from his hand.

"Your son's where? Red Army isn't he? Defending Stalin?"

"Well, he's in the army. He's a soldier, so. . ."

"So, to victory! Over the bolsheviks," specified Guzh.

Cursing the world to himself, and especially this plug-ugly visitor, Petroc drained the vodka from the glass almost with disgust.

"That's the spirit!" approved the polizei. Now get your teeth round that.

Guzh was behaving like the host at the table and Petroc had somehow been imperceptibly transformed from master of the house to no more than a guest. Of course he was intimidated by this unexpected irruption by the police, alarmed at Guzh's ominous hints and worried in case things turned out badly. Still, maybe it was for the best that he hadn't refused to drink;

the vodka gradually took the edge off his nervousness and he began to feel more in command of himself. If he wasn't allowed to play host, then he could settle into the role of fellow-drinker; he sat side-on to the table and gnawed a crust of bread. Guzh meanwhile was masticating his bread and bacon in broad, millstone jaws. He refilled his glass.

"Can't have too much of a good thing, eh, Bogatka?"

"Likely not. The first tot's like a blue-tit, but the second's like a swallow," babbled Petroc. "What about your mate?" He nodded towards Kolondenok by the door.

"He's all right," rumbled Guzh. "He doesn't drink. You're a teetotaler aren't you, Potap?"

"That's right," Kolondenok replied in a thin voice as everyone in the hut fell silent, listening. There came the sound of footsteps from the yard, and a hen started clucking near the sty.

"Now, then!" Guzh nodded to his assistant, still keeping the glass in his hand. Kolondenok leaped out into the passage but quickly returned.

"The aunty's arrived."

Petroc was furiously annoyed; he really was worried for Stepanida. Why had she trundled back here? He should have warned her not to enter the hut, but he'd got into this drinking party and now, it seemed, it was too late.

"I'll just. . .tell her to get something to eat," he half rose, trying to extricate himself from the table, but Guzh sat him back again with a decisive hand.

"You sit down! She can fetch it herself, she's not blind."

And so the passage door opened and Stepanida froze for a moment on the threshold, probably not recognizing the visitors at once.

"Come in, come in!" Guzh invited, playing the host and still chewing. "Don't be shy, ha-ha! Not shy are you?"

"Good morning," Stepanida greeted them quietly and stepped inside. 'Now they'll grab her!' thought Petroc fearfully, glancing sideways at Guzh. The latter, however, appeared to take no notice of the lady of the house. He cut another slice from the loaf and offered it to Kolondenok with a piece of bacon.

"Have a bit, Potap."

Kolondenok rose from the threshold and took the morsel with an expression of sleepy indifference.

"You're drinking and the Germans are walking about on the bridge," said Stepanida with faint reproach, mainly to break up the embarrassed silence in the hut.

"So they are," agreed Guzh. "Another couple of days and they'll be driving across. German efficiency!"

"And why should they drive here? Haven't they got enough roads of their own in Germany?" Stepanida grimaced unpleasantly.

Guzh glanced quizzically at her and snorted his displeasure.

"A sharp customer, I see! No wonder you were an activist. Haven't recanted yet?"

"What have I got to recant then? I'm no criminal. Let criminals recant."

"You hinting? Who're you getting at?" Guzh was alert.

"Some people. People who are one thing today and something different tomorrow."

'Shut up, woman, do!' Petroc urged her mentally. 'What are you nagging at him for? Can't you see who you're dealing with?'

Clearly Stepanida had more to say, but stopped there and merely flung a malevolent glance at Guzh, and then Petroc and Kolondenok. However, one glance was enough for Guzh it seemed; he rose menacingly.

"What are you doing loafing about? Why are you out spying on the roads? Why are you out of the yard when there's visitors?"

"I was grazing the cow. There's the master of the house here with you."

"What can he do, this man of yours? He wouldn't say boo to a goose! And we want something to eat."

"Anything else?"

"Eat, I said, something decent. Fit for the representatives of German authority!"

"Been that long, have you?" Stepanida burst out, and Petroc sensed that the irreparable was about to take place.

"Be quiet, woman!" he shouted, with forced severity. "Fry up some eggs! You hear what I say?"

Guzh sniggered approvingly from the table, as Stepanida turned silently and went out into the passage. The door remained open behind her, so Kolondenok shut it, remaining close by as before. However, Guzh swiftly wiped the smile from his face.

"There you see what sort she is, that woman of yours! Know what the Germans do with people like her?"

"Well, I've heard. Only it's. . ."

"Hang 'em! From the telegraph poles!" Guzh thumped his meaty fist on the table. Petroc felt a chill inside him and cringed, drawing his head into his shoulders. "The Germans don't mess about with the likes of her. And we won't either! We'll hang a dozen as an example to the rest," thundered Guzh.

"Oh, it's just talk with her, she didn't mean it seriously," Petroc feebly tried to justify Stepanida.

"Why say it then? Joking, was she? She's a communist," Guzh concluded abruptly.

"No, no. That's just what her tongue says."

"Yes, yes, tongue's right! Her tongue's the main part of her. Not been pulled out yet? It will be!"

Petroc agonized over what he could say to defend the wife whom these two could quite easily destroy. He knew she wouldn't take precautions herself, quite the opposite probably. She wouldn't give best to anybody, not the Lord God himself, especially if she lost her temper. Guzh obviously thought the same and suddenly changed the subject:

"You er. . .well, just be thankful it's me. If it wasn't for me, you'd have been a widower long ago."

"If that's the case, then thanks," said Petroc meekly.

He had gradually come to realize that this time it was going to be all right. It looked like they wouldn't be arresting Stepanida. For the moment. As long as she didn't go asking for trouble with the police.

"You don't get off with just a thank you." Guzh again switched his tack. Petroc became wary, submissively awaiting some new trick question from this relative of his. "Just for a thank you, I'm not going to protect you. Or fill you with vodka. You've got to get me the odd half-liter."

"Of course I would with the best will. . ."

"You're going to tell me you've got no vodka? Then get it! Buy it! Barter for it. Brew up some yourself. Can't you put yourself out for you own kin? I'm not exactly a stranger, am I?"

"Not a stranger, no."

'May you burn in hell, cousin of mine', thought Petroc despondently, already sensing that this new turn in the conversation was no better than the one before. Where could he get hold of vodka for him? There was none in the shops and none to borrow off friends. He had once tried to distil moonshine, when was that? The vessels and the long coil had all disappeared since then. Again, how was he to refuse Guzh? Petroc's excuses could hardly carry any weight here.

"That's it then. We're agreed, are we?" said Guzh, champing away at his bread and bacon. "You hear?"

"Yes, of course. Only. . ."

He just couldn't think what to say to the polizei; Stepanida came in from the passage and silently placed a bowlful of cabbage on the table.

"The Germans don't overfeed you then, that right?" she inquired cuttingly. Guzh's eyes widened malevolently.

"Any of your business? Or do you dislike Germans that much?"

"Oh, I like Germans. Like a boil on the backside."

"Stepanida!" shrieked Petroc. "Be quiet!"

"I'll do that."

"Be quiet! He. . .he's speaking as a relation. Being nice! And you. . ."

"All right," she spoke to Petroc. "You've had a skinful, so you're ready to lick his bum. You're a bit quick off the mark, I notice."

Her final words carried from the passage, a door slammed and in the ensuing silence, Petroc coughed apologetically. He was afraid of what Guzh would say next. Guzh, however, maintained a grim silence as he chewed. Petroc said softly:

"She's an old woman, we all know. What can you do?"

"Do?" the polizei caught him up savagely. "Get yourself a rope, thick as you like, with some bark on it. Then give her it. Otherwise she'll end up on a rope. Mark my words."

Petroc remained glumly silent, sitting by the table. He drew the heap of chopped home-grown to an angle and picked up the tobacco crumbs with unseeing fingers as Guzh munched his bacon, threatening and preaching to him on how to deal with his old woman. Half his age and look how clever he'd got under the Germans.

"One of the top brass has arrived," Guzh calmly informed him. "They call him a zonderfuhrer. He's ordered the fields to be completely cleared."

"Everything was cleared," said Petroc.

"Not everything. What was cleared isn't going anywhere. It's for the Germans' granaries. The potatoes are what's left. So they've got to be dug up. And handed in. For the German army. Got that? Like under the Soviets."

'Like hell you get them for the German army,' Petroc thought. 'Let them rot there.'

There wasn't much left in the bottle; Guzh poured it into the glass and tipped it into his mouth. He belched, wiped his greasy lips on his fist.

"And there's another thing. Lots of people drop in here, right? From the forest. Bandits!" Once more he stared at Petroc who went to pieces. "What, never? Alright, I'll believe you. But remember, if they do - it's straight to the police. In the township or the Settlement. At once, you hear? Any covering up. . .you know? You've been in the township?"

"Well, yes."

"Read the order? Death by shooting and confiscation of property. Germans, they're not joking. Understood?"

Petroc sighed sadly. What could you do? Trouble all around. Threats, shootings, confiscation. What sort of a life was it?

Guzh unhurriedly got out from behind the table, hiccupped from fullness and began pulling on the worn leather jacket.

"The omelet is cancelled!" he announced suddenly. "Another time. So be ready!"

4

Petroc sat on the bench leaning his head on his hands, staring absently at the table-top where fat autumn flies were crawling in the grease. He hadn't tidied away the dishes or the bread and Stepanida had kept clear. She'd given him a telling off from the doorway.

"Dishes out the hospitality! Bacon, cucumbers! Then he gives the orders: omelets for them! You going to lay the eggs yourself? Have you once fed the hens? If I wasn't here, how would you manage the farm? Didn't even get your horse back when everybody else got theirs. . ."

The horse had been his mistake of course, Petroc knew that and agonized over it as much as Stepanida did. But where could he get a horse? He'd done plenty of asking over in the Settlement, but what countryman would give up a horse? Everybody in agriculture needed a horse first and foremost. He'd had more luck in the township though and he now recalled his chief success.

"Who got his hands on kerosene then? Was it me or not?"

"Oh, kerosene! You'd make a cat laugh. People over there hauling off bags of salt, stocking up with matches, sugar even. But you brought back a bottle of kerosene - makes you laugh. . ."

"Well? During the winter, kerosene, you know! We've got some, not like a lot of people!"

"You be quiet! Kerosene. . .And you've found a fine relation, haven't you? A boozing pal! If he was my relative, I'd brush him out the door. He's bought and sold, and you drink with him, fill his face. The Germans are on their way, are you going to see to them as well?"

The door to the passage had been wide open summer-fashion. Stepanida kept passing through it to the stove and the boiler-house, clattering the mug in the bucket as she watered the livestock. Now they were alone, she was letting herself go and articulating everything that had been boiling up inside her about him, the war and life in general. Petroc was silent for the most part. What could he say, apart from objecting? He recognized the justice of Stepanida's feminine logic, but didn't want to abandon his own, which he sensed more closely and which sometimes rose suddenly in his heart.

"They'll come and you'll look after them! Where can you run?" he said softly, thinking perhaps his wife wouldn't hear. But she did and it was the last straw.

"That'll be your business! Not mine. I'm going to the forest with the cow, so I won't have to see."

"Oh that's terrible! Go on then, I'll manage."

"Oh, you'll manage will you? Think you'll do your boozing here? You'll get round them as well? They'll drink what you've got and give you sweet nothing in return."

Petroc was about to say something, but just waved his hand -Stepanida always had the last word. You couldn't get anything sensible into a woman's head. If it's as clear as day to you, it's night to her. Try to convince her that they'd been very lucky indeed with the polizei that day, that Guzh had mellowed after his vodka and not been too carping and that he really might shield them from the Germans. He'd said it himself - kinfolk! That's why they had to come to terms with him, be nice, make friends with him, like. Of course he was a bastard, a German toady and a thug, but he was the power in the land! As if he, Petroc, enjoyed drinking vodka with him and kow-towing to him - and listening to his preaching. But if you wanted to survive, you had to stand a lot more than that. When in Rome.

Of course, these expansive reflections were just a confused swirl in his drink-fuddled brain; aloud, he merely growled, knowing from experience that it was better not to contradict a bad-tempered wife; he wouldn't win anyway.

Stepanida, meanwhile, had got things off her chest, it seemed, and quieted down all of a sudden. When she had come into the hut, she'd even been alarmed at the sight of strangers, but her courage returned to her, especially when she got angry. Her anger was mainly directed against Petroc for his outburst against her, particularly in front of those mongrels. Let him shout his orders at her when they were alone together, like now, keeping quiet or mumbling his excuses to himself. She had detected in his shriek at her the undisguised desire to please Guzh and to humiliate her. She had never permitted anyone to humiliate her. She could stick up for herself. The Settlement folk to this day remembered her at the collective assembly, when she had exposed the thieving drunken storeman, Kolomits, in front of the district representative. He'd been dismissed from his lucrative job and there was even talk of prosecuting him. And when she had been a flax team-leader and Kondibisha's brother-in-law had spread rumors round the village that her women were stealing flax on the nightshift, she set up checks, even searches - several times stopping them on their way home and checking under their clothes; nothing was ever found and the suspicions against them were lifted.

She was energetically cutting the hay in the trough with a large knife. It was light in the open doorway, as the straw sifted down onto the beaten-earth floor and her feet. She was thinking bitterly that in these wretched times, Petroc was an utter liability. The main thing was, he hadn't a trace of hardness in him, no masculine independence; he was prepared to agree with anybody, be a yes-man to anyone, however brazen. You'd think being submissive had some good effect. The other way round, more like. If they didn't get put down straight away, these parasites would find a way of sitting on your neck and controlling you. She'd known Guzh from her childhood; he'd managed to escape the kulak expulsion during collectivization some-how, and now here he was again with a rifle in his hands, drinking vodka and seeking revenge for the past. But she hadn't forgotten her last encounter with him in 1930 and wouldn't ever forgive him either. He had a rifle, so what? Same for that Kolondenok; the whole village had detested him for long enough. When the war started he'd gone off with the first mobilization, but he'd come back a month later; the word went round that the Germans had released him from the prison camp. Kolondenok had turned up in the township all skin and bones, lousy and starving and now here he was filling his belly with police rations.

Stepanida wasn't afraid of them because she despised them. More than that, she hated them. Actually she kept well clear of them altogether. In this life which the war had forced on the world, Stepanida was sustained by the ancient integrity of the people, and while she retained the consciousness of that truth, she could look anyone boldly in the eye.

Her young chickens wandered restlessly about the yard, fence and garden, pecking here and there. There were only six old layers at the moment and Stepanida cherished them particularly: for a long time, the whole income of the farm had depended on eggs - money, wretched money, you couldn't do without it on a farm. She would collect two or three dozen eggs and take them into the township to sell or exchange for something useful. Without the hens they couldn't have carried on. Now she was thinking she ought to put out some chaff for them, but she was in a hurry to get to the fields and couldn't spare the time. She hastily made up half a bucket of mash for the pig and opened the low hatch of the shed. The pig, aware of his mistress, stirred quickly in the straw. Placing the bucket in the corner, she waited for a moment watching the pig champ away with gusto. A minute later he'd already got his feet in the bucket and knocked it over, but Stepanida made no move to set it right; she knew he would get every morsel as it was.

However, it was time to trot off to the fields - specifically to Sheep Valley, where Bobovka, tethered to a branch, was grazing. It didn't do to leave her alone for long at a time like this. Before leaving the farm, Stepanida nipped into the hut to snatch a crust of bread, for herself and as a treat for the cow. It was quiet and peaceful inside the hut. Petroc was sitting despondently at the table as before and didn't even look up at Stepanida.

"Feed the hens," she said, more softly than before.

As always after getting her grievances off her chest, she had calmed down and even felt sorry for the luckless Petroc, who sometimes exasperated her, or made her laugh, or, rarely, even happy. Still, overall he wasn't a bad man, not evil-tempered that was the main thing; just shiftless and unable to get on in life. Apart from which he was ten years older than her and hadn't been well for a long time. All his ailments stemmed from his everlasting smoking, she knew that for a fact and reminded him of it practically every day. A waste of time.

Stepanida ran along the garden path towards Sheep Valley, while Petroc sat on for a while, before heaving a heavy sigh and rising from the table. He'd had to drink vodka since morning, but hadn't had the chance to have a smoke. Now left on his own in the hut, he slowly rolled a cigarette. To get a light, he had to rake through all yesterday's embers in the stove before finding a live coal. He blew on it and at last, with long-deferred satisfaction, he inhaled. This was the only joy in his life, lighting up a cigarette; there was no other pleasure left in his existence it seemed. A good thing he'd sown some of his own in the garden that spring and not relied on shop supplies - there was none in the shops now. Although homegrown was somewhat worse than makhorka, it wasn't as bad as all that. Petroc was used to it and didn't really want any better.

He still felt a bit drunk and upset by what had passed; from time to time he swore quietly, almost soundlessly: to blazes with it all! Never mind the Germans, whether they got to the farm or not, but their own people had! And who? Kinsman Guzh. You'd never hide the pig from that one, he knew about the pig, and the cow and the hens, and all about Petroc's former life, there was no concealing anything here. Guzh had the power now: if he wanted he could take him into the township to the police station and hang him on the first telegraph pole, as was normal nowadays. So what was there to do, beg him to leave them alone, show mercy? That would hardly work. Even when drunk, Petroc had noticed his predator's eyes flash when he'd started talking about Stepanida. So he'd have to be kept sweet with little things - eggs, bacon-fat, gherkins and cabbage, since they had nothing else. That wouldn't be enough, surely.

Once upon a time, before the collectivization, Petroc had made a not very successful attempt to produce illicit booze, then all of a sudden, there'd been a government push on the flax front. Everything suitable had to be handed in under the production plan, but that wasn't all; regional representatives arrived, going round shaking out all the cloths in the yards and tossing the straw about in the sheds - looking for flax. They didn't find any, but they did come across the distilling gear in the boiler-house - the kettle and the fine coil of copper tubing, which they immediately requisitioned. Then he had to pay a fine and go through the ritual disgrace at the assemblies; he cursed the poorly-esteemed business of homebrewing. But all that had been long ago. Nowadays, when everything in life had altered so drastically, probably attitudes to homebrewing had as well. Petroc felt in his bones that vodka was going to be virtually the only thing of value around, something you couldn't be without. Drinking man or teetotaler, vodka-making was going to be essential.

He went through the passage into the boiler-house, coughing and leaning against the door-post. As usual, it was semidark in there and full of persistent odors, so intermingled as to be indistinguishable. The strongest smell, however, was of old clothes, dust and mouse droppings. Through the little window cut in the timber, the feeble light of the overcast morning scarcely penetrated. Petroc surveyed a row of wooden storage-bins under the blank windowless wall and the empty straw baskets that were filled with grain in good years when the bins couldn't hold all the harvest. In the corner by the door, nestled the old millstones, thin and worn and thickly powdered with grey flour. Alongside, gathering dust, was an ancient spinning-wheel and a brand-new aspen-wood clothes chest, its hoops already rusting, stood white and gleaming. There were tubs, empty for the most part, while neatly, stacked against the wall awaiting their hour were Stepanida's looms, complete with reeds, threads and rollers. On a shelf above them, a row of dusty bottles glinted dully; looming darkly important at the end was the large basketed bottle containing the kerosene. Next to them, near the window hung last year's strings of onions; then a few birch brooms near the soot-blackened ceiling and bunches of medicinal herbs prepared by Stepanida during the summer. The little boiler-house, its walls blackened by a hundred years of smoke, its corners swathed with dense cobwebs, was crowded with all kinds of domestic effects, but where the kettle was he just couldn't remember. Petroc prowled round the boiler-house, peering into all the dark corners, rummaging through the rubbish behind the stove-cum-fireplace in the far corner, before finally dragging out a blackened vessel, corroded by rust after ten years of disuse.

Out in the passage by the door where it was a bit lighter, he examined it meticulously. The thing was in good condition, generally speaking; the main thing was it had no holes and if the rust was cleaned off and sanded, it would do perfectly well. Now he needed some kind of tub or vat, that one Stepanida used to wash the potatoes in for instance. The potatoes could be done in the iron pot.

There was one drawback - no coil.

Petroc squatted down on a low bench near the buckets of water and began figuring out where he could get hold of a coil. In the old days, he'd have called into the township to see Leiba the smith, who used to shoe horses, fix up axes, sharpen the womens' sickles and could tin a bowl or repair a lock as well. Leiba was a master craftsman and would have helped out Petroc, his friend of many years. At all events, Petroc held him in respect and always addressed his as Leibochka - being called Petrochek in return. Apart from anything else, they were of an age and had known each other virtually from early childhood. Leiba had done all his forge work for him for years and Petroc hadn't been niggardly about paying: in money, eggs, bacon-fat, sometimes corn - whatever the farm had at the time. If there was nothing, Leiba might do it "on trust" and wait for a month or six, till the wheat was harvested or the beast was slaughtered. There had never been any misunderstanding between them, let alone grievance. Leiba would certainly have bent the wretched coil for him, only his smithy had been incorporated long ago into the collective and he'd moved to his relations in Lepel. Now it wasn't clear if anybody was working the smithy, which had been closed since summer.

Over the road in the Settlement, there was another man, Kornila, also a master metalworker and he could probably have thought something up or found something in his vast collection of spare parts. Petroc, however, had not been on friendly terms with him for a long time - worse in fact, they'd fallen out and never spoke if they met. Stepanida was the cause of all that; there'd been something between her and Kornila when she was a girl, before she'd married Petroc. Incidentally, she'd done the right thing there. The young Petroc hadn't been a bad sort at all; he played the fiddle what's more, not like that sullen old vampire, Kornila. That one was a difficult character all right and hard to please. If he took a dislike to someone he'd keep it up to his dying day. He was tight-fisted and greedy, too, even though he lived pretty well and didn't join the collective - he worked for the fire brigade. He was a real handyman - he could lay a floor, fix a window frame and even install a stove in a hut; still better not get involved with Kornila. He'd have to ask somebody else from the Settlement if he got the chance.

Having smoked to his heart's content, Petroc cleared his throat. Indeed it was time to get started. Yes, first off - feed the hens. Locating an old wooden corn-measure in the boiler-house, he scooped out some barley chaff from the end bin and carried it out into the passage. The hens had obviously been lying in wait for him and as soon as he appeared with the pot, they came racing in from the garden and out from under the fence and the shed. He flung the contents far and wide, so that they would all get a share. While the birds were pecking enthusiastically over the trodden part of the yard and searching through the grass, he pondered the twists of fate which had wrought such changes in a man's existence. The one-time master of Yakimovschina could never have descended to feeding the hens of a morning! Or didn't he have anything more pressing to do round the farm? There'd been more than ten head of livestock here alone: a horse, a young mare, two cows, not counting calves, six or eight sheep. And pigs, of course, never less than two - a boar fattening up and a smaller one for next year. Of course, there'd been a few more working hands. But it had all dwindled down to practically nothing; the only things he had to concern himself about were the cow, the little boar piglet and these hens. The collective had relieved him of responsibility for the horse and the sheep had gradually gone; who was there to see to them? The children had flown the parental nest when barely fledged, there was no getting them back. And this war would probably finish the farm off for good.

Still coughing, he stood for a while on the footworn stones of the threshold before deciding to get to grips finally with the potato clamp. The potatoes were giving a good crop this time; they'd dug them all up in the garden and filled the cellar. Water sometimes got into the cellar in spring, however, so he had to earth up the extra in a clamp on the mound at the end of the garden - that was the habit in these parts in good potato years. Potatoes had to be looked after; since time immemorial they had been the main produce of the field - grain didn't always grow and was often exhausted by spring, but the good old potato always lasted. If they were picked in good time and kept safe from frost and water, there would be enough for them and the livestock - people had been saved from famine by the potato more years than one.

5

Several days in succession the autumn sky had piled up threateningly with heavy rain clouds; a strong and variable wind blew. Then things settled down, the night was warmer and towards morning persistent rain began falling. Waking at dawn, Stepanida heard the indistinct monotonous sound beyond the hut wall and thought that today she would have to delay taking the cow out to graze. Petroc was lying on his bed in the corner and not even coughing, so he must be asleep. She rose and went out into the passage. At the door she could hear it, the quiet dripping from the roof, and a dark pool had already formed on the earth floor of the passage. For the hundredth time Stepanida recalled her negligent husband with annoyance and moved a pot under the place in the roof where the steady dripping came. Accustomed to getting up early, she knew that she wouldn't get any more sleep now, especially as Petroc was already moving about and coughing behind the sacking as he searched for his tobacco pouch - he couldn't start the day without a smoke. With a sleepy yawn, Stepanida picked up the new maple milking-pail, bought that spring, and went off to the cowshed to see to the cow.

Meanwhile it was almost dawn. The rain was drifting densely from the low heavy sky, but it was a thin autumnal fret, almost windless, and hadn't caused much mud in the yard as yet. There was a shining dung-puddle near the cowshed, but that hadn't dried up since summer.

A crow began cawing on the lime tree, now wet and drooping as it lost its leaves. Let's hope it doesn't mean misfortune, thought Stepanida, uneasy. This had been the fourth or fifth morning it had flown in and settled on the top of the tree, before lowering its wide black beak over the farm and uttering a piercing cry, as if calling to someone in the forest. A couple of times Stepanida had thrown a lump of firewood at it, but the crow was barely disturbed. Now, after crying out, it fell silent of its own accord and sat quietly for a little, before spreading its wings and flying off to the gully. The branch she had disturbed gently rocked its single russet leaf.

Stepanida took her time and carefully milked Bobovka, seeing with satisfaction that she had grazed well the day before in Sheep Valley - the pail was full to the brim. No getting away from it, the cow had turned out a great success, still young and not persnickety about feed, she gave milk in plenty. Stepanida cherished the animal and regarded it as her own most treasured possession. In times like these, such a cow was fortune indeed.

She left the cowshed, thinking she ought to throw the cow a handful of grass, make a fuss over her for a while, then boil up some soup or potatoes, seeing it was raining. For some days now she hadn't had the stove on to make hot food. However, she hadn't managed to cross the yard when her ears picked up a powerful rumbling sound, muffled by the thick weather. Not yet realizing what this could mean, she glanced out through the gates and stood petrified - rocking ponderously on the ruts in the misty rain, something huge, grey and bull-headed was moving from the road to the farm. Stepanida did not at once recognize it as a machine. Behind it rolled something smaller, with a tall pipe like a samovar; the wind was already carrying a smell of smoke to her. There were various white numbers and letters on the streaming sides of the vehicle and its huge wheels couldn't fit the track, so that it was crushing the verge on one side. Slowly, but with a sense of inevitability, the machine came nearer to the farm, until with a heavy hot breath it halted at the approach to the gates. Here the exhaust was more detectable and a stench of petrol filled the yard. A skinny figure in a hat and long, wet overcoat leaped down from the high cabin-step and Stepanida immediately recognized the township teacher, Sventkovsky.

"Good day, Mrs Bogatka," he greeted her with unusual courtesy and an enigmatic saccharine smile on his thin, aquiline face. "Guzh has ordered a German detachment to be billeted here. Well, just see everything's all right."

Stepanida, however, was silent in a kind of torpor, gazing in bewilderment at the vehicle, whose tarpaulin top had bent aside some of the lower branches of the lime. Just then came the metallic clang of the cabin doors and two men jumped out. Without examining their clothing or their faces, Stepanida realized that these were Germans by a certain elusive watchfulness about their stance. It was only as they came towards her across the yard that her mind took in that they walked like people, on two legs, and even seemed to be unarmed. The one who had jumped down from the near side of the machine was wearing a rather tight uniform with a lot of buttons. His head was close-cropped at the back and bore a rather wide cap; slender arms protruded from his short sleeves. The pale, young face behind round, black-framed glasses glowed with good-natured boyish interest, curiosity almost, in everything he saw. True, the other man who nimbly hastened out from behind the machine was quite different from the first - plump, much older and with a rather too swift, preoccupied glance, with which he

instantly took in the yard, cowshed and hut. He suddenly shouted out
something ill-tempered and imperative. She didn't understand and, totally
disoriented by the excitement, stood mute with her milk pail in the middle
of the yard.

"O mleko!"

The Germans jumped down one after another from the tarpaulin top into
the yard and it gradually dawned on Stepanida that they had not called in
just on an off-chance, but were to be billeted here as the teacher had said
and were already asking about the milk. She didn't grudge the milk -she
hoped it choked them. They didn't make a rush for it, however; the teacher
said something to the tubby one and she listened with amazed interest to
this language she had never heard before, though she comprehended not
a word. Sventkovsky likely knew German well but the German didn't know
Russian at all and said something to the teacher in his own language.
Sventkovsky turned to Stepanida.

"The German gentleman feldwebel is asking if the milk is fresh."

"Yes it is, why shouldn't it be?" she said and set the pail down on the
grass. The milky foam had still not settled and was lapping at the rim.

Sventkovsky and the Germans exchanged a few words and the young one
ran to the machine, returning quickly with a white mug in his hand.
Sventkovsky cautiously dipped it into the pail and handed it officiously to
the feldwebel. He accepted it and, bending forward so as to not to dribble
onto his protruding paunch, drank down the milk and turned the mug over.

"Gut, gut."

The teacher became quite animated all at once and dipped again to
supply the young one in glasses. Extending his arms from his short-sleeved
uniform, he also drank his fill. Then the mug was taken by another German,
a rather foolish-looking one with spots like chicken pox on his face. He
drank the lot too, but the fourth, tall and thin as a rake, wearing a kind of
smock-overall, merely tasted the mug before making a face and spitting the
milk out onto the grass. 'Don't like it? To blazes with you, then,' thought
Stepanida. With a feeling compounded of fear and curiosity, she meekly
stood by her pail, surveying the unexpected lodgers. Her heart thumped
painfully in her chest, though their faces seemed far from threatening.
Maybe they would just have a drink and move on, came the involuntary
thought as she repeated mechanically: it's good milk, good milk. . .The,
Germans, however, paid no attention to what she was saying or to her either.
While the rest were drinking, the feldwebel nimbly trotted round the yard,
glancing at the firewood and going round the boiler-house. She thought he
would go into the hut but he didn't, he turned away towards the cowshed
and suddenly halted by the well. Sventkovsky in his polished calf-leather

boots moved towards him through the dew-laden grass and she heard them discussing something in the language she didn't understand.

The rest, having drunk their fill, also moved over to the well, one by one; something had attracted their interest there. She remained standing by her pail, not knowing what was best - get away as far as she could or wait around? All the same, the master of the house should be here; he'd disappeared somewhere and wasn't going to show himself. Or he hadn't seen who it was who had called on him, thought Stepanida, vexed.

"Mrs Bogatka!" Sventkovsky called her again. "The German feldwebel wishes to check your water. Be good enough to bring a bucket."

"A bucket? Right. . ."

'So they've really got here at last,' she thought as she ran into the passage, beginning to get irritated. Once there, she called out in a voice of subdued alarm: "Petroc!" Then, tipping the contents into a bin, she took the new zinc bucket into the yard, where the young one in glasses took it from her. Attaching it to the chain, he deftly released the windlass; as soon as the bucket touched the water in the depths, he began to turn the metal handle to bring it to the surface. The rest stood around without moving, waiting. They were ignoring her again and it occurred to her that Petroc really had to be got out here. But at that very moment he appeared himself out of the passage, old shoes on bare feet, walking past her to the well, where he doffed his cloth cap with its floppy brim in a gesture of timorous respect.

"Er, good water that. . ." he addressed the Germans, his voice trembling and nervous.

Meanwhile, the Germans had hauled up the bucket and poured it into a sort of flat, green pan, talking among themselves in constrained voices. Nobody, apart from Sventkovsky, even so much as glanced at the farm-owner, and it was only after the teacher had said something in German that the spotty-faced one measured Petroc with a leisurely noncommittal stare. The latter bowed again, at which the young one in glasses, standing nearer than the others, took a packet of cigarettes from his pocket, selected one for himself and held one out to him. Petroc still awkwardly crushing his cap, accepted the cigarette in horny fingers, then stood as if not knowing what to do with it. The German used his lighter but didn't, however, offer it to Petroc.

They were discussing something, no doubt evaluating the well, so Stepanida took the milk pail and went off into the passage. She was a little afraid to shut the door behind her and from the shade of the passageway she began to watch the Germans, listening to their talk and noting to herself the servile way Petroc was giving explanations and pointing things out. He hadn't replaced his cap and the thin drizzle was drifting down onto his balding head and its few pitiful grey hairs. They were listening to him without interrupting. This easy relationship with the Germans was not to Stepanida's liking and she wondered whether he was going to conduct them into the hut as well. She was extremely averse to that; she felt the hut was her inviolable retreat, to be defended against outsiders, especially total strangers. If only they would clear off soon, she thought. But to all appearances, no one was disposed to do that - they'd unhooked their field kitchen from the vast vehicle and everybody except the feldwebel began dragging it into the yard with red, sweating faces. Petroc too gave a hand, straining and pushing at the huge rubber tire, then indicating the best place to set it up. They finally found a suitable site next to the well and Stepanida became totally despondent. What she had always feared more than anything had come about. Yakimovschina had failed to keep clear of the Germans. Now what was going to happen?

However, things took their course, independently of anyone's will, according to the laws, often strange, often terrible, dictated by the war. After setting up their kitchen in the yard, the feldwebel and the teacher set out for the passage with that fool Petroc trotting ahead pointing out the path to the hut. The feldwebel paused on the entrance steps and before entering, gazed round the interior in fastidious distaste. Sventkovsky explained something volubly as Stepanida shifted a bin away from the entrance and the German came into the passage. She went on through into the boiler-house to get out from underfoot, still tormented by the question of what it was they wanted. But here was Petroc opening wide the hut door and the lot of them moved in there with a sort of curiosity on their animated features. It was as if she saw her hut through the eyes of others for the first time, long past its best with its leaning partition, the darkened timbers of the roof, and the walls plastered over with old yellow newspapers. She hadn't washed the floor in a long time and gazed in annoyance at the grimy boards by the door with their dried-on scraps of potato skin and the sooty pots by the stove. Alien feet were trampling all over the hut, rough leather boots leaving wet, dirty marks on the dry floorboards: she wondered what the devil they were looking for? She remained standing in the passage in tense expectation of them clearing out at last. But they were engaged in leisurely conversation in there, glancing out of the windows, examining the icons, while the feldwebel pushed back the sacking and looked behind the stove. His lip curled in disgust.

In any event she didn't wait for their emergence as her attention was distracted by events in the yard, where the field kitchen by the well was smoking away fustily from its damp wood fuel, and the skinny German in the overalls was crouching down picking about in the firebox. Then he strode off purposefully across the yard, and she was afraid he'd heard the piglet squeal. But no, the piglet was keeping very quiet apparently; the German soon reappeared bent double, carrying a whole armful of firewood for the kitchen. Stepanida felt a chill in her soul on seeing him - they were the birch logs she'd been keeping for heating the hut in the winter, just a little heap right under the eaves next to the pigsty. And he'd found them! Her first instinct was to go out and say: that's not right, young man, that's not your property is it? But Stepanida swallowed what seemed a thick lump in her throat and told herself: let it be, let's see what happens now.

She had by now come to terms with her first anxiety and felt superfluous here; she wanted to get away somewhere, where she didn't have to watch things and get upset: let them organize things the way they wanted. She couldn't hinder them anyway. But she knew she couldn't leave the farm either, there was the cow, the pig and her nine hens and no rooster. As ill-luck would have it, she hadn't managed to get the cow away into the fields - thank heaven she had contrived to smuggle the pig away, so it wouldn't be easy to find in the nettles behind the hut. A good thing she hadn't let the hens out of the coop either - hungry or not, they could sit things out safely for the time being. There was no point hiding the cow, sooner or later they would find out about it. It had to be taken out to pasture. No sooner had Stepanida started looking for the rope in the passage when Petroc raced out of the hut, his wrinkled stubbly face alive and glowing, almost joyful.

"Woman, eggs! Eggs now, hurry!"

'Eggs', she repeated to herself. Of course, they couldn't manage without eggs. If they start with eggs, where on earth will they finish? After an interval, however, she opened the boiler-house door and from under the millstone sieve retrieved her old basket in which two dozen eggs gleamed dimly. She wanted to give them to Petroc, let him see to them himself, but Petroc had already returned to the hut and she had perforce to follow. Not knowing who she should give them to, she placed the eggs on the end of the bench. At once hands reached out for the basket and Stepanida, stepping back a pace just couldn't take her eyes off these avid, alien hands. The first to slip deftly in was a delicate, white, little hand probably that feldwebel's, feeling the topmost rounded shell of the speckled hen's egg. The German wasn't satisfied for some reason, so he put it back and took another, the same only smaller and perhaps cleaner or yellower than the first. The round one was seized at once by fat fingers like cow's teats, with brown stripes near the joints: then another, from the edge, was taken by a young driver's hand with dirty marks on it; it protruded from the familiar short-sleeved battledress blouse. Stepanida couldn't watch any longer; she lowered her eyes to Sventkovsky's clay-spattered, calf-leather boots. Then came the sound of an eggshell cracking; chatting among themselves, the Germans had started cracking the eggs and sucking them loudly without bread and salt. Sensing a faint squeamishness, she turned away to go into the passage and almost collided with the feldwebel who was tapping his little, yellow egg with a small knife away from the others.

To her own astonishment, she had speedily regained her composure, perhaps because the Germans had not turned out to be at all fearsome; they hadn't sworn or threatened and they behaved themselves coolly and confidently just like owners of the farmstead. Well, what was odd about that? They were the victors and had conquered this land, now it was their right to do with it what they wanted. To all appearances they were well aware of their rights and made full use of them. But it was precisely this confidence in their right, together with their sense of impunity in doing what was wrong, that at once disposed her against the intruders.

When they poured out of the low doorway, leaping down from the threshold steps, she was standing by the cowshed in the yard, waiting. She was deliberately mounting guard on the path to the firewood so as to intercept the one in the overalls, who was fiddling with the field kitchen - feeding in the birch logs. She couldn't say anything to him, she just wanted to look him in his shameless eyes. He didn't go for any more wood, however; his cooking machine was going well by now, emitting mighty puffs of smoke and occasional showers of sparks into the sky. Stepanida was worried: as long as there wasn't a fire. All these years she had feared a fire breaking out from the stove or a lightning strike; she'd often dreamed at night that Yakimovschina was on fire, while with legs of cotton wool she ran helplessly round and round unable to do anything.

The Germans came out all together, the feldwebel slightly apart from the others talking to Sventkovsky, who listened with exaggerated attention. Then the feldwebel issued a command to the cook, who at once left the stove and stood to attention, uttering the single word, "jawohl." What they were talking about, Stepanida had no notion and wished in her heart they might all drop dead together.

Meanwhile the remaining Germans had unloaded a number of yellow wooden cases and three heavy sacks stamped on the sides in black; next to them on the earthen parapet, they placed two short rifles on yellow slings. Clearly all this was to stay here with the kitchen, as the big vehicle was preparing to depart. The young one in glasses with the short haircut was already getting into the cab and soon the vehicle gave a snort and started to quiver. There was a strong stink of petrol. The feldwebel jumped aboard on the other side and the machine moved heavily backwards, excavated a pit in the soft earth and with a hellish racket, turned away towards the road.

The field kitchen and two Germans, the skinny one in the overalls and the older one with the spotty face, remained in the farmyard. They started hauling water up from the well as Petroc, awkward and sheepish, came up to Stepanida.

"Oh dear, oh lord!" he complained softly. "They're to be billeted for a long time."

She said nothing, although his words had made a grim impact. Petroc glanced round as if someone might overhear.

"They said to clean the floor. And get the stuff out of there."

"Where to?" Stepanida was astonished.

"The boiler-house, they said. We've got to get ourselves out too."

"What is this - summer? The boiler-house? They think. . ."

"That's what they said. All done by tonight. Their CO's coming."

"Let them clear it out! The lot! Let them choke", she said, angry, recalling how Petroc had put himself out to please them. And it had all been a waste of time, they were being thrown out.

The morning was getting on; the sky lowered over the desolate earth, but it was no longer raining and the wind had dropped. The smoke was catching at her throat as it enveloped the hut and the boiler-house, while a livid smoke blanket crawled across the potato field and over the garden. Stepanida opened the door of the cowshed with a flourish and led Bobovka out. They could do what they liked, she had to graze the cow, how long was it supposed to stand in the cowshed? To avoid seeing the Germans again, she led the animal past the firewood and through the garden straight onto the field. Bobovka glanced back anxiously once or twice, sensing strangers in the yard, and Stepanida pulled her halter in exasperation to get away from that yard as quickly as possible.

She took the cow past the edge of the potato field and along the overgrown gully whose steep slope abutted on the farm's vegetable garden. The gully was deep, with a winding gurgling streamlet at the bottom. On the other side about a dozen fir trees rose up in an intrusive small copse, standing out sharply against the thinning yellow foliage of the hazels, birches and aspens which grew far and wide on both hillsides. The gully was also regarded as part of the farmstead; you could hide yourself away from trouble here, sit down away from the war for a couple of days, away from the malevolent eyes of strangers. If it were not for the livestock. You couldn't sit for long if you had animals. They needed to be fed. Pity about the farm buildings as well, with their peasants' bits and pieces; they mightn't be much but you couldn't take them along with you and without them how could you live out in the woods? Especially now in autumn with it dripping down your collar and the cold weather coming on. So you had to hold on to the roof over your head. But the Germans had looked it over as if they couldn't find anything better anywhere around! Obviously the bridge was to blame for everything; they'd wanted that badly and the farm went along with it.

Having starved since morning, the cow avidly seized on the wet grass at her feet, pulling the rope from Stepanida's hands; let her, she thought. Not much point being angry at that fool of a Petroc, what could he do now? Whichever way you turned, once they'd given the order, you had to carry it out and prepare the room for the uninvited guests. But Petroc wouldn't wash the floor, that meant they would both get it in the neck. She ought to go back to the farm.

In a small clearing by the very edge of the gully, she fastened the end of the rope to a hazelnut tree and after watching Bobovka for a while, went back by the field's edge.

She felt grief and disquiet in her heart: the possibilities of human life had dwindled down to nothing. The war with its voracious claw had crept ever nearer and now it had slid into the hut, under the icons, behind the table. What was there left to do but suffer and weep. But the earth was overflowing in these days with tears and blood. So what was left - bear all in silence and wait for better times? A long wait. She felt it in her heart: after a small misfortune, a major calamity would come, then you'd cry your eyes out and no one would help you. . .

6

While the two Germans were busy with their kitchen, Petroc squatted down by the window in the hut and from sheer misery rolled himself a big cigar the size of a bean-pod. He stuck the yellowish German cigarette, squashed from being in his pocket, behind the angle of one of the icons for later. Time to get down to it: tidy up the hut, haul out the inessentials to the boiler-house and scrub the floor, that was the main thing. He was angry with Stepanida for her lack of cooperation. Just leaving it all and running away. Damn that cow, it could have stood in the cowshed for one morning! No time for cows when those. . .drove into the yard. Still the devil had landed him with all this worry and sent the Germans - as if they hadn't enough towns and villages big and small, they had to get to his god-forsaken farm.

Barely suppressing a cough, (his chest had ached all morning) Petroc glanced through the window at the soldier-cooks at work by the well. One of them, thin and fair-haired in overalls which bagged round the backside, was sprinkling something white into the kitchen boiler, eliciting clouds of damp steam; meanwhile the older spotty-faced one was laying out eatables of some sort on the lid of a wooden case covered with a white tablecloth. 'Just look at that, all refined!' thought Petroc with envy and sighed despondently: for that refinement he now had to set to with bucket and cloth and make a start on the dirt inside the hut. It wasn't enough for them to be warm and clean as well. Refined. . .

His cigar had come unstuck meanwhile and he didn't know how to light up; he wanted to ask the Germans for a light but couldn't screw up courage to do so. At length his desire for a smoke overcame his reservations. He went out into the yard and halted about five paces from the kitchen holding his unlit cigar in plain view. He thought they would notice and offer him a light, he felt awkward about asking, and a little fearful. But it was as if they hadn't noticed him. The lanky one went on stirring his mixture, while the kitchen steamed and smoked over the whole farmstead; the squat one, who was clearly his assistant, was cutting up bacon-fat with an enormous knife. Petroc coughed quietly and moved two paces forward.

"Er. . .Gents, if you've got a light. . ."

They seemed to comprehend. The short one in the white, grease-stained apron turned his broad, spotty face towards him and good-naturedly growled "ja, ja". Petroc didn't understand, but since the German said nothing more, he guessed that permission had been granted. Approaching the kitchen, he used a piece of birch bark to grub out a live coal, rather clumsily, scorching his fingers. He lit up his cigar and after the first few drags, sensed that his homegrown was defeating all those other foreign odors in the yard.

"Wass? Wass?" The cook's assistant turned in keen interest and abandoned his knife on the tablecloth. Petroc understood and readily brought out his tobacco pouch.

"Sure, aha, yes. It's my own, homegrown, if the gentleman wants. . ."

The German tore off a small piece from a rolled-up newspaper and Petroc measured out a good pinch of tobacco. Thereupon the German rolled a cigar fairly expertly, licked it assiduously and lit up from his own lighter - a little thing with a tiny gleaming tongue of flame. Petroc watched him with an almost childish trembling, so keen was he that the German should like his tobacco. Now the German inhaled deeply, then let it out and Petroc thought: now he'll cough. However no cough was forthcoming, he simply blinked his eyelashes, light as if bleached by the sun.

"Ist gut!"

"Gut?" Petroc remembered the word from the last war and felt glad. "I. . .er. . .good, that's it. My own, so. . ."

"Gut," the German repeated and said something to the cook, who was stirring the boiler with an enormous oar. He, however, merely barked something once or twice, and the spotty one laid the cigar on the edge of the table and picked up the knife. Petroc reckoned that was enough. They were at work after all and hadn't time to chat. He backed away somehow crabwise and went off towards the porch.

The cleaning-up had to be done, but still he delayed, not knowing where to start. He had never tidied the hut, Stepanida had always done that, and in recent years Fenya had given her a hand. He had had other male concerns. Now the war seemingly had levelled things out, womens' work had fallen to him as well. Well then, the first thing was to clear the floor so that nothing would get in the way of the cleaning; he began dragging all the pots and jars, the fork, the poker and the broom out into the passage; he shifted the bench from the corner, where a vast pile of domestic odds and ends had accumulated: ragged old shoes, an empty rusty flowerpot, a bin lid, various rags and some woodchips, probably for kindling the stove. All this had lain there for long years, everything in its place, bothering nobody. Why was it

in the way of these newcomers now? Petroc took away sundry garments on
a pole near the stove into the boiler-house and took down the case from the
wall and picked up his violin. This shouldn't be taken away, it had to be
protected from damp. Petroc carefully slid it behind the icons. His little
fiddle was wholly hidden there: let it lie and wait for better times, he
thought.

The hut had become roomy, almost empty. Petroc heaved a little sigh as
he brought a bucket of water in from the passage and found an old rag under
the stove. Still vexed at Stepanida, he poured the water over the most used
area in front of the stove, let that loosen the dirt. The water at once spread
far and wide across the boards, gradually collecting in a dark, murky pool
by the threshold. Petroc stood in the middle of the hut. He had to get out
to the passage for the broom, but he couldn't step across the pool and he
didn't fancy taking his shoes off or getting his feet wet through his broken
boots. He had to wait till the water drained off somewhere from the
entrance.

"Heavens, what's this? What have you been up to?" came Stepanida's voice
from the passage.

"Washing the floor. . ."

"You want that rag wrapped round your head! Who washes floors like
that? Have you gone mad?"

Standing beyond the doorway, Stepanida was slapping her sides in
exasperation and scolding him - of course he'd done everything wrong, in
his own way, which always earned him a telling-off from his wife. Still, as
she'd got here, let her do the cleaning herself; he'd done his bit, cleared
everything out - nothing left to do, just wash the floor.

"So why did you go off with the cow?"

"I don't need your permission. . ."

And although their quarrelling was rather more restrained than usual
because of the presence of strangers in the yard, they could still be heard.
Stepanida was waving her arms about in the passage, unwilling to cross the
pool herself, when the curious, spotty face of the German appeared behind
her. He giggled, said something even, so that she lost the thread. The
German, however, returned to his kitchen and Stepanida tossed a rag across
the threshold.

"Mop the water up! All of it, every last drop!"

She had to be obeyed and Petroc, groaning with the effort, crouched
down to the puddle. He swirled the dirty water about with the cloth and
then wrung it out over an old smoke-blackened pot. There was still a great
deal of water left, the pool had hardly diminished. Stepanida meanwhile
had gone off somewhere again, so he decided to be done with this tedious

labor at one fell swoop and began sweeping the water around the floor -
into the corners, under the stove, anywhere just to be rid of the pond. This
was more successful than sopping it up with a cloth and Petroc was already
getting to the old, worn threshold, when the shadow of the German once
more appeared in the doorway, this time with a bucket of lightly steaming
water. Petroc understood at once and gazed at the foolish, faintly-smiling
face of the German in unaffected gratitude.

"Thank you, sir. Thanks a lot. . ."

The German handed it over the threshold and straightened up.

"Bitte, bitte."

"Thanks a lot," repeated Petroc, overcome. Kindness such as this should
be requited surely, he thought. One good turn deserved another, that he
understood. "Just a moment, sir," he said and slipped along the passage to
the boiler-house, where there were still a few eggs left. Only he didn't know
where they were, those eggs, and while he was looking through the baskets
and bins, the shouts of the senior cook echoed in from the yard:

"Karl, Kom! Karl!"

Petroc realized that he wouldn't have time - Stepanida knew how to hide
things, and sure enough, the German ran out to the kitchen and an
exasperated Petroc emerged into the passage where he bumped into his
wife.

"Look, Karl brought some hot water."

"Hot. . ."

Apparently not in the least pleased, Stepanida crossed the step in silence
and picked up the cloth from the floor. She hadn't had time to drop it into
the warm water before the lanky cook appeared in the passage. With a
hushed, malevolent whisper he seized the bucket through the doorway and
emptied it out with a flourish over the floor. A thick cloud of warm steam
shot up to the ceiling, shrouding Stepanida's stony face. The bucket clanked
briefly, and the German shot out of the passageway.

"Drop dead, misery-guts," said Stepanida in a low voice, shaking out her
soaking skirt. Petroc glanced round - what if they heard, maybe they'd
understand. That thin one was a bad-tempered swine most likely, best be
on your guard with him.

"Quiet, woman! They give the orders, what can you do. . ."

"I hope they choke on their orders. . ."

They washed the floor with cold water - a good job it had been in the tub
overnight, there was no going to the well. Petroc didn't want to go near it,
nor did Stepanida. She scrubbed the floor with the broom, washed the
benches, scraped the old, long table with a knife and wiped the windowsills.
Petroc tidied up in the passage and carted out the bits and pieces to the

boiler-house or under the shed or onto the parapet, and threw the tow up into the loft. The place had probably never known attention like it; even before holidays they had never cleaned it so meticulously as they did now under duress. Petroc wondered if it would all be to the Germans' liking. And what would happen if it wasn't.

Meanwhile dinner was cooking over by the well. The smoke had virtually ceased by now, as had the steam. The round lid of the kitchen pot was loosely fixed, and the smell of fried onion and bacon-fat, the flavoring constituents of German soup, drifted out over the yard. The morose, evil-tempered cook was bustling about over there like an automaton, he never sat down once. After his brief clash with the cook, the subdued Karl was gloomily hanging about by the table. Now, however, the lanky one paused to take out a watch on a shiny chain from his trouser pocket and said something to his assistant. Petroc did a bit of clearing up in the passage, while keeping his eye on them and couldn't help feeling sympathy for the kindhearted Karl. All appearances suggested that he'd received a blasting from his superior, otherwise he wouldn't have turned away from Petroc with such demonstrative indifference when the latter came out onto the porch to brush round the entrance. He hadn't finished his task when an echoing rumble came from the highway and the familiar vehicle with the tarpaulin top swivelled towards the farm, rocking from side to side in the ruts. Petroc rushed into the passage with the broom in his hands.

"They're coming! Woman, you hear? They're coming!"

Grabbing something as she ran, Stepanida leaped out of the hut and closed the door. They both froze in the passage, waiting and listening. The machine swayed ponderously on along the track, before halting in the entrance under the limes. Petroc was waiting for someone to jump from the cab, but instead, something clanged inside the vehicle and about ten Germans one after the other spilled out from the tarpaulin chassis. They were variously dressed, in tunics, abbreviated jackets, two in camouflage capes, and all with a sort of shallow pan at their waist or in their hands. For some reason their weapons were not visible. The Germans, however, did not make a rush for the kitchen, where the two cooks were standing. They spent some time adjusting their straps, tugging at their uniforms and setting their little forage caps straight - presumably awaiting orders. Meanwhile a man had emerged from the cab in an oilcloth raincoat and wearing a cap as high as a cock's comb, with a white insignia above the peak. He said something to the lanky cook, who braced his shoulders then at once relaxed. No doubt it had been some sort of permission or command to stand easy.

"The officer!" Petroc surmised.

Stepanida stood behind the lintel by the open passage-door and said nothing, watchfully attentive to all that was taking place in the yard. But nothing terrible was happening for the moment; the soldiers besieged the kitchen and the long handle of the cook's ladle waved above their heads - dinner was being served. It was all exactly like last summer at the halt by the river, when our Red Army boys were having a meal before retiring eastward. Now about a dozen Germans were thickly crowded together near the well, they were chatting cheerfully and laughing, some rinsing out their mess-tins in the bucket standing near the fence. The officer, however, moved some distance away into the middle of the yard and looking upwards at the roof near the boiler-house, extracted a slender, gleaming, cigarette case from his pocket. While he lit up, Petroc attempted to catch his glance, but the officer's eye was invisible behind the peak of his cap, broad as a horse's hoof. The German puffed away, slightly lowering his head to listen to the familiar rotund feldwebel, who was talking fast and unintelligibly, pointing in all directions. His arm chanced to indicate the door at last and the officer, spotting the owners in the passage, became noticeably more alert. Petroc touched Stepanida on the shoulder.

"Look, they're coming!"

"Let them come."

They were rather at a loss, not knowing what to do - just stand, get out of the way somewhere or perhaps meet their guests on the step. When Petroc finally pulled off his cap and crossed the step, the Germans were already on their way towards him. At this, he recoiled and retired into the boiler-house, staring at the officer's face with tense anxiety, guessing at his intentions, good or evil, as he entered the hut. However, the clean-shaven, youthful face betrayed nothing beyond interest and the usual firmness of command. The dark eyes beneath black brows merely slid indifferently over the owners and paused longer on the shadowy passageway and the pile of potatoes in the corner. The fussy feldwebel, however, had already opened the hut door and the officer unhurriedly crossed the threshold. He didn't close the door after him and Petroc from the passage could hear them talking about something; the voices were measured and unruffled. Thereupon with his customary, fussy efficiency, the feldwebel sprang out into the passage and called someone in from the yard ("Kom, kom") and two soldiers came trotting into the passage in their heavy boots. The feldwebel issued his orders and the others nodded ("Jawohl, jawohl!") and doubled out to the vehicle under the limes. 'Discipline all right,' thought Petroc with grudging respect, not understanding as yet what those inside were planning. Soon all became clear. The soldiers hauled out some folding metal beds, head-boards gleaming, wire mesh of woven aluminum, bundles of sheets and blankets and began carrying them into the hut. Petroc retreated again so as not to be in the way as they made themselves at home on the farmstead. With might and main, bustling and shoving, they trampled over the still damp floor, shifting benches and banging the beds. Everybody ignored him and Stepanida, and Petroc had begun to relax, thinking it might all pass off harmoniously. Of course the two of them had worked hard and tidied things away good and proper, now they would be satisfied. The thought had just crossed his mind when the bouncy feldwebel appeared from behind the doorjamb and crooked his finger at him, like a bairn.

"Kom!"

Sensing a sudden weakness in his legs, Petroc went into the hut. In place of the table, now shifted to one side, stood a splendid bed with a bundle of sheets on the wires; a young sickly-looking German lad was busy with the other bed. Obviously a job had come up for Petroc, and the officer, legs splayed wide on the floor, stared at him, waiting for him to approach. Their glances met and Petroc's heart gave an uncomfortable lurch, foreseeing imminent trouble.

"Was ist das?" demanded the officer with concealed menace, pointing at the wall, plastered over with yellowing newspapers, torn in places. Scarcely daring to look, Petroc almost died of fright; in the space where the violin case had hung was a darkened newspaper picture of the May Day holiday in Moscow and on it the faded face of Stalin was clearly visible. "Was ist das?" repeated the German.

Petroc understood and was silent - what could he have said? He merely swore softly to himself - trust him to drop himself in it! They'd scrubbed the floor, the table, the benches, cleared out the corners and never looked at the walls once. They were going to pay for it. . .

"Stalin, sir," he managed to get out in a faltering voice, ready to take his punishment.

"Stalin good?"

"Well, you know. . .We're just ordinary folk. . .Good for some, not so good for others. . ." Petroc tried to wriggle out of it, thinking to himself: may you be struck by lightning, what are you getting on to me for? He didn't take his eyes from the officer, however, as he tried to guess what would follow and what form his chastisement would take. A harsh anger flickered in those dark eyes, though the firm, swarthy face was unchanged, imperturbable and calm. But now his hand reached for the belt at his waist, where a leather holster was fixed prominently next to the buckle. Petroc, as if hypnotized, was unable to take his eyes off that hand, which was already drawing out a small, black pistol, with a short blunt barrel.

"Well, this is it!" thought Petroc dismally. "What a stupid thing though. . .If I could say something to Stepanida at least."

With all his former deliberateness, the German twiddled the gun which gave a couple of bony clicks before he raised his arm. 'Now he's going to fire!' thought Petroc and closed his fingers to cross himself for the last time; the officer paused for a second and a deafening explosion rang through the hut. Petroc rolled to one side in fright as the smell of powder filled the air and the blue smoke from the barrel floated slowly towards the window. On the wall, a black mark had appeared in the center of the photo. Just to make sure, Petroc crossed himself in good time and prepared for the worst.

"Kaput!" spat the German coldly and blew on the barrel of his gun before inserting it in the holster. His face once more expressed nothing, his eyes gazing icily out from under the wide horse-hoof peak. Totally unnerved, Petroc stood by the window, while the feldwebel pushed him firmly, though not roughly, towards the door.

"Weg!"

Staggering across the step, barely able to move his leaden legs, Petroc made his way to the boiler-house. In its dusty gloom, Stepanida was standing rigid and Petroc leaned feebly against her shoulder.

7

After eating from their mess-tins, the Germans out in the yard spent some time crowding around the kitchen, talking and smoking before climbing back into their vehicle. This time the feldwebel went with them, the officer shutting himself away in the hut. No sound could be heard from him, he was clearly busy or had gone to bed. Petroc, head down, was sitting by the millstones in the boiler-house, not smoking even; after what had taken place, even smoking wouldn't have helped. Stepanida gradually recovered from her fright and placed herself quietly by the tiny window, ears pricked towards the yard. Only the two cooks were left there, however; the rest had gone off to the bridge. After waiting for a while, all senses on the alert, she went out into the passage and listened. Beyond the hut doors everything was dead quiet, not a sound to be heard. It looked as if the moment had come to feed the pig, otherwise it would start squealing in earnest and there'd be no saving it; it would be for the slaughter. Thus musing, Stepanida cut up some potatoes into a pot and sprinkled them with bran, then added yesterday's boiling and mixed the lot up together. Now she had to get the pot out to the shed without being noticed.

"Petroc, have a look out there," she whispered to her husband, but he didn't even raise his head. "Hear anything?"

"Ah-a-a. . . .You won't save it! Makes no odds. . ."

"What d'you mean, makes no odds?"

They went on quietly talking in the boiler-house. The recent shot in the hut had clearly so shaken Petroc that he was completely unnerved; it was as if he had fallen into some morbid stupor. On another occasion, she would have bullied him out of it but there was no time for that now, she realized; the old man had suffered enough. Stepanida quietly peered out of the passageway.

The yard was deserted except for Karl bent over the kitchen, washing out the boiler; the bad-tempered cook was standing by the boxes with his back to the hut. Anyway, why shouldn't she go out, she thought, she could have anything in the pot, what business was it of theirs?

And so she did - running quietly past the boiler-house and the woodpile, she slipped into the garden with its mass of burdocks. The piglet was marvelous, didn't even respond to her footsteps, just moved about in the straw when she began opening the lower hatch of the shed. To save time she pushed the pot across the threshold and leaned the old plow up against the decrepit door.

The piglet shuffled about a bit behind the plank wall, its champing barely audible and hardly making a sound otherwise, while Stepanida stood among the docks reflecting that this wasn't a very secure hideaway; there were so many folk in the yard, anybody could come round this corner on a call of nature even and hear the pig. And the hens as well! Somehow she hadn't thought about them at first, and here they were wandering aimlessly about below the fencing among the nettles, searching and scratching and pecking about. She didn't know what to do for the best, shut them all up together in a shed or drive them away from the farm? The Germans of course weren't blind, they'd spot them and there wouldn't be one left to breed from.

However, she took no steps to conceal the hens: she was far more bothered about Bobovka, left this time with Yanka's herd. Once it was getting dark, Yanka might drive the herd to the Settlement. Along the damp trodden path across the potato field, Stepanida walked to the edge of the gully, then followed the slight traces in the grass. The day was ending without the sky having freed itself from the enveloping clouds, suspended low over the grey expanse of field and woodland. It wasn't cold though, the wind had dropped, it seemed; a watchful early evening silence embraced the withered bushes in the gully. The damp grass was uncomfortable to bare feet at first, but her legs warmed up as she walked. She was quickly approaching Sheep Valley along the field margin, thinking that no matter how bad things were now, they would clearly get worse. The Germans wouldn't stop at moving the farmer and his wife into the boiler-house. If they spent a long time on the farm, anything might happen, but that they'd strip the farm to the bones was a certainty. What were they going to live on then? How could she save the cow, the pig, the hens? They might not take the grain or the potatoes - what did they want grain for? - but they'd burn up the firewood. How could they get any more here without a horse? How could they keep warm in winter?

There was plenty to worry about, and be alarmed about, grim forebodings kept tormenting her mind, but Stepanida bore up and remained outwardly calm. She wasn't the sort of woman who burst into tears at the first hint of trouble; she knew that there would be troubles enough and to spare to spend her small hoard of tears on, not that she hadn't wept enough of them in her time.

Yanka's small herd was grazing in the thickets near the hollow log by the oak tree. The cows were ranging among the alders as Yanka, catching sight of Stepanida, started muttering something with earnest fearfulness pointing to the field at the same time. Had he seen something? It was quiet and deserted there now as twilight descended and it was time to take the cow home. Stepanida separated Bobovka from the herd and only then realized that she'd brought nothing for Yanka. She'd not eaten a bite herself today either. Standing among the thickets, Yanka was still talking in his own incomprehensible tongue, flapping his arms anxiously. Suddenly two brief comprehensible words burst out from his lips:

"Bunch! Bunch!"

Stepanida, however, didn't try to work out what he wanted to say and smartly drove Bobovka on with her switch. She had to get the cow milked while there were no Germans about on the farmstead.

Even sweating a little by now in her thick kerchief and quilted jacket, she drove the cow on towards the fence by the potato field and realized she was too late. The tarpaulin-topped machine was already visible beneath the limes in the yard; the audible talk and the usual shouting indicated that something was going on over there. She halted, puzzled, while Bobovka raised her head and slowed down. The Germans could be seen over the fence milling around their vehicle dragging something bulky and heavy from it. One of them, glimpsing her beyond the palings called out cheekily in a youthful voice:

"O matka! Mleko!"

There was nothing for it, she slapped Bobovka lightly with her switch and the cow stepped over the lower rail, her usual route, and headed for the cowshed in the yard.

What Stepanida had dreaded above all was taking place on the farmstead: the Germans were settling in for a long stay. They had rolled a bulky grey tarpaulin out of the machine and stretched it out on the trampled grass, where they were now jostling about hammering short pegs into the ground. The two on the extreme outside were bent almost horizontal, pulling on the ropes with all their strength as the tarpaulin roof of the tent obediently straightened out, forming a taut and roomy structure for the soldiers in the event of frost or inclement weather.

Petroc was standing crouched over by the woodpile, peeping round the corner; noticing his wife, he spread his hands mutely. But Stepanida made no response. Blast them, she thought, maybe they would be less of a bother if they lived in the tent. The main thing was that they shouldn't take over that area of the yard nearest the outhouse, the hencoop, the woodpile and the way through to the shed. Still, it was probably too muddy for them over there, they needed somewhere drier. Yon end of the yard was raised somewhat, so naturally that was the better place for them.

Bobovka, evidently, was as aware of the unusual presence of strangers in the yard as her owners and had no sooner resolved to pass the woodpile than she halted, undecided, and snorted - she was afraid of them. Stepanida stepped out ahead and tenderly stroked the cow's neck, which trembled at her touch.

"Don't worry, now. . .Go on, go on. . ."

"Mleka! Mleka!" shouted one of the Germans drunkenly.

She hadn't reached the gate before Karl, the assistant cook, swaying on his short, bandy legs, was on his way to meet her, carrying a wide, tin pail. Three or four Germans were watching him from the direction of the kitchen, among them the plump, florid feldwebel, who was also present, bustling about, shouting and issuing orders.

As a rule, before milking, Stepanida would throw Bobovka a handful of grass so that the cow would be busy eating and stand quiet. At this moment she hadn't anything to hand and the Germans, to judge by appearances, were in no mood to wait. She was going to tell Petroc to bring some grass but changed her mind: let it go! Something angry flared up inside her, stung by their insolence - she was under no obligation to supply this gang with milk from her own cow, let them find other cows. Bobovka meanwhile kept pawing the ground and looking about her as Stepanida sat down to the udder. The cow clearly disliked the presence of outsiders; Stepanida sensed this and the quiet resentment within her grew and grew. She managed somehow to fill a half a pail all the same and got to her feet. Karl was standing next to her in his greasy tunic; his puffed, unhealthy face registered nothing but patient, indifferent expectancy.

"That's it, that's the lot!" said Stepanida, handing over the pail.

The German took the bucket and waddled off with it to the kitchen. Petroc sidled up to Stepanida and glancing about him whispered:

"I dare say that's not enough. . .For them to. . ."

"It'll do!" She cut in emphatically and slapped the cow on the rump, urging her into the cowshed. But then she winced as there rang out an immediate sharp cry of outrage from the kitchen.

"Halt!"

It was the feldwebel again. Flushed with anger, he seized the bucket from Karl in an access of rage, and while Stepanida was guessing what it was they wanted from her, raced right up to her, pail in hand. He was saying something short and malevolent, shaking the half-empty bucket as she listened, already comprehending what had annoyed him.

"There is no more milk. That's the lot."

"All? Alles?"

The plump little feldwebel added a further stinging comment then turned briskly towards the kitchen, picking someone out; he nodded - kom! The same Karl, as before, waddled up to the feldwebel without haste, retrieved the bucket and tentatively walked towards the cow, which was staring about in bewildered alarm. When he came near her, the cow hastily turned round as if divining his intention so that Karl had to go round her again and come in from the side. This was repeated two or three times until the feldwebel shouted at Petroc to grab Bobovka by the horns.

Stepanida already knew what would happen next and she began to be rather fearful as her deception was about to be disclosed. At the same time it was disgusting to watch a soldier set about milking while her fool of a Petroc gave him a hand. Poor Bobovka, what were they going to do to her - her eyes couldn't bear to watch. But somehow they wangled it and milk was starting to tinkle in the pail; bandy-legged Karl was bent over the cow looking down awkwardly at the udder. Bobovka was pawing at the ground and twisting her head as if to free her horns, but Petroc held on tight. Stepanida, tensed up in mute anger, stood some way off without raising her eyes. She could see everything anyway and mentally cursed the Germans to herself, most of all that round-bellied feldwebel, who was following intently all that happened near the cow. Finally, after some five minutes, she glanced in the bucket and shrank even more - the amount of milk had perceptibly increased. You little idiot Bobovka, why do you give them it? But clearly the cow had no choice, she was afraid too, and so was Petroc; his half-bent legs in their knee-patched trousers trembled faintly as he struggled to hold the cow. Stepanida quailed still more, aware that this was going to end badly.

"Genug!" suddenly commanded the feldwebel, the pail was filled to the brim. Karl straightened up and carefully, so as not to spill any, placed the milk before his superior officer. The feldwebel stared at Stepanida in hatred and clamped his jaws tightly. "Kom!"

She already knew what this brief word meant and slowly approached him as if in a trance; she couldn't take her eyes off the milk in the pail. She expected shouts and threats, but the feldwebel didn't shout; he merely moved his heavy holster nearer his belt-buckle.

"Sir!" Petroc suddenly cried out in a hoarse, alien voice and fell to his knees on the muddy earth, now churned up after the rain. "Sir, please don't!"

Only now did she realize that the German intended to get his revolver, and her heart gave an unpleasant lurch. But she did not move from the spot and kept watching as he struggled clumsily with the gun, unable to unfasten it presumably. Petroc continued to beseech him, moving nearer on his knees, his crumpled cap in his hands, grizzled, unshaven, terrified. She stood immobile and wooden as if impervious to death and ready any second to embrace it. The feldwebel, however, unhooked from his holster a long, white chain, and before Stepanida could take anything in, a sharp pain burned her neck and shoulders. She flung up a hand and at once the stinging pain took her hand and fingers; the next blow was across the back, a good thing the quilted jacket softened the impact on her shoulders. The feldwebel, incensed, kept cursing loudly in German and slashed at her several more times, but her fingers took the brunt; after the second blow, her back had almost ceased to hurt. She had by now found a way of shielding herself from the blows - not with her fingers, more with her elbows, and the German after delivering another couple of blows with all his strength realized he could make no headway like this. So, letting the chain fall, he screamed at her, his blond face purple with the strain of his anger. She, however, no longer heard his shouting or wished to understand him; it was as if she had gone deaf. Out of the corner of her eye, she saw that the soldiers had congregated near the kitchen and the tent; some of them brayed with laughter, it seemed the punishment struck them as funny, a matter for amusement, no more. All right, go on laugh, damn you, have your fun, she thought, beat an unfortunate woman with no one to protect her. Just remember, this woman has a soldier-son and he'll remind you of this. Maybe not now, later, but there will come a time when he'll settle accounts for his mother's pain and humiliation. Petroc, it's not becoming for you to crawl in front of them. Let it be! She had been whipped here in her own yard and laughed at by alien soldiers, but she would bear it. She would bear it all. You do the same.

Her neck burned with pain under the ear, likewise the fingers on her left hand as, filled with unspoken resentment, she moved slowly towards the woodpile to hide from these brazen eyes and perhaps have a cry. But somewhere where they couldn't see. She very much wanted to cry, if only she had tears to shed. But she had had none for a long time, there was only anger, suppressed by the force of her will, which made it especially hard for her. But let it be, all the same, she consoled herself; let everything be that was meant to be, then we'd see. Maybe they wouldn't kill her, she wouldn't be shot before evening, we'd live a bit longer. . .

8

Petroc tossed and turned all night on his rough bed of bins, trying to get to sleep under his sheepskin. At first he kept on listening to what was going on in the yard, where, although it was getting dark, the sound of alien voices went on for a long time - shouts, German laughter - for some reason they carried on tirelessly till very late. All the while, the passage doors kept banging as people ran into the hut, clattering pots and pans as they served the officers. It quieted down there around midnight as the soldiery dropped off to sleep in their tent. Sleep refused to come to Petroc, however, as the grim thoughts pressed in upon him: what to do? God had visited chastisement upon two old folk, but why? Petroc wanted to ask his wife, but she had not responded to his whispered invitation and he couldn't bring himself to raise his voice. He had been schooled all his long life to be a bit afraid of everything, and now he had reason enough and to spare!

He did doze off before dawn, just for a short while it seemed, and had an awful nightmare. For a long time there had been a wide rat-hole under the millstones in the boiler-house, and in his dream a horrible creature with a tusked snout like a wild boar peered out of the hole. Petroc flung a broom at it, then poked about inside with a stick, but to no avail; the rat had hidden away, but reappeared immediately and bared its fanged maw, partly in menace, partly in mockery. Almost in despair, Petroc seized an old rusty chopper by the door and launched it into the corner, where it caught the millstones. They collapsed in a roar, raising a cloud of dust in the boiler-house.

Petroc awoke at once and realized that something had crashed nearby in the real world. It was light in the boiler-house, morning was coming on. His battered old boots lay in the middle of the hard earth floor, the millstones were standing in their usual place in the corner, but there was no sign of Stepanida. Her rumpled mattress lay on the trestle-bed under the little window. Petroc, barefooted, just as he was, rushed over to the window and through its dirty cobwebbed glass made out the yard, the field-kitchen and the emaciated evil-tempered cook standing with a rifle raised aloft. He clattered the bolt and threw his cigarette on the ground before walking to the gates. He hung the rifle with its yellow sling on the palings by his kitchen. Fearing for Stepanida, Petroc threw his sheepskin over his shoulders and raced barefoot out of the passage; nearby, a soldier peered out of the tent, suspenders over a sky-blue vest and a forage cap on his head; he spoke to the cook, who had meanwhile vanished behind the fence. Soon, however, all became clear: the cook appeared in the gateway holding in his raised hand the crow, beak all bloodied and still fluttering feebly in the air.

Petroc transferred his gaze to the cowshed. The doors were open wide, signifying that Stepanida had already driven Bobovka away. This reassured him; he didn't care about the crow, to hell with that, it shouldn't have kept flying in and croaking like that. Brought it on itself, croaking like that. . .

He returned to the boiler-house and closed the door behind him. He sensed it would be better to appear as little as possible in the farm yard so as not to draw attention to himself; best sit quietly in his decrepit retreat. Trying not to knock against anything in the semidarkness, he quietly slipped on his boots and wrapped his sheepskin tighter round his shoulders before taking up a position by the window. He felt like smoking but there were no matches, so he waited patiently for whatever might happen. It had grown quite light meanwhile and the Germans had gradually wakened and started bustling about the yard in their underpants and blue and white vests; some ran to relieve themselves behind the cowshed, some lit up cigarettes and some were briskly limbering up near the tent doing their morning exercises. One with suspenders dangling drew a bucket of water from the well and began washing by the fence to one side of the kitchen. Others there fixed up little mirrors on the fence and shaved with special small razors of some sort. The lanky young one in glasses with the short back hair was strolling at his ease round the yard, peering into the corners with a certain interest before glancing at the roof and halting in front of the woodpile and noting something down with a pencil in a little black book. He put it away. Then he went over to the cowshed and looked inside the open door. It seemed to Petroc that he was searching for something, but the German merely took the notebook out of his side pocket and carefully wrote something down. 'A scholar,' thought Petroc. 'But what's there to see in the cowshed?' He waited for the soldiers to get ready and move off to the bridge, they had work to do after all. But time passed, the kitchen started getting up smoke and smelled of something unfamiliar and appetizing; the troops were still crowding together in the yard, in no hurry to get to work it seemed. There was no sign of the officer or the feldwebel either, still asleep in the hut no doubt - no one had put his head out into the passage since dawn.

The morning was unseasonably warm; somewhere beyond a thin layer of cloud the sun glimmered, ready at any moment to shine out brightly. Feeling the sun on their backs, the Germans were in no rush to get dressed. One with a sunburned back was washing himself at length and with relish at the well. Another, backside quivering in his underpants, was pouring water over him from a mess-tin; both were laughing as young men will. Decked out in clean white jackets, the cook and Karl were busy in the kitchen; Karl was bent over at the firebox, while the cook was mixing something in a pan with its lid open. Two Germans, dressed but without forage caps, were skewering the crow they had killed on a stake: they folded its wings neatly, so it looked as if it were alive, but the dead head wouldn't stay straight and kept flopping over to one side. Then one of the Germans brought a thin wire and used it to straighten the head, though the crow still looked dead. As soon as this German stepped back to admire his work, there came a loud knocking at the passage door. Petroc became alert and peered sideways out of the window. The officer was standing on the steps, uniform unbuttoned and with a black unruly curl on his head. He surveyed the farmyard, where the soldiers at once stopped their noise and stood to attention; he said something to the one working on the crow. He answered, a broad smile on his youthful sunburned face, and went off to the tent.

Petroc pressed closer to the wall logs, striving to see what happened next, though it was clear enough as it was. The officer aimed at the crow from the porch, the short barrel wavered slightly as he lined the target up in his sights, then paused before the shot rang out unexpectedly and feathers flew up above the bird.

"Bravo! Bravo!" The Germans clapped their hands, the one washing at the well and one off to the side with soapy cheeks, along with someone else whom Petroc couldn't see from the window. The officer aimed and fired again. This time the bullet knocked off the head and beak. The officer put his pistol back in its holster with satisfaction and fastening his uniform as he went, headed for the kitchen. From somewhere the spry feldwebel appeared at his side and began an incomprehensible conversation, which Petroc ignored.

Standing by the window, he heard something else, which disconcerted him for a moment, not knowing what to do. Beyond the thick wall of the boiler-house, where there was a small garden, someone was shaking his apple tree; the loud rustling of foliage could be heard and the frequent thud of his apples hitting the ground, the antonovkas he had patiently saved for the winter. Of course he didn't expect anything good of these soldiers, but adult people didn't act this way surely? They could have taken six or a dozen, a couple of capfuls. Why shake down the lot before they were ripe? And why didn't the officer stop them?

Seized by a sudden resentment, Petroc hurried out of the open passage door and ran into the garden past the tent, pegged out on the parapet itself. Of course he'd been right. One German, bandy-legged in his boots was sitting up in the apple tree and shaking a branch; the ripe apples were thudding heavily down onto the beds, where a ginger-headed, sickly-looking German was gathering them up in his cap. Petroc stood on the verge and stared at them reproachfully, but they didn't even glance at him, as if he were just another tree and not the owner of the farm.

"This isn't right, is it?" he said, trying to stay as cool as possible. "I'll complain to your officer. This isn't right, German gentlemen."

The ginger-haired one, still a boy to look at, stood up, stared provocatively at him and giggled as he threw a half-eaten apple at him. Petroc barely dodged the apple which struck the wall behind him and ricocheted into the nettles.

"You're villains!" cried Petroc, almost in despair. "Well, just wait!"

He turned on his heel with the firm intention of complaining to the officer, but he hadn't got as far as the shed past the burdocks when two shots rang out near the woodpile and the hens came rushing through the fence, clucking wildly. Having lost one of his boots in the furrows, Petroc hurried towards the little shed on the near side of the boiler-house. Another shot rang out and the lanky German vaulted the palings with ease, arms wide, and rushed out into the long grass. Behind him the feldwebel stood by the old trough with a revolver in his hand. He was speaking excitedly to two or three soldiers, who bared white teeth as they laughed. Further off, the officer was pacing to and fro, observing the proceedings indulgently; his tunic, still unbuttoned, displayed the black holster on his belt.

Instantly bereft of his recent resolution, Petroc halted - who was he to complain to? What the soldiers were doing was not   apparently anything forbidden, their commanders were cut from the same cloth. All this seemed quite normal to them, by right of conquest. The tall one was climbing back over the fence by this time, holding up the wounded hen by the legs as it still desperately beat its wings. The feldwebel, revolver in hand, looked about him, probably seeking out more hens. The hens for their part had hidden all over the place in their fright and there wasn't one visible in the yard. Conscious of his complete impotence, Petroc wandered morosely around near the woodpile not knowing where to put himself so as not to witness the pillage going on all over the farm. However, he had caught the eye of the feldwebel, who relinquished his pistol and his good-humored hunter's animation to bark:

"Kom!"

Well, of course he would start finding fault, hit him, maybe even shoot him, what was it to them. Petroc halted just as he was with one bare foot, by the firewood.

"Mleko! Warum nichts mleko?"

The feldwebel expected an answer; two other Germans stood nearby and the officer in his many-buttoned open tunic was coming over as well.

"Well the cow is out grazing," said Petroc simply, somewhat surprised at the naivety of the question.

"Kom cow! Quick! Understood?" bawled the feldwebel, and Petroc thought: they got their milk anyway. Have they nothing else to eat that they're so keen on milk? "Kom cow! Nach haus cow! Understood!?"

"Understood", said Petroc dismally and turned back towards the garden. He would have to look for Stepanida and Bobovka in the thickets.

The Germans in the garden had already climbed a second apple tree and were stuffing their caps and pockets with the sourish apples which crowded its branches. Two others were searching on the ground, moving quickly round the beds trampling down the onions, beetroot and carrots as yet unharvested. This time Petroc said nothing to them - let them trample, squash and eat till they choked. He found his boot in the ditch and went off by way of the beds to the gully. It was obvious that the fruit and vegetables, everything on the farm in fact was going to disappear, there was no saving anything. Keep your head on if you could!

He walked along the path, taking his time and waiting to hear further shooting from the yard, one hen no doubt wouldn't be enough for them. No sooner had he reached the bushes at the edge of the gully when he heard three bangs one after the other. Petroc looked round. No, nothing could be seen from here, the shots came from the farmyard on the other side of the buildings. A good job if they had shot each other, less of them left on earth. No, things wouldn't get as far as that, but the hens would be for it, that was certain. And it looked as if they had no intention of going to work on the bridge. Or they had the day off today or a celebration of some sort, thought Petroc. He really felt like going away and never coming back to the farm, especially since the weather had been fine since morning. The sky had cleared and the sun was starting to warm things up; the wind had veered round to the south and there was such belated tenderness in nature. That rarely happens in autumn and when it does it fills a peasant's heart with peace and goodwill. How his heart would rejoice if it wasn't for the war and these unbidden guests on the farmstead.

Still he had to find Stepanida.

He had already passed along the thickets by the gully above the field and paused for a moment by the white trough, made out of a barked oak tree, and listened. Stepanida and the cow seemed nowhere about but he couldn't be too late or what would the Germans say? Even from the previous war, Petroc had heard people say that the Germans got very annoyed if their orders weren't obeyed at the double, and woe betide anyone who dawdled or wasn't prompt and efficient. If you didn't come up to scratch you were shot, like a hen, and you wouldn't quiver either.

After a deal of trotting about in Sheep Valley, he suddenly heard Bobovka rustling the bushes ever so quietly on the edge of the swamp. Stepanida was standing close by. With a sort of remote hunted look, she stared at Petroc from afar off and waited for his approach, sensing naught for her comfort.

"Well, you're tucked away, aren't you! Could hardly find you!" he said wearily, forcing his way through a stand of young aspens, almost leafless now. "They want milk."

Stepanida thought for a moment, listening.

"You should have said no. They had the lot yesterday."

"They said I had to bring the cow. I suppose they're going to milk it themselves. They're shooting the hens. Shaking the apples down. . ."

Stepanida calmly took in this grim news. Asking no questions, she pulled the kerchief closer round her neck.

"They're getting nothing," she said finally and went over to the cow who was quietly grazing among the undergrowth. Petroc thought she would rope up Bobovka and they would take her home. Stepanida, however, had something else in mind and she sat down close by the cow.

"What are you up to?"

"You'll see."

Well of course she began milking the cow onto the grass, Petroc was alarmed.

"But the milk!. . ."

"Nothing I said, no milk. . ."

And that's what they would get, he thought, bewildered, watching the white streams disappearing under her hands into the short grass strewn with fallen leaves. He knew his wife's character only too well and realized that she wouldn't be moved, especially after the humiliation of yesterday's whipping. So he stood meekly some way off among the bushes till she had finished milking the cow.

"Ye-e-s. . .What now?"

"Now you can take her. Let them milk it now."

Stepanida threw the rope over the cow's horns and thrust the other end into Petroc's hands.

"Now, take her away!"

He led the cow as far as the edge of the woodland where a path lead to the farm, Stepanida lagging behind a little; Bobovka was unable to understand the whims of her owners and would walk, then stop to munch a clump of grass between her legs, clearly short of pasturage and unwilling to return home. It was as if she knew that little good awaited her there and it was a long time till evening. Petroc made heavy weather of striding along in wet boots, reflecting uneasily that it was no good bringing in a cow without milk. Still, what could he do? The cow wasn't his property, it was more that of his wife. But after yesterday's events Stepanida was mortally affronted and with good reason. He wouldn't have stood it either if he'd been lashed with a revolver lanyard. Fortunately they had only frightened him so far. That wasn't the first time it had happened to him, he'd got used to being afraid a long time ago and had learned to recover himself quickly. Otherwise he couldn't have stood it. Especially in this war.

As if sensing something, Bobovka had a fit of obstinacy near the farm and was reluctant to proceed from the garden into the yard: she splayed her legs wide, and twisted her head in the halter to look back at her owner. Petroc shouted at her a bit and jerked on the rope, but until Stepanida touched her with the switch from behind, the cow paid no heed. From as far as the gully it had been clear that the Germans had no intention of clearing off the farm that day - the bustle was at its height, there came the sound of laughter and something thudding in the air, regular and subdued. Petroc took a look at the antonovka near the boiler-house. There were a few small apples left at the very top of it, otherwise the whole tree was denuded and a heavy, broken bough hung downwards to the earth. The entire garden had been trampled by boots, the vegetable beds crushed: in the cucumber patch the seed gherkins had been smashed. 'It's a judgment from God,' thought Petroc, bitterly, 'but for what sins though? And why has all this landed on me?'

While still in the garden, Petroc divined that there was a game going on in the yard - through the lively chatter and shouts, the taut thudding of a ball could be heard amid laughter. Soon a mighty brown ball the size of a pumpkin bounced over from behind the shed and a young blond German, flushed from the game, leapt after it. He glanced briefly at the owners, seized the ball and disappeared into the yard behind the boiler-house.

Petroc led Bobovka past the woodpile and halted in silence to await the feldwebel, who had already fixed him with his eye from the kitchen. He barked something briefly and Karl hurried over to the cow with his shining bucket. Petroc began to feel extremely uncomfortable, almost fearful, as he looked at the bucket and thought: I hope there's some left in Bobovka otherwise there's going to be trouble. At the other end of the yard about five Germans, stripped to the waist, were knocking the ball in the air, flattening the grass near the tent; the portly feldwebel was starting to discuss something with the cook as Karl slowly approached the cow. Without releasing the rope, Petroc took closer hold. As before, Bobovka looked anxiously round at the Germans, her full eyelashes reacting sweepingly to every smack of the ball. As yesterday, Karl squatted down on his haunches close to her and elbows wide, began milking.

Actually there was nothing to milk and the cow didn't want to stand; although Petroc was holding her, she kept jerking about and changing legs. After about a minute, Karl picked up his empty bucket and rose. It seemed to Petroc that he shot a worried glance at him, then looked round at the woodpile, where Stepanida had peered out then disappeared. He brought out just a couple of incomprehensible words, overheard, however, by the feldwebel, who sped over to the cow.

"Was ist das?" he indicated the bucket. "Warum nichts mleko?"

"Who can tell?" shrugged Petroc with affected sincerity, almost devotedly gazing into the baleful eye of the feldwebel. The latter's red face turned a shade of purple.

"Warum?" he barked louder, reaching automatically for his holster.

"It just won't give any, it's calving. It's expecting," Petroc lied awkwardly, getting himself mixed up and mentally cursing Stepanida: what did she have to milk the cow for! Let it choke them, Petroc had no desire to sacrifice himself for it.

The Germans in the yard broke off the game; one with the ball under his arm came nearer and the rest followed, curiosity written all over their sweaty faces. Each in turn stared into the almost empty pail; there was at most a mug-full of milk gleaming white at the bottom. The feldwebel exchanged words with the bad-tempered cook, who also hauled himself over and stood there staring more at Petroc than the bucket or the cow. During a short pause when nobody said anything, the feldwebel loosened his holster with a squeak and slowly pulled out his revolver with the slender barrel and the black bone handle.

Seized with sudden terror, Petroc thought they were bound to ask something at least before they shot him, and he wanted to say something before he died. Even if only to curse. But disconcerted by the unexpected turn of events, he simply forgot all the words he knew and stared sightlessly as the feldwebel swiftly clicked his revolver.

"Weg, verfluchter. . ."

With a sharp blow of the elbow he knocked Petroc aside and grabbed the rope. Bobovka shook her head and squinted her eyes, seeming to sense her destruction as the German deftly, almost casually, blasted the shot into her ever-sensitive trembling ear.

Petroc waited for the cow to jerk about or start bellowing, but she very meekly slid down onto buckling knees and stuck her moist muzzle in the mud. Slowly subsiding onto her flank, she threw her head back, the pupils of her large eyes rolling, as a brief, soft gasp burst from her throat. The whole of her body with its enormous belly stiffened immobile on the earth. A rippling shudder ran along her skin several times, then all was still.

Petroc's hands trembled faintly as he wandered on legs of cotton-wool out of the yard, where the feldwebel was already briskly shouting at his soldiers, doubtless issuing orders.

9

To her own astonishment, Stepanida was not too distraught over the cow
- however sorry she might be about Bobovka, she felt that something
immeasurably greater had been destroyed. An implacable danger was moving closer and closer to them both. The danger had started at a distance -
from the yard, the road, through the milk, the hut, the well, but it had crept
up so close now that there was no room left for doubt: the Germans would
have them both by the throat! It was true that for all her pondering, she
couldn't reach any clear notion of the real motivation of their actions and
intentions; these were wholly hostile to her, but how was she to understand
which of them would bring the final calamity upon her? Of course that might
be kept at bay somehow; she could hide her feelings, curry favor with the
invaders, try to please them in important or minor ways, but that wouldn't
help matters, she reflected. From childhood, she had never been able to
compel herself to act against her inclinations, particularly if doing so
involved humiliation; she had never possessed the capacity for it and she
couldn't even see how it was possible - to come to terms with the Germans,
especially when they performed acts like this. The humiliation they had
inflicted on her on their first appearance prevented her from feeling anything other than hostility, and subsequent events had added to her outrage
and hatred. It was true, nothing like this had ever happened to her before.
People had annoyed her, frustrated her, even humiliated her, but no one
had ever raised their hand against her - not her father nor her kinfolk, not
even Petroc. Now these people had, though she was old enough to be
mother to many of them.

Stepanida was sitting in the boiler-house, not even looking out of the
window; she could hear well enough what was going on around the farm.
Shouting and pushing, the Germans had taken the cowshed doors off their
hinges and laid them out in the middle of the yard before setting about
skinning Bobovka. No doubt it was Karl again doing the flaying. She heard
his name being spoken amid the shouting and laughter of the soldiery; when
the feldwebel spoke, the rest shut up except for someone's terse "jawohl";

the troops panted in their efforts and the rending of Bobovka's skin could be clearly heard. Petroc had disappeared somewhere, he wasn't in the yard otherwise she'd have heard somebody shouting at him. So she sat alone on her mattress under the window in the cool, semi-darkness of the boiler-house. Now she had nowhere to go, nothing to do. It was quiet and peaceful in the boiler-house; outside a beautiful autumn day was coming to an end. A shaft of sun through the window, sickle-like, slid along the cracked, earthen floor as far as the millstones and shed oblique light on the black, fissured logs of the wall. This golden beam, however, became ever narrower, melting as it were and transforming itself into a thin, shining splinter before fading altogether as the sun vanished behind the Settlement hill. The boiler-house at once got darker and the corners with their assortment of utensils were drowned in shadow; the anxious night drew on. In the end the Germans had not gone to the bridge at all, they had spent all day hanging about the farmyard; it really must have been some sort of holiday for them. Stepanida waited for them to get tired or at least get working at something - she had to have a look at the shed and feed the pig to stop it squealing from hunger and landing up in their voracious kitchen, like Bobovka. All day long Stepanida had been waiting for a suitable moment and now it was evening.

She winced at the sound of a heavy, dull blow out there in the yard, then a second; something gave a crack, like a dry tree branch as she rose to peer out of the window. Four soldiers were busy around the flayed carcass of Bobovka, small somehow, as if it were a calf. A narrow-shouldered German, tunicless and sleeves rolled up, was chopping at it with an axe and the cow's legs were drumming against the door planking. The head had already been severed and lay on the trampled grass by the palings; the black crumpled horns standing out against the evening sky.

Stepanida looked out once or twice but no more, she just couldn't bear to watch all that. They were a long time hacking at Bobovka's bones, ribs and spine and every blow of the axe echoed painfully in her heart.

The twilight heralding the approach of night continued to fill the cramped and cluttered boiler-house. She ought to occupy herself but what with? And anyway what could she do here where she had no rights of any sort and no control over anything - just the contrary, she was the one controlled. And yet her active nature could not reconcile itself to her own powerlessness; she yearned for some outlet, some possibility of not giving in, of asserting herself.

She looked out again; they'd finished with Bobovka it seemed. The bloodstained doors lay on the ground and Germans were sitting and standing round their kitchen, where supper was cooking and giving off the unbearable sickly smell of boiling meat. Petroc was still nowhere to be seen. She went over to the blank wall of the boiler-house and listened hard. No, there was no sound from the garden; maybe this was the time to nip out to the shed in the twilight. While she was listening, her gaze passed casually over the dusty side of a bottle on the shelf and it came to her: the Germans would burn the place. Of course, when they needed light they'd grab the kerosene. To hide it away from prying eyes, Stepanida took down the heavy bottle from the shelf and pushing it well under the millstones, covered it up with a tub. She then transferred yesterday's boiled potatoes from the tub to one of the pots, covered that with her apron and cautiously pushed open the boiler-house door.

There was no one about in the passage or on the step as she noiselessly crossed the threshold and went along the boiler-house wall to the woodpile. She didn't look at the Germans, expecting and fearing their shouts, but they were busy round their kitchen and probably had no eyes for her. She caught her breath behind the firewood heaps before climbing over the fence into the garden. The henhouse was open wide, the door support lay on the ground and there wasn't a single fowl to be seen - surely those swine hadn't shot them all, she wondered. Perhaps the hens had hidden themselves? Or gone out to the gully, as they sometimes did in summer? Ears pricked for the explosion of comradely laughter among the soldiery, she quietly knocked away the door-prop of the shed; her piglet came bundling out against her legs with such joy that she got worried; what should she do with him? Meanwhile, grunting quietly, he nuzzled her feet with his cold, blunt snout, as if demanding something; she made off through the docks, then along the path across the garden to the gully. The piglet hurried after her, surprisingly nimble, like a little puppy, but inclined to make short pauses which made her wince for fear that someone might emerge from the yard and see them there.

But all went smoothly; nobody appeared from the yard and she led the piglet by way of the garden to the fence where she got over the palings while the animal snuffled and squeezed underneath. Now he was concealed by the artemisia and blackberry bushes. Close by was a ditch fringed with bushes; on the edge in the fading light stood a familiar figure. It was Yanka, which surprised her: what was he doing here? Get away from here! Run away, she gestured. That was all she needed, for the Germans to catch sight of Yanka and his herd, they'd shoot the cows, what did they care? But the herd wasn't in the vicinity, Yanka had obviously driven them over to the Settlement while he had come across to the farm for some unknown reason and was running to meet her. They had stopped at the edge of the gully barely concealed from the farmstead by the last alder bushes. As usual, Yanka was in agony trying to communicate something, but she understood nothing and mumbled in her turn:

"The piglet here, where to hide it?"

Oddly enough, he guessed her meaning. For an instant his face darkened with concern, but soon he began waving his arms indicating the far recesses of the gully, now shrouded in twilight, towards which the winding path through the bushes led. Stepanida didn't grasp this but he seized her jacket sleeve and began tugging her along the path. While she was making up her mind, the piglet had already set off after him, pushing impatiently at his bare heels.

They began a slow descent of the steep, in places precipitous, path down into the gully. The piglet didn't lag behind, though he let out a squeal of fright at the steepness of the descent. Yanka knelt and from below caught hold of the animal across his body. When the going levelled out, he put it down and it scampered after the youth without straying from the path.

Soon they found themselves among the damp undergrowth down by the stream where lofty alders with thinning foliage towered above their heads. Yanka pushed further on, leading Stepanida and the piglet deeper into the hushed evening fastnesses of the wooded ravine. Surprisingly enough, the piglet trotted after him more willingly than if Stepanida had been leading it. When Yanka shortly turned off the path, grabbed a hazel branch and swarmed aloft, Stepanida guessed where he had brought them. Somewhere round here on the gully side was a badger den. The Boklagi brothers from the township had hunted it out with dogs long ago and the burrow had been four years empty. Little boys playing there had enlarged the entrance, but it was so deep they hadn't got to the end of it.

Here they had to scramble across the face of the cliff through clumps of hazel bushes. The piglet clambered awkwardly upwards with occasional brief pauses to recover its strength, and where it was really steep Yanka took it into his arms, and ignoring its puny squealing, forged ahead on knees and feet. Stepanida held the pot in one hand and with the other grasped the dark branches so as not fall as she hastened after the boy. So they made their way with difficulty as far as a fir tree root, tangled and exposed; nearby, beyond a small patch of gravel, yawned the black mouth of the den. Once released, the piglet settled down and began joyously sniffing around the sand churned up by boyish feet and the tree root itself. However, as soon as Stepanida placed the pot on the ground, it fell avidly on the potatoes, oblivious of all else.

"I - I - !" Yanka was waving his arms again. "I - oo - oo" came the effortful noise from his chest, but there was nothing coherent, and as Stepanida was considering how to block the lair so as to prevent the piglet slipping out into the gully, "- I - eh!" Yanka tried to explain once more and with a wave of his hand set off up the cliff-face.

Stepanida stood by the tree root, listening to the piglet champing away in the pot and the rustle of fallen leaves on the slope. The rustling, however, receded until it died away completely. It was almost completely dark in the gully, just the edge of the sky on the opposite hillside still glimmered in the last rays of the setting sun. Stepanida didn't know where Yanka had run off to - home to the Settlement or maybe he was looking round here trying to help her. While the piglet was still eating, she stood there, listening to the mysterious, disquieting, nocturnal noises of the gully. The thought came to her suddenly: what had she come to! Running away from her house, hiding away in the gully and looking for refuge where she usually experienced only fear, especially in the evening or at night. But that's how it had turned out. She felt more at ease here than on her own farmstead, whether in the hut or the boiler-house, and this sweet creature, an obedient little pig, seemed closer to her than any human being, a child almost. Especially after Bobovka, whom she had so stupidly failed to protect that day.

Stepanida sat down on a projecting section of root and became still, ears pricked. The piglet had consumed everything in the pot and lay down contentedly at her feet, his hot flanks bringing a pleasant warmth to her chilled feet. She began tickling him under his belly with her toes. Willingly submitting to this human caress, the piglet slowly rocked over onto its side, contentedly grunting. She remained sitting there until she heard the leaves in the grass rustling again; something in the gully was making a considerable racket alright, a fallen branch had just snapped. Stepanida jumped up, listening hard. All around it was dark, and down below where the streamlet ran, lay an impenetrable murk; up above too, the trees and bushes had melted into a solid black mass over the gully, the far edge of the sky just barely visible. The rustling above grew louder and there was a clatter to one side of the burrow as Yanka leapt down to the tree root. Crouching low to the earth, he was dragging something bulky and probably too heavy for him.

"E - e! I!" the weary herdsman announced himself and threw down a wooden harrow with teeth intact, doubtless found in the fields.

It wasn't too bad - the harrow at once screened off all entry into the burrow, though it needed a support from outside to stop the piglet butting it over. The two of them pushed the pig into the deserted badger lair and swiftly stuck the harrow over the entrance. The piglet began grunting anxiously, pushing feebly at the harrow, but Stepanida held it firm, while Yanka broke off a suitable branch nearby, and they both worked hard to ram it up against the harrow.

"That's the boy," said Stepanida softly. "Just you stay there and don't grunt or they'll eat you up and won't say thank you."

Yanka pulled something out of his pocket and passed it through to the pig which began champing with relish in the darkness of its lair, as they began making their way up the slope. Actually this was nearer, though less convenient than the path along the stream. At length, hot with exertion, they reached the top of the mound and passing the bushes found themselves on the edge of the potato patch. Night lay on fields and farm alike; it was pitch dark and not a thing could be seen from this distance; the sloping mass of Golgotha not far away merged almost completely with the dark sky, in which a single, tiny, reddish star was twinkling. The trees and bushes nearby formed a solid, black, jagged wall with a gap here and there disclosing the misty gash of the gully.

"Thank you, Yanochka," said Stepanida, touching the boy's shoulder, thin beneath his light shirt. Yanka tensed, stopped and drew nearer, looking questioningly into her face while muttering something comprehensible only to himself as usual. She decided she should have said something more to him but could find no words and went on towards the farm. The path was level here along the rim of the gully at the field's edge. Yanka stayed behind. Of course he'd be off to his Settlement giving the farm a wide berth, no poking your nose in there. A verst at least for safety.

Still a long way off, Stepanida suddenly saw a bright, almost blinding light in the windows: that's no lamp, she thought, they've switched on their electricity. With an unpleasant sense of trepidation, Stepanida approached the farmstead and entered the garden along the path. Here it was dark and quiet, it looked as if the Germans had tired themselves out. It was only from the hut window that the bright oblique beam of light fell on the trampled beds. She saw a similar beam in the yard as she came in past the woodpile. The black kitchen with its tall stack stood diligently cleaned and tidied and covered with a broad piece of tarpaulin; by the fence a row of buckets could be seen. To one side of them was something vaguely gray in the darkness, no doubt the rifle with the new, yellow sling, forgotten since that morning. Stepanida took all this in with one swift glance as she slipped into the passage through the unlocked door. From the hut could be heard the even, guttural tones of two or three Germans as she quickly slid along into the boiler-house.

Petroc was already there on the bins and responded at once from the darkness, as soon as she had closed the door behind her:

"Dear me, where've you been till this time of night? I've been scared stiff here."

"So where did you disappear to half the day?" she said quietly, fumbling for her mattress in the darkness.

"Guarding the hens. Those two were shot and the others holed up in the pit behind the threshing floor, you know, the one with the brushwood. They're sitting tight so I gave them some feed there, they can stay down there tonight."

"How many are left then?"

"Well, seven. Just the speckled one with the black head's gone. And the old yellow one. Still I don't think they shot that one. She's hiding in the nettles somewhere."

"Let's hope she is," sighed Stepanida, thinking of something else now. A new idea was forming in her mind, displacing any thought of hens or pig - the farmyard was the powerful focus of her attention. But she hadn't decided on anything yet and for the moment just listened to Petroc tormenting himself.

"Dear oh dear! What are we going to do? What are we going to do?. . .Here I've got this crust. You have some, you've likely not eaten today."

In the darkness he passed over the rough crust and she took it with an unexpected pang of pity - not for herself, for him. What a day, no hot meal, just dry stuff for that ailing stomach of his - poor old Petroc! In times gone by he would be railing against his lot or blaming her, but now he was resigned and getting by with a tough old crust. He'd come to that! But then so had she. She hadn't had so much as a poppy seed in her mouth since the previous day and now a lump of bread seemed a delicacy. She lay down on the mattress and, covering her legs with her jacket, began breaking off pieces of bread and putting them into her mouth, chewing quietly. But mainly she was listening. Everything had settled down in the yard and the tent; true, along the passage the subdued evening conversation of the officer and the feldwebel was still audible, they weren't asleep yet. She very much wanted them to drop off; a secret, hazardous plan was taking urgent shape inside her, making her tremble even, but she knew it was irresistible. Not that she had any intention of resisting; on the contrary, she had mustered her courage and would carry out her plan even if she had known for certain it would go wrong. Anyway, for the moment she had to sit it out: while those two were still awake, she couldn't leave the boiler-house. Stepanida knew how to wait. That's all she'd ever done in her life. Sometimes in vain, but now and again she'd been lucky. Only very rarely had she ever renounced her own intentions, that was how she was: it often cost her more to do that than to carry them out.

She had chewed all the bread and was now lying sleepless on her pallet.

She didn't know whether Petroc was asleep or not, but there was no sound from him, no breathing or movement; worn out by his day, he'd obviously fallen asleep. The guttural conversation from the hut seemed to be dying down. After lying for another few minutes, she rose quietly, and resting her hand against the wall, peeped out of the window. No, the bright strip of light was still shining across the grass outside, patterned by the black shadow of the window frame; it almost reached the buckets under the fence. The rifle couldn't be seen from here, but she sensed it was still hanging where it had been. Stepanida squinted at one side of the yard, then the other. There really seemed to be no one about. She lay down on her mattress again, encouraging herself: never mind, sooner or later, those in the hut would go to bed as well. All she had to do was wait it out.

She lay there for another hour or so, listening to the nocturnal sounds near and far. Somewhere, over in Zabolotye, probably, beyond the gully, a dog kept barking endlessly, then abruptly squealed and went quiet - somebody had struck it or let if off the chain. The talk in the hut ceased, but in the silence came the sound of footsteps on the floorboards. The door banged briefly and someone went outside, soon to return. As the dim reflection on the black rafter up above blinked off, she guessed that the hut light had been extinguished. The murk of a moonless autumnal night reigned in the passage, the farmyard and the boiler-house. Stepanida lay on for a considerable time, mulling over the distressing events of the day with the edge of her mind, as it were: her own action over the milk, which caused Bobovka to perish, the pillaging of the farmstead, the shooting at the hens and her unexpected success with the pig. Maybe at least he would survive if these villains didn't get to the gully and drag him out of the badger's lair. So she thought things over severally and at once, as if gradually gathering strength to embark upon the most difficult undertaking.

She seemed to doze off for a little and came to suddenly from some subconscious inner prompting, ears pricked. A rat was quietly moving about under the millstones and Petroc was whistling as he breathed hoarsely on the bins. She sat up on her mattress, feet on the floor. Now she felt nothing but a stubborn determination to reach to her goal - to do that which she could no longer not do. It was some cruel compulsion rather than her own will which made her rise as quietly as ever she could and lift the latch of the old oak door of the boiler-house. Luckily it didn't creak, just rustled a bit and she left it as it was without closing it. Then she tiptoed towards the half open passage door with its faint draft and listened again. Inside the hut, somebody was snoring sleepily, not loudly, lulled rather and measured. She had to be more venturesome. After all, didn't she have the right to go into her own yard if she needed to or had she ceased to be a person at all? So what if there was a war on, and Germans. . .People lived before this war and they'd live after it, and whether these would survive was a matter for conjecture. Those who took up the sword against others could end up spiked themselves. Gingerly feeling the earth with her toes, she moved down off the steps to the cold damp grass then slipped round the corner and hid - she thought someone in the tent had moved. They must have been dreaming, at any rate nobody came out. There was no sign of a sentry in the yard and this gave her heart. Naturally they were full of confidence, the new masters. What did they have to be afraid of anyway, who could harm them here?

And yet she was more fearful than she had ever been in her life, perhaps; it was particularly terrifying as she left the woodpile and approached the fence on tottering legs. She didn't need to peer into the darkness, she knew exactly where the place was and touched the rifle at once, seizing it by its thin cold barrel. It was heavier than she had thought; let's hope a weight like that plopping into the water won't wake everybody up, thought Stepanida anxiously. This circumstance rather disconcerted her, but she had no strength to alter her intention now - she was totally given up to it. Stepanida ran on tiptoe to the well and rested the rifle on the woodwork. Before completely letting go of it, she glanced at the hut and the bellying shape of the tent, but all was peaceful in the night, no one visible anywhere, so she released her fingers.

Stepanida recoiled from the well as the splash echoed in the depths sufficiently to bring everyone to their feet. Distracted, Stepanida raced to the boiler-house and slipped into the passage in its shadow. Here she felt a terrible fear when she found the boiler-house door shut, but recalled that it sometimes closed itself and much relieved, raised the latch.

Before closing the door behind her, she paused for a moment - no, all around was calm and quiet. It seemed she'd pulled it off. 'What'll happen?' she thought feverishly, shivering with a sudden chill, only now perhaps truly frightened. Fear possessed her with such strength that her teeth began to chatter and so probably woke Petroc.

"What's the matter, got the shivers? Cover yourself up," he said half-asleep and at once from the bins came his steady breathing.

She, however, had not fallen asleep by dawn.

10

The Germans rose bright and early, before dawn. Petroc heard them by the boiler-house, coughs, hoarse voices out in the yard. A bucket clattered in the well - they'd started drawing water for the kitchen. It seemed yesterday's celebrations were over and to all appearances, they intended to get to work today.

Petroc lay on the rags covering the hard boards of the bins, jacket pulled up over his head, listening to the bustle outside and thinking how differently from us they went about things, these Germans, they had their own alien style. Yesterday night even, when they were having their celebration, the electric light shone brightly in the hut, they ate from plates with forks and drank something from small white cups, got a bit merry and talkative but almost as usual; there wasn't a drunk to be seen. The officer and the feldwebel ate apart from the others in the hut and had stuff brought in to them on shining plates, covered with white napkins, and these two were restrained as well, talking quietly and sitting no longer than usual at supper. Probably it was an hour or so after the supper had started when the feldwebel came out onto the steps and gave an order. The yard cleared immediately - the lot vanished into their tent. 'That's discipline all right, bugger me!' thought Petroc, quietly envious. The officer's word was law, everybody ate, slept and prayed only on the word of command. Hardly surprising they were winning. Organization!

So they'd eaten Bobovka. Petroc was somewhat angry at Stepanida, thinking this over: she shouldn't have meddled there, give them all the milk, let them get it down them if they're so fond of it, why play tricks? Because of Stepanida's tricks they were left without a cow. Of course, Petroc knew that they might have taken the cow, milk or not, - if not now, later, when they left. Of course it would have been better to have hidden the cow. But how could they have done it? A cow wasn't a hen, you couldn't hide it in the nettles. And anyway, who could have known they'd suddenly descend on the farm like that? There were none of them in the Settlement even.

From outside, a pleasant, sweetish almost familiar smell drifted into the boiler-house and Petroc didn't realize at first it was coffee. Well, of course, he'd heard from the first war that Germans drink coffee first thing in the morning, not kvass or tea like the Russians. Petroc had never tried the beverage and now imagined it to be very tasty. Anyway what was coffee when there were only three handfuls of salt left, how could you eat potatoes without any salt? They wouldn't go down your throat. Nothing but trouble!

It was getting a bit lighter outside, but the sun wasn't up yet; all that could be heard was the rustling of the nagging wind over the roof. Yesterday was the last of the good weather, apparently. Overnight the frail boiler-house with its rotting corners had become cold and by morning Petroc, chilled, fidgeting under his sheepskin jacket, didn't want to get up. Out of the corner of one eye he glanced over at the mattress by the window. Stepanida was lying hunched under her quilted jacket like one dead: fretting over Bobovka, he thought. Of course, what life would it be without a cow? Without the cow the old woman was done for.

Just as he was thinking about getting up, the door to the passage was yanked open to reveal a German on the threshold. It was the evil-tempered cook again with his forage cap screwed sideways across his head; the young one with the glasses peered out behind him. Petroc made shift to sit up on the bins, feeling for the sleeves of his jacket. The cook, without a word, shone a torch in his eyes and began searching the boiler-house, illuminating in turn the dusty millstones, the shelf, the large storage bin in the corner; he leaped over to the corn bins, took the lids off all three and looked inside. Two were completely empty, while there were about a hundred pounds of barley in the third. Then, with a barked "weg" he sprang over to Petroc, who leapt barefoot onto the cold floor, while the German threw aside all his clothing and the bin coverings as he searched through every one. He bent down under the millstones for some odd reason, flashed his light over the walls, corners, the ceiling even, then dashed out into the passage without a word.

Petroc got into his sheepskin sleeves somehow and cautiously closed the door behind the cook. He turned to his wife who was sitting on her mattress with a stony expression, eyes lowered.

"What did he want then?"

Stepanida shrugged and tucked her kerchief in without a word and leisurely donned her quilted jacket. She seemed not to be at all surprised at the odd behavior of the German; only her eyes betrayed the fact that she was paying close attention to every outside sound. Quite at a loss, Petroc looked out of the window. The Germans out there were discussing something excitedly, even fearfully, huddled together round the kitchen; a few were wandering near the cowshed for some reason and over by the woodpile. What were they looking for?

"Looks as if they've lost something," said Petroc.

Stepanida had no time to answer before the Germans near the kitchen moved towards the hut en masse, tramped through the passage and this time not one but three together burst into the boiler-house. Then it started. . .With expressions of grim, incomprehensible resolve on their faces, they began turning everything upside down, bins, containers, the lot; they took down garments from their hooks; they raked through the potato pile out in the passage with their boots, hurled the chest lid to one side with a crash and instantly dumped the contents. Petroc mutely fidgeted by the doorway; nobody asked him anything. He just stared as the lanky one in the broad boots angrily rummaged through all the baskets and the hemp bin, and overturned all the pots at his feet. Leaping over to Stepanida, he pushed her aside and felt the mattress on the bench with his knee. Glancing through the window, Petroc saw several soldiers clambering onto the sheaves in the shed and searching there, throwing the sheaves into the doorway.

"What are you after, gentlemen?" asked Petroc as politely as he knew how, addressing no one in particular.

The lanky one measured him with an icy stare and shouted something incomprehensible; Petroc inquired no more. He squashed himself still deeper into the corner furthest from the door and watched the proceedings in silence. At length the Germans piled out into the yard, leaving a jumbled havoc behind them and spent a long time prowling along the walls, peering under the eaves, then over the fence into the nettles and even onto the moss-grown boiler-house roof.

'Have they gone barmy, or what?' thought Petroc in wonderment.

Still, things had to be put in order somehow and Petroc was busy replacing the containers when he heard the familiar twang of strings and froze in alarm. They'd found his violin. 'Oh God, that's terrible!' thought Petroc, ready to weep at this new blow. But what could he do? Maybe they'd amuse themselves a bit and give it him back? Surely they wouldn't smash it and throw it away, what did they want with a fiddle? Without much thought, however, he rushed out into the passage at the very moment when the officer was hastening outside in his tall cap with the plump feldwebel in his wake. They ran into Petroc, who spoke up, tongue-tied with excitement:

"Officer, sir, can I have my. . .well, violin back. . .Because it's mine, my own. . .Bought it, you see. . ."

"Weg!" barked the officer, his voice a whiplash.

Cursing the world and everything in it, Petroc backed off into the boiler-house and quietly opened the door. Stepanida was standing by the window, tensely watching.

"The fiddle's had it," Petroc said, crushed. "What the devil's got into them?"

'Something bad's happened,' thought Petroc, as he heard the sharp command from the yard and watched through the window as they formed up in two ranks, rifles in hand. Everybody lined up, including the feldwebel and Karl, with only the officer in front of the parade and, next to him, the cook standing rigidly, arms by his sides and a crushed expression on his face. His white jacket was belted around with a strap which sagged with the weight of a pouch on either side of the buckle. Head hanging, the cook stared straight at the ground in front of him. Only when the officer roared at him did he raise his narrow, deathly-haggard face and utter two quiet words. The officer at once, briefly and without flourish, smacked him across the cheek. The German swayed a little but did not recoil and did not even raise his hand to defend himself.

"Stepanida, Stepanida, look at this!"

Stepanida merely shivered as she wrapped her jacket around her and sat down on the mattress, while Petroc kept watching through the window as if some absorbing film was playing out there. The Germans were silent and downcast, the stricken cook likewise, who had now taken his place at the end of the line. The officer, clasping his gloved hands behind his back, paced before them and spoke jerkily. He would say something, walk three paces, halt, say something more, then stop. Judging by the soldiers' morose expressions, what he had to say was naught for their comfort; he was likely giving them a good ticking-off. Petroc guessed that something had happened and the cook was to blame. It was all very interesting, but Petroc began to worry whether this turn of events might rebound on Stepanida and himself. Everything indeed depended on the officer. Petroc already knew that the officer was the senior man here and that no good need be expected from him; as for evil, he was always ready enough for that, judging by all that had happened.

However, the lecture in the yard was over, the parade was dismissed; some of the Germans had lit up cigarettes, while the rest headed for their vehicle. If only they'd clear out altogether, Petroc thought hopefully, but it was too soon for that. The gray tent and the field kitchen remained behind in the yard, the officer waved his arms about in front of the feldwebel, who made off at a run for the steps. Petroc's heart lurched: not here in the boiler-house, surely?

But it was. The boiler-house door swung wide and the feldwebel beckoned him from the doorway like a puppy.

"Kom! Kom-kom. . ."

"Me?"

"Ja, ja. You," confirmed the feldwebel.

Petroc straightened his cap and followed him out through the passage into the yard. The troops were already getting into the machine, one after the other scrambling over the tailgate, while the officer stood by the open door of the cabin. The feldwebel squeezed through the fence into the garden and trampling the beetroot in the beds, began mincing his way across to the far end of the garden. Petroc trailed after him, puzzled.

"Klozet nicht?" queried the feldwebel, halting all of a sudden.

"Who?" Petroc was lost.

"Klozet nicht? Ferstehen? Klozet, klozet?" persisted the feldwebel, but obviously realizing the hopelessness of his attempt, got down fussily onto his haunches and pronounced distinctly: "A-a-a. . ."

"Ah!" It dawned on Petroc. "The whatsit?"

"The whatsit," repeated the German. "Make!"

"Well if you. . .If somebody needs it, I'll. . ."

Petroc wanted to go into more detail about this delicate matter and pointed to the cowshed, now empty and surplus to requirements. The feldwebel, however, ignored him and with his short little legs measured out three broad paces by the blackcurrant bushes under the fence.

"Ofitsirklozet!" he announced decisively. "Drei hour time. Ferstehen understood?"

"Right, understood," said Petroc, not wholly confident.

Well, after all it wasn't the worst that might have happened - digging them a latrine; Petroc was pleased even that everything had passed off so straight-forwardly. And he'd been thinking. . .He'd even been afraid that this pit might be his last resting place.

He returned to the yard and retrieved an old rusty spade from under the planks on the woodpile. It was no easy task digging with it, but he'd manage in three hours, probably. He'd have to because hell only knew what would happen to him if he didn't finish in time.

The vehicle could be heard revving up, everyone no doubt aboard. Just to make sure, Petroc peeped round the angle of the woodpile. The yard was practically deserted, as the machine turned round under the limes, ripping up the garden soil with its enormous wheels. Only Karl was left by the kitchen, and Stepanida next to him on a bench by the fence was settling down to peel the potatoes. Naturally, they've handed out work to everybody, thought Petroc, noticing the half sack of potatoes in front of this wife, obviously from his stack in the passage. The vehicle was receding as it rumbled its slow way towards the road and Petroc went out into the yard

with his spade, somewhat relieved at getting rid of his lodgers at least for a
time. He rejoiced too soon, however; between the tent and the windows of
the hut stood a young German with an icy expression on his young acned
face and a broad shining bayonet on the end of his rifle. There you are,
they've posted a sentry, reflected Petroc, reverting at once to his usual mood
of careworn gloom. You couldn't expect things to get any better round here,
of course, he thought, heading across the yard towards the garden, then he
heard Karl's voice.

"Vater, kom!"

Karl was standing on a large white tub. As Petroc approached, he raised
the lid to disclose that there was meat inside. Bobovka's meat of course.
Taking a hefty chunk, he handed it to Stepanida first, but she shook her head
fastidiously.

"I shan't."

Then Karl turned to Petroc who accepted a nice piece on the bone from
his hand. The meat gave off an appetizing, filling smell and Petroc was sorely
tempted, but Stepanida looked at him with such contempt from the fence
that he felt confused.

"Er. . .Maybe later, sir, Karl? Actually I'd rather, you know. . .have a smoke."

"Smoke!" Karl understood. "Ja! Jawohl."

He got out a packet of cigarettes and they unhurriedly smoked one apiece.
Petroc inhaled greedily, still holding the meat in his left hand.

"I'll put this. . .for later." He indicated the meat and the boiler-house.

"Ja, ja," Karl agreed.

Petroc set off quickly towards the passage, but as this point the sentry
strode forward from the tent.

"Halt! Verboten!"

"What?"

"Halt! Zuruck!" he barked in metallic tones, smartly barring the way to
the threshold. His youthful face was stony.

'God, more trouble!' thought Petroc. 'Now we can't get into the hut; how
can we survive here?' That was it: they couldn't get into the boiler-house
even. Petroc hung about in the yard till he'd smoked Karl's cigarette to his
fingernails. Karl glanced at him once or twice without expression and began
fussing about his kitchen. Stepanida peeled potatoes by the fence. She had
turned her back on the kitchen, presumably so as not to have to see anybody
in the yard.

There was nothing for it, Petroc laid the meat on the metal lid of the vat
and went off to the garden. The officer's latrine had to be dug.

The digging was easy at first; the spade bit deep into the garden topsoil
which Petroc tossed over to the fence. After that, though, the soil got harder,

then came the clay which was really tough going. It involved twisting the spade around awkwardly in the tight narrow pit.

Although the weather since morning had been chilly and windy, Petroc warmed up quickly and unbuttoned his sheepskin. He had only dug knee-deep before he felt tired and realized that he might not finish on time. In fact half the time allowed had passed if not more. His back grew damp beneath the sheepskin, and Petroc sat down on the edge of the pit to rest up a little.

It was then that he heard voices in the yard, familiar voices it seemed. Petroc glanced round. Out from behind the hut, across the beetroot beds, Guzh came striding, his boots spattered with mud and a rifle across his shoulder. His crumpled white armband had slipped below the elbow of the same old, ginger leather jacket. 'This is a bit too much' thought Petroc apprehensively, anticipating yet more bad news. The polizei came up to the pit and slid his rifle off his shoulder.

"Digging are we?" he said without greeting.

"Yes, well. . .as you see. . ."

"You're digging the wrong thing."

"It's what they said. Nowadays we do as they say, you know."

"So here's my orders: you get over to the potatoes. To the Settlement. Everybody's been sent there, there's only you and the old woman left."

'That's a new one' thought Petroc. 'To hell with you and your potatoes!' He didn't fancy going out in this cold, with nothing inside him and working the whole day in the fields, but he didn't know how to refuse.

"Maybe they'd let us off? Eh? Not feeling too good, you know, these days. Get this stitch in the side, so. . ."

"What's that to me!" Guzh broke in harshly. "He's got a stitch. If we don't get the potatoes in, the Germans'll unstitch your head. That's the order: dig every last potato and cart them to the station. Deadline - by Sunday."

"But that's. . .Aren't there any younger people?" Petroc became agitated. "Women, girls. I'm past sixty you know. . ."

"Come on, come on!" Guzh prodded the earth impatiently with his rifle-butt. "No more backtalk."

After a pause, Petroc began climbing out of the unfinished pit. He didn't feel at all like going off God knows where, to the Settlement fields, but it looked as if he would have to. These boys wouldn't let up. They'd drag you out from underground and force you to do what the Germans had ordered them.

Laying hold of his spade, he meekly followed the polizei to the hut, feeling the ache in the small of his back; then a sudden thought occurred to him: it might even be better this way - well away from this trampled, despoiled farm and out into the clean fields. At least he'd be among his own sort there, away from this constant hustling and belittlement. As always, he tried to discover some advantage in any new circumstance, how could you live if you didn't adapt? Things would never be as you wanted them, that was certain.

They pushed their way through the hole in the fence and found themselves in the yard, where the kitchen was smoking away and clouds of steam were coming from the boiler. Karl was mixing something up in there, while Stepanida was peeling potatoes by the fence with silent concentration, her expression unchanged.

"Well, activist, how long are going to be?" Guzh barked impatiently.

"You can't drive me, I'm not in harness," replied Stepanida calmly, hurling a potato into the pail.

"I'm not driving, I'm ordering. Get your baskets and march after me!"

"Where can I get them?"

"The house! You've got some baskets in the passage, haven't you?"

"Who's going to let me in there?"

"What d'you mean, who? That sentry won't let you in, is that it? . . .Hey, friend!" Guzh addressed the sentry in a different, much softer tone. "I'll see to them. We need a basket. Understand, a basket!"

"Zuruck!" barked the sentry and unhitched his rifle.

'Well good for him!' thought Petroc to himself. 'Serves you right: zuruck! What did you think?' and stared with something akin to sympathy at the dense face of the sentry, who had thwarted the arrogant polizei in so timely a fashion.

"Well, hell!" Guzh brought out anxiously. "Grab a sack, then, a bucket or something. . ."

"Where do I get a bucket? That belongs to them."

'Yes, you can't catch Stepanida with your bare hands!' Petroc thought of his wife admiringly, perhaps for the first time in years. 'Once she makes her mind up, you'll jump. I'm not going to help you. Force her if you can!'

Amid these exchanges in the yard they didn't hear the enormous German vehicle turn off the road and roll up to the gates. It hadn't stopped before the roly-poly feldwebel dropped from the cabin. His flushed face was animated; for good or ill, it was hard to know.

"Was ist das?" barked the feldwebel, halting in front of Guzh. The latter tried a clumsy salute, an effort spoiled by his rifle whose sling slipped off his leather shoulder and dangled from his elbow. "Was ist das? What is this?" reiterated the feldwebel, really angry by now. One hand on hip, there he stood, short and round, in front of the awkward, long-armed Guzh.

"Orders for potatoes, officer, sir! Potatoes!" Guzh explained. "To get them picked by Sunday."

"Was ist das?" squealed the feldwebel furiously, ignoring Guzh's explanation and moving a step nearer the polizei.

"I was telling you, officer, sir, everybody's ordered to the potatoes. The burgomaster, sir. . ."

"Was ist das?" pursued the feldwebel, and Guzh bit back his words this time. Straightening up and putting on a fixed stare, he stood in silence before the German gathered himself and with a neat upwards movement, hit him twice, first one cheek then the other. The polizei staggered back with his rifle, hugging it to his side, and blinked his eyes, flustered and no doubt expecting further punishment. The feldwebel, however, did not strike him again; he simply pointed a stubby finger towards the gate. "Weg!"

As Guzh left the yard, whether in fear or relief, the feldwebel contemptuously hissed through his teeth:

"Stinking polizei-swine. . ."

"That's right, what you did. He's a bad man. . ." Petroc couldn't resist saying, well pleased with this turn of events. He was fairly trembling with pleasure, but the feldwebel gave him an odd look, as if seeing him there for the first time. His eyes narrowed unpleasantly.

"Ofitsirklozet fertig?"

"Eh?"

"Is it ready there?" he indicated the garden.

"How could it be when that bloke stuck his nose in?" Petroc recovered himself, guessing what the German had said. But he added nothing more as he noticed the German edging round to the side and before he caught on to what was happening, a sharp pain from a booted toe in the backside propelled him three paces towards the fence. 'Oh, my gawd!' he had just time to think and flew through the hole into the garden like a scalded cat.

11

Stepanida herself didn't know how she had lived through that terrible pre-dawn hour when the Germans were going over the farmstead, overturning everything in sight. It was clear she hadn't been spotted the previous night, but that didn't make things easier and all kinds of possibilities flooded into her mind. The rifle had gone missing here on this farm, and that was probably sufficient reason for dealing severely with the owners. It was odd that the thought hadn't occurred to her the night before, when she had been seized by that irresistible yearning for vengeance. Towards morning the possible consequences frightened her considerably.

But for the time being, it had blown over. The Germans had cleared off to work, leaving Karl on his own; she had orders to help him. At first it was potato peeling (three whole buckets), then washing out a couple of dozen mess kits and lids; after that Karl made her sand off two blackened vats and then wash through some dishcloths with soap and hot water. Working with deliberate lack of haste, she reluctantly did all this and gradually, as her fear of the morning subsided, her worries about the piglet increased: how was it getting on over there? It had to be fed, otherwise it would be squealing for the whole district to hear. Somebody might come across it and let it out or make off with it - what would be left of the farm then?

Karl, however, wouldn't let her budge an inch from the kitchen and kept finding tasks for her; she performed them all without demur. The Germans didn't turn up at the farm for dinner; perhaps there was some problem with the bridge, or they were working to make up for the holiday the day before. They arrived at twilight and besieged the kitchen immediately; all of them were clearly tired, starving and chilled by the wind. Petroc was digging out the officer's latrine in the garden and putting a fence around it, while she slipped away from the kitchen to the passage; the sentry stood aside and permitted her to go into the boiler-house.

Stepanida went in and held her breath, she had been terrified of attracting the Germans' attention; she kept thinking - what if somebody found out or guessed that it was she who had taken the rifle? Unless she had been compelled to, she wouldn't have left the boiler-house, which now represented refuge and sanctuary for her and was still upside-down after the morning's search. Petroc hadn't returned yet from the garden, so she busied herself restoring containers to their appointed corners along with the various utensils and rehung garments on the wall. The chilly autumn day had deteriorated towards evening and drizzle had set in. The Germans were disinclined to wander about the yard and after quickly sorting out their mess kits and meat, they betook themselves into their tent.

Once the yard had emptied, Stepanida transferred the remnants of the old, boiled potatoes from the tub to a pot, sprinkled them with bran, and looked out of the window. The yard and the immediate vicinity of the farm were quickly fading into a dank autumnal twilight. There was no one near the kitchen except for Karl who had put his camouflage cape in a skewed wedge over his head and was cleaning up. With the pot covered by a flap of her quilted jacket, she marched out of the passage only to run straight into the sentry - a middle-aged German with a long nose and a wet hat pulled down over his ears. He was standing by the door under the roof and immediately stuck his leg out across the threshold.

"Es ist verboten! Not allowed!"

"Not allowed!. . .So that's the way of it. . ."

She made no attempt to appeal or persuade him - harsh words from the feldwebel came from the hut, meaning that either he or the officer had ordered the sentry not to let her into the yard. 'Drop dead the lot of you!' she thought to herself and returned to the boiler-house.

She set the pot down by the door, sat down on her mattress and remained there till Petroc entered. There was a cold, wet smell about him, though Petroc himself seemed neither cold nor weary, on the contrary, he appeared cheerful and pleased with himself.

"Woman, we're all right!" he said from the threshold with, for him, unusual vigor. "Did the latrine, that there closet. . .The officer was pleased."

"Maybe he was giving you a good telling-off?"

"No, he was praising me, honest. Clapped me on the shoulder like that. Gut, he said."

"You're really sucking up to them, aren't you?" said Stepanida sarcastically, marvelling to herself: what a thing to be pleased about.

"Oh no I'm not, blast them!" Petroc said, voice dropping to a whisper. "I just thought they might give me my fiddle back."

"They won't," she said. "Otherwise they wouldn't have taken it."

"What do they want with it? They can't play it, can they?"

"Maybe they can."

"If they could, they'd have played it by now. I know."

"Well, go on then, Ask them," she said, her mind occupied elsewhere.

The piglet was surely done for; in this weather it would just curl up and die in the badger's den if it didn't perish from hunger before that. What could she do about it? Apart from asking for leave of absence from the farm on some pretext, that is; they might let her go. But what convincing reason could she think up? She racked her brains but nothing came.

"Right, I'm going." Petroc had mustered his courage, but remained where he was.

It was then that she recalled her surviving hens, who had probably run away from the farm somewhere or were scattered about the gully. While she had been busy round the kitchen during the day, she had kept an eye on the various nooks and crannies in case one turned up, but not one of them did. They'd lost themselves good and proper.

"While you're there, ask them to let us out to look for the hens. Say they got scattered yesterday and we've got to round them up."

"Well, why not? So, God have mercy on me!"

It was too dark to see, but she knew Petroc had crossed himself and tentatively opened the door. Then, after an interval, a quiet knock on the hut door could be heard from the passage. Stepanida was on edge: hell knew what would happen. At least let her Petroc come back in one piece.

Apparently they let him into the hut, where he spent a considerable time. She waited, listening, but almost nothing could be heard beyond a few foreign words, none of which she understood. Then suddenly one string of the violin began singing, then a second and a third, before they all blended into a melody in which she recognized Petroc's touch. He wasn't much of a hand at anything else, but he could certainly play the violin, that she knew. Surely they wouldn't give it back to him, Stepanida thought, joy and sadness blending. However, Petroc did not return; instead, the melancholy music of "Kupalinki", her one-time favorite, began to flow melodiously. Stepanida listened and listened, trying to cope with something compassionate in her that threatened to overwhelm her emotions completely, but couldn't resist. One by one, the teardrops rolled from her eye, as she quickly wiped them away with the edge of her rough kerchief and once more held her breath as she listened. Petroc was playing cleanly and with great attention as he had at one time at parties in the Settlement, with Zamoshye and Guschi, with Lavrik on the cymbalom. When he had finished, there was more talking, but it soon went quiet again as a new strain commenced, a song about the Volga, popular before the war. The audience could be heard joining in, raggedly falsetto in their foreign tongue. Stepanida kept on listening, though her first unwitting capitulation to the spell of the music had begun to give way to annoyance, even anger - why was he playing for them? Some audience to entertain! Couldn't he have refused? He could have said he couldn't play, it wasn't his violin, it belonged to somebody else. Instead he was overjoyed: the officer had praised him for the latrine so maybe he would be called in to play whenever the officer was in. Well at least let him come back! As long as he didn't earn another kick up the backside from them.

Time passed. They were obviously in no hurry to administer the kicking, his playing was clearly much to their liking. He went on for a long time; after the songs came dances. He played the "Kazachok" the "Levonikha" and the "Cracoviak". Stepanida thought she heard someone clapping once or twice and someone saying "bravo". 'Just fancy that' wondered Stepanida. 'Just you wait, I'll show you how to deal with those carrion-crows!'

Perhaps an hour later, the doors banged, one, two. Petroc came back into the boiler-house and spoke quietly, but with total satisfaction:

"Well. I told you didn't I. . ."

"You got it back?"

"I did and you didn't believe I would." He passed something over to her in the darkness and she fumbled before grasping the violin's slender neck.

"And you asked about the hens?"

"Ah, the hens. . .Forgot. I forgot. . .you can't get much over to them in there you know."

In an abrupt gesture she flung the violin at the millstones; it hit something soft and rebounded with a faint twang of strings. Petroc was stunned:

"What are you doing? Why do that?. . ."

"I'm doing nothing. It's you who're doing it as far as I can see," she said bitterly in an undertone. "You've made your peace, playing the fiddle. Who're you playing for, have you thought about that? Maybe they've killed your children. Where's your daughter? Or your son? Not a word for a month, maybe they're buried already and he plays for them!"

"What else could I do? They told me to! So I played. They gave it back to me anyway."

"Gave it back to you! Now you'll be playing for them every night, I suppose?"

Petroc had no time to reply before a shot crashed out somewhere close at hand, echoing in the nocturnal stillness, followed by a hubbub of voices - alarmed, loud and German. Doors banged in the hut as everybody leapt outside into the dark yard; more shouts of alarm ensued and two more shots thundered out in close succession. Stepanida sat as if turned to stone, unable to comprehend who they could possibly be shooting at, when suddenly a dazzling light, like electricity being switched on, burst over the farm and the yard; a bright fiery beam struck in through the window and fled along the floor, crossing the bins and Petroc himself, stock-still and clutching the red violin, before going out on the wall under the black ceiling beam.

"Flare," said Petroc cheerlessly. "What on earth's going on? They'll set light to. . ."

She didn't know what was going on either and since she was unable to see anything, listened fearfully to the mysterious comings and goings round the farm buildings. It sounded as if the whole hullabaloo had moved round behind the hut in the direction of the gully; there was a rush of boots on earth and more shooting in the distance. When another rocket burst, its distant light flickered dim and uncertain over the lime tree boughs and the bulky top of the vehicle parked beneath. 'Who've they seen there?' wondered Stepanida. 'Not the pig surely? Had it got out and come running? If so it'll be shot for a certainty.'

She couldn't stay sitting on the mattress any longer; she knelt up to the window and peered into the darkened yard. She tried to go outside but at once returned to the window, deciding that was unwise: only too easy to get shot in the dark. She strained her ears for the shouts and running about near the gully or the garden on that side of the farmstead. Several more gunshots were heard and a sharp stentorian word of command.

"Good Lord! What is all this?" asked Petroc completely at a loss.

"Quiet you! Listen. . ."

Well, of course, what else could they do but sit and listen? And amid this endless tension, when things were quieter for a moment, she overheard a brief conversation by the porch as someone spoke to the sentry. She understood only one word "banditen." 'How could there by any bandits here?' she wondered. 'Maybe the Germans had been attacked from the forest, seeing as they had rushed off furiously towards the gully? But if so, why were there no shots from the other side, from the gully itself?. . .'

"What's going to happen, eh?" Petroc went on grumbling, till she quietly rejoined:

"What will be will be. Surely you know that."

"As long as they don't set light to the farm."

"They might just do that," confirmed Stepanida. "I wouldn't put anything past them."

She thought somebody had run past the boiler-house wall towards the yard or the tent; voices were once more audible, but this time restrained and the newcomer's boots came thudding back across the earth and receded. There were no more shots, but further rockets went up and their distant fitful radiance briefly relieved the gloom of the yard and boiler-house. She could make out Petroc's face as a piece of white linen, as he stood holding his useless violin, seemingly at a loss to know what to do with it.

"They're coming!"

Petroc tensed his whole body in the darkness: she sensed it almost physically as the distant chatter of excited Germans reached her ear also. The voices were getting nearer - a contingent, or perhaps the whole detachment, were on their way back to the farmstead. Yes, they were certainly returning, the voices were becoming clearer, while one, a little louder than the rest, the feldwebel perhaps, broke in from time to time. Stepanida listened closely. No, it was a different voice; it was busy explaining or perhaps justifying something.

Soon the boots came tramping along the path past the boiler-house and woodpile; the yard was lit up by several torches flashing as the Germans found their way. They poured into the yard, seemingly the whole crowd of them, before halting in the middle. Somebody ran into the hut (Licht, licht!), and electric light suddenly blazed out from the window.

Stepanida stood by her own window, already aware that any moment now something extremely unpleasant would become apparent, though she couldn't foresee what it was. There was little to be seen in the nocturnal murk of the yard through the window's dirty glass, apart from what the electric light from the hut lit up. She could see the Germans hauling something heavy and throwing it down onto the grass. Some were laughing, others shouted their excitement. Behind their backs and forage caps, the only thing visible was the tall hat of the officer in a shiny cape. The torch threw a pool of light on the earth by their feet.

"They've killed somebody," Petroc said, now by her side. He had no time for further observations before an uproar broke out in the passage and the weak beam of a torch played about the boiler-house and dazzled them as they stood on the mattress peering out.

"Vater, kom! See ein bandit! Identify ein bandit," said the feldwebel, instantly correcting himself.

Crossing himself as he went, Petroc made for the door, leaving Stepanida in the dark, no longer looking outside. She stood in the middle of the hut as if petrified, already knowing that something frightful had occurred and awaiting confirmation of her premonition, like one condemned.

Petroc soon returned, but Stepanida did not inquire WHO. She would have been grateful to Petroc if he had said nothing and kept his counsel till morning. But Petroc was not a man to be quiet about something important for long and barely closed the door behind him before confiding in a frightened whisper:

"They've killed Yanka!"

Stepanida felt as if she had collapsed into utter darkness; her heart grew heavy and painful, but Petroc obviously interpreted her silence as an unspoken question and hastened to elucidate:

"You know, that little shepherd boy. From the Settlement."

To prevent herself from actually falling, she felt for the edge of the mattress and sank down onto it.

Her conscious mind really did seem to have fallen away from the boiler-house and this fearful night; she ceased to be aware of herself in this world of turmoil which was narrowing about her, diminishing like a trap soon to snap shut for ever. She knew her end was approaching, inevitably and soon; her only thought was - why? What had she done wrong against God and conscience, why had such chastisement descended upon her and mankind in general? Why, into a life already replete with hardship, had these aliens invaded to turn everything upside down, depriving people of even the smallest hope for the future?

Why, what for, she continually asked herself, without finding an answer and her thoughts turned back in upon themselves, into the depths of her lived experience. Things had quieted down in the yard beyond the wall; the soldiers' rough boots had ceased their tramping. From time to time, German sentences could be heard, but she no longer listened to the repulsive alien sounds. As her spirit grew calmer she already saw another time, and there heard other voices, voices which had accompanied her all her life. Perhaps it was only in these that she could find consolation, if such a thing as consolation could any longer be found in this world. . .

12

On the farm no one had eaten dinner that day; Stepanida was waiting for the children from school and Petroc hadn't been home since morning - at dawn he'd gone with the men to the station with the voluntary rate contribution. He wasn't due back till late evening. It was very muddy underfoot - it had been thawing for almost three days and outside everything was sodden; a thin rain drifted down from the sky. Mornings saw the onset of frost - the fields, the road, the trees were covered in an icy carapace and one branch of the lime tree had failed to withstand it; it was broken across and dangled its ice-sheathed twiglets over the snow. Through the partially melted window Stepanida could make out a figure in the field beyond the sagging branch. He would run swiftly along the Settlement path, then pause to slide along the sledge ruts, flapping the long sleeves of his homespun coat. When this figure had run across the main road and was heading for the farm, Stepanida recognized him as the Settlement youth, Potapka. Potapka was a backward child and hadn't been to school that winter as he had no shoes; he used to sit for days on a bench in the hut where the village soviet met. There he would listen, mouth gaping, to what the men were discussing. If they needed to send for somebody, the leader of the soviet, one-eyed Levon Bogatka used to send Potapka. The youth wasn't all that keen, but he would go, walking or running where he was sent; when he came back he would sit down again by the door, full of precocious interest in everything the elders said.

After a brief sojourn at the window, Stepanida left her spinning wheel in the corner and adjusted her kerchief. Obviously Potapka wasn't running to the farm just for fun. He was on an errand. Recently there had been meetings over in the Settlement practically every evening since Epiphany, where the village activists and district deputies were urging the peasants to join the collective farm. It was wasted effort. The day before yesterday they had sat up all night arguing and swearing and only dispersed as dawn was breaking. Still only six establishments had signed up for the collective.

Seeing Potapka, Stepanida thought he was running over to let her know about another meeting. So, there'd be no literacy class today. She was rather sorry about that because today she had written out a page of her exercise book, and for perhaps the first time that winter the words had been fairly neat, almost all in a line; likely she'd have been praised at school. Last time the teacher had ticked her off for carelessness - it had been getting dark and she had been writing after getting the children off to bed. The kerosene had run out in the oil lamp and Petroc kept grumbling behind the stove that she'd got all worked up about literacy at an awkward time - bedtime. Now, alone in the hut, she sat down at the tidied table and unhurriedly crafted out her eight lines: 'We are building machines, we are building collective farms.' Still, there it was, there'd be no lesson that day.

Meanwhile the door slammed in the passage and Potapka tumbled into the hut without pausing to wipe his feet. He was a strapping, palefaced youth with a rope belt round his patched secondhand jacket. Without preamble he snuffled a couple of times down his reddened, cold-infected nose and neighed:

"Auntie, Levon's asking for you."

"A meeting or what?"

"Na, not a meeting. There's going to be a poverty committee."

"What, now?"

"Yes."

"I'll get ready and come," said Stepanida, somewhat puzzled by this announcement. The poverty committee hadn't met since the autumn and people had been talking about electing a new one. So now the old one was of some use after all.

Potap snuffled again, set his crumpled sheepskin cap straight on his head and slid out of the door. Before he closed it, there came the clump of bootheels on the step and Stepanida recognized the footwear of Levon himself. Back in the soviet hut, the council leader was now doubtless ensconced further back behind the table, with his feet tucked under the bench so that no one should see the president without boots. Still, in the matter of footwear it was no better on the farm. In fact it was a real problem: there was none to be bought or sewn at home either for herself or the children. All the family had was one pair of patched felt boots and Petroc had put them on that morning before setting off; now she would have to make do with bast sandals. Certainly she wasn't too concerned about her appearance, she wasn't off to church after all. If she was going to a poverty committee, there was no point in being fastidious. Just so long as her feet were warm.

She got ready quickly, put on a newish, woolen skirt and tied on a fresh,

white-spotted kerchief before giving her bast sandals a final adjustment. She
didn't make too much of dressing up: she wasn't young and though God
had spared her health, she was forty after all, a wifely age, not like twenty.
She took down from a nail by the door her chief article of finery - a fur jacket,
embroidered down the front. It wasn't new, but it was warm and decent,
suitable for all occasions. She didn't lock the hut; the children would soon
be due home from school - she might even meet them on the road. The
school was close at hand, also in the Settlement to which led the narrow
sledge path from the farmstead. As she walked, Stepanida glanced up ahead
to see if her two little ones were visible. Fenechka was going into the third
form, Fedya into the second. There was no sign of the children, however,
and the path was as slippery as glass. Stepanida kept an eye on where she
walked at the same time so as not to slip and fall over, placing her feet
carefully and worrying about what lay ahead at the committee.

If they'd sent for her, there must be something doing.

The previous night, towards morning, in the impenetrable smoke of the
village soviet hut, something had started which, she felt, could not end with
peace and goodwill all round; something was surely going to happen. It had
all begun with the tense guarded attitude of the peasants, the district party
man and the village council president, Levon; during the election of the
presidium and while the day's agenda was settled - the same as it had been
ever since Christmas - an atmosphere of anxiety, almost of menace was
building up towards a climax in the hut. When the district deputy Kosmachov began to speak, all present lowered their heads and hid their eyes;
they listened and said nothing. Kosmachov spoke competently, with the
emphasis on the political side, and put forward as an example the prosperity
of the collective farmers in some village near Lepel: after good harvests for
the second year running, they were building a club, two tractors were in use
in the fields and they'd obtained a threshing machine and reapers. It was
time for the people of the Settlement to stop hanging on to their thin, little
strips of land, dragging out a poverty-stricken existence, now that their own
Soviet government was offering them similar possibilities and ready to meet
poor and politically conscious average peasants half way. The entire country
was amicably moving in the direction of collectivization, were they going to
fly in the face of that? Kosmachov spoke soberly, appealing to the social
conscience of the average peasant who should enter the collective along
with the poor and against the kulaks and their hangers-on. He chose his
fine, intelligent words carefully and looked intelligent and reasonable
himself. He really was a capable administrator: before working for the
district, he had been a history teacher and was good at his job, so people

said. He was trusted. But trust was not enough for the Settlement peasants, it turned out; they wanted evidence right before their eyes and such an example was just what was lacking in the vicinity.

Alongside Kosmachov, his chest slumped heavily across the table sat Levon Bogatka, with his narrow black eye-patch askew. Levon was a native of the Settlement, with plenty of children and very little land. Like her and Petroc he had been allotted five acres of the Yakimovschina land by reason of poverty. Levon had lost his eye in the Polish campaign, somewhere near the Vistula, in a saber fight with two Polish uhlans. He had had a pretty bad time in that war, barely survived in the field hospital and had returned home an invalid - one leg crippled, one eye gone and two fingers missing on his right hand. Levon couldn't speak reasonably at all, his usual way of talking was like boulders rolling into a field, while in practical affairs he had the reputation of being stubborn and unyielding. After Kosmachov's speech, there was a sort of confused vote for the organization of a collective farm, with a lot of abstentions, but once the matter reached the signature stage, everything ground to a halt. Here Levon rose clumsily in his sheepskin above the sooty lamp and spoke, raising his hand:

"If that's the way it is, I'll be first. Why not! And I call upon Bogatka Stepanida to follow."

This was something altogether new. On previous occasions, Levon had also put his name down first but hadn't called on anyone to follow his example; Stepanida had put her name down next, then Antos Nedoseka, then the demobilized Red Army man, the landless Vasil Goncharik and after that came a pause. Nobody else put their name forward, they just sat in silence, smoking. Another speech by the district man, more swearing from Levon on political awareness led nowhere.

Then Stepanida rose from her bench by the wall and said she was willing to go into the collective.

"And who do you call upon to follow your example?" Levon stared at her tensely with his one good eye. Stepanida was rather disconcerted. However, as she stood there by her bench above the bent backs of the peasants and surveyed their heads, balding, gray or shaggy, and those shoulders stooped with years, toil and now this new anxiety, all those sheepskins, waistcoats and overcoats it came to her: she should nominate someone who would certainly join and in turn call on someone suitable to follow. At first she wanted to choose Kornila, who was sitting three away from her. He even glanced in her direction, sideways from under the shaggy collar of his sheepskin, but she detected no support in that glance, rather fear and malevolence. She couldn't make up her mind.

"Well, I call on Ladimir Bogatka," she said after a pause, without even considering whether this was a wise move or not.

Ladimir wasn't the poorest man in the village, nor the richest either; he had about three acres more than Stepanida and Petroc. His youngest daughter Anyuta used to go with Stepanida to literacy classes and the two sat at the same desk in school.

Tall and thin in his short waistcoat, Ladimir rose from his bench fingering his mustache with a trembling hand. With considerable reluctance, almost as if he were ill, he forced something out which the comrades on the presidium interpreted as agreement to join the collective. Thereupon he similarly strained every fiber to think who to call on to follow his lead, before nominating Antos Nedoseka. Still young, lively and active, Antos immediately agreed and called on his neighbor across the street, Ivan Guzhov, known simply in the village as Guzh.

Things were moving, the ice had broken, thought Stepanida and was even glad that Levon had hit upon this effective way of pushing the collective idea. It was so simple: one after another in a chain, following the lead of the activist, or a neighbor or one's in-laws. This way it was a lot more cheerful and reliable, not like standing up on your own with the agonizing thought - what if the others won't follow suit and support you, and you're left looking like an upstart and an idiot. There was no profit in going against the whole village. After all, though the idea was attractive, taken as a whole, government-sponsored and devised by clever people, it was something new and unprecedented in these parts, wholly untried: who could tell how it would turn out? Maybe it had been a success in some places, but perhaps they had better soil than round here with its clay, sand and bog, and the people more hardworking, not like in the Settlement. Everybody here was a loafer or a weakling, some were far too greedy, others cross-grained and quarrelsome, feckless or just stupid. If they couldn't cope with working on their own, how would they get on in a collective? Stepanida had few fears for her part, she was like the rest and if she was first to volunteer, it was probably because if things didn't work out, she had little to lose. She was poor and knew poverty in full measure on five acres of clay across the main road by the gully. She had had enough. She'd had enough of working like a dog for six years as a hired hand for Pan Yakimovsky, without sparing herself. And what had she to show for it? All right, she'd been given five acres and a hut. How could she have survived otherwise? With Petroc, a laborer like herself, and two children to provide for.

That evening in the village soviet hut, Stepanida felt her spirits rise: things were moving, matters were afoot, there was going to be a collective; why cling to unrelieved poverty, was it not time to trust to the new? Especially as clever people were advising it. She respected clever people, especially those from the city, working class folk who wouldn't recommend anything bad. It was a good thing Petroc hadn't objected particularly either, although he'd stopped coming to the meetings; he sent her instead and groused good-naturedly in the mornings when he was getting ready for the threshing or to see to the animals. Still, what did Petroc know after his two winters schooling; all he could do was his signature and even then it cost him sweat to grind out his simple surname. She had rejoiced too soon, however, though she had known long enough that good would not come of it. Old Guzh did not take up Nedoseka's call and refused to join the collective. So the chain that promised so much was abruptly broken.

Once more Kosmachov talked to them, once again Levon banged the table, and the meeting began to get rowdy and disorderly; it was as if something evil had broken through in people. Ladimir started a quarrel with Kornila and nearly came to blows. Old Guzh, his face covered in tufts of stubble, sat as if facing death, straight and silent, lips tightly pursed and gazing into the corner where the icons had once hung and where now a portrait of Karl Marx with a nail in each corner was just visible through the haze of tobacco smoke. No further progress was made and at dawn everyone dispersed singly.

While still in the Settlement street, Stepanida could see a bay horse with a gaily-colored saddlecloth, harnessed to a neat green sled-carriage in the council yard. She guessed that Novik had arrived. He had been going around in this fine conveyance since the beginning of winter, after his summer move into town to work for the regional committee. This Settlement Bogatka had made his way up quickly and once a chief, his first act was to change his name to Novik; he disliked his former name now for some reason. He had been an intelligent child and got good marks at school before going on to teacher-training college in Vitebsk. He hadn't fancied teaching, however, and put in for administration. He's no Kosmachov, thought Stepanida, turning in to the village soviet, he can see through everybody here. Despite being a local boy, he dealt sternly with people, a real manager type, principled and practical, so people said, very much a party man. Well, Stepanida mused, that's the sort of man that was needed now, the locals couldn't be dealt with any other way. If there was one thing they understood, it was the iron fist, the hard man.

The village soviet hut stood close to the street in the heart of the village - a long low shingled building with a faded cloth slogan in white letters along the wall: "Closer ties between town and country!" There was no passage into the hut. On opening the door, the visitor found himself directly in a large rather empty space, where at one time lived Konon the psalm-reader, now deported: the ailing Kolondenchikha was now billeted here with her son, Potap, somewhere between a boy and a youth to look at. Approaching the step, Stepanida lightly scraped her sandals and opened the door to be met with the warm smell of the stove, as a cloud of frozen air swept into the hut under her feet. She hurriedly closed the door and stood there, trying to make out who was there first of all. There were several men seated on benches by the wall and gray clouds of tobacco smoke floated and curled beneath the ceiling. The loud male conversation ceased at once.

"Well, here's Bogatka," said Levon from behind the table. He stopped.

She greeted those present and sat down on the end of a bench near the door; she knew there was no point in asking questions at the moment, all would soon be revealed in any case. She merely gazed at the worried, even harassed, countenance of the president, who was sitting before a piece of paper. She then turned her eyes to the fine, spruce figure of Novik, who was wearing a broad military belt and a camouflage field jacket; she took in his dandified boots with their high uppers, in which he was striding vigorously between the window and the little stove, obviously saying something important before she came in. A stiff black curl kept falling down over his forehead and Novik vigorously shook his head to send it back. Potapka was poking about in the firebox by the door, shoving in thick, resinous logs and the flames roared away pleasantly inside the stove which had once been whitewashed but was now scratched and scraped by peasants' backs. Nedoseka, like Stepanida, a member of the poverty committee, was observing him closely from his bench. His peeling, patched sheepskin was wide open; the hut was pretty warm.

After a silence, Novik took three resounding paces and turned decisively to the table.

"I've already said: the chief danger at this stage is any leaning to the right. The collectivization impetus cannot be allowed to slow down. Still less grind to a halt. But that's just what's happened here: halt! What a mess! Eight meetings and you can't organize a collective farm. Flabbiness and indulgence towards the class enemy. Comrade president, how many kulaks have you dispossessed?" Novik suddenly turned sharply on his heels and loomed in front of Levon. The latter, puzzled, raised his big one-eyed face with its blue scar on the left cheek.

"Who is there to dispossess? They're all poor, the lot of them."

"Ah, poor is it? So why on earth are your poor people boycotting the collective?"

"Because they're afraid. They don't know what it is. What it's like in a collective. It's a serious matter. . ."

"The party has said what it'll be like. It's written down in the decisions of the congress of Soviets. Or haven't you explained that?"

"Yes we have. The politically literate part of the peasantry are for it. There's just not many of them."

"Not many of them?" Novik seized on this. "First of all you've got to be politically literate yourself. As it is you're infected with the spirit of deviation, yes you! The way I see it, private property interests are more important to you than party decisions."

That Novik was angry was obvious from his nervous movements and the way he walked, frequently pausing to hurl wounding accusatory remarks at Levon. But Levon was also clearly becoming exasperated: his ravaged face grew more flushed and the single eye under its bushy brow filled with rage till he could no longer restrain himself:

"Don't call me a deviationist! I'm as keen on the collective as you. I've shed blood for the new life. It's all right for you to ride about demanding this and that! You sit where I am and you'd find out! Get them to agree voluntarily. No waving pistols, like some folk. . ."

Novik probably realized that this was the way to a quarrel, in public at that. He said nothing for a while and sat down at the edge of the table.

"All right. I'll show you how," he said, calmer now. "Where's the poverty committee?"

"Well, this is Bogatka, Stepanida; Goncharik'll be here directly. Semyon can't attend, he's carting grain to the station," Levon replied in a quieter tone, checking his feelings.

"Well all right then, it'll be a plenary session. The village soviet, the poverty committee, regional representative - a plenary session. We have to decide. Smash the saboteurs! It's been an unholy mess up to now!. . .Declare the joint session open."

"This. . .Joint session is declared open," growled Levon and said no more.

"There is only one item: defeating the wreckers of the collective farm movement." Novik carried on. "I propose as the first point the dispossession of Guzhov, Ivan. As kulak sympathizer and saboteur."

Novik struck the scarred edge of the table to emphasize his words, glanced at Stepanida, then stared long and hard at Levon's face. Levon slumped forward, chest on table, and said nothing.

"Under what article though?" he asked after a pause. "He's got ten acres of land, you can't be more average than that."

"I know," said Novik. "His strip is next to ours. It's not a lot of land, I agree, but he's a saboteur, he broke up the meeting. So he's a wrecker. When he digs his heels in, you can't shift him. I know him of old. . ."

Stepanida said nothing - she hadn't expected this turn of events. In her eyes Guzh was no different from the rest: he was no richer than them, maybe put a bit more into his work, besides he had two strapping sons to help him, and three men working the land aren't the same as three women. Threw their weight about, oh yes -but why dispossess them?

"He didn't egg the others on. He didn't go in himself that's all, so why's he a wrecker? Or a saboteur?" Levon argued tensely from the table, shifting his bit of paper about.

"Can't you really understand?!" Novik turned to him brusquely. "If you can't move him, the others won't shift either. Everybody in the village always looks to him - he's an authority! So that's where we strike! Then they'll sing a different tune. They'll be a bit scared."

"But is it right or not?" said Stepanida, getting up her courage. "Dispossess those who are kulaks. Guzh is a middle peasant. No I don't agree."

"So speaks the leadership! The activists!" Novik was stung into leaping up from the table. "You're just bunglers! He's worse than any bloodsucker, don't you see? He's a saboteur! He wrecks collectivization in the Settlement, that disrupts the program in the district and the district wrecks the region, you understand what that means? Nobody's going to pat our head for this, not ours and not yours!"

"Just as you like, but it's not fair this," Stepanida persisted. This had stuck in her craw and she was preparing to dig in, but at this point Novik began to tremble and shouted as if she had insulted him:

"What fairness are you on about, auntie? Your head's full of old-fashioned rubbish, obsolete conceptions about classless justice! We have to lead with the only class justice there is: no mercy for the enemy! If someone stands in our way, he's an enemy, and we will break his back. Otherwise we'll never get to see the new life. We'll be ground into dust ourselves. You've got defeatist, right wing, deviationary attitudes that must be rooted out mercilessly!"

Stepanida said nothing, thinking maybe that was it, maybe Novik was right. Of course he was brainy and educated, not like her going to the second literacy class. But Stepanida imagined the dispossession process, the crying, the grief, deportation, so she got confused again. What should be done?

"How'm I going to tell that to the villagers here?" Levon was fidgeting tormentedly at the table. "What's a saboteur? Will they understand that, eh? No, they won't. Because I don't either," he said, still moving his paper about, towards him, away from him, to one side then the other.

At this point the street door was flung wide and a husky youth bounded into the hut, wearing a greatcoat with bright raspberry tabs on the collar; he took off his pointed helmet with the broad star on the front. He looked tired and out of breath from running, but his eyes held a lively sparkle and pleasure at the youthful strength which filled him and his reserves of spiritual generosity.

"You're late, Goncharik," came Levon's morose rebuke. "We've been waiting ages. . ."

"I've just run over from the township, mother said the poverty committee."

Vasil Goncharik first shook hands with Novik, then Levon, Nedoseka, touched Potap on the shoulder and pressed Stepanida's hand with his chilly fingers.

"I'll sit next to you, auntie."

"Sit you down," Stepanida shifted slightly. She wasn't concerned with Goncharik - matters of much greater moment possessed her anxious soul.

"What are we on about?" inquired Goncharik, still grinning and showing the attractive dimples on his red cheeks. He'd just got back from the army the previous autumn after active service in the Far East and was intending to get married. No one answered his question; all were anxiously frowning, so he wiped the pleasant smile from his face, sensing something amiss. Stepanida whispered:

"It's dispossessing Guzh. . ."

"So that's it!"

"Yes, dispossession," shouted Novik again. "And no bones about it. The collective is in danger of being wrecked. And Guzh. . .did he have any hired hands?" Novik asked suddenly tense as he waited for the answer.

"What hired help could he have?" said Levon, brushing this aside.

Here Antos Nedoseka stirred on his bench by the stove.

"There was that. . .when he put that three-sided shed up. He took somebody on, so he did. An old bloke from Zagriazye. They fell out over the pay. Guzh twisted him out of three roubles."

"You see!" Novik came alive, bending over Levon. "Did he?"

"But anybody. . .built a three-sider! If that's all. . ."

"No, no, it all fits. Hired labor - the first principle of the exploiter. Doesn't matter if he's not got much land."

"And there was. . .help with the harvest," Nedoseka went on, pleased at his contribution. "I don't know whether he hired anybody, but he had help. Portnov's daughter Marusya was there."

"Still better!" Novik was even more pleased and sat down at his former place by the table. "It's all clear enough. Let's put it to the vote."

Stepanida was so nervous she didn't notice how many times she'd unbuttoned her fur jacket and started fastening it again. She understood; Novik was right: Guzh was being pigheaded and wouldn't be moved. Others would look to him for a lead; maybe there had been hired help, for building or the harvest, but all the same. . .It was a pity about the old man, and his womenfolk even more - aunty Fruzyna, his ailing daughter Nastulka, with whom Stepanida had taken turns to graze the village herd last summer. No, she couldn't transgress against this pity even for the sake of enormous class interests. And she didn't know what to do.

"Well all right then," mumbled Levon, head down. "If that's the way it is, let's vote. Who is against dispossession, leaving. . ."

"Not that way!" Novik recollected himself. "Not correct! Who is for dispossessing Guzhov, Ivan raise your hands," he announced and raised his own hand high.

Over by the stove, Antos readily raised his hand. (Potap Kolondenok on his knees by the stove looked round open-mouthed in curiosity as the voting proceeded). Stepanida averted her eyes, as she glanced sideways at the table to see how Levon was voting. He was leaning even more heavily on the table and had not raised his hand.

"Two altogether," said Novik, displeased, and lowered his arm. "Who is against dispossession?"

Without raising his head from the table, Levon raised one wrist in the air and Stepanida also partly raised an arm.

"Two against two then!" stated Novik, disappointed. "What a business! And what about you, Goncharik?" he suddenly stared at Vasil and Stepanida realized that the lad had not voted either time.

"I abstained," said Vasil simply.

"What d'you mean, abstained?" trembled Novik, leaping from his bench. "What d'you mean, abstained? You a komsomol, a demobbed Red Army man? You want to serve in the red police force yet you abstain from the heat of the class struggle? What are you doing, consciously playing into the hands of the class enemy?" he cried angrily, coming closer to Vasil. The latter blinked his beautiful, girlish eyes helplessly.

"What if I don't understand it?"

"Get it understood! The collectivization plan is threatened by wreckers. Half the poverty committee is infected with right wing deviationism. The village soviet is displaying opportunism. The activists are bunglers. And he hasn't understood! You've got three minutes to think it over and define yourself. For collective policy or against collective policy? Define your political face."

Stepanida was shaken, almost feverish; her body became unbearably hot, and cold sweat trickled down her back. She felt that a decision was imminent. The fate of the Guzhovs and perhaps the collective as a whole depended on Vasil's vote.

Vasil pondered for no more than three minutes indeed, weighing things up, face inclined to the floor; his fingers trembled slightly on the knee of his blue tunic trousers. Novik, standing opposite him, waited.

"Well?"

"All right. I'm - for," decided Goncharik and rose to his feet.

Novik turned sharply to Levon.

"That's it! Decided! By a majority. Write it into the record. Guzhov, Ivan is to be dispossessed as a kulak."

13

If only it were granted to man to peer even a little way into the future and see what lies in store for him, what will become manifest in all its detail with the passing days, but as yet lies concealed behind the strata of time. Not so! Nobody can know what the future holds; he may even rejoice over something soon to become a source of grief or weep bitter tears over what will later merely serve to raise a smile.

Stepanida did not miss her literacy class that evening after all and although she got no praise for her neatly written lines (there was no time to run over to the farm for her exercise book), she did read her piece well, only stumbling once over the word which nowadays was on everybody's lips. "Collectivization," Rosa Yakovlevna corrected her. The literacy teacher repeated it: "Collectivization! Everyone remember how to pronounce this word properly."

Well of course she remembered it, as did all the others present in the unheated school - boys and men in the literacy class, and just the two women Stepanida Bogatka and Anna Bogatka, or Anyuta as they called her in the village. They weren't related at all, it was just that half the village were Bogatkas and the rest were Nedosekas and Guzhovs, with a small family of Gonchariks. When the lesson was over towards midnight, they left the school together and strolled unhurriedly towards the fringe of the Settlement.

Anyuta had been depressed all evening and made mistakes in her reading. Stepanida even had to prompt her a couple of times: "To work, all who feel strong under the red banner, the banner of freedom," but she still couldn't remember it. Something mysterious was going on. Stepanida was not one to pry into another's heart, she had worries enough of her own. Anyuta couldn't contain herself, however.

"You know, aunty, I've every reason to be happy. And I'm not."

"Why not?" Stepanida was surprised.

They were walking along the narrow street, worn smooth by sledges, with the moon looking down over the rooftops full and round, and stars densely clustered in the sky; the sharp frost nipped their cheeks. Stepanida hid her fingers in the sleeves of her jacket, hands clasped across her stomach. It was very slippery and they made their way in short uncertain steps. Anyuta took Stepanida's elbow to steady herself.

"Vasil Goncharik and I have agreed to get married on the eighth of March. He was here yesterday talking to my father."

"Well, what on earth's the matter then?" said Stepanida. "Vasya's a good lad. They say he's going to be a policeman."

"That's right, he is. He's so clever, and sweet. . ."

"You love him?"

"Oh, aunty, I don't know how much! Ever so much!"

"Well, that's all right then. What're you all sad about then. You should be glad."

"Well, I would be. But he doesn't want a church wedding."

"That's no problem! They do komsomol weddings these days, without a priest. You just register at the village soviet. They do a bit of speechifying and that's it."

"That part's all right. . .It's father!" sighed Anyuta. "He doesn't want it without a priest. He says it'll bring bad luck. I don't want that, do I? I wish him so much happiness, if you only knew aunty. . ."

"Oh, don't you listen to him, Anyuta. There's not much luck attached to a priest. . .In the old days everybody got married in church, and did they all live happily ever after? Oi, oi! What's a father nowadays? You do it the way you want."

"That's true. Still. . ."

Anyuta fell silent, having got her unhappiness off her chest, while Stepanida pondered: what a time for this! Not married yet and the girl was already shrivelling up with grief and anguish. Of course, Anyuta wasn't one of those brides who would be content to get their own way and marry who they wanted. She needed those around her to be happy too, her parents to be pleased that everything had gone off with dignity. But Goncharik would hardly agree to a church wedding or celebrate the marriage with match-makers, in-laws, best man, boozing and kissing, like in the old days. It wouldn't look right for a komsomol to do that, certainly.

"Aunty, how would it be if you were to come and ask father maybe. He'd listen to you." Anyuta halted suddenly. Her gentle voice was so full of sadness and hope that Stepanida quickly consented:

"Well, all right. Tell me when. . ."

They separated at the edge of the village. Anyuta turned onto the path to her own yard and Stepanida went on along the road, down from the hillock and across the highway to the farm. She reflected that notwithstanding her talk with Ladimir, it would be the young ones' decision. Their time had come. It wasn't like under the old regime when young people could do nothing without their parents' consent, and none dared contravene the age-old customs of their forefathers to which the old folk clung. Those former ways had collapsed, for good or ill, who knew. Maybe people would regret it later on, but at the moment there was no way back - just onward and onward like in the song.

All around stretched the dim whiteness of the fields; the sky was filled with shining, twinkling stars. She could see for miles across the wide, snowy expanse with the straight line of the highway slicing across her path. At the end of that expanse against the dark wall of the gully thickets on Golgotha, stood the buildings of her own Yakimovschina, the farm which had become her destiny. Who could have thought it? Once upon a time as a young girl, she had gone there as hired help for the harvest to an unknown farmer on an unknown farmstead, and now she was running towards it as if it were her only refuge. A twist of fate indeed. Like a fairy tale! Stepanida never clung to the past - she would have been hard put to find six months of bearable human existence there; there had always been the burden of work and before that beggary as an orphan and lack of rights. How many years had she toiled as a laborer for Pan Zhulega and old squire Yakimovsky, tilling the soil of others, having none of her own. What alien soil meant - anyone who has tasted the bread of charity, from the hand of strangers, would remember to their dying day. True, after the revolution, everything had changed radically and reversed positions, like herself: Zhulega had fled to Warsaw, old man Yakimovsky had ended his earthly journey, and she and Petroc had received five acres of the farmland from the new authorities. To begin with, they had done quite well, eating their own produce not the squire's, acquiring a horse and cattle. Petroc, who had been an unpaid laborer in his father's impoverished family, devoted himself so much to the management of his own land that she feared for his health. But his own land made its demands and he put his heart into every operation: he plowed, broke up the clods, manured every heap of soil, then did the scything himself, carted it in, then plowed again, sowed and harrowed. Their young mare fell dead the very first spring, a great sorrow which lasted until they earned enough to buy another horse. Then at once misfortune befell Petroc. When Fenya was born, Stepanida was negligent about her health and he had to harvest, scythe and pull for the two of them and strained himself. He was somehow dragging hay in from the water-meadow, when the cart overturned on the edge of the gully. In putting his shoulder to it, Petroc broke his collar bone. He was in hospital for two months and the doctors barely pulled him through. Meanwhile the spring crop bolted in the fields, and in autumn they harvested about two loads of barley and barely got their seed back. That year was a hungry one; the bread held out till Easter and it was the potatoes which saved them. There were other poor grain years, either too much rain or not enough, too little in the way of seed, manure or animals. Petroc didn't give in, however, working like a man possessed so that his fellow villagers in the Settlement often made fun of him; he really did put his back into it night and day and the results were miserable. Still he couldn't get enough of working his own land in freedom; he grew thin, shrivelled even, his breathing grew hoarse, but he kept at it, going to bed after everyone else and rising first. He was his own boss, you reaped what you sowed, you got what you deserved in this world, he used to enjoy repeating when she tried to persuade him to slow down, rest and conserve his strength. Stepanida herself, after a series of defeats in this endless battle with the soil, told herself: no, this isn't how you get rich, you just lose your health and get carted off to the village cemetery among the pine trees before your time. Whatever it might be like in a collective farm, it couldn't be worse than this. We'll be like everyone else, there's a chance we won't come to grief in a collective. It would even be therapeutic for Petroc and give him maybe an extra year in this harsh world.

In the distance by the wood, a little red light began to glow, that means Petroc's come back, she thought and was glad with a young woman's happiness, knowing the whole family was together after the day's alarms and her heart could be at peace till morning. Hastening her steps, she ran across the highway and up the narrow track to the farm. In the moonlit yard stood the sledge with its wisps of hay; the horse had already been seen to and was feeding in the cowshed. Maybe Petroc had got hold of some kerosene, Stepanida thought; there was very little left in the lamp, enough for one evening, no more. She'd also told him that morning to ask about some boots at a Jewish cobbler they knew at the station. There wasn't much money available for boots, of course, ten roubles in all, but he might have done a trade-off for a shoulder of lamb or a couple of pounds of butter or whatever else they might have bartered with. They couldn't get by on one pair of felt boots between the two of them; when one wore them, the other had to stay at home and not stir out of doors. Yet you had to go out, like today for instance, and there was always something every day like that; if it wasn't one thing it was another, always a summons to take on this, run and do that - over to the Settlement, to the village soviet or to the township, to the district committee.

The passage door was open as she crossed the step; she closed it behind her and entered the hut. She realized at once the children were asleep; it was warm and peaceful in the smoky semidarkness, and smelt strongly of kerosene and tobacco. The lamp was blinking at the end of the table and Petroc was picking over some papers by its light, receipts probably, checking the bills: which ones he'd paid, which ones delayed, how much the fine had risen and what was left.

"Been back long?" asked Stepanida quietly.

"Not long."

"Had anything to eat?"

"We ate there. Buckwheat cakes."

She began taking her things off, hung up her sheepskin on the nail and removed her warm kerchief.

"How's the commune?" asked Petroc from the lamp. "Got anything organized yet?"

"Passed a resolution to dispossess Guzh," Stepanida answered indirectly. "Novik was there. For sabotage and because he hired labor."

Petroc raised his wrinkled, stubbly face from the lamp and regarded her closely. His eyes expressed anxious surprise at first, soon giving place to the gloom of disagreeable reflections.

"What's the world coming to?" said Petroc slowly. "Hired labor! What hired labor?"

"Just that," she replied. "They helped him to build a three-sider. He hired them. For cleaning up as well."

"For shame!" Petroc sighed. "Hired labor!. . .That means chairman Levon hired labor as well. For the threshing, yon Ladimir's bairns gave him a hand. He can't use a flail, the hand he's got. Are they going to dispossess him as well?"

"There's a matter of sabotage included," said Stepanida. "It was him being pigheaded the other night at the meeting, wrecked the collective farm idea."

She squatted down on the low bench and began undoing the strings on her sandals, iced over from her journey. Petroc was still uneasy.

"If it's reached the likes of him, what's it going to be next? Who're you going to dispossess in a year or two?"

"Maybe there won't be anybody. They'll all be in the collective."

"Maybe they will. What about the class war then? The class war won't be cancelled, will it?"

"Maybe. When there's no enemies left. A fat lot you know!" Stepanida interrupted, irritated.

What did he know really this ignorant peasant, who didn't even go to the meetings, rarely read a paper and never talked to the leadership! Dead keen to argue about everything, all mixed up, with his little peasant brain!

"There's something about your lot, not like ordinary people." Petroc was still musing, staring at the flickering flame of the lamp. "Over at the station,

I was talking to a man from somewhere near Ula. Nothing going on over there, all quiet. Nobody's heard about any collective, nobody's been to see them, nobody's forcing them into anything. Nobody's been dispossessed yet."

"Just wait, they'll get there. Probably lives out in the sticks somewhere. Across the bog."

"Maybe he does. What about us?. . ."

"We're right under the district's nose here. We get the region as well, we're just off the road you know. It's a good thing we are here, there's a lot of advantage in that," said Stepanida and remembered: "Did you buy kerosene?"

"They were giving some out. One liter. Rations. Will it keep us going?"

"While it lasts. They'll be bringing some more. The road's clear now. Did you ask about the boots?"

"Boots?" Petroc threw a frightened glance at her, as if just now recollecting about the boots. "There aren't any boots," he said and rose from behind the table, small in stature and thin, with the sunken chest of an old man. Yes, an old man for his fifty years. Petroc shifted the bedding behind the stove and took something from the bed they shared. "This instead of boots."

"What is it?"

Bewildered, she took a tiny, neat, black case from his hands, like a child's toy, and didn't take in at first what it was.

"It's a violin!" said Petroc.

"You've gone crazy!"

"Happen I have."

"It must have cost a lot?" Stepanida said, alarmed. "So there's nothing to put on our feet. Fedka's shoes have fallen apart, and he buys a fiddle! It costs a canny lot. All of a tenner, I bet?"

Petroc shifted uneasily around her, took the case and undid the catches with his work-calloused hands. Trembling like a child, he took out a shining little red violin with a black sounding board and handsome curved openings along the sides.

"It was you who wanted one," Petroc apologetically reminded her.

"Whenever was that? When I was young and had no children. Now. . .Well, you're off your head! What are we going to put on our feet, go barefoot, and he buys a fiddle! When are you going to play it - winter's nearly over, soon it'll be the sowing. . ."

"Well my sowing days are over obviously," said Petroc, head hanging, and went off in a huff to sit on the bench. The fleeting mood of elation had completely evaporated. On the table next to its case lay the violin, untouched by bow. "I paid a tenner, and owe two more. My word on it. A Jew at the station."

Stepanida wrung her hands.

"Three tenners, ai-ai! You're out of your mind! You've gone daft in your old age. We haven't paid the insurance yet, have we? We've just paid the tax for this year and they've sent another demand. The fine for nonpayment's piling up. We've got no shoes. No kerosene. Not a spoonful of sugar till autumn and Fenechka won't eat anything that's not sweet. If he'd just bought a loaf, but a fiddle! Where are you going to get your tenners? Who's going to give you them?"

"We'll earn them in the commune."

Stepanida was furious to the point of tears, what was he saying this madman, why a violin? And at such a time? Once upon a time he'd learned to wield the bow a bit, asked a gipsy at the fair in the township to let him have a go, while she stood by and applauded. Now this, he'd got the idea into his head: I'll buy one! And he'd found the time and money to buy one - but not to bring them joy, misery more like. What did she want with a violin? A violin when they were coming sooner or later to take the horse into the collective farm, and they would have to give up their seed, hand in the harness, sledge and cart and rebuild their lives in a new, unfamiliar, irrevocable direction. Who had time for music?

Life was changing before their eyes in every way. What remained of the time when they had both been young, with peasants' strength in their hands and passionate hopes for the future?. . .

14

That was a very hard spring, memorable indeed though now far distant, which brought alarms in plenty to lives already replete with hardship and unease. A long, drawn-out, agonizing war had just come to an end and the young men and boys were trickling back to their villages, townships and farms in their pointed Budyonny helmets, battered boots and puttees, proud of their victories over the whites, Germans and Poles. The rucksacks on their shoulders were poorly furnished, but they had grandiose hopes for the new life which they had won at the expense of the old regime. It remained to grapple with the land, to plow and sow to provide food for the year ahead. The earth awaited its workers and seemed prepared to resume its immemorial task - to grow bread for mankind. From Annunciation the sun gave friendly warmth and melted the snow within a week; it was mild and almost dry out in the fields. On Palm Sunday, Stepanida and Petroc were going to church and had been bickering since morning whether to get dressed up or go in summer clothes. Petroc had got warm in the sun and felt hot in his satin shirt, Stepanida had a job to make him throw a waistcoat over his shoulders. Somewhat annoyed and taciturn with each other, they left the boiler-house to take the path through the winter crops to the township. Old man Yakimovsky was standing in the yard by the parapet, stooped and hunched in his black kaftan with its dense row of neatly fastened buttons; he was leaning on a fashionable cane with mother-of-pearl mountings and stared after them rather oddly, almost enviously, with his washed-out old man's eyes. It was just a week before that he had let them onto the farm because life had become impossible for them with Petroc's family in the Settlement. Stepanida immediately smoothed matters over with her in-laws and had asked Pan Yakimovsky the day before to give her the boiler-house; she was already running the farmstead anyway and the new laborer, Petroc, could help her. How could they manage without a hut and some land and stock of their own? Earlier that spring, Petroc had been laboring on the Polish farms and it was a problem where he could pick up a living wage now. Stepanida asked so sweetly that Yakimovsky, bearing in mind her four year dedication to the farm, agreed, saying: all right, there's room enough, it's warm in the boiler-house. Especially now it's spring.

The spring was indeed gathering strength and the young grass was pushing through on the slopes and verges. Boys and girls in the Settlement discarded their bast shoes and went barefoot until the feast of the Intercession. For several days and nights after Annunciation, the cranes' gabble of delight and alarm could be heard over the farm and Golgotha. Their long uneven wedges trailed helplessly across the windy sky to the north. On the water-meadow in Sheep Valley, one long-legged stork had already peeled off and was gradually making his way across the bog, thoughtfully eyeing the frogs. One sunny morning above the winter crops, the familiar trills of the lark came sifting down and Stepanida, busy with the cattle in the yard, trembled with joy at the bird song, the advent of spring and the sense of imminent happiness.

It was the first spring of her life with Petroc, not on their own land perhaps and in a stranger's hut, but nevertheless in love, peace and harmony. She already carried burgeoning life beneath her heart; at times she could sense its throbbing, and her thoughts flew on into the future when they would be three. The unseen skylark had touched a chord in her that resonated to the spring song and Stepanida surrendered herself completely to it, listening to the polyphony of other birds and the sounding strings of her own heart. This did not last long, however. That very day, towards evening, a biting north wind got up, and gray besieging clouds moved in from the direction of the gully; it grew much colder and by nightfall there were flecks of snow. All nature underwent a sudden change; chilled with its light powdering of snow, it turned gray, and there remained not a trace of spring. The boiler-house was wintry-cold and refused to be heated: the stove-fireplace had once been used without a chimney and the smoke had escaped through the little window under the roof, now boarded over. For the night, Stepanida fetched coals from the hut in an iron pot which warmed them up somewhat, as she mused: how are the larks getting on in the fields? She heard no more of their song after that. From their snowed-in nest on the old maple in the Settlement, the storks' heads with their long bills protruded complainingly; at night a hard frost struck, pools were covered with a thin layer of ice and for several days the wind howled tirelessly round every corner. People expected it to get warmer with each passing day, but in vain: the snow had ceased to lie and had melted away but later on more came intermixed with rain and it was a dismal scene indeed; a piercing north wind blew across the fields. There was no venturing into the yard; people just scuttled out to see to the animals, then hurried back into the hut to shelter in the warmth and wait.

One day, when Stepanida had gone out into the passage to mash some potatoes for the pigs and Petroc was busy sorting out some farm gear in the boiler-house, she hear unfamiliar voices. Throwing the pestle down, she half-opened the door to see three men approaching from the wicket gate. The leading figure, smirking and mustachioed in his army cap, she recognized as Tsiprukov, an official of the area committee; the second, poorly dressed in a peasant overcoat was Grishka, a Settlement komsomol. The third man, who carried a yellow cardboard folder under this arm, was a stranger to her, perhaps from the province maybe or even higher up. The men shook hands and inquired if Adolf Yakimovksy was at home.

"Pan Adolya!" she called, half-opening the hut door so that the master could come to meet his visitors, but they moved towards the door without waiting to be invited. She remained where she was, in the passage above the kettle of boiled potatoes, but couldn't help hearing the conversation in the hut. Petroc stuck his head out of the boiler-house as well and both listened in with bated breath.

Anyway it all became clear soon enough - the visitors were going through the farm description. They began with the land, checking the plots and boundaries against the documents, how much land was under crops and what they were, how much was leased. The numbers of laborers and lease-holders were ascertained and everything was written down in the cardboard folder.

Adolf Yakimovsky was descended from an ancient family of Polish gentry, once accounted rich but gradually becoming impoverished, dwindling towards extinction as Yakimovsky used to say. Once, being in a good mood, he showed Stepanida some old yellowing papers bearing coats of arms, studded with red seals, in which were inscribed the domains of Yakimovsky ancestors here and elsewhere. His grandfather had owned farms near Drissa, Podzwil and other places, but this tiny farm was now the last refuge of the reduced line. Although Adolf strove with all his old man's strength to preserve, if not the riches of former times, then at least some fragment of its former dignity, he was barely able to do so. His two sons, born on the farm, did little to help their father; once grown, they both went off to town, Vilnius apparently, and visited him on the farm occasionally for a fortnight or so, not more. As soon as the war with the Germans broke out and Vilnius was on the other side of the front line, there was no further news from his sons. Pan Adolf didn't like to talk about it, but Stepanida knew this was his last hope. His wife, old Adolikha, had died still waiting to hear from them. The household duties and the animals were Stepanida's responsibility; part of the land was rented out - about half, depending on negotiations - and he hired seasonal laborers for the rest. He was a taciturn man, calm and even-tempered, something Stepanida prized in him above all else. Although life on the farm was hard at times, she knew that there was none easier to be found. Now, hearing the discussion in the hut and comprehending something of it, she suddenly sensed that she was at a decisive point in her life, though she couldn't work out whether it was for the better or the worse. That the hour of change had arrived, however, was most certain.

Having concluded their business in the hut, the men went out into the yard to inspect the farmstead. Pan Adolf did not go with them; he remained, head down, on the bench by the table, as she went to the officials to show them the grain in the barn, the cowshed, the two horses and the piglets. The visitors reckoned it up and wrote it all down on paper - the grain in the granary racks, the flax under the canopy, the animals - and Stepanida asked Tsiprukov why they were doing the check. He explained that this was expropriation - the possessions of the exploiters were now to be transferred to the people. Stepanida couldn't grasp all of this, though she could guess, and with a tiny secret hope, asked: "And the land?" Tsiprukov said that it would be divided between the landless peasants and the laborers and that Petroc should go next morning to the area executive committee where it would all be decided.

She remembered shaking, as if with fright, at this stunning news and long after the men had left the yard, couldn't screw up her courage to talk to Petroc about it. She was ready to dance for sheer joy: just think of it, they would have some land - no money, no argument, no court case or petitions, they would get it and that was all there was to it. By right of expropriation.

When she told Petroc about it, at the woodpile, he dropped the log he was holding and sat down next to the chopping block, just plumped down in the mud. He recovered himself at once and started brushing off his pants, as she laughed happily, noticing, however, the swift change in her husband's facial expression from bewilderment to one almost of fear. She turned and behind her stood Pan Adolf with the inevitable cane in his hands; down his furrowed unshaven cheeks rolled the tears of an old man.

"You're plizzed? It's heppiness for you?"

They had no time to realize what had happened before he turned and went towards the porch. His legs, bent with rheumatism, trembled slightly at the knees.

From that moment on, Stepanida didn't know how to conduct herself or what to think. Her joy was dimmed and she felt awkward as if she had been caught doing something forbidden, and she knew she was guilty. If only in her thoughts and hopes, she had coveted what wasn't hers, something she had not permitted herself during all the years of her service at

Yakimovschina; with all her strength, through poverty and need, she had kept her integrity so that no one ever, in any particular, could reproach her. And she could have taken a great deal without asking; one could say she had all the running of the place in her hands after all, but when she needed anything she went to the master and couldn't remember an occasion when he refused. He wasn't a bad man, Pan Adolya, and prized her as a conscientious worker and respected her moreover for her scrupulousness in regard to her responsibilities. Now all these changes had disturbed her conscience. What was she to do? How could they live if they didn't take the offer, refused the land? And if they did take it, how could they look the master, her benefactor, in the eye.

The sleepless night, coming after a wretched day was full of pondering, anxiety and hesitation. Both of them were worn out in the boiler-house and had had their fill of whispering and silence and still not thought up a way of stilling their conscience. In the morning Petroc had to go over to the Settlement, to the area committee; it was at dawn that he dangled his bare legs over the bedstead and after some more thought, decided:

"I'm not going. Blow it. . ."

Stepanida leaped up from beneath the blanket.

"What d'you mean, not going? What happens then?"

"I'm not going, that's it. I just can't. . ."

No, that she couldn't agree to; this morning she felt surer of herself - there weren't just two of them in the family now, there were nearly three, so that meant she had two votes, her and the bairn against one wavering Petroc. While he was getting ready to see to the animals, she swore at him roundly, even shed a few tears but there was nothing for it; she quickly got herself ready and ran across the fields to the Settlement.

Out of the extensive farm holdings, five acres were set aside for them and the rest went to other poor and landless folk, of whom there were a goodly lot in the Settlement to be satisfied out of one expropriation. Stepanida didn't go to the distribution herself; she managed to push Petroc into going and waited behind the railings in the yard, keeping her eye on a group of men in the fields trotting back and forth measuring and calculating. From time to time, Yakimovsky's shadow, all in black, passed by the window and his exhausted faced peered out. At such times Stepanida would hide round a corner or by the woodpile; it was awkward, almost agonizing to have the former master of the farm looking out on all this. In the last few days he had hardly shown himself outside the hut and had not spoken to them. He just sat there in permanent resentment having seemingly lost interest in the farm and life in general. She and Petroc kept away from him as well, asking no questions and appropriating nothing, as before. They got by with what they had. Activity on the farm died down, there was only a young mare left in the stable after they took the stallion away to the area committee; there was only one cow left in the cowshed and the piglets were taken off to a diner in the township. The rest - harness, various implements, domestic utensils - seemed to be nobody's; Yakimovsky had lost all right to them, but Stepanida and Petroc had not taken them over. They would have liked to manage with their own things, but this wasn't always feasible and they had to have recourse to the master's stores: first it was a bucket, then hay for the cow, then starting a new potato clamp, when the first was exhausted. On such occasions, Stepanida would open the hut door and ask Pan Adolya, as he sat on the bed with its neatly folded blanket, a waistcoat thrown across his bony shoulders; his thin stockinged feet resting on the floor, once painted but now peeling. Without raising his completely bald head, he would throw out:

"Take it. It's all yours now."

She would turn and leave the hut, noticing, however, the untouched food on the corner of the table - the bowl of cold potatoes, the jug of milk and two slices of bread she had fetched him that morning. The old man had ceased eating at all, how did he think he was going to survive? This way, there was nothing left but to die.

She was sorry for him and this pity cast a considerable shadow over the great joy of starting to farm their own land, the happy awareness that the young black mare belonged to them, just like the easygoing piebald cow, not as young as she was of course, but still giving plenty of milk. Ahead lay a life of liberty with lots of worries and hard work, but a life without compulsion, where, everything, bad or good, would depend on the two of them and no one else. This was happiness, raising them up to the heavens, good fortune beyond their wildest dreams.

If only that living reproach didn't sit next to them in the hut day after day, his legs dangling from the bed, that shrivelled, emaciated, old man, crushed by life.

Somehow she couldn't stand this, and one evening after she had seen to the animals, she told Petroc that they had to talk to Yakimovsky, this was no way to go on; they'd lived so long together in harmony and agreement, but now. . .They had to tell him again that it was no fault of theirs, it was a government matter, that although they'd been given the five acres, they hadn't asked for them, had they? They'd taken them, yes, but if they hadn't they'd have gone to somebody else - there were plenty of poor people in the world. Good relations had to be restored with Yakimovsky, hidden resentments had to be got rid of; as for living, he could live in the hut, they'd rough it in the boiler-house, till they could afford their own hut somehow.

When they got on their feet. She would look after the old man, couldn't she repay him for his land with kindness and attention!

Petroc groaned a bit, feeling embarrassed, but he was obliged to go into the hut as she listened in from the passage. But Petroc couldn't be relied on to do anything properly. He started well off the point and a lengthy and wide-ranging conversation got under way: they recalled life under the Tsar, the way of life in the township, various happenings in the forest and hunting anecdotes. Unable to contain herself, Stepanida wiped her hand on her apron and crossed the threshold. Clearly sensing something in the manner of her entry, Pan Adolya rose and got into his black kaftan and did up the whole row of buttons. She sat down on the bench by the door while he groaned and settled back in his old-world armchair opposite the large dim mirror between the windows.

"You must forgive us, Pan Adolya," said Stepanida, when he had adjusted the skirts of his kaftan and placed his long thin hands on his knees.

"The Lord Jesus will forgive you," said Yakimovsky, staring sternly at the doorway.

"You know it wasn't us. We didn't ask for it did we?"

"But you didn't say no."

"How could we say no, Pan Adolya? They'd have given it to somebody else. Look at the Gonchariks, they got nothing."

It seemed she had hit the mark there. Yakimovsky was silent for a minute, probably not knowing how to reply to this. Then he brought out, in a harsh and suffering voice:

"It's a sin to covet another's goods."

She said nothing from the doorway and he nodded his old, bald head, yellow as a bone, pondering on something or reproaching them silently to himself. These words of his, not about himself, about them, found an anxious response in Stepanida's heart; she sensed a sort of prophetic truth in them which depressed her spirits.

"But there's nothing to be done," he said after an interval. "I don't wish you ill. May Jesus and Maria help you. . ."

"Thank you for that," said Stepanida, almost touched. That was the main thing for him not to harbor a grudge against them and wish them ill. They could have coped somehow with anything else. They had a horse, a plot of land, seed corn had been left in the barn for them to sow their five acres of winter wheat, and maybe there'd be some barley left over for groats and some peas for soup. There was an adequate supply of potatoes on the farm and there were two bins of bacon-fat, saved for the seasonal laborers who would now no longer be coming. They would have fed him, the old man, like a live-in relative, a grandfather. Let it go. They didn't wish him harm did they?

The changeable spring, with its cold snaps lasted nearly till Easter; only after that did it start to get warmer, still irresolute and tardy. On Saint George's Day it was really warm and Stepanida and Petroc got up bright and early and went to the cowshed according to age-old custom. In olden times, the animals were driven out to pasture on this day, but there was nowhere to drive them these days; except for some dry gray grass and toad- stools, there was nothing growing on the grazing grounds yet. Petroc stood in the doorway as Stepanida, using the end of a processional candle put by since Candlemas, rubbed the cow's udder to keep off evil spirits and to insure the year's milk supply; then Petroc set light to a tuft of dry gospel-grass and vigorously fumigated the cowshed and mangers, as had long been the custom on the farm. Towards noon it got still warmer. After tidying up in the hut, Stepanida got some consecrated willow twigs and tied a piece of sweet loaf saved from Easter in her kerchief. Putting on their cleanest clothes they set off to inspect the fields, which had been steaming damply since morning under the benevolent sun - they were waiting for the plow.

The inspection started with the winter crops by the pine wood, where the long rye meadow was bright green with young shoots. Petroc was walking in front and grinning discreetly under his short-clipped mustache. He was no longer young but not yet old: forty years, not yet a man's span. He still couldn't get over this unlooked-for joy: he'd come to the farm as a laborer after all, and here he was now - the boss, inspecting his meadows and pasture land. Of course he realized you couldn't get rich from five acres, but they could live on their own bread all the same. He was a little worried that the winter and especially the long cold spring might damage the winter crops, but it seemed the worst was over -the shoots had survived the cold snaps and covered almost the whole field with bright green. Only the lower part near the road was still darkish, probably where the water persisted. Petroc stepped off the verge to pull up a shoot and have a look at the root. No sooner had he stretched out his hand to the pale wilting stalk when he caught sight of something else gray among the clogged lumps of earth and his puzzled fingers lifted a tiny bird by one extended wing. It was a skylark, probably one of the luckless ones deceived by the first breath of spring and paying with its life for its premature song.

"Look, Stepa. . ."

Stepanida ran up to Petroc and in surprise took the little dead thing from his hand; the spread wings dangled feebly in the air, like the head and tiny open beak.

"Heavens. . .Petroc! What on earth is it? It's a bad omen, you know. . ."

"Is it?"

"Oh yes, it means bad luck! It's a bad lookout for us." Stepanida was ready to burst out crying.

Petroc was also disagreeably struck by his discovery but tried to appear calm, unwilling to credit that misfortune could come upon human beings through the agency of this tiny bundle of feathers.

"What d'you mean, bad luck? It got frozen, that's all. The frost and all. . ."

"Lord, Lord! Why did you have to touch it? Why did you see it?" Stepanida lamented, beside herself at this unmistakable harbinger of disaster.

For a while, they were at a loss and stood stupefied over the little dead bird, with its curved claws, pale as rye stalks. Stepanida began weeping a little and Petroc did not try to console her, feeling no better himself. They buried the skylark in a hole by the verge and stuck a willow twig next to it. They couldn't think what to do with the rest of the willows, all desire to carry them round the winter crops had evaporated at once. They were totally at a loss and for some reason filled with apprehension. Dejected and with no trace of their previous interest in the fields, they skirted the farmland and turned towards the buildings.

Had they known what awaited them at home, they would most likely have run away somewhere far away and never come back. But ignorance is a mighty force and means as much to man as the most certain knowledge and ability to predict the future. Evidently, ignorance can protect us too, preserving the spirit and allowing man to go on living.

In the boiler-house back at the farm, Stepanida undid her kerchief with the Easter cake, cut off a piece and took it into the hut for Pan Adolf. She thought he must be asleep behind the stove, as there was no one to be seen, so she placed the cake on a plate on the table. A settled silence brooded in the hut but she paid it no attention. In any case she wasn't accustomed to dally in there - she would perform whatever it was or take something out into the passage, but there was no reason to disturb the old man beyond that. They ate what was left of the Easter cake and washed it down with milk before Petroc went out into the yard. Spring fever still gripped them and the plow had to be got ready; however, he couldn't find the swingletree without which the horse couldn't be harnessed up. Stepanida for her part began mixing a special drink for the cow in an iron pot; she liked it just so, lightly mixed with flour, and was never partial to water by itself. She was stirring as she squatted by the pot, when Petroc, swaying oddly, stuck his head in the door and cried out to her in a crushed voice, anxious, even alarmed.

"Stepanida!"

She did not at once leap to her feet, thinking merely that Petroc didn't feel too well. He had certainly gone white in the face and the hands extended towards her were disturbingly shaky.

"Stepanida!"

She rushed over to her husband, but he stepped away, backing towards the yard to direct her attention towards the barn. Her glance moved further on and she saw that the barn doors were wide open - something that had never happened before; a great rusting black padlock had always hung there and the huge key had hung on a nail in the hut. Sensing something wrong, she ran to the gaping doors, glimpsing while still in the yard the dim shadow of a man amid the gloom of the barn. Adolf Yakimovsky was standing motionless on his long bandy legs as if just stooping over the bins. In an unrecognizable voice, she cried out, "Panochka Adolya!" but there came no response. At this, she rushed into the barn and realization dawned. From the beam up above stretched a taut rope; Yakimovsky's head and neck, yellow as ivory, were twisted unnaturally to one side and his arms had fallen along the thin pendent body; one shoulder had jerked upwards and the whole corpse was bent forward. She seized his shoulders, bony beneath the kaftan, and the body turned over, heavy and reluctant. He was hanging so low that his bent legs in their calf leather, Sunday-best boots scraped a line in the earth as she pulled at him. Despite her fears it occurred to Stepanida incongruously that even here there wasn't enough room for a man to hang himself.

Two days later, she and Petroc knocked together a coffin of old unplaned boards and carried it to the Catholic cemetery for burial. The day after that, Matskievich came out from the township and loaded the bulky oak armchair into his two-horse wagon, along with the narrow-case clock and the fine mahogany bureau, saying it was in settlement of debts. Stepanida and Petroc made no objection - take the lot! There was far more left - virtually the whole farmstead, five acres of land, the young mare and the cow. Surely that was enough in times like those?

After an interval they transferred their bits of belongings from the boiler-house and began living in the hut.

Old man Yakimovsky gradually began to fade from their minds. They would recall him sometimes, but it only made them feel depressed, so they tried to dismiss all thought of him.

And indeed they succeeded, especially as there were travails and anxieties enough in those hard and troubled years. . .

Winter crops grew by themselves, no worries there, but there were only two little fields of them; the main part of the holding up on the hill had to be plowed for spring sowing. It was all right, they could have coped somehow, but the very top of the mound had lain fallow since the year before last; Yakimovsky hadn't plowed it. He had let it go because the soil up there was hopeless - stones and clay-loam that went rock-hard in dry years. Yakimovsky could afford to let an acre or two lie fallow, of course, he had better land elsewhere, what was it to him? It was a dry spring, almost rainless and when the weather grew warmer, Petroc harnessed up the young mare and set out to plow up the fallow land.

He struggled on up there from dawn till noon. Stepanida, busy with other tasks about the farmstead waited for him at dinner, but he did not appear. With some foreboding she abandoned her chores and ran by way of the gully edge to this ill-starred plot of theirs.

While still some way off, she caught sight of her husband on the hill fussing about with the horse, having left the plow in a furrow for some reason. The mare was standing, head drooping among the dry stems of last year's grass and weeds; her flanks were damp with sweat. Stepanida ran up onto the narrow little plowed furrows and let out a cry as she spiked her feet on the lumps of clay lying red across the plowed land like bricks among the grass stalks and heaps of dried dung. It was hardly surprising the mare had had enough; a good experienced horse would likely have burst a blood vessel pulling a plow up here. Their dark mare had turned jet-black with the sweat trickling in rivulets down her prominent ribs and her flanks were heaving in exhaustion as her head sank closer and closer to the ground. Barefoot in his unbelted homespun shirt Petroc glanced around at her with his shoulders drenched in perspiration and jerked the mare's bridle; the animal staggered, splayed its hind legs out and subsided in its traces onto the rough furrows.

"Oh dear, this is terrible, what's to be done now?" Petroc, distressed, was trying the raise the mare with a mixture of threats and coaxing. Before long the front legs gave way as well, and the mare stretched out in its harness, scrabbling convulsively at the clay with its hooves. Petroc anxiously hurried to unbuckle the animal from her harness, but couldn't manage to free the collar which had ridden up over the horse's head; Stepanida meanwhile uncoupled the swinglebar from the plow, so loosening the traces. She was now fully aware that misfortune had suddenly burst into their independent life, so recently begun.

So it transpired. The mare did not rise again, however much they assisted her or tempted her with hay, grass and a crust Stepanida had fetched from the farm. The head on the long scrawny neck finally rested on the earth; only the eyes rotated in their sockets as if beseeching help, but she was past saving now. Towards evening the mare tensed herself and thrust her legs out for the last time.

For her part, Stepanida stood petrified with grief, clearly envisioning life on the farm without a horse, just at the season when it would be most needed. Petroc, wet through, also stood for some time, then silently sat down with his hands across his face and wept. Stepanida made no move to console him as she wiped away a furtive tear of her own and recalled the recent field inspection and the frozen skylark under the verge.

"There's a curse on this hill. We had no land, but this isn't land either."

Little by little Petroc recovered himself, sat for a while longer, then got ready to go home. They had to consider how life was to be from now on.

As evening came on, he returned to the farm with the horse collar, took out a spade and headed for Sheep Valley and the pine hillock where people used to dig sand and bury any dead village animals. He excavated a pit on the edge of the pine copse, then fetched Ladimir's stallion from the Settlement and dragged the mare off. Stepanida did not accompany him, unable to watch such things; her mind was concentrated on ways of overcoming these disasters. Where could they get hold of a horse to plow that accursed hill? They couldn't let it lie fallow again, could they, what would they have to live on?

Petroc dragged himself home at length and answered her questions in monosyllables; he had some soup and sat down on the passage step. She tried to say something to draw him into conversation, but he was in no mood for that so she busied herself with other things to avoid getting on his nerves. Later she snuggled down behind the stove and when she woke at dawn, Petroc had already gone out somewhere - to the Settlement she assumed, since a horse had to be obtained somehow to finish off the hill. Other folk had finished sowing and here were they not even able to plow.

But there was no sign of him at breakfast. Worried, she peered through the fence up at the hill and almost wept as she saw, far off across the fields, the solitary figure of her husband, swaying rhythmically from side to side as he dug the earth. She wanted to run over there, but the potatoes were already boiling on the stove and couldn't be left unattended. Nevertheless, after a quarter of an hour, she made a sort of breakfast - bowl of potatoes, piece of bacon-fat, bread and a jug of milk - then fastened her kerchief and went up to the hill.

Petroc had been digging by hand, with his spade, rooting up, beating down, chopping the wretched clay through the young couch grass starting to grow up through last year's crop and had already fined down a decent wedge in from the edge of the field. As she glanced at his face, Stepanida could scarcely recognize her husband, fierce, aging, with a dark growth of stubble on his cheeks. His flat chest had got even more hollow, his shoulders grown sharp from emaciation. His sweat-soaked shirt flapped loosely around him as if it were hung on a pole and his round suffering eyes held a mute reproach towards someone for all the failures of his life.

"Petroc, what in the world are you doing?"

"What you see," he replied without interrupting work; exhaustion made his voice indistinct.

"You can't dig the lot up?"

"What ese can I do?"

"Maybe somebody could lend us a horse? You should go and see people."

"I've done that already. Who's going to give us a horse to bury?"

She stopped harping on this, realizing that Petroc was more or less right; you couldn't get a horse from people who needed it themselves; then again, who would give up their carefully tended animal to anybody else - on land like that too? So what was there for it but to dig it with spades? There was no alterative.

As she recalled, she even started crying then at the vivid picture she conjured up of the peasant's lot without a horse. Petroc stopped digging and rested wearily on the spade.

"What else can we do though? We've got to live. . . somehow. . ."

Four days from morning till night they smashed at the clay with their two spades and overcame it at last. Of course they had no strength left. They had reached the limit of exhaustion, but they had managed to break up the soil all the same, though in some places they had only just got their spades into the surface. They worked all day in silence, holding on to their spades as they got their breath back. Then Petroc lifted and broke up the bigger clods and so one fine morning they loaded themselves up with half a sack of buckwheat apiece in plaited straw baskets. They broadcast the seed quickly, as Levon had loaned them a horse for half a day to get the harrowing done. His plot bordered on theirs a little lower down and the soil there was no pleasure either, if slightly more workable and sandy. They got the job done on a Saturday as it happened, on an evening of quiet beauty, and Stepanida reckoned on giving her swollen, blistered hands something of a rest; Petroc, however, after sitting on the earth parapet for a while hefted his axe and set off somewhere towards the gully. She asked where he was going, imagining he was off for firewood as they were short, but he just disappeared round the angle of the boiler-house without a word.

He got home as she was milking the cow and lay down behind the stove without his supper. When she had finished the evening chores, she went into the hut to find him fast asleep snoring; without questioning him she lay down alongside.

Next day the same thing happened - he disappeared at dawn, where she did not know. Still, a peasant had plenty of tasks in the spring, especially after a disaster such as they had suffered. Maybe he'd gone to the Settlement asking about a horse again to get the manure carted out for the potatoes, plow the kitchen garden plot, get the peas put in - there was always a ton of work on the land in spring. Stepanida tethered the cow by the edge of the gully and on her way back to the farmstead, glanced up at the hill and shuddered at what she saw.

The dawn sun was just up and at that moment was passing into a low purple cloud. To one side of it, against the bright edge of the sky, a human figure showed dark - someone was stooping and apparently wrestling with a recalcitrant post or tree. Stepanida quickly realized it was Petroc, but what was he doing there?

Turning off the path, she rushed straight up the hill, jabbing her feet against the clay shards of the sown field as she ran to her own strip. Here she began to make out, on the highest point at the end of their plot, a huge cross of rough-hewn logs, leaning at an angle as Petroc, braced against the earth, raised it aloft. She ran closer as he cried to her in exhaustion: help! She seized the rough trunk of the young oak in both hands and lowered it into the deep pit Petroc had hastily begun digging for it. The cross was damp and she had only to lean it out of true for the huge weight to push her to one side; she was terrified but managed to hold on as Petroc threw earth into the pit.

"Lord, help us, do not withhold thyself from these thy servants," he said, crossing himself and wiping the sweat from his face, worn out by these hard days of toil. Stepanida also crossed herself, thinking: maybe it really would help to deflect misfortune from this land of theirs, cursed by God and man.

The cross stood through all that spring and summer on the topmost point of the hill, above the gully and the wood, set well back from the road so that anyone walking or riding along the highway could see that sign of human calamity. It was at that time that somebody from the Settlement called the hill Golgotha, and the name caught on: Golgotha or the hill of Golgotha, Petroc's Golgotha even. It was the same even after the Settlement Komsomols, Kopylov, Meyerson and Hlasko toppled the cross in the autumn. They just came to the farm and asked to borrow a saw; as Petroc fetched it from the boiler-house, Stepanida gave them some kvass, good stuff which had stood for a decent long time. The lads had a drink and a joke and went on their way. She had thought they were heading for the gully or the woods, but they turned along the verge up to the hill and in the space of ten minutes or so, they sawed down the cross. After they brought the saw back, they read them a long lecture on the evils of religious belief. Petroc scowled in silence and didn't answer back, but Stepanida had a furious row with them, remembering how Petroc and she had broken themselves that spring toiling on Golgotha and nobody had made a move to help, but now that the barley was ripe, these oafs had up and taken against the cross. Still what was the use of talking to them, they just laughed at her ignorance and went off to the Settlement conscious of duty done.

But the name of the hill remained and likely will for long enough, precisely defining the grim reality of that patch of earth, so unsuitable for raising bread, and consecrated by tears, toil and a years-long peasant calvary.

15

Winter was turning into spring, the blizzards were at an end and the days were warming up. On the sunward side of the yard, the roofs dripped at noon, though severe frosts persisted at night, and the corners of the hut would crackle. The morning would begin with a broad flood of crimson sunrise covering half the sky; the red sun would rise from behind the woods in a cloud of frosty mist, then gain strength and soon the whole stretch of the field with its thick carpet of post thaw crunching snow was striped with the immense shadows of trees, hills and poles. Far off in the frosty morning, the woods glimmered a tender gray-blue, alongside barely perceptible speckled clearings, while all around was a white, dazzling enough to hurt the eyes. It was mild, gaily colored and peaceful.

Stepanida, however, was not disposed to drink in the beauty of a fine winter's morning; she barely noticed it in fact as she fussed round the stove and instructed Petroc in what she hadn't managed to finish - water the sheep, mix the mash for the hens - before she set off across the fields to the Settlement.

In her old patched up felt boots it was easy to run along the trodden ice of the path and she imagined that this time she would return only at twilight - the collective farm business was getting into full swing now that it had finally been organized the previous week. It had meant an all night sitting, but they had managed it in the end - over half the Settlement had agreed to go in. Novik had been right in his own fashion: dispossess one as a kulak and a lot of people would think it over. That they'd done, then came a bit of discussion and finally agreement. Now three days running the collective committee had been going round the farmyards, making an inventory of seeds, horses and equipment. As a rule Stepanida ran over bright and early to the village soviet and the group of four went round the village missing nobody, into every yard, - past weeping women, under the tensely anxious gaze of old men and the silent attention of children - everything was noted down. It was hard but it had to be done.

That day she didn't think she would find the president in and she would have to catch up with the commission somewhere in the village; she was mightily surprised when she opened the door of the psalm-reader's hut, long as a cowshed, to find everyone in his place. Levon was sitting silently at the table opposite a squat peasant in a black fur jacket; this was his neighbor Kornila, who had also been co-opted onto the collectivization committee. Face turned away towards the window, Vasya Goncharik was standing in his Red Army greatcoat. The room was cold and full of smoke and a certain tension could be sensed among the men; Stepanida caught this at once and greeted them guardedly:

"Good morning."

"Good morning," returned Kornila.

"What the hell's good about it," said Levon, directing his good eye at her. "It's a rotten day, couldn't be worse."

Stepanida was taken aback.

"What d'you mean, its nice out. . ."

"Too nice. Spring'll be early. But. . .well, read this."

He handed her a small, very creased sheet of the district paper "Red Herds". Still in the dark, she began reading with difficulty the headlines sprinkled across the page: "Raise higher the banner of industrialization," "New directions!" "Export plan for forestry industry in danger of wrecking." There was a little cartoon on the other side, showing a Red Army man, legs set wide, prodding a snarling, fat-bellied bourgeois with his bayonet.

"Not there," said Kornila. "Over there right in the corner."

Sure enough, in the corner of the page, there was a heading in quite small letters: "In the Settlement they pander to the class enemy - the kulak." Stepanida fixed her eyes on the small letters and began reading. The piece stated that whereas a severe struggle was in progress throughout the country against the kulak as a class enemy, this was being ignored in the Settlement; they had dispossessed only one kulak, for hiring labor, Guzhov, Ivan. Other farmers using hired labor existed, however, namely: Bogatka, Kornila who hired the poor peasant Fruzina Kolondenok for two summers harvesting the rye; Prokhorikha, who had hired help for three years running for plowing, sowing and harvesting and Bogatka, Ladimir who had hired labor for threshing. There were witnesses who could swear to all this. "No mercy to the class enemy!" - the slogan ended the piece. It was signed simply and mysteriously: "scholar."

Stepanida at once realized what had cast a gloom on the men, especially Kornila, and indeed the president Levon. She felt somewhat fearful herself and wanted to read the article again, to make sure she'd understood everything properly. Kornila, however, reached out for the paper.

"See that? Me, a class enemy!"

"And I'm pandering to him!" Levon grinned wryly.

Stepanida sat down on a bench; there was something she still didn't comprehend; what was written in the paper was true, but still. . .Where that truth was leading, though, was terrible to think.

"What swine could have written it!" Levon struck the table with the three fingers of his crippled hand.

"I told you who! It was his work!" Kornila burst out, obviously on edge, and rose from the table. Goncharik turned back from the window, dignified in his uniform, over which hung a heavy holstered pistol at the hip - a significant emblem of his new job as policeman.

"I'm going to the district. I'll find out who."

"No need," Kornila insisted. "It's Kolondenok, I'm telling you. Bet you what you like."

"Maybe it is," said Levon. "He's our scholar alright. But that's not the point."

"What else can it be then?" Kornila spoke heatedly. "Somebody slanders me, that's alright is it?"

"The point is, it isn't slander. It's true! You hired them, didn't you? Yes. So it's hired labor."

Everyone in the hut was frowning, staring straight ahead in silence. All were well aware of what hired labor was and its consequences too. Stepanida was also silent although she realized that something had to be done; could they complain to someone? It was true that deep in her heart she couldn't believe that the worst could happen because although those named in the article had hired hands, how could they be called enemies? Nor wreckers either, as they'd gone into the collective along with the others; Prokhorikha was just a poor old woman living out her time in a moldering hut. How could she do the sowing and harvesting herself on twenty acres? So she'd hired outside help to work about a third or a half of it. How did that make her a class enemy?

"Where's Potap, though?" Goncharik asked.

"Run off, the puppy! He knows he's safer out of the way, the sod," Kornila pursued his theme. Levon drew avidly on his cigarette butt and hurled it to the floor.

"It was me who gave him houseroom as well! Let him live in the village soviet hut. . .Bastard! Just let him wait!"

"What'll you do to him?" inquired Kornila. "You can't throw him out."

"Harassing a village correspondent is a criminal offense," Goncharik reminded him.

"What village correspondent?! He's nowhere near being that. He's just dabbling in it."

"He's the one responsible. But that's just it, he's got no responsibility! Puts slanders about and then he's off and away. And we're the ones who worry, get scared, think of the consequences. It's surely not going to end here, is it?" asked Kornila.

"It surely won't."

"I'll have to go to the township," said Levon, raising his mangled face to Goncharik. "Let's go together."

"What about the inventory?" queried Stepanida. "There's still all yon end of the village to do. Or should we leave it?"

"No," said Levon, "you do it. We won't be back till evening."

"Alright then."

Sunk in gloomy reflections, Kornila slowly paced the length of the hut, halted, weighing up this and that. Naturally, nobody could be elated at such a time and Stepanida had some sympathy with him. Kornila was about to say something, put on his new gloves, sewn from sheepskin, then took them off again. But he'd changed his mind obviously and with a wave of his arm he grasped the doorknob. Stepanida followed him out.

So, in silence, Kornila in front and Stepanida behind, they went along the street to the far end of the Settlement, which lay in a hollow behind the hill. Kornila stayed quiet for a long time as he strode out across the close-packed snow in his black felt boots. The boots were still quite new and rough and looked ponderous in their crude galoshes made out of thick motor tires. Of course he hired people now and again, though he didn't have a lot of land, but in the village he had the reputation of being a thrifty, calculating sort of a peasant; he liked doing carpentry and kept a few beehives. It was also said of him that he was a miser and not fond of lending things to his relatives, let alone fellow villagers. He didn't reject the collective farm and went in with the rest; Levon wanted to install him as a foreman - he certainly knew how to farm, unlike some. But now this in the papers. . .

"They talk about leaders, leaders!" he said, turning to Stepanida who hurried to catch him up and walk alongside. "But I'm telling you: you'll never find worse than the folk round about. Nobody can do you as much harm as your neighbor. Your own folk are the ruin of you."

"Happen so," agreed Stepanida. "That's because they're close by, at your side."

"At your side, keeping their eye on everything, green with jealousy. Specially if he's a failure himself. He's not pleased when he buys a horse himself, but he is when yours pegs out. It's true! I know these neighbors. You've got to eat your crust under your coat to keep it from them. Even then they're jealous. Envy always finds its mark when you don't expect it. I'm not a kulak, not rich. And I haven't got much land. But I love the work. And keeping things right, neat and tidy. Not like some I know: give up, run away. If I start something, I go on till it's well done. I love my land more than my kid. I crawl over every lump of soil on my land, sieve it through my fingers. I don't go round any rusty wire, I pick it all up. How else should land be farmed, eh? And some people don't like it."

"Did Potap really write that?" said Stepanida doubtfully.

"Who else, then? Scholar! Remember him reporting Prokopikha? About the flax?"

Stepanida recalled that well. It had been the talk of the Settlement, indeed and the whole district, for a year. People had even quarrelled about it; some of the young ones had almost come to blows with their elders, who abused the boy. Some were envious of him because the paper had written about him, praising him throughout the region. It had all happened in late autumn of the year before last, when the district was well behind in flax production. The flax crop was poor; it simply hadn't grown because of the lack of rain since spring, but the quota was due and all the peasants went into arrears. Two deputies arrived from the region straightaway and started going round the yards with Levon, looking for flax - but what could they find if the peasants had given up every bit and not kept a stalk for themselves? Spinning wheels and looms stood idle that year. To keep to the plan somehow, people unravelled old ropes, horse whips - anything. Old Prokopikha, of course, didn't even have an old rope that would do, and the region men were sorry for the old thing as she wept and complained at her luck, her ailments and old age in general. As soon as the commission had left the unheated hut and gone into the yard, however, Potapka Kolondenok, who had got used to the company of the top men, went up to the senior region official, a young fellow in a black beaver coat and whispered that the old wife had some flax hidden away in the cowshed. They didn't believe him at first, but they glanced in the open doors of the empty shed as Potapka clambered up onto a beam and pulled out from somewhere under the roof three hanks of first-class flax. This was sabotage and although Prokopikha justified herself by saying she had nothing to wear and that this was for underclothes when she was buried, they drew up an official report with a view to taking her to court. She got away with that, actually, the judge was sorry for the old dear, but Potapka Kolondenok's class vigilance came in for praise from the district newspaper "Red Herds." It was after this episode that Levon let Kolondenok live in the council hut along with his mother, who had resided till then in the public bathhouse. The villagers began calling Potapka "scholar", some, as a mark of praise and envy, others, ironically. As for Potap, he interpreted this after his own fashion and on several more occasions short pieces appeared in the paper concerning the Settlement:

one was about how well the campaign against illiteracy was going in the village and the other stressed the importance of wood-ash as a fertilizer.

They had arrived at a sloping little hut under a moldering roof. Kornila touched the wicket gate, bolted on the inside. Here dwelt Bogatka, Boris, a poor peasant with a numerous family who had been almost the last to sign up for the collective at the assembly and had at once disappeared from the village. Rumor had it that he had gone to live elsewhere. The gate wouldn't give at all until Kornila shook it till it almost fell off its posts and finally sagged open. The two of them entered a littered yard, rust-colored from domestic slops, and in the chilly passage found the door to the hut.

"Good morning. Anyone at home?" Kornila sang out.

Boris's wife, Lizaveta, took her time in appearing from behind the stove, carrying a baby hastily wrapped in some kind of sacking; the child pressed its dirty face to its mother's emaciated breast. Lizaveta stared at the newcomers with eyes red with weeping.

"Lizavetka, we're making a list of what goes into the collective," said Stepanida, trying to be as gentle as possible. At this, Lizaveta's face flared with sudden anger.

"List? Make a list, then! List this lot! Manya, Teklya, Ganulya, come here! Here you take them and feed them in your commune. . ."

Out from behind the stove, two barefoot toddlers in threadbare little kaftans ran out to their mother and clutched her dirty skirt. The eldest, Ganulya, also emerged and stood shyly behind her mother, staring at them sullenly. Hens could be heard clucking in alarm under the stove and something was smelling strongly in the comfortless, neglected hut.

"Alright," said Kornila. "No need to put on a show for us. Where's Boris?"

"Do I know where that Boris is? He didn't tell me. If he's signed up for the collective, you can write him down. But I'm not going and I'm not giving up my cow! It's mine, part of my dowry from my dad. You've got no right to take it away."

"Just be quiet, Lizaveta!" Kornila lost his temper. "We're not going to list your cow. Just the horse. And the bits of harness. The seeds as well."

"There's no seeds. And no horse either."

"What d'you mean?" Kornila said, alert. "There was a black horse, wasn't there?"

"There was, but not any longer. It's gone."

"You've got rid of it? Sold it?"

"What if we did," Lizaveta wiped away her tears. "Are we supposed to give it to the collective just like that? Did we get it for nothing? We paid good money for that horse."

"You're as much good as a leaky boot, you are!" said Kornila. "Build a collective farm with people like that, I ask you! You should get your wits together for a start and pull yourself together as well. The hut needs a good cleanup, the kids are filthy. You're as lazy as sin, young as you are! You're no good for anything but producing bairns."

"I am what I am!"

"Come on, show us where everything is. So we don't have to rake about like burglars."

"I'm showing you nothing. Look for it yourself."

She began wrapping the little one in sacking and Kornila spat at his feet in frustration.

"Well, you watch, we'll list everything. And no whining afterwards."

He stepped out into the utterly filthy yard with Stepanida and looked about him.

"Where do they keep things here? That's the brewing hut isn't it?"

But as they turned towards the old outhouse with its rotted corners, there came a child's breathless voice from the street:

"Uncle Kornila, daddy said you had to come to the village soviet."

On the other side of the wicket gate stood Olechka, Levon's youngest daughter. From her face, flushed with running, Stepanida guessed that something had happened.

"What's up with him then?" asked Kornila, guarded.

"Ai, there's come. . .well a man from the township, he's got a black collar."

"Kosmachov?"

"Mm. And another one with him. So daddy said. . ."

Kornila's face darkened as he thought hard and finally cursed savagely:

"Bloody hell's flames! I knew it!. . ."

He said no more, as he stepped out along the icy street; Stepanida had a job to keep up with him. Olechka was left puffing far behind.

At the village soviet, as if everything was as usual, there were no horses to be seen, maybe they were round in the yard somewhere? They went into the hut together, letting in a blast of cold air. Stepanida fumbled with the heavy door as she closed it behind her and looked over into the corner. The two men were already present, Kosmachov by the window and at the table under the portrait of Marx, an unfamiliar man with a hard, cleanshaven face. He wore a shiny leather jacket, with a cross-belt - for a holster was it? The man was staring at his hands laced on the table in front of him, twirling his large fingers one after the other; the effect was slightly comic. Kosmachov in his black collared waistcoat was looking anxiously at the entrance; Levon was sitting on a bench between the windows, head in hands, elbows on knees, in a haze of home-grown tobacco. Alongside him sat Vasya Goncharik. An oppressive silence reigned, as all present thought furiously, and the atmosphere immediately communicated itself to the newcomers, who said their helloes quietly and took a seat by the door.

"Is this a meeting or what?" asked Kornila after a pause, more to break the awkward silence in the hut.

"Dispossession!" growled Levon.

"What? That's been done already!"

"Yes, but not everybody!" Levon burst out, his voice breaking into a shout as he turned away towards the window. "I said it wouldn't stop at one, didn't I?"

Kosmachov turned sideways-on at the end of the table, then leaned his elbow on it again; he was obviously laboring under emotional stress, though he tried to appear calm, and, as always, rational. He was making a poor fist of it. For no reason at all, Levon suddenly came out with a vile and savage oath and hurled his cigarette butt to the floor. The stranger, without raising his head from the table, gave him an intense, mistrustful look then glanced at Kosmachov. In response, the latter turned to Levon and rebuked him:

"One must be able to rise above personal considerations in the class war."

In the hut the oppressive silence returned, no one seemed to be breathing. Stepanida plucked at the seam of her jacket with her calloused fingers, thinking that all this was a misunderstanding soon to be resolved and that trouble would pass them by.

"So who's going to be dispossessed?" Kornila tensed himself to ask in the silence. Levon sprang sharply away from the window.

"It's them who made use of hired labor! Them named in the paper! Got it?" he was shouting, though whether he was angry at the kulaks or out of sympathy for them was unclear.

Kornila clenched his powerful jaws and slowly lowered his head. After sitting a while, he rose and slowly wandered to the door in silence. When the door closed behind him, Stepanida felt a pang as she thought: what on earth is going on?

"What him as well?" she asked addressing them all. Her voice trembled slightly, tense with emotion.

"Him as well. And Ladimir. And Prokhorikha," Levon threw out.

"Dispossessed as kulaks?"

"Not getting a prize are they?"

A feverish trembling came over Stepanida; her back perspired under her jacket and a thick mist came before her eyes. For a minute she didn't know what to say or what she should think. And all present - the man at the table, Kosmachov close by, one-eyed Levon, even Goncharik - were silent in a sort of strained attention, as if just waiting to hear what she would say. Quite out of key with her feelings, she gave a forced unnatural laugh which frightened her as she realized how she was going to end it.

"Idiots you are!" she shouted suddenly as she stopped laughing. "Clods! Who are you dispossessing? Why not everybody? Every last one? There'll be no need for a collective then. No more worries. Go on do the lot! Me as well, Pan Yakimovsky's laborer. And him over there, landless Goncharik! Everybody! Every last one!"

She shook as if in a fever, blearily looking round those present in the hut, thinking they would come to their senses shortly and realize the stupidity of their proceedings, the blatant injustice of it all. But they all sat on like so many tree stumps, calm, strong and unmoved.

"That's enough, aunty," said Kosmachov, calmly.

"Policy has to be consistent."

"Where's the consistency?" She lost her self-control and leapt up from the bench, stung by the very composure of his manner. "What consistency? What about justice? Poor peasants now is it? Is that fair? You're educated men, can't you see that? Ask the peasants. . .any ignorant old boy, ask him and he'll tell you: it's wrong! It's wrong to punish your own people! Have you gone crazy with your book learning, is that it, so you can't see. . . Everybody else around can see it but not you?"

She was shouting incoherently, leaping from complaint to accusation, mainly addressing herself, however, to the man in the leather jacket. She wanted him, as an outsider and probably some kind of boss, to understand that an injustice was being committed and that he should intervene. She was avid for justice. But silence still reigned in the hut, and the stranger said nothing, keeping his eyes stubbornly averted from her. She began shouting louder:

"It's pure madness! Levon! You'll have to go to Moscow, to Kalinin himself. You're one of us, a local, how can this happen? It's all wrong! It's inhuman. This isn't the Bolshevik way! It's going to far, you must see! We're hurting ourselves!"

"Now, now, calm down, aunty!" Kosmachov cried angrily. "What are you standing there for comrade Goncharik? Quiet the lady down!"

"To hell with the lot of you! Do what you want! But count me out!"

She turned and rushed for the door, banging it behind her demonstratively. It didn't shut so with a sigh she had to come back and close it.

Stepanida ran along the trodden path to her Yakimovschina, tears streaming down her chilled weather-beaten cheek; her insides were still clamoring and she didn't know what to do. She just felt with a rare clarity that something had to be done; she had to run somewhere, see someone, but where and who?. . .

Novik maybe? After all he was one of them, a villager and something of a big bug these days so they said. Last time he'd just been on about Guzh, he hadn't mentioned anybody else. He knew these people, how could they be kulaks? Complain to him and get him to cancel the dispossession order. So what if the paper had printed it? Who'd written it - a wretched half-wit, a eunuch, a boy-girl, bastard. Were they going to listen to him?

Stepanida ran into the farm, glancing into the cowshed where Petroc was usually seeing to the animals, but he wasn't there and neither was the sledge. He hadn't gone for firewood at last, had he? He'd been planning to long enough, saying that while they still had the horse, he should get the firewood in at least. Alright, if that's where he was. She ran into the hut for the three-rouble note she had hidden away wrapped in a handkerchief in a corner of the trunk. She had been saving it for an emergency but there wouldn't be more of an emergency than this, most likely. She thought for a moment and picked up a basket as well and threw in a fresh kerchief and cut a slice of bread. Polotsk was a good way off, might take some time. Still, somebody would be going there from the township. Drop in on Leiba, he was a coachman, maybe he'd take her. If she hadn't enough to pay, she'd owe him, then pay him in eggs or something. Leiba was an accommodating sort of man, he could wait till spring or summer. He didn't swear or tell her off like some others.

Time was passing. The sun had descended into the western clouds and the frost had given, night would likely see a thaw. Crows had settled in the branches of the limes and were squabbling there, cawing away in advance of the thaw or the rising wind.

Stepanida made haste. To save time she turned off the road onto a path across the young pine wood, cutting half a kilometer off her journey. The path was not much trodden - a few pairs of feet had passed across the snow - but after the thaw and the frost, the snow was nice and firm; it was on the powdery side only among the young pines and she fell in a couple of times. As she got warmer, she loosened the scarf round her neck, at the same time bending her head to avoid the prickly branches; as she waded through the hollow towards the highway, she thought to herself: I hope I catch Leiba at home, he might be out somewhere on a trip and she would either have to spend the night in the township or return to the farm.

She was just about to run down from the hillock onto the easier going of the road when she glimpsed two shadowy figures among the roadside firs. It was dark, however, and she only saw one bent double scuttling away from her as the other, a tall hefty individual in a black shaggy hat and short fur jacket, strode forward to meet her.

"Where to, Stepanida?" he asked matter-of-factly, very calm, as she recognized the youngest Guzh son, Zmiter. The Guzh family has been dispossessed a week before and their belongings confiscated, but they hadn't been transported anywhere yet. Now this Guzh was barring her path, so she came to a standstill, not knowing how to answer. "Where are you running off to, I'm asking you?"

"The township. What's it to you?"

"Why the township?"

"Well, business."

"At this time of day?"

"Well, what of it?"

"You're going back, understand?"

"Why should I go back? Can't I go to the township now or what?"

Guzh came right up to her, thinking doubtless she would turn back or move to one side. She stayed where she was and stared angrily into his large, youthful, not too sober face with its white eyebrows. The face was impassive, however, no special rage or menace; the eyes, though, were very cold and intent.

"What's in there?" Guzh nodded towards the basket and grabbed it from her hands before she had a chance to reply. "Kerchief, bread. . .What about this? Money? That'll come in handy."

He began stuffing her scarf with the three roubles into the pocket of his black breeches then suddenly swore savagely.

"Now run! Back to the farm, run! Bloody activist. . ."

"What are you doing? What are you doing? I'll scream, you're a bandit that's what you are!" Stepanida began wailing. Guzh vigorously pulled something out from under the hem of his jacket and before she knew what was happening, a black gunbarrel without a sight was pressing against her heart. Guzh's great hand grasped the sawed-off wood of the butt tightly.

"You're lucky you're a relative! Otherwise. . .get me?"

Yes, she probably did, though not at once. Especially as somewhere near at hand in the hollow, plainly rustling the branches, someone else was concealed, closely observing the skirmish on the path.

Stepanida turned away and headed into the heart of the pines in the direction of the farm, not once glancing behind her, though somewhat afraid of getting a shot in the back. She knew Zmiter was capable of anything. When he was a boy he used to raid gardens, make fun of the younger ones and stamp on vegetable beds in the Settlement. When his neighbor Kornila got hold of a little dog which stopped Zmiter going on the rampage at night, he caught it, throttled it and hung the animal on Kornila's apple tree. He had shown pity to nobody since the day he was born. He was a total contrast to his kind and scrupulous elder brother and even his severe but decent father who was a distant relative of Petroc's.

"And no word to anybody! Understand? Otherwise your roof's on fire! You know me," came to her from the distance.

Like a beaten dog, she got back to her farm again and gave way to tears of helpless exasperation. Not to be able to stick your nose out of doors. They'd robbed her like some stupid old woman, a mile from her own house, and taken her last bit of money. And who was responsible? Again it was one of their own, someone she'd threatened to thrash with nettles when he was a snivelling brat for annoying the little ones out on the common pasture. There was no thrashing him now; he was the one doing the threatening and that made it utterly mortifying. She didn't care about the money, it was the brazen threat that humiliated her; she had had to give in because she knew he would stop at nothing. If he had gone this far already, he was quite capable of setting fire to the farmstead or killing her in the pine grove.

So what now - put up with it?

Putting up with it was alien to her nature, she would decide on some course of action come what may, get something done. First thing was to tell Petroc all about it and run over to Goncharik at the village soviet in the morning. There was such a thing as Soviet order in the world after all; justice would be meted out to the bandits in the woods.

It was quite dark by the time she reached the farm. The red light of the kerosene lamp glowed in the tiny window of the hut - the children were sitting at their homework. Petroc was watering the horse in the yard, just unhitched from the sleigh standing near the woodpile with three considerable logs aboard, probably from Sheep Valley. If they were careful, they would last till spring. Any other time she would have been pleased to see the logs but now she barely noticed them as she went to Petroc.

"Petroc! Oh, Petroc!. . ."

Petroc probably sensed something was amiss straightaway from her tone of voice - it wasn't often she used this tone to him. Throwing the bucket down in the snow, he strode towards her anxiously.

"Piotra, what on earth's happening!" she said and broke out into sobs. Petroc stood facing her, at a loss.

"Who. . .what's the matter?"

"They're going to kill us, I know. And set fire to the hut. . . They're like wild beasts! They stole my basket as well. . ."

Petroc seemed to slump at this; he frowned and sighed.

"You as well, then?"

"What d'you mean, you too?"

"Me as well. . .in the pine plantation, right?"

"That's where it was."

"Listen. . .listen to me. Not a word to anybody! And don't stick your nose anywhere. Stay at home. Because. . .they threatened me as well: one word and they'll burn us out."

Stepanida lowered herself onto the rough fir log on the sleigh, she had no strength left to stand. So Petroc had been in their hands too and he was telling her to keep quiet. Otherwise. . . it really was terrible to think what might happen "otherwise". . . Where would they live after that? Where could they go with the children?

Petroc finished watering the horse and led it into the shed before returning to the yard. It was now completely dark, with a mild wind gusting round the corner of the boiler-house; no stars were visible. Stepanida had cried herself out and sat exhausted on the log thinking over what to do. It didn't look as if she and Petroc could stay out of harm's way, but as long as it didn't touch the children and scorch their tender souls. . . Later of course it would be the turn of the children to learn of the crookedness that abounded in life, but that could wait till they were older. Now was too early, now she was prepared to shield them with her own body against the spiteful stings that life could inflict.

"Well, woman of mine, things have come to a pretty pass!" Petroc came up to her. "Who'd have thought it! Here I'm going along, just turned the horse off the road to come straight across, then out they come: hand over the horse! What d'you mean, can't you see I've got a load on? Hand it over, that's all. And a gun under my nose. He'd have taken it as well but I says, but the collar straps are weak, look I says, the straps are frayed. . . He had a look and let me go. Well, you're kin after all, he says. Relative - he can drop dead, he can. Still if we do anything they'll set light to us. That's the sort they are. They're all worked up to it. What's it to them? They've got nothing to lose. Like wolves."

"Were the brothers there or what?"

"Hell knows! But there was more than one. I saw. . ."

"So what do we do? Keep quiet?"

"What on earth else can we do? Complain? Have some pity for your kids!"

Stepanida said nothing. She would have pity for her children, of course, but who would have pity on her? They had humiliated her and now she would have to abase herself, bear with what was unbearable, keep silent when something inside her was crying out. Could she do that?

All through that long windy night, behind the stove, she lay open-eyed and motionless, pondering. Her reflections were endless, gloomy and oppressive, filled with unanswerable questions. The world had got confused somehow, good and evil were mixed up, or one evil with another still greater. Or had something changed in her, snapped and crumbled into dust? There was a lot she didn't understand, but one thing she was intensely aware of: what was going on was wrong, it was inhuman and therefore something had to be done about it. Not just lie down, wait and be resigned - tomorrow she had to hurry off to the Settlement, the township, region, Polotsk, to get to the good people. The sight of Novik, who had demanded the dispossession just of Guzhov kept recurring to her. He hadn't said a word about the others. She hadn't voted against Guzh and had been very sorry for the old folk, but now after yesterday's encounter with Zmiter, her pity had evaporated. Let them be dispossessed and that wolf taken out of the village, so that no smell of him remained. There would be peace here once that happened.

But what about the others?

About them she couldn't think without heartache, especially remembering Anyuta Ladimirova, old Prokhorikha, and Kornila too. She had had a special relationship with Kornila for a long time past. It had almost led to their fates being joined. It had not turned out that way though. . .

She had just been a girl then, working for old man Yakimovsky. She lived in the Settlement and went over every day, getting up at the crack of dawn to run across the main road to the farm. She had to milk two cows and drive them out to pasture, make up the feed for the pigs and geese - there were a good many of these grazing the stubble on Golgotha. Old Yakimovsky practically never interfered in the running of the farm, just groaned to himself sitting on the parapet or behind the stove, while she got on with her own work. There were laborers on the farm apart from herself but they worked out in the fields and were no concern of hers. She had enough on her hands with the farmstead itself, the kitchen garden, the animals to keep her going winter and summer without a break. It was no picnic, but what could she do without land, without a dowry, a poor hanger-on in the harsh and almost landless family of her elder brother in the Settlement?

One day she had been late getting up and was running quickly along the dewy path through the potato patches towards the main road when she heard Kornila's voice raised in anger from his yard; the frisky Kornila cow was leaping about and not letting anyone get near her. Kornila had been widowed about a year with two sons to look after. He did all the womens' work about the house, not too skillfully, at times even clumsily, and the village wives used to make fun of him doing the washing or mixing the dough for baking. Some were openly sympathetic though. Stepanida halted, realizing that the cow wouldn't let herself be milked and Kornila was wasting his time running after her with his bucket, threatening and cajoling. Rather timidly Stepanida went through the gates and in her quiet voice gradually calmed the excited animal. Kornila fetched bread sprinkled with salt from the passage as Stepanida began milking. There wasn't much milk to be had and the job was soon done. She handed the bucket to its owner, smiling. Kornila, instead of taking it, advanced on her rather oddly. Here was a stocky powerful heavy-handed young man, shirt open across his chest and Stepanida was quite alarmed till she caught the complete helplessness, almost bewilderment, in his darkened eyes; she laughed as she repelled his arms.

"Now then, Kornilka, you're forgetting yourself."

This seemed to sober him up. He walked over to the fence and stood for a while with his back to her, barring the way out through the gate, however. She was rather disconcerted: what should she do? Turning to her again, he said in a sad hoarse voice:

"I could do with a wife like you. . ."

She laughed again.

"So send the matchmakers, that's the way. . ."

"And you would?" Kornila regarded her keenly.

"I'll think about it. I might. Don't know yet. . ."

In truth she didn't know, though she had nothing against him. Kornila was a hard worker, but he was a widower and two children as well. She was one of the girls. She hadn't picked out any of the boys yet and nobody had sought her in marriage. What should she do? For several months she waited, dreaming up various pictures, fantasizing, even getting to hate herself, and Kornila too. But Kornila never did send the matchmakers and after Lent fetched over an old maid from Kukhnali, and this Vandzia began looking after his household. Stepanida had a cry into her pillow and got over it, though she never forgot that little episode in his yard.

Perhaps this was God's punishment?

No, no, why should anyone be punished for a thing like that? And anyway why would Ladimir or old Prokhorikha be punished? Or the Guzhovs for that matter. . . Actually, if you thought about it, maybe everything had started with that Guzh. If he hadn't been pigheaded at the meeting and called on someone else, Novik probably wouldn't have come over and demanded his dispossession. Even that wouldn't have gone through if Goncharik hadn't voted for it and carried it. If Guzh hadn't been dispossessed, the paper wouldn't have carried those notes and then. . . they might not have touched the others.

But whose fault was it then? Guzh? Novik? Or Vasil's compliance? Surely one raised hand couldn't be the cause of it all? It was just terrible to think how much in one's life or other people's destinies sometimes depended on a word, an arm, someone's innocent glance even. Especially in times like these. How reasonable you had to be, even-tempered and fairminded! Spite against someone close at hand could fall back, ever so heavily, on yourself - and oh dear, how painful that was!

In the morning when she got up, Stepanida was shattered, worn out with thinking. The children had to be got ready for school, otherwise she wouldn't have got out of bed at all. Petroc could feed the piglet and the sheep, good job the cow hadn't calved yet, she didn't have to be milked. By the light of the oil-lamp she scraped a pot of potatoes and lit the stove. The children were still asleep, Fedka snuffling sweetly in the dawn light and Fenechka had quieted down too after tossing restlessly all night. Petroc had gone out into the yard, most likely to see to the animals. She had noticed him spending more time with the horse than he had ever done before, knowing that soon it would be time to part. They were loath to give up a good horse they'd only got the year before. . . She understood Petroc's feelings. Meanwhile the morning was advancing; the windows had turned blue and the hut was lit up by the glow from the stove; she was just about to blow out the lamp when there came a knock on the window. She thought at first it was Petroc, but no, the knock had been too quick and anxious, frightened even. Stepanida thought: if anything had happened, the master was about somewhere. She went over to the window and through the frosted and half-melted pane made out with some difficulty a female figure standing near the parapet.

"Aunty. . ." came the muffled voice, as if from the world beyond, and Stepanida recognized Anyutka. She hastened to open the passage door and Anyutka ran into the hut, stumbled onto the bench and spoke, crushed and inconsolable. Her black plush coat was unbuttoned, her kerchief had fallen round her neck and her loose blond plait lay across her shoulders. "Oh, aunty, we're in trouble. . ."

Stepanida had guessed already. Yesterday's meeting had made it clear enough what sort of trouble was in store for Ladimir, Anyutka and her grown-up brothers, and now Stepanida wanted to comfort her somehow. The young girl, however, suddenly stood up, stopped crying and, wiping the tears from her face, spoke up for herself.

"Oh, aunty, they came for Antip and Andrey in the night. The police came and arrested them, they searched everything, they were looking for Guzhov, Zmiter as well, but he was cleverer. Zmiter's hiding somewhere but they got our two and they've taken them off somewhere. . ."

"There, there, there," Stepanida repeated automatically, guessing what had happened. "Had they been with Guzh?"

"Oh, aunty, how do I know, but these past few days they've been missing. When Zmiter came for them they disappeared, didn't come home for two nights. But today. . . maybe you heard what happened on the high road last night? Oh, it's awful. They say somebody stopped Kosmachov, you know the one from Polotsk, and shot him. He was wounded, they say - good job his horse carried him off. It bolted and took him as far as the township. Well, the police turned out and I don't know what! During the night. . . They arrived just as my brothers got back. They'd just started taking their jackets off when - knock, knock, and them asking: where've you been? Home they say. Then they ask me. . . And what do I say, I don't know anything, do I?"

Stunned by what she had heard, Stepanida sat down on the bench, feeling how everything had got mixed up at once in her head as well as her heart. Little by little, however, she began to realize something frightful had taken place. She sensed also a vague link between this terrible event, what had been happening in the Settlement and yesterday's encounter in the pines. She looked silently at Anyutka, who had calmed down after her cry, and started straightening her kerchief. The significance of these extraordinary events was dawning upon her. The children were getting up behind the stove. Fedka had put his drawers on and peered out through the sacking, alarm on his sleepy face.

Anyutka meanwhile was talking away, wringing her hands in despair.

"I don't know what to do now! Father's crying, says: why do this in my old age? And when they took Andrey and Antip away, he really started beating his head on the floor, I got frightened and ran over here. What should I do now, aunty?"

What to do? If only she knew. Well, there was really nothing to do now. It was too late! After this it was certainly too late. There was no escape now. It gradually came to her what had happened in the pine wood when she had been running to the township and they had stopped her: they didn't want the three roubles - they had been WAITING. And she could have got in their way. But to go to such lengths, to dare to do that! And now. . . what would happen now?

16

Stepanida gradually calmed down and pulled herself together, though the sense of injustice continued to torment her and despite the fact that there was nothing she could do after the events of the night, something as yet unsaid and not fully acknowledged demanded elucidation, some outlet or acceptance, if only for her own peace of mind.

Now some distance from Ladimir's yard, she realized she was not heading towards Yakimovschina but to the other end of the Settlement; she did not change direction, however. Just ahead she noticed a familiar spot, once the site of their own hut, but where now four birch trees froze uninvitingly in the chill breeze; a row of cherry trees had put out thin branches on the farmstead verge. The hut had long since rotted away and its remains used for firewood, but the kitchen garden had passed to Bogatka, Demyan their neighbor, who had solicitously placed a neat birch fence around it. Stepanida didn't linger near their former dwelling; she trudged on further, past little huts, log walls, fences, street trees, all familiar down to the last detail. She skirted round the stout bole of the Melanins' maple, sticking out into the street, then descended the hill, continuing till she stumbled across the new fence near Avsiukova's hut, where the school was now and where she had so recently run three times a week to literacy classes. Fenya, Fedka and another thirty or so children attended here in four rows of desks, one class per row. Stepanida leaned her chest against the fence, her mind still working. Let the children study, maybe things would fall out better for them than it had for their parents: knowledge would bring them bread and a chance to make their mark in the big world, but it was over for her, she wouldn't be going to classes any more. After Anyutka went she couldn't sit at that desk on her own or even cross the school threshold. At the beginning of last autumn, Anyutka had talked her into going to classes, convincing her: it was a disgrace not to be able to read and write when the whole country was studying. She had tried very hard to excel in literacy herself and Stepanida knew why - before he was called up, Goncharik had reach form four in the township, Anyutka could hardly lag behind him. When she was a little girl she hadn't had the opportunity and at sixteen she'd had to take the place of her mother in the home; her mother had died of TB and her father hadn't married again. Antip and Andrey, her twin brothers, had been in no hurry to take wives; they'd looked around, dithered and now obviously they wouldn't be marrying at all.

When a joyous hubbub rose inside the school, Stepanida realized it was recess and moved herself away from the fence. There was no point standing there; she wandered away back along the street and up the hill. As she passed the psalm-singer's hut, she took it into her head to see Levon. He seemed to know something she didn't; he'd tell her something to reassure her. The village soviet hall, however, was deserted apart from a cloud of dust; this was Potap Kolondenok raking a balding broom across the floor with its filth of ages. She paused on the threshold.

"Levon hasn't been in?"

"No, he hasn't looked in."

Ignoring her, Kolondenok toiled away with his broom, sweeping dust and rubbish towards the door and she saw he was wearing some decent second-hand boots on his bluish, bare feet. They were not Levon's, however.

"Earned yourself some boots, have you?"

"Requisitioned," replied Potap in a thin voice, giving her a look of dislike through the rising dust cloud.

"Work away, you little sneak!" she said to herself, furious.

She walked along by the fence reflecting that here was a person, young and literate (even too much so - he'd got to the third or fourth form), always acting honestly as the times demanded, who got nothing but hostility from everyone in the village as a consequence. Here he was writing in the paper what was probably no more than the truth and what was the result? She hadn't enough words in her head to tell him what she felt, but she despised this taciturn youth who could hardly understand what he had accomplished by his diligent efforts, that much was certain. He was no Zmiter. One look at Zmiter and you could tell what he was capable of, but just try and guess what this goody-goody would do tomorrow. She recalled that even the village children left him out of their games, and though he was not malicious and didn't annoy anyone particularly, his peers gave him a wide berth. He was always by himself, alone whether in the village, on the way to school or out with the herds. When he was growing up, he began taking an interest in the complicated affairs of his elders, attending all the meetings, hanging about the village soviet from morning till night, listening open-mouthed, in silence. What was he thinking about though?. . .

"Oh, I wish you'd just drop to bits, wretched boy!" mumbled Stepanida in exasperation.

She had already passed the end huts of the Settlement and Ladimir's yard, lonely and deserted, was already visible, isolated, its gates wide open, when from somewhere behind Goncharik's hut there rose a woman's heartrending shriek. She shuddered and came to a stop in the middle of the street. From round the corner of the hut ran Ulyana, Vasil's mother; she was dishevelled and screaming wildly over and over again "People! People!" and frenziedly beating her breast with her fists. Seeing Stepanida, she rushed to her, still shouting something Stepanida couldn't grasp; it was clear something terrible had happened. Amid the weeping and lamentation, Ulyana kept pointing to the hut's bare windows, with their thick coating of ice. Stepanida ran towards it and from the yard she could hear the same appalling shrieking, this time from Ulyana's little son Yanochka. Stepanida rushed through the gaping doors into the passage and flung open the hut door, thinking Yanka had to be rescued from some kind of accident, but she couldn't make out at first where he was in the gloomy unfamiliar interior of the hut.

But she could see something else and for a moment froze in horror where she was.

By the window, slumped forward against the end of the bare table, Vasya Goncharik was sitting motionless, dressed just as he had been, in his Red Army uniform, greatcoat, belts; his fair tousled head had fallen unnaturally against his shoulder. The musty air of the hut bore clear and frightening witness to a recent shot and a pistol lay on the floor by the table; somewhere in the corner by the stove three-year-old Yanochka wept unceasingly. . . . . .

17

And so that autumn the ill-starred race of Settlement Gonchariks, few as
they had been, dwindled to nothing.

The youth's thin, puny body, his clothes tucked round his stomach, lay
beside a bench close to the fence. Petroc was stunned by the killing and
couldn't understand why the little dumb shepherd boy had turned up on
the farm that night. What had he wanted here? Petroc was literally speechless
and even stopped railing at life; fear held him tight. As indeed it did
Stepanida, sitting on her trestle-bed under the window.

The Germans had long ago worn themselves out, likely, and were sound
asleep in their tent; the sole exception was the sentry who stood near the
entrance or quietly patrolled the yard. When the window turned somewhat
gray, there came, as always, the rattling of pots and pans in the field kitchen
- Karl setting about his business. Petroc took note of these familiar sounds,
as he surfaced from oblivion half asleep. He had to get ready for fresh fears
and calamities - what else could a new day bring with it? However, no sooner
had he set his feet down from the bins and felt his dried-out boots than his
ears caught a distant, intermittent, thunderous roar from the direction of
the highway. Once upon a time motorcycles used to sound like that, but
there hadn't been any of them over there for a long time. The bridge must
be finished if there's motorbikes on the road, thought Petroc despondently.
The dense roar died away at intervals but at once got louder again, now
close at hand, by the limes it seemed, then abruptly cut out. Somebody
started talking to Karl, then to the sentry by the entrance; Petroc listened
with bated breath. There'd never been a motorbike here before, so this man
had rolled up from a good distance with an order of some kind, obviously -
perhaps heralding some change on the farm? It really did seem as if a
despatch-rider had arrived: there came a subdued knocking at the hut door,
where the officer was sleeping and after a pause it was opened and then
closed. The Germans' quiet conversation was barely audible in the boiler-
house. When they emerged, however, the sentry in the yard shouted something and the bustle around the tent began - Germans started stamping

about, bawling and sprinting around the yard. There seemed no particular panic about this, maybe they were just responding to an unusual command and hopping to it.

Petroc was glued to the window, very much wanting to see what else might happen. Stepanida, however, apparently indifferent to everything, sat on her mattress and leaned up against the log wall. Her eyes were closed, but the quivering of eyelids told Petroc she wasn't asleep and was, like him, keenly listening to events in the yard.

This time only two or three Germans took a hasty wash near the well, while the others left the tent in their greatcoats, and even carrying rifles; some had bags and haversacks and gathered near the field kitchen expectantly, chattering and smoking. It looked as if they had no idea of breakfast or work which prompted Petroc to a thought which made him tremble.

"Woman, I say woman, can you hear? They're leaving."

"Just wait, you'll see if they do."

"No, honest, they're going! Look, they're taking their odds and ends out of the tent. Over to the lorry. . ."

And they really were hauling boxes, bundles and clothing out of the tent and tossing them into the truck. A minute later, two soldiers pulled some pegs out of the ground, and the tent's taut hump sagged, wrinkled and collapsed on the ground.

"So-o, they're on their way, are they! Ai, thanks be to thee O Lord!" Petroc was seized with a sudden access of joy as Stepanida half-rose to peer outside. What she saw first was not at all what was enthusing Petroc.

"Just lying there. . . They might have covered him up. Like an animal. . . Beasts they are."

Of course she was referring to Yanka. But Petroc was afraid even to glance in that direction, beneath the fence where the youngster's thin body lay, now a matter of concern to nobody it seemed. Shot him and threw him aside. But why? Of course it was easy to kill a deaf mute - he wouldn't hear the sentry's shout and couldn't respond anyway. But why did they kill him? What harm had he done them?

He had supposed the Germans would take Yanka with them; if they'd killed him they must have had some purpose - they wouldn't have done it just for fun. However, they loaded their gear into the lorry without any of them going near the body. There was just one, middle-aged and heavily built in his greatcoat, haversack over his shoulder and rifle slung, who walked aside from the kitchen and looked towards the fence; it seemed to Petroc that he heaved a sigh as he moved back towards the lorry. Despite the departure preparations, Karl was continuing with his daily routine, pushing wood into the stove and stirring the copper where something was already boiling; the wind blew the steam across the palings into the fields. The steam prevented Petroc from seeing the cart which had approached the gate unseen and pulled up near the lorry. Guzh jumped down from it, rifle in hand, still wearing his ginger leather jacket.

At that very moment, the officer appeared from the passage in his oilskin coat and halted on the steps, surveying the yard with a possessive air. Guzh ran up to him, straightening clumsily as if at attention. 'He'll give him one!' thought Petroc maliciously, remembering yesterday's clash with the feld-webel. But it appeared that something had altered in the German relations with the polizei. The officer mildly looked about him. Petroc couldn't see his eyes from the window, shaded as they were by his broad peaked cap, but his expression seemed placid and good-tempered. Guzh was explaining something to which the officer listened, putting in the occasional "ja". Then he came closer to Guzh and raised his hand. Petroc again experienced a brief pang of gloating: he'll smack him one! But no, he didn't, he patted Guzh approvingly several times on the shoulder - Gut! Gut! - just as the feldwebel had patted Petroc the day before for his hard work in supplying the officer's latrine which, by all appearances they wouldn't be requiring any more. So, the polizei had earned praise for something, thought Petroc, and his elation began to ebb rapidly - Guzh's arrival promised nothing good. Especially after being praised by the officer. Now wait for trouble.

The Germans meanwhile had packed up their belongings in quick time, the last things being their white folding beds; now they began hooking their cumbersome kitchen onto the lorry. About five of them strained to roll it to the gates; as they turned it round, hot coals spilled from the firebox and everywhere smelled of smoke. Clouds of raw steam swirled in the wind over the yard. Guzh lent a hand as well, as Petroc stood by the window and thought: 'Bust a gut, go on but I'm not and I won't either unless they chase me out of course. I wish I'd never set eyes on you lot, brutes. Shot up the hens, ate the cow, killed that boy - what for? Is that the way human beings behave? If you're not afraid of men, you should fear God, he sees everything. He'll remind you of the crimes you committed in a country not your own.'

At last it was all over. The soldiers got into the lorry under the tarpaulin, the feldwebel ran round the yard for the last time and got into the cab. They had forgotten about the owner, thank God; they didn't say goodbye, so they can't have felt the need. Nor indeed did the owners. Bouncing heavily in the potholes, the vast lorry and its kitchen crawled towards the highway. Petroc felt like crossing himself from very relief when from under the limes a roan horse appeared, wrenching awkwardly at a cart in which polizei Kolondenok was tugging the reins. Guzh, at once assuming an air of brazen assurance in his movements, was already, boss-like, pointing out where it should park itself in the yard. Petroc spat at his feet in bitter exasperation.

"Hell's flames. . , The first are hardly out of sight, now these. . ."

But there was nothing for it, he couldn't sit it out in the boiler-house, he had to be out in the yard. "Well?" Guzh drilled him with a glance. "Working in with the bandits are we?"

"Me?" Petroc was taken aback.

"Yes, you. Who else? The German unit over there was out beating all night."

"Beating? And how was I supposed to know? I was there in the boiler-house. They saw me there."

"Saw you there?!" Guzh mocked and pointed towards the fence. "And this one? How did he get here?"

"Am I supposed to know?"

"You don't know?" Guzh shifted from foot to foot, swapping his rifle over. "Well, call your old woman!"

"Stepanida!" called Petroc and walked to one side.

Stepanida appeared from the passage, tied her kerchief under her chin and huddled into her jacket from the cold.

"You grazed cows with this one?" Guzh nodded towards the fence.

"Yes, so?" replied Stepanida, hiding her hands in her jacket sleeves.

"Did Kosmachov turn up? To see him in the alders?"

"What Kosmachov?" Stepanida raised her eyes.

"*The* Kosmachov! He's marching about the place. Stirring up partisan activity. I'll show him partisans."

"I never saw anybody. Nobody came round."

"Why did that one stop a bullet then?"

"How should I know?"

"You don't know, he doesn't know!" Guzh exploded and waved his rifle menacingly in the air, tossing it neatly from hand to hand. "Don't play dumb with me. I can see right through you. Especially you, activist. It was your hands on that little rifle wasn't it?" thundered Guzh piercing Stepanida with a ferocious glare. Stepanida held her breath, keeping her gaze fixed somewhere beneath the limes.

"Talk's easy," Petroc resolved to intervene. "But it's not right to accuse somebody without reason. We were sitting in that boiler-house over there. Under arrest more or less. If anything. . ."

The cart was standing in the yard and the roan dozed between the shafts, head drooping dismally; nearby polizei Kolondenok waited silently in his cross-belted greatcoat. As soon as Guzh turned towards the cart, however, he was all attention.

"Alright," said Guzh, "Leave it for now, there's no time. Let's get the boy on board," he said more calmly to Petroc as he made for the fence. Kolondenok threw the reins onto a pile of hay in the cart.

Suppressing the fear in his heart, Petroc timorously approached the youngster's outstretched body in its somber work-worn clothing. The head was thrown back and there was a dry spot of dirt, or it might have been blood, on the temple, not far from the ear. The brown suffusions on the earth-stained belly had also dried up. Petroc halted indecisively, not knowing where to get hold of the body. As he stood, Kolondenok seized Yanka by the bare, dirty ankles and hauled him indifferently, like a log, over to the cart. The boy's arms lolled wide and awkward while the head on the scrawny neck bobbed about as if it were alive. 'God! God!' Petroc was horrified as he trailed along behind. 'What are things coming to?'

"Grab hold, what're you waiting for?" barked Guzh from afar when they were both standing by the cart. He himself stayed out of the way and began rolling himself a cigar from a piece of newspaper.

Petroc and Kolondenok somehow lifted Yanka's rigid body over the side and into the cart, where Kolondenok sprinkled a light covering of hay over him, though it was still obvious there was a dead body there. Petroc thought the others would be on their way now and stood to one side out of the way. Guzh, however, burst out:

"You're going with us!"

"Where?"

"To work, that's where! You've had your sunshine holiday, now it's work time! Finishing off the bridge. Well, naturally! There's the township folk doing their stint every day and you playing the squire with the Germans."

'I hope you play the squire like that for the rest of your life, damned cutthroat,' thought Petroc despondently, knowing he would have to go all the same. That was something you couldn't get out of, especially after what had happened here on this farmstead. He should think himself lucky he was just being chased out to work and hadn't been arrested outright.

The polizei leapt into the cart as it moved off and Petroc walked behind, cursing in his heart. Kolondenok guided the horse, while Guzh sat behind with his legs dangling nearly to the ground, keeping an eye on Petroc, to see he didn't run away, no doubt. And where could he have run to? He'd spent half his life here, brought up two children, lived through so many anxieties, fears and sorrows and perhaps some joy too. Where could he clear off to? He was a weak sort of person, dependent; all his life he'd had to do what other people told him. They had the power, hadn't they, and what did he have? A pair of work-worn hands, rheumatism in the leg joints and sixty years on his shoulders, what could he put against their greedy will? Maybe you could hoodwink the Germans a bit but not this lot, they were their own folk and there was no tricking them. Stepanida's tricks with the Germans back then had very nearly got them into trouble. Better to be open and straight, no tricks.

On its way down to the highway, the cart skirted a large yellow pond and climbed up to the embankment as Petroc made his way along the path by the roadside ditch. The pine wood began soon after this, then came the bend in the road, then the bridge. To blazes with the blasted bridge, it was the cause of all these descents on Yakimovschina, thought Petroc. It had been fine when it was shattered by bombs and nobody had come here mounted or on foot. Now. . . now all hell would be let loose, that was certain.

But they didn't get to the bridge, didn't reach the bend even. Off to one side of the highway, in among the pines where the peasants of both Settlement and township used to dig out sand for their own use, stood three carts. A number of peasants were loading them up and taking their time about it. Kolondenok swerved onto the roadside verge and halted the horse and Guzh sprang down from the cart. The peasants ceased digging, first one then the rest doffed their caps uncertainly and stood still and silent before the polizei.

"Why so slow?" asked Guzh severely. "How many loads have you sent off?"

"Six, I think," said an aging man from inside the pit, his face thick with gray stubble.

Petroc recognized him as Ignat Dubasei from Zagriazye. At one time, before the collective farms, Dubasei used to deal in sheepskins and Petroc had gone to him about the very jacket he was wearing now. Shifting awkwardly from foot to foot, Petroc was in two minds over which was better, take his hat off or stand as he was. Finally, so as not to stand out from the others, he slid his cloth cap off on the sly.

"It should be twelve, blast your souls!" Guzh suddenly burst out savagely. "You've got to move yourselves, not loaf about, you're not under the Soviets now! You've had a few smoke breaks I dare say?"

"Yes, we. . ."

"No more breaks! The road's got to be sanded before dark. You!" he rapped at Kolondenok. "Jump down here and watch them. See nobody goes anywhere! Work I want, work!"

Kolondenok laid the reins in the cart and retrieved his long rifle from under the hay. Guzh took his place. He took a last look of hatred at the pit and the three silenced peasants inside; then he noticed Petroc on the roadside.

"You, Bogatka, give them a hand! And schnell, schnell, schnell! Alright?"

Guzh and the cart moved off towards the stream and one of the peasants swore under his breath. Another sighed deeply. Petroc descended into the pit down a crumbling slope and picked up a broken-handled spade which was sticking sideways out of the sand. The empty cart stood close above them. His rifle under his armpit, Kolondenok stood stiffly on sentry duty. His eyes had disappeared into his forehead it seemed, his thoughts far away from there.

They began hurling the sand aloft into the cart, very likely no faster than before. It was awkward work - the pit was pretty deep by now and they had excavated all the sand near the roadside and were digging further and further away. Petroc quickly warmed up, but soon began to tire; he felt a disagreeable burning sensation in his chest and slowed his pace before stopping altogether. He had barely drawn two steady breaths before Kolondenok appeared on the edge of the pit, quivering.

"Dig!"

"It's just. . . I'm worn out. . . Rest. . ."

"Dig!"

"It's just. . . Sonny. . ."

But 'sonny' had already seized his rifle and clicked the bolt, ready to let fly. Petroc was alarmed and his hands picked up the spade of their own accord; he slung a little sand into the cart and Kolondenok lowered the rifle. 'The rat!' thought Petroc. 'Why didn't his mother suffocate him when he was a baby? He's worse than Guzh. At least you can swear at Guzh, put your side. But the least thing and this one grabs his gun.'

After four loads, Petroc had trouble straightening up. The cart was moving out onto the high road and it seemed to be the last; there could be a bit of a rest. He had barely time to feel pleased when the sound of hooves came from around the bend and soon a new driver was backing his horse and wagon into a convenient position. It was Kornila from the Settlement, as always taciturn and frowning - not badly kitted-out though, his woollen waistcoat was barely worn. Recently he'd grown a shaggy black beard, quite the grandad, though he was five years younger than Petroc. For many a long year they hadn't spoken or said hello to each other, but spying Petroc in the pit, Kornila nodded slightly.

"Good day," and Petroc surprised himself by responding with pleasure: "Aha, morning. . .They chase you out, with the horse as well?"

"Well, we're pitching in," mumbled Kornila into his beard, taking a spade from the cart. "They're in a hurry, they need the bridge."

"Maybe they do, but as far as we're concerned that bridge can go up in a blue light. . ."

Kornila glanced swiftly at Petroc and sideways at Kolondenok, who was already paying heed to their conversation; he spoke loudly, doubtless for the benefit of the polizei:

"Have to help the German army, have to. 'Course we do."

Petroc said nothing, at a loss as to how to interpret these words. An observer would have said he spoke sincerely and meant what he said. But Petroc knew that Kornila was too wily a bird to be taken at face value. Whatever he said, he always had an unspoken meaning of his own. His secretiveness dated from the time ten years before when he had been excluded from the collective and dispossessed as a kulak. True, he hadn't been exiled and he'd started working in the township - first in an industrial workshop, then about four years in the fire service. As it turned out he did no worse than those in the collective farm, maybe better.

They dug on without drawing breath till noon, then past noon; carts kept moving back and forth from the bridge, conveniently near at hand. Those with the horses got a short break on the journey from the bridge, but the horseless Petroc and Dubasei didn't get a minute's rest and thought they would drop from exhaustion. Ignat at least was lightly dressed, only wearing his old kaftan but Petroc in his sheepskin was soon sweating like a pig and thought: I won't escape pneumonia this time. He'd contracted pneumonia once after catching cold on the tree felling, when they were hauling logs from the forest and the sleigh had broken down; he'd had to put his back into it and work his guts out. Three days later he'd fallen into a fever among strangers in the village where the lumbermen were billeted; he never thought he'd pull through. Maybe he wouldn't if they hadn't got him to hospital. Once there and improved, he'd been almost glad to be ill and not have to go out: just lie there in the warm with decent food provided, treated decently, not like in the forest, out in the frost with the horses, inadequate clothing and bast shoes perpetually wet. There'd been timber felling every winter these last few years, supplying shaft supports to the Donbas mines, and he'd been really lucky to fall ill when he did. He did stagger about from weakness for a long time afterwards, but he was younger then and recovered himself bit by bit; spring saw him properly put to rights. But there were doctors then, and hospitals - and now? If you were ill who would cure you? That half-wit Kolondenok would drive over and shoot you and tell you you'd sinned against Germany.

Ignat Dubasei doing his bit of digging alongside, kept on grumbling to himself in the pit, and Petroc lent an ear: the old man was moaning on that they'd forced somebody of his age to come here when others were left untouched to stay at home. Petroc, somewhat surprised, asked him why.

"Heh, why? They poured moonshine down that rat's neck, that's why. Moonshine's power these days."

Petroc was already aware that illicit vodka meant influence and silently agreed with the old chap. There was a knack to everything though, some could produce good moonshine and others couldn't. You had to have the equipment, that was the thing.

"My gear's bust, damn and blast it. Where can you get stuff nowadays? A coil, say," Petroc lamented and fell silent, secretly hoping for an answer.

"Ha, gear! There's our Timka Rukati yonder; before the war he could fix up the devil himself if you gave him enough cash. I don't know about now. What would he do with money now?. . ."

"Is that the hut by the elm? On the edge away from here? There's a stork's nest there as well, isn't there?. . ."

"That's the one, near the stork. Nice hut. Shingles."

Petroc would have liked him to be more specific but Kolondenok had overheard their talk from above and his thin voice squealed:

"No talking! Dig!"

"We're digging, so we are. Get. . ." muttered Dubasei quietly; then aloud and more politely, addressed the polizei: "Sonny, call of nature. . . in the woods, eh?"

"Dig!"

"I have to, Sonny. . ."

"In the pit."

"What d'you mean the pit? I'm not an animal, am I. . . I have to. . ."

But Kolondenok appeared to have gone deaf; he rolled up his eyes and seemed to see nothing around him. The old man stuck his spade in the sand and with an anguished grimace on his stubbly face started crawling up the slope out of the pit to where the young pines were growing on the hillock.

"Back!" squealed Kolondenok from the road, but Dubasei had already reached the pines and from below Petroc could see only his head in its shaggy black cap. Suddenly the cap flew up oddly to be followed at once by the echoing crack of a rifle shot from the road; Kolondenok, slender legs wide apart, was reloading his weapon. "Back!"

Old Dubasei slid backwards down the slope, bringing the sand cascading down; Petroc was horrified to think he had been killed. But no, it seemed he was alive, though capless and pale with fear. Crawling to the bottom, he began feebly rising to his feet.

"Dig! Quick! Schnell!" squealed the polizei from the road, holding his rifle in both hands.

With unseeing eyes filled with tears, Dubasei looked round the pit, blindly poking about with his spade.

"Good God, God almighty!" his lips whispered. "What's it come to, eh? What's happened, eh? I was a friend of his father's, I was. We were called up together. His father was a real man. . ."

'The little snake,' thought Petroc wearily sticking his spade in the sand. 'Why didn't some disease carry him off when he was a kid? So many good men gone the journey and this one still alive and chucking his weight about. There's no justice in this world. . .'

Petroc could hardly remember him as a child; he seemed just like the rest as a kid but once he started school, there began to be talk about him in the village. That was when he got beaten up by the youngest Lukashonok, who found him up in the loft with a stolen salami under his shirt. Just before Christmas word had gone round the village that meat and suchlike was disappearing from peoples' lofts; at first they pointed the finger at Kornila's lazy old cat and even tried to kill it with a fence post. They would have succeeded too if it hadn't climbed up to the very top of the maple and sat there till evening. In the morning it was discovered that the cat had nothing to do with it; it was the ten-year-old Potapka Kolondenok scouting through the village lofts on a regular basis. He'd got it in the neck from the powerful and furious Lukashonok and was in hospital for a week. When he got out, he stopped going to school and kept away from people for a good long time. As time went by, however, people forgot about Potapka's boyish transgression; Potap though did not, seemingly, and was now revenging himself on others for his own escapade.

Kolondenok permitted them no smoking and no rest: the carts kept coming, and they kept on digging and digging. The pit was now man-deep and it needed a good swing to reach the cart; arms were failing to respond. Dubasei was working without a cap and the wind toyed with the white fluff of his scalp; the old man's eyes were filled with tears which he wiped away on the sly with his horny hand. Up aloft on the road, Kolondenok stood ramrod-stiff. He was obviously cold and had shoved his hands in his pockets; the skirts of his greatcoat were flapping around his boots in the wind, but the polizei retreated not one inch from the pit.

Still, somehow they lasted out till evening, though they were exhausted to the last degree and had lost count of the number of loads they had filled. When evening came on and twilight was gathering down in the pit, Guzh arrived on the road. His ginger jacket was open across the chest and his face was deeply flushed. There was a wolfish gleam in his eyes - sure sign of liquor.

"Genug, loafers! Genug for today! Tomorrow the order is - either here or potato picking. Dismiss!"

On the command, Petroc's knees gave way and he collapsed against the sandy slope where he stood, totally exhausted, wasted after a whole day working without food. Dubasei began crawling out of the pit and barely made it to the pines and his bullet-holed cap. Petroc too clambered out after an interval.

It was already dark and his overheated body cooled quickly in the wind. Petroc bent low and made the best of his way home via the high road. He realized that if this was to go on, he couldn't reckon on living much longer; he would have to knuckle under and the sooner, perhaps, the better. He was afraid of dying though and wanted to live for a bit longer, if only to be around to see these people get the Russian boot up the backside, watch them howl. That time would come, surely. It had to come, it mustn't be otherwise. Pity he mightn't live to see it. . .

It was pitch black when he dragged himself into the frozen farmyard, stumbled into the passage and didn't know whether to go into the hut or the boiler-house. But the hut door swung open of its own accord and as he saw Stepanida he crossed the threshold. Inside everything had been tidied up and stood in its former place, as it had been before the Germans came. The stove was going and the cracks round the lid glowed brightly; it was warm. Petroc subsided, just as he was in his sheepskin, onto the bench opposite the stove.

Stepanida said something about eating, but he had got past being hungry and had stopped thinking about food altogether. His body yearned for just one thing - to collapse and lie down in the unlooked-for warmth of his own hut; but he couldn't allow himself that luxury. . . He had realized that day down in the pit that you had to give thought to the morrow if you wanted to survive for a while and see better times.

"Bring the violin," he said to his wife in a faint voice.

"Violin, why? You going to play?"

"My playing days are over. . ."

He said no more and she went into the boiler-house with a lighted splinter, returning shortly with the violin and bow. Again saying nothing to his wife, Petroc went out with it into the yard and took the path across the garden, before shinning over the wall and heading in the direction of the gully.

Further on he had to skirt a field and find his way across the end of the gully. Beyond Sheep Valley, over by the forest, lay Zagriazye where Timka Rukati, the man who could fix you up anything you wanted for money, lived in the hut under the elm tree.

18

Fate or chance had given her a breathing space, shifted the worst to one side as it were, allowing Stepanida to take heart. There had been moments when she had already bidden life goodby and only regretted having been too timid to inflict more damage on the Germans. What she had plucked up courage to do hadn't always turned out right; things had been stupidly bungled. She'd lost Bobovka out of stupidity; the hens had been lost because of her lack of foresight and it had probably been her fault that Yanka had met his end. If she'd had more sense, she'd have got it through to the lad somehow that he shouldn't come near the farm. Still what could you do when the right idea usually came too late to be useful?

However that might be, life went on and she had to find something to eat today and give some thought to the morrow beyond surviving till evening. The cold weather was coming; the autumn skies were closing in day after drizzling day and the potatoes lay in a pile at the end of the garden. Petroc had still not managed to get around to that, so after a pause for thought, Stepanida got hold of the spade. It wasn't all that much of a job, though it was always reckoned man's work, clamping up two cart-loads of potatoes. Stepanida levelled out the heap, raked them together, packed them tightly round with straw and began covering them with soil.

She had no other worries on the farmstead. They had gradually got six hens back in the coop - the Germans must have eaten the others. Yesterday morning, as soon as the polizei had cleared out of the yard taking Petroc with them, she made it her first task to run to the gully and find her starving piglet in the badger's lair; he was so glad to see her that he rushed at her legs forgetting all about how hungry he was when she scratched his thin hollow stomach. He hadn't made any noise all the time she led him out of the gully; then he jogged along the path to the farm and with considerable reluctance slid once more into his cramped little pen. Then she gave him a fine meal of potatoes, not grudging the extras; after drinking a whole pot full of water, he settled down.

Earthing up the clamp wasn't hard, though Petroc might have done it quicker. He, however, had been busy since morning on another matter. Up before dawn, he'd spent a long time clanging about with distilling gear before disappearing somewhere. On his return he picked up his buckets, yokes and whatnot and started transferring his mash. She thought he was going to set up in the boiler-house or maybe the barn, but he took himself off even further, not telling her where. When he'd got it all fixed up, however, he came to beg a match. His voice had become quite hoarse and he looked tired, more exhausted than he had been for a long time. She gave him two matches and told him not to stay out in the cold too long; it was chilly and damp out in the yard, it would get to his chest and then what use would his moonshine be?

"Ah, to hell with it," Petroc waved this aside wearily. "What's it matter now. . ."

Stepanida started earthing up one side of the clamp, slapping it down with a spade as she levelled the layer of soil on top of the straw. All this time, whatever she had been busy with- household chores or seeing to the pig - she couldn't stop thinking about Yanka. She now bitterly regretted having met him that evening near the gully; he could have grazed somewhere in the thickets, why did he have to come near the farm? It seemed some evil power had drawn him to the danger which resulted in his death. Stepanida couldn't rid herself of the grim sense of having been involved in his destruction in some way, though she realized that what she had done with the rifle had affected no one but herself - not even Petroc. She saw no link there with Yanka. She could make a guess at what had drawn the youngster to the gully at night - most probably he had been on his way to the badger's lair - but why so close to the farm? Couldn't he have approached from the other end of the gully? Couldn't he really see how things might turn out for him?

She hadn't finished the clamp when she heard a voice from the yard calling for her. There was no need to guess who it could be at this hour; it was the same spiteful brutes again. Tensed up inside and ready for the worst, Stepanida stuck her spade in the earth and went through the garden to the woodpile.

She had not been mistaken. On the very spot where the German field kitchen had stood, there was now a cart with the familiar droop-headed horse between the shafts, and Guzh and Kolondenok shouting her name and peering in at the windows. Close by the cart, with an expression of bored indifference on his swarthy face, stood polizei Antos Nedoseka, his rifle slung on his shoulder.

"Ah, there she is!" said Guzh, catching sight of Stepanida. "Where's Petroc?"

"You mean he's not here? Then I don't know," she lied, realizing at once that this visitation was not on her account. They were after the master of the farm.

"Open the doors!" ordered Guzh, but got in before her, lifted the latch and slammed the door wide. While she was catching them up, Guzh had looked inside the boiler-house, glanced around the passage, even sniffed at something with his broad fleshy nose and then swiftly rushed into the hut. In there he began by peering out of all four windows.

"Where's Petroc?"

"I said I don't know. I'm busy with the potato clamp yonder."

"So, you don't know? Well we do - he's making vodka! Where's he doing it?" Guzh was suddenly alert and turning towards her so as to blot out all light from the windows. She didn't try to talk him out of it or swear she didn't know where Petroc was. She said quietly:

"He didn't tell me."

Guzh pondered, then his broad jaw snapped, wolf-like.

"Alright, bitch, I'll see to you later! I'll hang you at last. With great pleasure. I'll enjoy that!"

"And what would that be for?" she inquired coolly, keeping her eyes lowered and staying by the door. Her jaws also had tightened of their own accord, but she gave no hint of this and continued to regard the floor. They had trampled relentlessly over it in their filthy boots, just when she had cleaned it after the Germans. Still she didn't care about the floor; what she wanted very much was to answer this German bootlicker in his own coin. She repeated sharply: "What for!"

"You know what for! You!" he barked to his henchmen. "Just you have a poke around the farmstead. He's at it somewhere around here."

Kolondenok and Nedoseka surged out of the door as Guzh sat himself down at the table, fixing Stepanida with a menacing glare.

"You know you should be hanged as a bolshevik activist, don't you? And still got plenty to say for yourself! What do you expect to get by that?"

"I don't expect to get anything by it. I'm just an ignorant woman!"

"Oh, an ignorant woman, eh? And who organized the collective farms? Who chased the wives into the reading hut? Ignorant woman! And the dispossession?"

"You won't forget that of course," she said pensively, leaning up against the stove. She was in control of herself and met the polizei's gaze boldly.

"No, I won't! Till my dying day I won't. And I'm going to remind a few others. Pity Levon's not here. I'd make it hot for him!. Dragged the boots off my father!"

"Best to forget about that now," said Stepanida, after a silence. "Best for you. You wouldn't be so worked-up."

"Sod that! I won't forget. And I won't forget whose kindness sent me to far away places to try and keep body and soul together. Why d'you think I worked my way back here?" said Guzh in a tense, almost uncontrollable rage. "You don't think it was to do the Germans a favor, do you? To blazes with them. I've got some scores of my own to settle. Those collective laddies, damn and blast them! Living off the fat of the land while my dad was dying in Solovki camp!"

"Fat of the land indeed! We worked. . ."

"For matchsticks!" Guzh guessed. "Serves you right! Why a collective farm? You egged them on to join, didn't you?"

"That wasn't hard. You know that surely?"

"So what the hell did they join up for, if they didn't know anything about it? Land of plenty, eh? Now they've filled their bellies on matchsticks, have they seen sense?"

"They saw sense then. But having too little land's no better. How could you live on five acres with a family?"

"Was it any better on fifteen hundred? Five acres wasn't enough for them! Now, see, the Germans give you as much land as you want. Up to thirty hectares. To those who earn it, naturally. Earn it with the German authorities."

"They'll certainly give it to you. You've earned it!"

"Me? What would I want with land? I've detested it since I was a boy. To hell with it."

"What're you putting in all the effort for then?"

"Oh, no flies on you I see! Have to know everything! Let's say just for the power they've given me. Power! All my life I've been ordered about, helpless. Couldn't do anything. Now I've got power! Complete. For your lot I'm higher than the village council. Higher than the district council, than the People's Commissars even. I can shoot anyone I like. Everything's delegated to me. I can dish out rewards as well. What do you need? The cow the Germans guzzled? There'll be one! I'll bring it tomorrow! A pig? Same thing. No horse? I'll drive two over from the Settlement tomorrow. I'll choose them from somebody's stock and fetch them. Didn't think I could, did you?"

"We don't need somebody else's."

"I'm not giving you them! You're an enemy, aren't you? An enemy of Germany. You think I don't know whose hands were on that little rifle? Those Germans were idiots thinking it was the dumb kid did it. I agreed with them:

let it go! But me, I'm thinking. I'm thinking of you, Stepanida. I'll have a little hunt round here. In a certain place. You know where!"

He practically shouted as he stared at her, hard and merciless. She was disconcerted, for the first time during the encounter. Surely he hadn't sniffed it out, had he, German jackal?! But her mind was disturbed; it looked as if he'd found something out - either he'd had a look himself or someone had tipped him off. Her reason told her that he couldn't know anything. Was he just scaring her? Testing her? Maybe, but it was nasty whatever it was.

"Petroc now, he's cleverer than you," said Guzh after a calming pause. He leapt to his feet. "Taken up distilling. Good thinking. Just don't let him think he can keep it from me. I'll screw his head off and say he was born that way. He swapped a fiddle for a coil and thinks he can keep it a secret. Won't work, I've got my agents!"

There came the sound of footsteps in the passage and long-legged Kolondenok strode across the threshold, accompanied by the stocky, broad-shouldered Nedoseka.

"Well?"

"He isn't nowhere!" squeaked Kolondenok.

Nedoseka assumed a deeply worried expression and started elucidating, with gestures:

"We've been all through the place. In the grainshed, in the cowsheds. No sign. Who knows where he's got to?.."

"Like hell you've been through it!" Guzh interrupted. "Well, alright. There's no time now, otherwise. . ."

He glanced quickly through all the windows and grabbed his rifle.

"Nedoska, you're on guard! Sit and wait! He'll turn up, he can't get away anywhere." "Her," he nodded towards Stepanida, "no step outside. When he comes, the moonshine to me. Understood?"

"Yes, well," said the polizei hesitantly.

"That's it then! Let's go, Potap! And you remember what I said," was his parting remark to Stepanida. "Before it's too late."

She stood and looked out of the window as they turned the cart and jumped aboard as it was moving out of the gate. Only then did she tear herself away to look at the silent figure of Nedoseka, standing patiently by the door.

"Sit down. What's the point of standing."

"Aha, It's. . . I will. Anyway my legs are my own, not official."

Nedoseka demurely slid down onto the bench and sighed. Both hands leaned on the muzzle of his rifle, whose woodwork was much the worse for wear.

"Were they after vodka or what?" Stepanida asked.

Nedoseka registered genuine puzzlement on his good-natured, rather attractive face with its level brows.

"Who the devil knows? He's the one. Either it's vodka or it's something else. Doesn't tell us."

"He really never says?"

"Na-a," Nedoseka blinked, round-eyed. "Well, when we were smoking the Yids out, he told us then. He gave detailed instructions: how many cartridges to take and where everybody had to stand. Some in the cordon, I mean, and some taking care of their stuff."

"Where did they go?"

"Drove them out. Zondercommando drove them out to the quarry. There. . ."

"All of them?" Stepanida hung on his words, feeling an inner chill.

"You can reckon the lot. Not many left."

'There it is then, they've met their end!' thought Stepanida with something approaching horror. She had heard towards the end of summer people saying that the Germans had driven all the Township Jews into three streets specially marked off down by the river. Some of them said: oi, it's only temporary, they'll beat us up anyway if we don't, better run over there. Others argued that they wouldn't be killed; the Germans were people, they believed in God - it was written on their belt buckles. The clever talkers were very plausible and people paid heed to them. When you want to believe something, you'll always find a reason for it to convince yourself, then others. Or vice versa. So they'd sat it out till the quarry.

"So many people dying for nothing and nobody lays a finger on that swine. It's your mate I'm talking about, Kolondenok. He was a sod before, now he's one ten times over," said Stepanida.

"Sod's right," agreed Nedoseka simply. "Guzh wanted to smash him at first. Came to his hut one night, put me on guard. Well, they had a talk and took a fancy to each other. Next day he even gave him a rifle. That's the way of it."

"A quick way it is too. He hadn't even taken his Red Army uniform off. Birds of a feather. . ."

"What I think: what else could he do? Everybody round here detested him from way back. What could he do but join the police?"

"Just the police, that's true enough," Stepanida confirmed. "Direct road. And what brought you in? Or did you just like them?" asked Stepanida, emboldened.

"Get away!" Nedoseka avowed artlessly. "Who could?"

He sighed sadly and quietly scraped at the floor with his rifle butt.

"I thought you must, as you're so keen."

"You've got to! Yesterday on the bridge, the German bossman yelled at him, at Guzh I mean. And Guzh threatened to shoot me. I'd missed one of the Zagriazye peasants doing off in his cart."

"There's time for that yet," she said. "If that's the way you go on. Or our people will."

"Maybe they will," Nedoseka agreed. "But what can you do? I've had it," he concluded, then suddenly asked: "Could you let us have something to eat, Aunty? Haven't had a bite all day."

Stepanida was astonished: a polizei asking for something - not something you heard often nowadays. Guzh of course wouldn't have bothered asking, but this one came straight out with it, like a lamb. She had a pot of cabbage soup in the stove for Petroc, but after some thought she opened the door and took it out.

"Why didn't you have breakfast today, then?"

"Oh, there wasn't time. Guzh got us up in the night, job on. Looking for a bomb. Hell knows where that is. . ."

"What bomb?"

"The one lying by the bridge after the raid. Didn't explode. Somebody towed it away. Apparently it was wanted."

"So they towed it away, so what?"

"Ah but suppose somebody put it under the bridge? Whoosh! Then who'd be responsible? The police. Oversight."

She poured out a bowl of cabbage soup and put a piece of bread on the table. The rifle was obviously in his way, so Nedoseka leaned it up against the stove and started tucking in to his soup-mixed with bacon-fat. Gradually he warmed up and unbuttoned his grey woollen waistcoat. He kept his cap on; his face was animated in a homely sort of way, clearing like that of a young man. Stepanida stole a glance at him and recalled his brother-in-law in the township. Antos had moved into his hut before the war. The brother-in-law hadn't lived in the hut for ages; after the civil war he'd stayed in the army and served all the prewar years on the Japanese front, where he was an officer. Sometimes Nedoseka, not without pride, would show the peasants his letters and photographs with two red collar tabs, indicating senior rank. Of course they envied Antos, especially as his relative would send a hundred or two now and again before feast days - for a large family of children that was very handy indeed.

"I've just remembered your brother-in-law," said Stepanida, catching Nedoseka's quizzical look.

"Brother-in-law? What about him? He's doing alright, but what about me. . . It was because of him I got dragged into all this. . ." He shifted his elbow with the armband on the sleeve. "All because of him."

"Who forced you?"

"Guzh, that's who! What could I do, then? Just lie down and die? With him as a brother-in-law. . . Once it was honor and respect. Now the only safe thing is the police."

"I doubt you won't save yourself."

"Maybe not. Who knows? If a man knew what was coming to him, but he doesn't, does he?"

"Maybe it's for the best," said Stepanida. "Otherwise there'd be such doings. . ."

She was standing by the stove, looking out of the window at the same time to see whether Petroc was coming and beginning to feel sorry for this whining polizei. He really had got himself into something with no safe road out.

"Have you hanged anybody yet?" she asked.

"Na-a. Not yet. God forbid, horrible!"

"What if they tell you to?"

"If they do, well, I'll just have to!"

"Your own kin as well?"

"Why my own kin? Na-a. Just communists. Bandits as well."

"And what would your brother-in-law say to you? If he came in now? You thought of that?"

"Yes, I have. He'd say nothing good."

"Well, and what if they captured him and ordered you to hang him? Would you hang your own brother-in-law?"

"You're a funny one, aunty! No idea of discipline. They order it and you do it. Otherwise they hang you."

"And you've got children."

"That's the whole point, the children. If it wasn't for them I'd - oh! I'd light out for the forest. But with six children you're tied."

"There you are then, you're doing your best for your children. And you think when they grow up and start thinking for themselves they'll thank you for it?"

"Who knows? Depends which," Nedoseka laid down his spoon, confused.

"They'll curse you for the rest of their lives."

"What d'you mean curse?" Nedoseka blinked in bewilderment. "It's for them, isn't it. . . I'm suffering because of them, doing all this."

"Antoska!" she surprised herself by saying, almost solicitously, touched by the obtuseness of the man. "You'd do better to die for them."

"Me?"

"Yes, you, Antoska! You're ruining their whole lives for them. And yourself first and foremost."

"No, no, there I can't agree," said Nedoseka, offended. "Maybe I am doing for myself, but them na-a. What would they be eating now if it wasn't for me? I fetched them two sacks of flour. Three pairs of boots. Little coats. I'm not like some I know - just getting drunk. I take care of them. Six, after all, no joke. Eldest only fifteen. . . easy for you to talk, aunty, but for me. . . And my brother-in-law as well. Ach, if it wasn't for my brother-in-law. . ."

Stepanida made no further objection, just listened to his incoherent explanations, thinking what a fool he was and maybe a scoundrel as well. Her sympathy for him had rapidly given way to anger: life taught such people nothing, they understood nothing about it because it was not granted to them to see further than their trough. People like that were naturally blind to the least glimmer of humanity, thinking only of themselves, sometimes using children to justify their conduct. Lord, what could be expected of such children, what would they inherit from fathers like these? Better if he was shot straightaway, there'd be less harm done and more benefit to his own people. And his own children too, that he kept so tenderly supplied with flour and footwear. . .

19

Petroc was making vodka.

He had selected the most secluded nook to be found in the vicinity of the farm - a shallow, twisting, little gully beyond the badger lair. It was thickly overgrown with young firs and inside it was still, hushed and secret. He had set up his uncomplicated equipment in a small narrow clearing among the trees: kettle of mash, tub of icy cold water from the stream, then a long job maneuvering the copper coil into place before he laid his small fire. The dry kindling readily caught light from his carefully shielded match, igniting in turn the small birch logs, an armful of which he'd prudently fetched from the farm; greedy flames began licking playfully round the old, smoke-grimed kettle. The dry wood gave off little smoke and Petroc for the first time that morning felt pleased as he looked up into the frowning autumn sky above the pine tops, thinking that he would hardly be noticed from a distance, unless someone stumbled across the clearing by chance. The wood swiftly took hold. Petroc, on his knees in front of the kettle, anxiously adjusted the sticks to get a good blaze going underneath. He warmed himself too, because although the weather was still, a forest dampness crept up from the stream below, chilling his hands and knees. It was pleasant by the fire, though he had to make sure he damped it down at the right time, otherwise the mash would be burnt and the whole batch spoiled. Of course, this wasn't the first time in his life that Petroc had undertaken a job like this, he'd had some experience. But that had been in the long-ago days before collectivization. In recent times, before the war broke out, there hadn't been much illicit liquor made, people were more worried about getting enough to eat. There, the kettle was warming up slowly; out in the woods wasn't the same as in the barn or the boiler-house, where everything would be to hand, but there was no doing it there nowadays.

For the hundredth time over the last few days, Petroc bewailed the fact that the farm was in such an awkward place, so close to the road. In peacetime it wasn't so bad, convenient even, being near the main road, village and township, but in these last prewar years that convenience had seemingly come to an end: they'd started incorporating farms into the village. The street of farm buildings in the Settlement had at once extended and this summer had been the turn of his own Yakimovschina. They'd already dismantled the threshing floor and hauled it away; after the hay harvest they had been going to dismantle the whole farm. The war had put an end to that and now he could only envy those who were inside the village fold and not out on a limb like he was. Although there were places even now where people lived in clover as they had before. Zagriazye yonder for instance. It wasn't far from the township either but tucked away behind its swamp it kept clear of trouble; even Guzh didn't come all that often and they'd never seen any Germans at all. Then think of Yakimovschina. The Germans had stayed for a few days and ruined the whole farm you could say. Well, never mind that, worse had happened - they'd killed the youngster, a harmless orphan lad, not to mention Stepanida and him barely getting away with their lives. So much for the Germans, they'd come and gone, but the problem was with Guzh; he could see right through you and harbored a grudge from the past as well. He was barking up the wrong tree with Stepanida though, she had nothing to do with it; she'd actually been against the dispossession. Still he'd latched himself on, comes riding in driving people to work; he'd stick close in the future as well most likely, till he'd finished Petroc off completely; inhuman bastard, like some savage dog on a chain. Now, blast it, Petroc didn't grudge either grain or effort just as long as he could fill up that insatiable throat with illicit booze.

Good God, thought Petroc, gazing at the frisking dance of the flames along the kettle, what had the world come to? This terrible war which had started with such horrors, and what lay ahead? Terrible times! Before the war had been bad enough, struggling against this or that. Petroc had only a vague idea of the complexities of the nationwide struggle, but as regards his own village, he understood more than any bigwig deputies. They used to enjoy Antos Nedoseka's speeches in the assembly, probably thought he was very class-conscious! But Petroc knew his class-consciousness was based on the fact that he'd recently put in an application for assistance to be given to those with large families as well as landless folk. That's why he was so keen. And if Boris Bogatka voted for the collective, that didn't mean at all he wanted it organized there and then, he just wanted to spite Guzh, who'd been his enemy for long enough and feared the collective farm like the devil fears incense. Even his Stepanida, though she was always on about a new life for the whole village, was more concerned about herself, when you came down to it; and for him, of course, since she'd come to the conclusion that it was impossible to live on five acres, and you'd ruin your health for certain. But the way things had turned out, Boris had run off to his Leningrad relations straightaway, Guzh had been dispossessed as a kulak and sent into exile, and now Petroc Bogatka had to answer for everything and everybody because his wife had once been on the poverty committee and had been in the presidium at meetings. He hoped those sessions wouldn't weigh in the balance against her now.

Petroc prodded two sticks under the kettle and added a birch log at the side, thinking it would soon start precipitating. The copper liter jug had been waiting for a long time under the tube end, but it was still dry as yet; not a single drop had issued from the coil. Petroc glanced up again. A magpie in the fir saplings on the lip of the gully was fidgeting about, fussed and anxious, continuously twittering about something; Petroc pricked up his ears - was someone creeping up the gully? Or perhaps the bird was disturbed by him? Still, just to be sure and for his own peace of mind, he stood up and took a look through the trees. It didn't seem as if anybody was close at hand. The magpie was still agitated though, coming closer, then circling the glade and squawking her unceasing alarm. Bending down, Petroc crawled through a clump of firs and down by the stream saw Rudka, the shepherd boy Yanka's well-known dog. Now masterless, Rudka was obviously doing the rounds of the area and had been attracted by the fire. On seeing Petroc, he wagged his tail vigorously, without taking his pleased but questioning gaze off the man.

"Well, then? What're you standing there for? Come here," Petroc called to him softly and the dog pushed his way obediently through the pines to bound out into the clearing. He didn't come near the fire though, but sat down some way off. "What, you're hungry? I've got nothing. There'll be something to drink, but not to eat." Petroc conversed gladly with him, as if he were human. Rudka, however, having made contact with an acquaintance seemed inclined to leave it at that and laying his head on his dirty paws gazed wearily at the fire.

And now the great moment was approaching when the first drops would fall from the tube to the bottom of the copper jug with a triumphant clink. Petroc at once raked out the unburned sticks from beneath the kettle; the embers with their feeble blue fire would suffice - there was no need for flames now. Meanwhile the droplets were falling ever faster from the tube as if a tiny threadlike stream had begun trickling down; a pleasant smell of spirit rose amid the acrid smoke in the clearing. From now on the fire had to be tended especially carefully, holding it steady so that the kettle didn't cool down, but didn't overheat either and burn the contents. The skill needed here was no less than in playing the violin. Petroc was even getting excited as he alternately pushed burning brands under the kettle and withdrew them; the smoke made his eyes water and he wiped away the tears with his toilworn fingers and kept glancing at the jug: was there much there?

At last the level rose to halfway and he carefully tipped out the liquid, clear as tears, into an old lemonade bottle. This was the first and strongest part of the batch He began to begrudge pouring it down Guzh's insatiable throat; happen he'd keep it for himself or some worthy recipient. Ruminating about this, Petroc stoppered the bottle with a screw of paper and went over to the wild roses at the edge of the clearing. There he dug a small cavity and placed the bottle inside before carefully earthing it in and covering it with dead leaves. It could wait there for better days.

Rudka, keeping his eyes fixed on Petroc and his doings round the fire, watched him lifting the jug with an expectant look, waiting for his share. There was nothing to give the dog, however, Petroc was hungry himself after his efforts with the kettle of mash.

There was enough for three more bottles before a rusty sort of mush emerged, no doubt there was only residue left in the kettle. It was time to make an end and Petroc stamped his old boots about scattering the embers; he hauled the kettle away into the rosebushes and carefully concealed it with leaves and several pine boughs on top of that. The coil, as the most valuable part of the apparatus, he had to take with him, the tub as well. He stowed the three bottles of liquor, still muddy and warm, around his pockets and under his coat. Finally, he lit up a cigarette from the embers and made his leisurely way back to the path.

As he walked, following the stream along the gully, Rudka ran along behind, but hung back when the path to the farm forked away; Petroc turned to call him quietly and Rudka rapidly caught the old man up and didn't lag again. It seemed he was a quiet polite sort of hound who respected people and never pushed himself in without invitation.

While he was still approaching the boiler-house by way of the garden, Petroc caught the murmur of somebody's voice apparently emanating from the hut; he listened hard but the voice immediately fell silent and Petroc thought he must have imagined it - who could be on the farmstead apart from Stepanida? All the same he felt a pang of anxiety, so he halted at the woodpile, threw the tub down on the chippings and, glancing round, stowed the coil and the bottles of vodka behind the pile of firewood. That was the safest place - anybody might wander into the hut, if not Germans then the polizei, still worse. Assuming an expression of weary indifference, he entered the passage.

Well, there were voices right enough, he hadn't been mistaken: one was Stepanida and the other. . . Unable to guess at once whose the other voice was, Petroc opened the door tentatively.

"Well, here we are waiting, thought you'd never come."

'You, the wolves over the mountain would drop dead before you gave up waiting for what you wanted,' Petroc thought, seeing polizei Nedoseka, who had risen from the bench to meet him, proffering a broad hand. Petroc pressed it lightly, reflecting to himself: 'They sniffed it out, then! That was smart of them. . . You haven't got time to think something before they're onto it.'

"If it's work I'm not going," Petroc said. "I worked my guts out yesterday, I'm done in."

"Don't go then," agreed the polizei readily. "You needn't go today, the Germans aren't here. Well, how did you get on? Got some?" he asked suddenly, all attention.

Petroc knew what he meant and was on the point of saying no and thinking up some lie, but first he shot a glance at Stepanida, as she stood in silence by the stove. Catching his glance, she said softly:

"He's waiting for you. Guzh was here. They know all about it."

For the hundredth time Petroc swore savagely to himself. Damn it all! There was no getting away from the man, though it was a good thing the senior polizei wasn't here in person, that cut out the explanations and excuses. All the same, he had intended to deliver the hooch to Guzh personally, so that it was clear who was giving what to whom - and maybe talk him round a bit as well. Ask him to go easy on the work side, not billet Germans on him and stop pestering his wife. There was no shortage of business with Guzh! But now he would have to give up the booze to Nedoseka and he'd drink it himself, bet what you like.

After a brief pause, Petroc left the hut and pulled two bottles, still warm, out from behind the stack. He decided to hang on to the third, keep something in reserve. As he walked back, he wondered if Nedoseka would stick out for more; then he would have to make excuses and swear that it was all he made - poor equipment, not enough mash. To his surprise, however, Nedoseka didn't say a word, just stuck the bottles in the pockets of his cavalry trousers causing them to droop down over his knees.

"Is it potato or grain?" was the polizei's only inquiry.

"Grain. I gave it a real go, not half! Nowadays, you know, you've got to work in with everybody, specially the authorities," Petroc said.

"You've always got to please them. Soviet or German, that's for sure." Nedoseka concluded and grasped the door knob. "Well, then it's goodbye for now!"

He went, apparently pleased with what he had got. Petroc followed him suspiciously through the window, before subsiding wearily on the end of the bench by the table. Stepanida reached into the stove for the pot and the remains of the soup.

"You think two bottles are enough to keep them quiet?" she asked acidly, looking askance at Petroc.

"Why? Too little?"

"You know it is. Let's hope he doesn't come pestering again."

"Well I won't give him it. What am I, a vodka factory?"

"Anyway, they know you're making it. And that you swapped your violin for a coil. Agents, he says."

"Is that so? I hope they drop dead then."

"They can't find the bomb though. There was one lying near the bridge, somebody's pinched it."

"A bomb? Who wants a bomb?. . . Not Kornila was it? Kornila for sure," said Petroc after some thought. "He needs everything. Whatever he sees, he hauls home with him."

Sitting in the very same place where Nedoseka had perched, Petroc ate his soup. He felt utterly exhausted, almost ill; there was a rasping in his chest, from the smoke likely, but for the first time in recent days, he felt a sense of satisfaction that he had accomplished something and purchased himself some peace and quiet; how long it would last there was no telling. But he'd bought himself off for today, Guzh would leave him in peace. Finishing off the soup in the earthenware bowl, he decided he would have a smoke, then relax in the domestic warmth of his hut; it would come to him what to do next. But, as always Stepanida knew better than him what should be done first and what next.

"We never got round to finishing the clamp. They stopped me today. And there's no bread either, got to grind."

"The potatoes can wait. Not frosty yet."

"What about bread?"

"Tomorrow," said Petroc.

After his meal in the warmth, he felt worn to shreds and simply didn't have strength enough to start on anything. No matter how urgent it might be.

"What if they drive us both out tomorrow, to the bridge or the potato field? Or somewhere else?" Stepanida nagged on.

"They won't."

"What d'you mean they won't? He's let you off has he? He'll sup that lot and be back again, he'll stick like glue."

Maybe he would be back, and stick like glue and issue his threats as well, but Petroc had so driven himself over these last terrible days that he had no strength left to do anything. After his meal he rolled himself a cigar, lit it from a pine splinter and wandered off behind the stove.

"Presently, I'll. . ."

Without taking off his boots, he lay down and fell asleep, his cigar still smoldering. It seemed that he had barely closed his eyes, when the forgotten Rudka started barking in the yard and footsteps were heard. Petroc dragged himself from sleep and rushed to the window. Over beyond the well, someone was tethering a thin chested bay to the palings; when he turned towards the hut, Petroc recognized Kolondenok in his greatcoat with his rifle slung behind his narrow stooping back.

"To hell with the lot of you," Petroc swore despairingly, already sensing what had brought the polizei to the farm.

Rudka continued to bark, first at the horse, which pricked up its ears watchfully without, however, stirring from its place, then letting fly at Kolondenok. He halted abruptly, grabbing his rifle. Petroc, just as he was, without his sheepskin, bounded out onto the steps and shouted at the little dog:

"Rudka, out of it! Out of it, pup! I'll give you what for! Don't shoot him, he won't bite," he went on, addressing the polizei, who had already slammed a round into the chamber. Rudka realized at last what was in store for him and hid behind the stack of firewood. He kept up his barking from there but without any great conviction and Kolondenok slung the rifle back across his narrow sagging shoulder.

"I've come for the vodka," announced the polizei simply, the wan expression unchanged on his hangdog face.

"But I gave it up didn't I! Nedoseka took two bottles," Petroc began to get flustered. "What d'you think this is, a factory?"

"Guzh said: another two bottles. Otherwise it'll be repression tomorrow."

"It'll be what?" Petroc was bemused.

"Repression. Well, that means we'll hang you. Or was it shoot you?" Kolondenok considered. "No, hanging, I think. Aha, yes, I remember, it was hanging. Repression means hanging, that's it."

"Amazing!" Petroc spread his arms. "So, where'm I going to get it from? I gave it up. Nedoseka. . ."

"Then get your cap."

"What for?"

"You're going to the township. Guzh said: if he doesn't give the vodka up, fetch him here by the collar. For repression."

"He did?.."

Well what else could he do with these gangsters? Petroc said nothing as he thought hard and realized with almost blinding clarity that vodka wasn't the way out either. No, moonshine wouldn't save him; it might do for him faster than anything else. He silently paced across the damp yard in his ancient boots and quite openly, with no attempt at concealment, pulled out the third bottle from behind the alder logs.

"There you are! And you said there wasn't any!" squealed Kolondenok angrily. "And the rest?"

"There isn't any, honestly, I haven't got any more. Search if you like. I didn't make a lot, the soaking didn't go right. . ."

"Well, alright," relented Kolondenok after some thought. "I'll hand it over and he can decide himself."

He untethered his horse and leapt on it sideways, stomach down, flinging his long leg over the other side. The horse trotted off friskily to the high road as Stepanida came out of the garden carrying a basket of potatoes.

"Vodka again?"

"Yes," Petroc confirmed gloomily.

"What did I tell you? Now they'll start coming. . ."

"I hope it chokes them! There's no more."

"It'll be the worse for you then."

"It can't be worse," said Petroc vehemently, without feeling any confidence in his own words, however. In his heart he didn't want to believe the worst; he kept thinking, maybe it'll all blow over. . .

20

Towards evening, as the light was drawing in, Petroc groaned a bit and after bickering with his wife, scraped the rye which had been drying on the stove into jugs and went off to the boiler-house. He had to grind enough for bread and vodka, as it was plain by now that there was no living without either.

The millstones were ancient and loose, with slender worn-down stones; they ground too coarsely and the only good thing was, they were easy to turn. As Petroc gently rotated the handle, from time to time feeding in the warm grains from the jugs, his mind reflected on that multitude of things, mostly disagreeable, which raced within his brain like midges on a summer's day.

The war was bad for everybody, you could reckon it brought sorrow all round, but if that sorrow was because of the foreigner, the Germans, it was nothing to wonder at; it was like disease, the plague or an ulcer - who could you be angry at? But if this plague came about because of your own, local, village people you'd known since you were knee-high and who'd changed from what they'd been all their lives and all of a sudden turned into brute beasts, obeying only the occupying Germans, was there any understanding them? Or had they suddenly turned into beasts under some kind of compulsion, crushing down all the humanity they had inside?! Maybe they weren't people at all, they'd just pretended all those years before the war woke the beast in them? Petroc was a quiet individual, like the majority in the Settlement: fairly cautious, considerate towards others, a little superstitious and pious. All his forbears had been like that, too. His grandad, for example, had never allowed himself to address a harsh word to the township folk, let alone his family - or indeed swear at a farm animal, unlike today when even youngsters shouted and used bad language to their horses and cows. God forbid that he should speak evil of anyone or take what was not his own from yard or field. And nowadays?. . . It was a good thing he wasn't alive now to see what the world had come to, what with this war. . .

As soon as the Germans appeared, Petroc had gone into the township to get salt, kerosene, matches and take a look at the "new order" but chiefly to find out what was going on in the world and weigh up likely developments. He recalled a group of peasants gathered near the fire station in the shade of the maple, sitting and smoking. The talk was gloomy and concerned a single topic. A few days previously, an important German official had arrived in a rust colored service jacket with a red armlet on the sleeve, so they said. He had appointed a new administration made up of local people. The peasants were pleased on the whole that it would be their own people in charge rather than some emissaries of the Germans. Shortly thereafter, the local administration established itself in the stone building of the former district executive committee; the German interpreter was seen in there, the inconspicuous bachelor and former schoolmaster, Sventkovsky, who used to lodge with Riva the Jewess by the bridge. Guzh, who had only just appeared in the township, immediately became chief polizei. It wasn't long before Antos Nedoseka also donned the polizei armband; this greatly surprised the township folk, none of whom could think of anything to the discredit of the man. A lot of people were openly indignant over the third polizei, as he had long been unpopular in the Settlement, but Potap Kolondenok was doubtless used to the villagers' funny looks and paid then little attention. Nowadays he had regard only to the Germans and his immediate superior, the senior polizei Guzh. As for Guzh, who knew whether he had changed or not? He'd been away for ten years getting schooled in the faraway Donbas, what had he learned there? Now he was openly revelling in the power he had been given over others; alongside the Germans he had wiped out the township Jews, looted their possessions and here he was parading about in the leather jacket that had once belonged to Efim Katz, the head of the district land bureau.

That was your local administration for you!

But how could such things be, thought Petroc as he rocked himself back and forth to the rhythm of the millstone handle. It was quite dark now; Stepanida hadn't lit the lamp as she was economizing on kerosene and he was in no mood to wrangle with his wife, he could work in pitch darkness if it came to that. How could such things be, he asked himself again; to do it to your own people! Since time immemorial, good neighborliness had been highly esteemed in the village; it was very rare that anyone other than some degenerate raised his hand against another or was at odds or quarrelled with such as himself, a tiller of the soil. Of course such things could happen in life for no reason at all but it was usually about land - plots, hay meadows and animals, say. But what about the land now? Who needed that land now; all enmity on its account had subsided, but people were no happier. They'd gone to the dogs, they had. In days gone by a young man wouldn't dream of passing an old chap without taking his cap off, now young folk were taking other peoples' caps off with the heads still in them. And they were frightened of nothing - neither the justice of man nor the wrath of God. As if it had all been laid down long ago, as if they not only had might on their side but right as well. Maybe they didn't need the right as long as they had bloodthirsty German might behind them? They didn't give a damn about right if it got in the way of their bloody misdeeds. Still right must get in their way all the same, mused Petroc, otherwise they wouldn't be looking over their shoulders at the Germans every time or drowning their conscience in vodka. They wouldn't keep grabbing a rifle when they couldn't find something convincing to say to country wives when they got into a slanging match. The men never crossed swords with them, they held their peace.

Petroc had got through about a quarter of the rye and was fingering the soft warm flour by the heated millstones, reflecting that as he'd got started he should grind some more to be enough for bread and vodka mash. Behind the even, muted hum of the stones, he was slow to detect Stepanida's voice from the hut; when he did hear it he realized she had been calling for some time and that her voice contained a note of unease. He ceased turning the handle and at once echoing blows at the passage door filled the farmstead with alarm - someone was battering at the door and cursing in a bass voice:

"Master, sodding hell! Open up!. . ."

Petroc slipped into the passage, felt for the hook with trembling fingers and lifted it from its ring. The doors swung wide almost knocking him off his feet; Petroc gave way and a large shaggy man tumbled into the passage with others behind him; a wave of vodka, onion and something else, alien and disgusting, swept over Petroc. He stood behind the open door, saying nothing, while they found the hut door and flung that wide, letting the bright red glow of the stove which Stepanida was stoking flood out into the passage; the four uninvited guests stamping, snuffling and swishing their wet clothing tumbled into the hut.

"Master!" barked the hairy bass once more, as Petroc racked his brain trying to guess who on earth it was. He failed, try as he might; they must be strangers.

"Here I am," he spoke from the passage.

"Master, light! Give us some light!"

"Where can I get light from? There isn't any. There's the stove there. . ."

"Take it from the stove! Light a spill from it!"

Petroc went into the hut, now crowded with the newcomers, squeezing in past the threshold, already aware that this nocturnal visitation boded no good for him. Stepanida was hurriedly fixing a long spill, lit at one end, into the bundle. Soon its light was flickering over the four clumsy, suspicious figures clumping massively about the hut, examining the walls and fingering the bench and table. Petroc tried again to identify any of them but without success. When the light had got going, the big one who had fallen into the passage first, turned his big-nosed stubbly face towards him.

"The master?"

"Yes, well, you know. . ."

"Any bandits come here. Quick now!"

"What bandits?" Petroc was lost. "The Germans have just left us, they were here for a week, you know. . ."

Two of them sat down on the bench, placing their rifles between their knees, two remained standing in the middle of the hut.

"Any bacon-fat?" asked the one with the nose and Petroc was about to reply when the one standing in front of him turned sideways, showing the white armband on his left sleeve. 'Ah, polizei,' Petroc understood; at first he hadn't known how to behave towards them, what tone to adopt.

"Oh, what're you asking him for that for?!" the polizei rebuked big-nose in a pleasant, open kind of voice; smirking, he asked Petroc: "Any vodka?"

"Where from? There is none," Petroc brought out, suddenly hoarse. The visitors glanced at each other conspiratorially.

"Stop playing dumb!" the polizei was getting annoyed. "Put the bottle out and we won't quarrel."

"There isn't any, honestly! Would I lie?" Petroc said, trying hard to sound sincere and therefore probably achieving the reverse. The visitors, however, had already caught the unnatural tone in his voice and their surprise grew.

"You saw?" the polizei addressed big-nose, after a brief pause. "He refuses!"

"You tired of living? Ever smelled that?"

Before Petroc could grasp what was happening, big-nose thrust the cold barrel of a pistol in his face. Petroc involuntarily wrinkled his nose at the acrid smell of burnt powder.

"Moonshine, and quick about it!"

"But I haven't got any," Petroc feebly stuck to his story, knowing his words wouldn't convince any of them.

"What moonshine?" Stepanida suddenly flared up, having tucked herself away in silence by the stove all this time. "Where's he going to get it for you?"

"He got some for Guzh from somewhere," said the polizei with the armband, almost tenderly. "But he begrudges us. That's not right. Not fair."

"What Guzh? Who told you?"

"Kolondenok told us," the polizei elaborated and Petroc guessed: these arrivals must be the Krinki polizei. Of course, the bridge was repaired now and the Krinki and Vyazniki lot and plenty more from villages near and far would be travelling around. And they would all be turning off into Yakimovschina, so unluckily near at hand, just off the road. Petroc was aghast at what he had taken on with this moonshine business. He couldn't keep supplying these dogs from all over the region; he wouldn't have time or grain even if his toilworn hands could take it.

"Kolondenok hasn't shown his face here for a month." Stepanida lied boldly as the polizei exchanged astonished glances.

"Not showed his face?"

"That's right. He hasn't been here. Maybe he got it somewhere else."

"You're not telling the truth," the armband smiled. "Kolondenok doesn't play tricks like that."

"Alright, search the place!" big-nose yelled suddenly. "Everywhere! Take the light with you - the passage, the cowshed, all over. . ."

"You'll set the farm alight, you can't go round with a flame like that. Are you out of your minds?" Stepanida lamented.

Nevertheless the two sitting on the bench leapt up smartly and seizing splinters from the bundle began lighting them in the stove. Their puffed, unshaven faces were lit up in the flickering smoky stench, and it was plain that both were well-oiled already; they could hardly be relied on to display much in the way of caution. They headed off into the passage with their brands and could be heard in the boiler-house. Cold air was drawn in through the doors and Petroc's shoulders, covered only by his waistcoat, began to shiver convulsively. The two who remained behind in the hut seated themselves more comfortably in front of the master.

"Now then, come here!" big-nose ordered roughly. Petroc walked in silence to the middle of the hut and halted, prepared for anything. "You going to give us vodka?"

"There isn't any," he said almost tonelessly, aware that proving it or swearing to God would be useless now. They were in such a state of blind drunkenness that his words would hardly be understood. Vodka was what they wanted.

"And if you find it?"

"If you find it, it's yours," said Petroc meekly, sensing he'd said the wrong thing, however: they'd still be thinking he'd got some hidden somewhere. Still where it was hidden they'd never find it, even if they turned the whole farmstead over and the gully to boot.

"We find it, you get a bullet. For gross deception," the polizei promised.

"And if we don't, we'll shoot you like a dog," added big-nose grimly. "So just have a good think."

"That's up to you," Petroc shrugged, knowing there was no way out for him. "But there's no hooch."

A short silence ensued; the polizei were obviously waiting for news from those rummaging through the boiler-house. Stepanida changed the spill in the bundle to brighten up the hut in which the smoke had settled in layers; there was a strong smell of burning. Petroc was afraid they would set something alight in the passage or the boiler-house, you couldn't expect drunks to take precautions. Of the two left in the hut, the polizei seemed less drunk, or less intent on plunder, so Petroc addressed him:

"You don't have to go looking, there is none, honest to God. Why should I grudge it, honest. . ."

"You're keeping it for the bandits?" rapped big-nose. "And we can go hang? Us servants of the people?"

"What're you reading him sermons for," said the polizei, cordially as before. "You're wasting time. Just put him up against the wall. If he wants to live he'll find it!"

At this he gave a good-natured laugh displaying a broad row of shining white teeth.

'There's your kindhearted man for you,' thought Petroc, disenchanted. He had been thinking of asking them to stop making game of him and believe that there really was nothing to find. Petroc had ceased to worry about his farmstead catching fire. Now he just wanted one thing - to get clear of trouble himself; he resigned himself to the fact that he couldn't do it, it just wasn't to be.

Brandishing their torches, the two out in the passage fell into the hut in their black hats, rifles in hand.

"Well, nothing?"

"No, not a drop; it's dark, and there's nothing like that anywhere. He's grinding out there, there's flour on the stones."

"Grinding!" big-nose was furious. "Grinding moonshine for somebody! But not for us! Right, against the wall! Move!"

It went dark before Petroc's eyes, he staggered whether from weakness or fear, sensing that it was all up now. Somebody pushed him hard in the back, then in the side, so that he instinctively took a step forward and found himself with his back to the wall between the two windows. Big-nose ranged himself opposite, settling his legs comfortably, then slowly raised his foul-smelling pistol.

"What are you doing, you brutes? What're you doing that to him for?" Stepanida shouted out from the stove. Big-nose lowered his arm.

"Ah, I feel sorry for him! Maybe I shouldn't kill him? Just fetch a couple of bottles! Move it!"

Stepanida began wailing louder:

"Where can I get it for you, we've got no vodka, I hope you may see your wives as much as we've seen that vodka."

"Shut up!" barked big-nose, and the polizei seized Stepanida by the arms and boldly pushed her into passage. There she cried out softly and fell silent. 'They've killed her!' thought Petroc, horrified, himself ready to say goodbye to life. "Right, we'll count to three!" big-nose announced pointing the gun at him again. "No vodka? One. . . Think on, I'm a crack shot, I won't miss. Two. . . Well, where is it? No?"

'They won't shoot will they, the dogs?' thought Petroc, gazing mesmerized at the dully glinting gunbarrel, wobbling perceptibly three paces from him. 'They haven't the nerve, surely? Or are they just trying to scare me? Anyway let it be over. Shoot if you're going to, I don't care, I can see I'm not fated to survive this war or see my children,' thought Petroc incoherently. Tears crawled down his long-unshaven cheeks towards his chin.

"Three!" snapped big-nose.

A piercing, red flame struck Petroc full in the face and jammed his ears tight; he didn't realize at first that he was still alive and standing where he had been with his back against the wall. Only some half minute later did he hear the quarrelling voices of the polizei far away through the dense ringing in his ears.

"What're you messing about with him for, wasting cartridges, one in the head and be done with it!"

"No hurry! I'll settle him like God did the tortoise. Now then, where's the vodka? Still not talking?"

Petroc made no reply - he was practically deafened and stood stupefied in a kind of feeble indifference to his farmstead, his wife and his own person; he could find no strength to defend himself. They were still messing about with something in front of him: one was lighting spills in bundles and the smoke swirled about the hut and poured out into the corridor through the open doors; the monstrous hunched shadows of the visitors swept along the walls and ceiling; the glow of the splinters kept flaring up and dying down to a glimmer blinding his streaming eyes and lighting up the squat figure of the executioner with the gun.

"Where's the vodka? Speak up! No?. . ."

A further shot rang out, louder than the first, it seemed. Something cracked in his ear and Petroc, unable to stand, collapsed onto the end of the bench. He hit his side with considerable force and his hands encountered something wet on the floor; his ear hurt dreadfully. The polizei, however, did not let him scrabble about for long; he kicked him in the chest and grabbed him like a pup by the collar and stood him by the wall. So as not to fall over, Petroc leaned his back against the ripped newspaper in utter helplessness, just where the three black bullet holes were.

'My God, why?'

"So, you bastard farmer! Lousy kulak! Still nothing to say? Right, this is for you! . . ."

'Just let it be now. No more torture. . . Straightaway. . .' The words spun around in his head. Petroc swallowed his salty saliva and once more experienced that gloomy indifference towards himself and life as a whole. He had no time to gather his resources or stiffen himself before his last breath, before there came again the roar, the fiery stench blazed in his face, once, twice, three times; he was blinded and deafened. His knees bent and, tearing the newspaper with his back, he slowly slid to the floor.

He seemed to lose consciousness for a time; his chest ached badly, he couldn't breathe and his eyes could make out almost nothing in the stench-laden, smoky darkness. With the furthest edge of his mind he realized he was still alive. Still alive for some reason. . . From somewhere, seemingly far, far away, the voices of his tormentors carried to him:

"What're you messing about with him for! Finish him and be done with it!"

"Just let him croak!"

"Let me. . ."

"Wait! He can still be some good," big-nose pushed the polizei aside, and walking over to Petroc, stooped slightly over him. "Understand,slug? We want vodka. Vodka, understand? If not today, tomorrow. A decent supply. Understand? Otherwise we'll come and you can say goodbye to life."

'They're not going to let me live are they?' thought Petroc, almost with alarm, limply rising to his feet as after his loss of consciousness. He leaned against the wall, raising himself on one knee, and surveyed the hut through the smoke. The spills were all burned out but the stove gave a little light, where the wood was burning through and the last embers were casting a crimson glow on the trampled floorboards. All four polizei disappeared one after the other through the wide-open door whence a damp chill crept into the hut. Petroc shivered. He kneeled up with an effort, trembling all over from his fearful experience, the cold and his inexpressible sense of outrage - why him?

"Water for the old woman?"

"To hell with her. She'll come round herself. . ."

These were the last words spoken by the polizei in the passage; presently they were trampling past the window, then the footsteps died away and on the farm all was still.

21

Petroc somehow rose to his feet and holding onto the tattered wall, made his way into the passage. Stepanida was somewhere there, alive or possibly already dead. As he crossed the threshold, he saw the soles of her bare feet in the half darkness. Stepanida was lying on a heap of potatoes scattered about the floor. To his astonishment, she also got to her feet and staggered drunkenly towards her bed behind the stove. She made no reply to his questions, just groaned faintly from time to time, while he kept tramping round the hut, bringing her water, covering her with the sheepskin, and complaining with genuine bitterness, but chiefly cursing the polizei, the Germans and the war. He didn't bother to close the door into the passage, let it go, let them come and beat him up, set the place on fire; there was no living with them in any event. Clearly life was at an end; why go on suffering when you were all in, and if you thought about it, there was no great necessity for it in any case. They wouldn't let a man die his own death, they'd finish you off violently. Of course before that they'd humiliate you till you felt like hanging yourself - because what was left for a man if his life had become torture?

That night he didn't go to bed at all. For a while he nestled up against a corner of the table and dozed off with his head on his hands, before waking at dawn almost from fright: a new day beginning and what would it bring? Actually it was obviously going to bring new agonies, perhaps death even; however much they played at murder, they would surely carry out their threat in the end. To hell with it, death; he'd already stopped being afraid of it, let them kill him, just as long as it was soon. One couldn't live like this. This wasn't life.

It seemed that Stepanida had calmed down somewhat behind the stove; she had stopped groaning and was perhaps dozing even. Petroc went out into the boiler-house and retrieved his sheepskin jacket from the bins by the millstones. So he hadn't milled the rye, not for bread or liquor, and he didn't intend to. There'd be no more mash, let them mill flour and distil booze themselves. He'd had enough. If there was no other salvation, moonshine wasn't the way out either. Let them finish him off just like that, no reason, if only because he was a human being.

Petroc left the passage and went into the yard without closing the door behind him. What was the point? Doors weren't needed any more, they'd just open them and go where they pleased. Who needed doors?

The late autumnal dawn was struggling to penetrate the settled darkness of the long night: the fields, hemmed in by the gray murk, the bare thickets on the edge of the gully, all seemed dismal and unwelcoming; the gusting wind carried bone-chilling damp and cold. The last remaining scraps of yellow foliage fluttered desperately among the twisted lime twigs, while the wet leaf-fall overnight had thickly covered the road and sprinkled the grass in the yard; leaves were stuck to the logs of the well cover and the bench by the fence.

That night had shifted something in Petroc's consciousness and broken it beyond repair, forcing his train of thought out of its usual circle of anxieties. Now he no longer knew what to do or how to go on from here. He wanted to hide away somewhere far away from the farm. He was afraid of being caught here again by the same crew with their rifles, and he would be put through the same agony again.

He was afraid to show his face on the road: this was the route of most danger now. As always, his wish was to get behind a corner and conceal himself from any rapacious eye. He went over to the woodpile glancing glumly at the open doors of the cowshed, where their Bobovka no longer stood; birch logs lay scattered in disorder and the chopping block had been tipped over from its place of many years. From the woodpile his eyes turned to the familiar path, leading across the trampled garden in the direction of the gully. Surprising himself, he walked along it, knowing well where he was going. On weak, unsteady legs he descended through the alder thickets to the stream; paying no attention to the wet boughs snatching at his cap and shoulders, he walked for a long time along the gully bottom, skirting the badger den up the slope, then ran across the stones to the other side of the stream before finally clambering into the mouth of another, smaller gully into an impenetrable thicket of young firs.

The familiar clearing was deserted and damp, the wet ash from yesterday's fire had settled into a gray heap between three smoke-blackened stones. Under the widespreading briar with its few wrinkled hips, he saw his black kettle partly covered with decaying leaves, and thought: blow it, let it rust! He would never lay another finger on it, the distilling was over. Glancing about him, he sat down by the bush and beneath the branch he had broken the day before, raked away the leaves and drew out the earth stained bottle by its dirty neck and wiped it off against the fleecy flap of his jacket. That lot over there had drunk and had a good time, while he hadn't even tried it. He'd kept it while trying for better results. Who for? Who was he worried about, idiot? Himself of course, but you shouldn't worry so much about yourself, should you? Old fool.

Petroc pulled out the paper stopper and took a cautious sip or two. It was good rye spirit alright, he'd done well not to give it up; let them drink that mush, muddy rubbish that it was. It would be all the same to them most likely. He'd treat himself to the first and best of the batch - after all, who else would? How else could he console himself if it wasn't with a cigar and this, distilled by him in his bitter need. True, he had no glass, so like a real boozer he'd take it straight from the bottle. But what a grim time it was, a good time to die, no good for normal human living.

He drank some more, then took a breath and thought how wretched it was drinking with no bite to go with it; he wanted to hurl the bottle far off into the gully, but changed his mind. He begrudged what was left. A certain relaxed lightness had entered his thoughts and his troubles ceased to seem bitterly hopeless, as they had been up to now. An agreeable self-confidence possessed him; even his body seemed to take on strength. What bastards they were, those polizei, thought Petroc, but he was no fool himself, not some half-witted oaf; he knew a thing or two about life, about war even, although he'd never seen it, mind. But he understood matters. He wouldn't let them put a saddle on him and ride where they liked, he could still stand up for himself. Where vodka was concerned anyway: he damn well hadn't given up his best bottle, he'd stood out against a firing squad, he'd stared death in the eyes and come through, he'd resisted and they had gone away defeated. He hoped they choked!

Without looking back at his clearing, he made his way through the prickly fir branches and came out onto the path, along which he made his leisurely way back through the gully silence. He hadn't thrown the bottle away; he kept it in his hand, thinking he'd chuck it in the stream after a few more swallows. At the bend in the stream where the path turned sharply, he collided with Rudka and came to a stop. The little dog was doubtless surprised at this unlooked-for meeting and began wagging its tail joyfully.

"Well, what is it? What, Rudka?" Petroc spoke in a low voice.

Actually it would have been good to talk to someone, but who was there? Rudka stared into his face with concentrated attention; his own expression was agonizingly uncomprehending; he whined quietly as if inquiring about something.

"You hungry? Yes, you are, of course. Well, let's go. You see there's not a crumb round here. There, see?" Petroc tried to turn out his empty pocket. "Nowt! There'll be something in the hut. Let's go, I'll feed you at home."

He went on his way along the path, having decided that Rudka must be given something this time; the dog had clearly been waiting for him in the gully since yesterday. Then Kolondenok had prevented him and driven the dog off the farmstead. He was lucky not to have been shot by the woodpile. Petroc himself had been within an inch of death. It was terrible to think of what he'd been through.

"That's the life we've got now, friend!" complained Petroc, turning to Rudka who once again stared at him earnestly wrinkling his little bushy eyebrows. "Life! They beat dogs like human beings and shoot people like dogs. The human race has turned into animals, that's how it is friend."

Well, what was it to them, thought Petroc. All they cared about was enjoying cruelty, shedding blood. Their throats would dry up without blood. And vodka wouldn't wash it away either. No, indeed it wouldn't. After blood they wanted vodka and after vodka they longed for blood. That's the circle they were locked into. Ah, beasts, beasts. . .

He was already walking purposefully along the path, firmly intending to give Rudka something to eat, masterless as he was and obviously a bit scared of people; the little dog had found a refuge in the gully here, where he had lost Yanka the night before last. He wouldn't see Yanka again. Yanka was far away now likely, in the sky. That sinless boy's soul would certainly be in paradise. And where would our sinful souls end up, eh?

Petroc hadn't drunk all the vodka, reasoning soberly that he'd likely had enough and the rest could help to revive Stepanida. After her experiences of the night, a glass of rye vodka would be just the thing to restore her to strength and activity. A glass of the first distillation was a medicine and not a bad one - doctors themselves were not averse to it. And doctors knew what they were about. Doctors knew everything, what to drink and what to eat with it. He wouldn't say no to something to eat, he really felt like a bite, especially after what he had drunk.

"We'll have something there," promised Petroc, looking round at the little dog, who was running closely behind him. "We'll have something to eat, don't worry. . ."

Breaking into a sweat, he struggled up the cliff path and emerged from the gully. The dog realizing now where Petroc was heading, overtook him and ran on a little way ahead, never straying far from the man, however. Petroc thought the first thing to do at home would be to fry some potatoes and bacon-fat, if there was any left in the tub. He'd come and scrape the potatoes, fry them and feed Stepanida, then look for something for homeless Rudka. Who else would do it if he didn't? Obviously Yanka had been killed somewhere in the gully and the dog kept hanging around the vicinity. You could say he was a local dog now. From the farm.

All of sudden Rudka halted on the path for some reason and stuck out his neck; his tail stiff and immobile. Petroc, stumbling slightly, did not reduce pace at once, as he raised his head. His farmstead was already visible behind its fence and there was a flash of something rust colored in the yard. Some sort of bedding seemed to be fluttering in the wind on the palings, but it couldn't be that, could it? Petroc rubbed his eyes and peered more closely. It was just what he hadn't wanted to admit to himself. They'd got there before him. In the yard, close by the fence, the roan and bay horses were tossing their heads, and although there was no one in sight, Petroc realized that THEY had already arrived.

Petroc almost wept from the exasperation, grief and fear which suddenly seized him. He went on very slowly along the path, looking round. He hadn't the strength to go on towards the farmstead because he was very well aware of what awaited him there. But where could he go? The open fields? Sheep Valley? The swamp? Back to the gully?. . . Meanwhile his wife would be abandoned, bruised and ill in the hut; the potatoes were there, and all his bits and pieces. The polizei would take a cruel revenge. There was no escape, was there?

And yet his legs turned back and he even ducked a little, sinking his head into his shoulders, and nervously tottered back towards the gully.

He hadn't even got to the nearest bush when the first menacing shout echoed behind him:

"Petroc, stop! Stop, you bloody. . . Back here!"

At once there came a rifle shot cracking close above his head, or so it seemed. The bullet flew on into the bushes at the lip of the gully and a twig sliced off by its passage dropped quietly into the grass. Suddenly sober, the final realization came to him that he couldn't run away. There was nowhere to hide from them.

In fact, they were already running through the garden, directly from the farmstead; he stopped and then turned back. They also stopped within the fence, near to the officer's latrine he had constructed, rifles at the ready to put a bullet in his back should he run. But he didn't; doomed, he dragged himself along the path towards his destruction. Everything inside him risen up in silent swelling outrage: what for? Incongruously, he felt the neck of the bottle in his hand; there was still some splashing inside, which he had been taking to Stepanida. She wouldn't see it now. Without drawing back his arm, he flung the bottle away, feeling a brief pleasure that they wouldn't get any of it, let it drain into the grass. Filled with despair, he walked resolutely towards the polizei, who emerged from behind the fence jostling each other to get to the path, Guzh in front in his leather jacket, and

Kolondenok in the rear with raised rifle. Sensing their hostile intentions almost physically, Petroc halted.

"Well? What? What d'you want from me?" he cried weakly, glaring at them through tear blurred eyes. A pressing lump came into his throat and he stopped five paces from the fence.

"Come on, a bit closer!" said Guzh quietly with the merest hint of menace. The long face of the polizei, sober this time, it seemed, was set woodenly. Petroc sensed that the game was up, it wouldn't blow over this time.

"What d'you want? Why are you always on my back? Just what the hell d'you want? Rats that you are, German bootlickers. . ."

"Just cool down!" snarled Guzh unslinging his rifle. "Otherwise we'll. . ."

"What? You'll what? Shoot me? Go ahead, and to hell with the lot of you!" shouted Petroc with unexpected, even frightening resolution, and waved his clenched fists in the air. "Shoot!"

"Plenty of time for that," stated Guzh, calmer now. "Come here!"

"Well, I won't! I won't come over there and I won't listen to you either, you bastards!"

Guzh coolly shouldered his rifle and gave the nod to Kolondenok.

"Alright, give him one!"

The slender, long-legged Kolondenok vaulted lightly over the top of the fence and approached across the trampled furrows of the potato field. He raised his hand. Petroc's ears rang, the farm rocked before his eyes and he found himself unexpectedly among the cold, rough potato stems.

"Get up!"

"Alright! Alright! I'm getting up. . . I'll get up. But what are you hitting me for? Aren't I a human being or something?"

He hadn't managed to get to his feet, however, before a second blow on the right ear dumped him on his other side in the mud of the furrow.

"Where's the vodka?"

"A dick's all you'll get!" said Petroc, spitting blood on the ground; they seemed to have knocked out his last remaining teeth. "That's for you!" he stuck up two fingers. "Go on, hit me! I'm not scared of you! Or that Hitler of yours either! That's for him as well! I hope you choke, the lot of you!"

Kolondenok leapt towards him and raised his hand once more, but Guzh shouted from behind the fence:

"Stop! That'll do for now. We'll, like. . . make an example."

"Repression, is it?" asked Kolondenok in his thin voice.

"Repression. On a rope end," said Guzh, climbing over the fence himself. "Now then, up on your feet!"

"I'm not getting up. Shoot!"

"You're getting up, you old dummy! Trading in hooch, eh? Dished it out to the wrong folk, eh? Now it's two fingers to your own kin! Oh no, I'm going to roast you. For deception. And for insulting the fuhrer. You know what you get for that?"

"What do I care? I'd spit in his ugly German mug! And yours as well, traitor!"

"Silence!"

Guzh booted him sharply in the chest. Petroc cried out and curled up on his side in the furrow. For some minutes he couldn't breath or say a word, everything spun before his eyes. Was this the end? Sooner the better, to end this misery; the thought flickered through his mind, still just able to react to his unenviable fate in perhaps the final minutes of his life.

"Up!"

But he couldn't rise, just as he couldn't shout, he simply gulped desperately for air, like a fish landed on a river bank. Coming closer, Guzh shook him roughly by the shoulder.

"Up!"

With a great effort, he managed to swallow air a couple of times as Guzh shook him roughly again. Then with Kolondenok, he stood Petroc on his feet and taking him under the armpits, dragged him across the garden to the woodpile. He could barely put one feeble foot in front of the other; his cap was left on the ground and his head with its white, downy tufts of hair felt very cold. It seemed, though, that he would no longer be needing his cap, nor his wretched health, nor even his head and he felt no self-pity. His only thought was: what else could he say to these bastards? But as if to spite him, the most important and necessary words refused to come into his head and he was reduced to dull mumbling:

"Just you wait. . . Just wait. . . You'll get it!"

"You're the one to get it! Just you wait a bit," promised Guzh, menacingly.

They didn't hit him any more though, as they brought him into the yard to the two horses tethered by the fence. Kolondenok continued to hold him under the arms, but Guzh ran into the hut for some reason. 'They're not taking Stepanida as well are they?' thought Petroc. He thought he would see her presently and they would go together to their Golgotha and accept death. Soon, however, Guzh emerged from the passage alone.

"Alright, get aboard!" he shouted at Kolondenok. "There's not much time."

Before mounting his droop-headed nag, Kolondenok led Petroc to the gate under the limes and squealed:

"March! There!" and waved in the direction of the road.

Petroc stood up. The cold and the marrow-piercing wind had allowed him to take a breather and recover himself; for the first time since his storm of excitement began, came an idea which frightened him: where? Where were they taking him? Those two were galloping out of the yard while he was standing in the gateway unable to move a step. Anyway, why should he go voluntarily to be tortured, let them kill him here, on the threshold of his dwelling place. Why should he oblige them by his obedience at the last?

"Come on. March!"

"I'm not going. Kill me. . ."

"What's that, not going?" Guzh was genuinely surprised as he rode round him on his horse. "I'll give you 'not going' - you'll run like greased lightning."

At this, he struck Petroc savagely across the head with his switch. It felt like scalding water across his bald pate and Petroc staggered but stood his ground.

"I'm not going you bastards! Do what you like but I'm not going!"

Once more an angry wave of outraged despair had risen up and possessed him, giving him strength and nerving him not to give in. He wouldn't budge, if they were going to kill him let them do it here.

Guzh kept his horse turning in the yard, clearly at a loss in this tricky situation, but he didn't strike again. He shouted out to Kolondenok:

"Come back, look, that rope there!"

'Tying up? Hanging? Let them! So long as he didn't leave here. Die, but die at home,' thought Petroc bitterly, quite prepared for death. There was still no sign of Stepanida, perhaps they'd killed her too.

"You wouldn't be sensible, so you'll hang!" threatened Guzh. His long legs in their mud-splattered boots hung low under his horse's belly. "For insulting the police. And the fuhrer."

'Alright! Alright! If that's the way it has to be, alright!' thought Petroc and made no reply. He no longer looked behind him at his farmstead or the yard, he thought to himself that he wouldn't ask for their mercy, however bad things might turn out for him. Just hold on. As long as it wasn't too drawn out.

"Hands! Hands," squealed Kolondenok by his ear and without waiting for him to comply, grabbed one hand himself, then the other, folded them on his stomach and began tying them together with the end of the long rope. Petroc heard him snuffling, tense with effort as he bent down in front of him, but made no resistance, simply gazing at the rope and musing: so that's what they've come in for. . . They were his reins. At one time, during the collectivization, he'd given his old ones in to the collective and hidden the new ones away in the boiler-house; he used to tether the cow with them sometimes or secure a load on the cart, but for the most part they hung on a nail in the passage. Now they were used to tie his hands. They'd come in useful.

At length Kolondenok finished off the job with a tight knot and slung the free end into the mud, churned by truck wheels and trodden by horses: Petroc was surprised - why? But it dawned on him at once as the polizei got onto his horse with it.

"Let's go! Move it!" ordered Guzh, staying close at hand, however. Kolondenok started off alone and the rope lifted from the ground, then tautened and dragged Petroc forward by the wrists. "Move it, I said!"

Guzh again slashed his head with the switch and pain shot through his entire frame. So as not to fall, Petroc was forced to run behind Kolondenok as he kicked his horse's flanks, meanwhile Guzh drove him from behind, flailing his switch.

"Faster, faster! Bolshevik dummy!"

Petroc couldn't keep up, he stumbled and almost fell headlong as he was flung from side to side. His old boot held him to the mud, but to fall now would be worse than death, surely. So he ran, hopping and holding on to the rope which took the skin from his hands as it pulled and hauled him towards the highway. His face was once more wet with tears and the wind gusting in his face was not enough this time to dry them.

"Bastards! Murderers!" Petroc shouted, his voice muffled by the choking wind. "Just wait! My Fedka will come! He'll show you!. . . Don't think. . . My son will come. . ."

22

Petroc was gone, vanished from this world, just as his farm, his wife Stepanida, Golgotha and the entire world had vanished for him. Only memories of him remained, that is if there was anyone to recall his human sufferings, his miseries great and small. All his life he had wanted only one thing - peace and quiet. Sensing his own weakness and dependence in many respects, he had yearned to keep himself away from the events which were lashing his world, wait them out somehow, sit tight. It was good thinking, but naive to depend on it. Life went its own way, in accordance with the harsh laws of a cruel epoch and once upon a time the will of chance almost drew Petroc Bogatka into the very epicenter of the human drama.

And what exactly happened to Petroc?

For good or ill, he was a man of certain defined qualities, probably poorly adapted to the modern age, who always acted in accordance with his character. Perhaps indeed that was why he had his fill of suffering in this life.

*   *   *

. . .Thick snow had fallen after Christmas that year and three days before Epiphany such a blizzard had got up as no one very likely had ever experienced since the beginning of the world. The yard was filled up with driven snow and for several days it was impossible to get out of the hut. Still, water had to be fetched, firewood chopped and the animals to be seen to; Petroc had to dig out the doors of the cowshed every time he wanted to squeeze in. After half an hour, however, there wasn't a trace of his work left; thick snow was piled up in the yard, tightly compressed by the wind.

That day it wasn't coming down from the sky, but it was blowing hard across the ground and a long snowdrift had formed from the cowshed to the woodpile, and a lesser one near the well, under the fence. The top of the well cover was level with the drift. Petroc had a job to get to it with his bucket, and to draw water was impossible - there was just a tiny black air hole like some animal's lair. Petroc swore to himself. He was in a bad mood as it was, having just had a row with his wife. It had started over the bread, which Stepanida had kept too long, mixing it with potatoes and scraps till it was impossible to put in your mouth it was so hard and tasteless. Of course Stepanida had a reason: there was only just over one sack of rye left in the rack and four months to go before spring and the first crop. What else could she do but economize! Economizing like that could lay you out before you saw spring, and Petroc wanted to live a bit longer and had told Stepanida so that day.

Treading the snow down near the well, Petroc attached the bucket to the chain; it got stuck in the tiny hole at once and delivered no water. He needed a stick to enlarge the opening. As he glanced round he stood stock-still over the snowbound well. Across the virgin snow, three dark figures were making their way from the road, indian-file; they moved slowly as the wind furiously whipped the snow from their boots, before bearing it off towards the pine wood, where two cars stood out black on the highway. Somebody was digging about near them as well. They were obviously stuck, people were always getting stuck there in winter, especially going into the pines. Cars wouldn't get through there now, thought Petroc as he took off his mitt to blow his nose. There was no doubt now that the newcomers were heading for the farm. He would have guests.

Pulling his bucket with its light load of snow out of the well, Petroc turned away from the wind and waited for a while till the people reached the gate. The first of them was already near at hand making long vigorous strides; his black leather jacket gleamed in the frosty sunlight. He carried a similar black briefcase under his arm. Nearing the gate, Petroc made out the second, a man of average height in a black beaver coat with an astrakhan hat powdered with snow; his face was red and weather-beaten and he had a short, clipped mustache, also white with snow. The third wore a long Red Army greatcoat and helmet, with the earflaps down. He carried a pistol on his belt, which bumped gently on his right hip in time with his stride.

"Can we drop in, master? Just to warm up a bit," asked the first as he came up to the gate.

"Surely, why not! Wind like this, of course," said Petroc guessing that these people were administrators and high up at that, regional or above.

He got hold of the wicket gate at the top but couldn't open it. It just sagged away a little in the snow and the visitors squeezed through one after the other into the yard. Then Petroc led them into the passage where everybody stamped about together getting rid of the frozen snow. When they opened the hut door, Stepanida emerged from behind the curtain with a cloth in her hand and exclaimed in surprise at so many unfamiliar men on the step. She rushed back at once behind the stove. Fenya had been lying there ill for the last two days. She'd caught cold and had a cough so they hadn't let her go to school: it was no joke dragging yourself three kilometers to the township in a storm like this. Fedya was alright and had gone to school, but they had kept Fenya off, hoping she'd get better. While Petroc was busy round the yard, Stepanida had been stoking the stove, but the hut was still cool and smelled of smoke. Of course, damp alder wood tended to smolder and smoke rather than give off heat.

Petroc closed the door and the visitors made themselves at home in the hut. The senior man shook the snow off his cap near the stove exposing a bald or close-shaven head and quietly sat down on the bench, resting his elbow on the corner of the table. The military man with the gun discreetly sat down next to him; he kept his helmet on. The third, the one in the leather jacket, noticing the ailing fire, bent over it and squatted down on the low stool.

"Eh, it's not catching! Not much in the way of shavings, eh, mistress?"

Stepanida came out from behind the stove, wearing a quilted jacket but without her kerchief; she surveyed her guests modestly.

"Where can you get kindling? We use the damp stuff as you see."

"Damp's no problem," said the stranger and attacked the wet stick-ends in the stove with a poker. "You don't put damp sticks in that way. Not like a cage, it's got to be a tent. I learned the way of it in Siberia one time. It has to catch like that, it can't do any other."

Rearranging the alder twigs, he closed the door, not all the way, just leaving a crack. He glanced round at Petroc, who was standing quietly by the door.

"Master, are you in the collective or a private farmer?"

"In the collective, naturally," Stepanida answered for the master as usual. "Since day one, we were."

"Well, how's it going? Is it a prosperous collective?"

"Prosperous, I don't think! No, it's pretty poor."

"Is it just the two of you?"

"Just the two. And two kids. The son's gone to school, the little daughter's not very well, got a cough."

Fenya coughed on cue from behind the stove and everybody stopped talking in the hut to listen. The one sitting near the table, who had not stirred a muscle all this time, lifted one black brow at the cough and glanced at the sackcloth curtain.

"It's easy to catch cold in weather like this," said his comrade by the stove. He opened the door again and began poking about inside the stove with a thin alder twig, rearranging the sticks in his own fashion.

"That's very true," said Stepanida lightly. "Her shoes let in, you know, and she's got no boots, just runs round in torn leggings, legs got cold, so here she is two days now, fever and cough."

"Learning's no easy business for peasant children," observed the one by the stove, sighing and he turned his strong-chinned, cleanshaven face towards the table. "And yet they study, don't they? That means there's an urge towards knowledge, towards the light."

Petroc thought that the older man, senior in rank perhaps, would say something now, but he said nothing, just sat on in silence, gazing at the stove. His face was stamped with pensive weariness, a kind of profound anxiety. It seemed as if his thoughts and attention were miles away.

"It's alright, aunty," said the one at the stove brightly. "We'll carry out the five-year plan, then there'll be footwear and a lot more. Life'll be more cheerful. Till then we have to work."

"That's what we're doing. As hard as we can. Like mad. We never worked for the squires like this."

"Well, that was for the squires, now it's for yourselves. For your own country of workers and peasants."

"True enough. The country does us no harm either, the Motor Tractor Station yonder's made a big difference, you can reckon it does half the plowing. If only things were a bit better organized."

"But that really depends on you," the visitor asserted firmly. "All together and each separately."

"What, you think we don't realize that? It's just we've got nothing to wear. Before we had flax but now we give it all in and don't keep any. If we just had a bit of cotton to make shirts for the children," Stepanida began complaining, probably aware she was talking to high-ups. Petroc took a poor view of this: why did she have to go on so? As soon as people were in the hut, bosses or not, out she comes with her troubles. People couldn't get warm in peace. He stood respectfully by the door, thinking the newcomers would probably explain that pestering them with questions wasn't the done thing.

Stepanida, however, seemed to have taken her courage in both hands, talking away, complaining that people hadn't been paid yet for the wool quota. It was the third time Smik had promised, naming dates, but still there was no money. Petroc scowled his embarrassment - people from Polotsk or even Vitebsk, what could they know about local problems - or Smik, the official in charge of quotas. The bald one by the table sat motionless, eyes closed, clearly warming himself through. But he was listening all the same and hearing all that Stepanida said. When she mentioned money, he opened his eyes and said to the one near the stove:

"Take a note!"

The man opened his briefcase and jotted down a few words in a blue exercise book.

"And er. . . they set aside the worst soil for flax, all clay; it'll grow, say they, a likely tale. When the weather's dry, you can't pull it out with two hands; there's not much of it anyway, and it's very short, class three, no better. . ."

'She's off!' thought Petroc. 'No stopping her now!'

The visitors listened, however, apparently with interest and without interrupting. The bald one had opened his eyes and was staring at her, tiredness forgotten, though he said nothing. The one in the leather jacket only intervened once, asking the name of the collective farm and noting something down himself without being told. Aware of their interest, Stepanida spoke a great deal about her troubles, the way things were done on the collective and the district in general. Then she recalled breakfast.

"Maybe boiled potatoes and pork crackling, if you haven't eaten?"

The bald one by the table snapped out of his immobility, said a firm "no" and turned to the soldier in the greatcoat.

"Have a look out there. . ."

He quickly went out into the passage while the one sitting by the stove opened the hatch to let out an even heat - the wood had caught after all.

"There, you see. Nice and cheery, Siberia style!" observed the guest briskly.

At this point Fenya began coughing behind the stove and Stepanida disappeared behind the curtain, while the bald man by the table sighed heavily. When she returned after quickly settling her daughter, the man in the leather jacket had risen and, it seemed, closed off half the hut with his broad back.

"The child needs treatment. Have you had the doctor in?"

"In this storm? She'll likely get better by herself. Trouble is there's no milk, the cow's gone dry. She's not eating any more," Stepanida complained.

"That's bad. You should buy some honey."

"Hmm, if we had the wherewithal. We haven't paid the insurance arrears yet." The soldier entered amid heavy stamping in the passage and said something. The man by the table rose at once and started fastening the hook on his collar, then suddenly stopped and undid a button. Petroc couldn't see what he was getting from his pocket, the one in the leather jacket was in the way, but he soon guessed. Stepanida spoke uncertainly:

"No, no! You shouldn't. . .", but began thanking him immediately in a quavering voice.

"Thank you very much indeed, if you. . ."

"For milk and medicine," said the official softly.

His tall astrakhan cap was already on his bald head; he closed his overcoat and headed for the door. Petroc stepped aside into the alcove ready to fall through the earth for very shame. Why had she accepted it? Like a beggar maid, from strangers - and officials at that. Even if it was for medicine, it wasn't right, was it?

"Thank you. But how can we repay it? How do we know who. . ." Stepanida said, flustered, as she followed them out.

"No need to return it," said the man in the cap firmly.

"But it's a loan."

"Just a little one."

"If we knew where you're from. . ."

The man in the overcoat was already leaving the passage and the leather jacket was close behind him. The soldier letting them both pass ahead of him, stole a glance behind and whispered to Stepanida:

"Minsk. Comrade Chervyakov."

Stepanida seemed petrified for several seconds, the ten roubles clenched in her fist, while Petroc felt a sudden bodily weakness: well the wife had got her way alright! Asking charity from the leader of the republic itself! Going on about flax and money. . . But the guests were leaving the passage and he had to see them on their way, however embarrassing it might be.

It was still blowing out in the yard but visibility was good across the fresh snow. The two cars were standing on the highway under the pines, with several black figures nearby; presumably they'd managed to dig themselves out and they could now proceed.

At the gateway, turning away from the wind, Chervyakov halted.

"Thanks for the warm up, master. Good health to your daughter," he said quietly.

Petroc stood in the snow, confused, not knowing whether to bow, say thank you, or what. His tongue seemed to have been cut off and he couldn't say anything or find the necessary words. Then Chervyakov asked his assistant something, who inquired of Petroc in turn:

"Your name, what is it?"

"Bogatka," said Petroc and felt embarrassed about his own name for the first time, it sounded so absurd - "Rich", in that wretched snowbound yard.

"Well, I hope your life will be rich, comrade Bogatka," said the chairman of the Central Executive Committee, and all three of them bent their heads before the wind and began to make their way back along their own tracks to the highway.

Petroc, bemused, did not answer as he watched these people and repeated in his head: 'rich, I like that, rich. . .' His former inescapable worries seized upon him with new force - only about four poods of rye left in the boiler-house; of course, the bread could last them till the nettles and sorrel, if they had had a few more potatoes. They, however, were coming to an end, it had been a bad harvest that summer - the wet had caused rotting underground. How were they going to live till the next harvest?

23

Still, somehow they managed to hang on till spring; not well-fed, in fact pretty hungry, but they survived to see the warm sunny days and green grass. Stepanida contrived to make a kind of brew out of the first nettles, which was palatable if eaten with bacon-fat. It was worse on the bread front - there was just no bread at all. However, the president of the collective, Bogatka, Levon wangled three clamps of last year's potatoes for distribution as a labor day supplement, and Petroc fetched a cartload of wizened sprouting tubers in time for May Day. Never mind, they ate them, mixed them with buckwheat flour and baked cakes, keeping the rest of the buckwheat as grits for the soup.

Finally came full summer and May brought plentiful rain and thunderstorms; even on the clay soils the winter crop sprouted with a will. The winter crop field was, as it happened, along this side of the highway, near the gully and on across the whole of Golgotha. Now and again, by chance or when he had a spare moment, Petroc ran his eye across the field and was glad: the rye promised well this year. If it wasn't a dry summer and didn't pour at Ilya, the weather would hold till Transfiguration. The hay meadows were ready and Levon got the peasants together to "try the scythe" in Sheep Valley, close by the stream. From not being used to it, or from malnutrition, Petroc lost his breath on the third swathe, as pain pierced his chest, but he knew this happened at the start, it would pass when he got into the common rhythm, he was as good as the next man, wasn't he? Take Levon, three fingers and all, squeezing his scythe blade in between them and swinging away like a man possessed. Out mowing nobody wants to look weaker than the others, so they try with all their might to keep up. That Saturday evening they divided up the plots deciding which brigades should operate where. They agreed to start the next day, Sunday at dawn and mow till the sun got high. Levon ordered the rivets on all scythes to be tightened and warned everyone not to be late. At the end of the day results would be compared and the brigade which cut most hay would be moved to the red half of the board and the other to the black half. The second brigade had the luck to draw the easier stretch, from the alders on the edge of the water meadow; the grass was dense there, though not very high. There was a real chance of overtaking the third brigade from Zagriazye and get on the red side of the board.

At that they dispersed late in the evening from the psalm-singer's yard, where the collective office had been located for the last three years. Petroc hurried off to his own Yakimovschina; there was the scythe to tighten up and his whetstone was no good - just a short piece jammed into a wooden holder. While you sharpened your blade with that, the others would be way ahead. Levon had promised though that he'd nip into the township tomorrow and get whetstones for everybody, the money had already been paid into the village shop and everything would be above board. It would take an hour on horseback and the job would be done.

Relying on his new whetstone arriving, Petroc didn't take his old "lump of soap"; once the mowing began, he became aware that his scythe was getting blunt and Levon hadn't appeared with the stones. The peasants had got through two swathes as the sun rose above the fir copse, though dew still lingered in the deep grass which was falling splendidly in a thick arc. Petroc glanced more and more at the edge of the firs, from where the path to the water meadow ran, to see if the chairman had arrived with the sharpening stones, but to no avail. It was towards breakfast, when the mowers had lost a deal of sweat, that Levon's youngest son Mateika, ran from out of the firs and halted, seemingly frightened. Petroc thought at first that the chairman had sent him with the whetstones, but the boy's hands were empty. After he had drawn nearer and one of the mowers had asked rather roughly after his father, the boy dropped to the grass, covered his face and heaved in soundless sobbing.

"What's this? What's the matter?"

"Father, last night. . . they've taken him. . ."

The mowers froze; the nearer ones silently stuck their scythe blades into the earth, while those furthest away finished off their swathes before coming over to the firs one by one, already realizing what had happened. How could it be? Levon Bogatka?. . . What for?

They calmed the boy somehow and mowed on at half strength and individually until breakfast, though they spent most of the time, sitting, smoking and putting forward various theories and guesses. The majority view was that it was a mistake: Levon shouldn't have been arrested, as he wasn't an enemy or a harmful element. He'd never acted against his own people and had suffered for the Soviet cause in the war. It was obviously an oversight, a mistake. The powers that be would sort it out and release him after a day or two.

When Petroc had trailed back to the farm with his scythe, Stepanida was nowhere to be found. She hadn't returned by midday and he had no idea where she'd gone or on what errand. This Levon business had bewildered everybody, they were simply stunned, not knowing what to think or what action to take. In the afternoon, Petroc didn't go to the mowing; he had lost all heart and was filled with anxiety over Stepanida in case they'd taken her as well.

Stepanida ran home towards evening, upset, no kerchief on her dishevelled head and with her cotton jacket soaked in perspiration. It turned out she had already dashed over to the township, inquiring about Levon at the district committee and the police station. It had been to no avail, however; they had all maintained a gloomy silence and told her nothing. She had had a row with Kapusta, the chairman of the executive committee, after she had asked him to intercede, only to be rebuffed with a "know your place" refusal. Out in the yard, she slumped wearily against the parapet and responded in monosyllables to her husband's eager questioning. When she had recovered herself somewhat, she mulled the matter over and came to a decision:

"Got to collect signatures."

"What signatures?" Petroc was surprised.

"For Levon. That he's one of us, a bolshevik, not a wrecker."

Petroc said nothing for a moment, he was thinking.

"Then what?"

"Then put it up to the NKVD. Let them look into it."

That same evening she wrote something on about three pages of Fenka's exercise book and ran off to the Settlement, taking her indelible pencil with her. The cow was due back from the fields soon; she had to be milked and here was the mistress, gone who knows where. Stepanida, in fact, was rushing round the Settlement yards and returned late that night, worn out and emotional; after a few household chores, she flopped down to sleep. Petroc also went to bed late, although the next day it was planned to start on a new meadow beyond the alders, quite a tramp, and he should have to get up even earlier. He rose at dawn when the sky was barely tinged with blue, but Stepanida had already left on her rounds and was nowhere in the hut. It was Fenya's job to drive the cow out, but she was sleeping so sweetly that Petroc eventually did it himself. Nevertheless he felt that things were not as they should be; when the mistress neglected the farm it meant ruin.

And she did just that. For the next three days, Petroc hardly saw her on the farm, apart from a glimpse morning and evening; otherwise she was missing. She got round three villages and collected a fair number of signatures; the collective farmers felt sorry for Levon: he was a plain-spoken, straightforward, good-natured type of man. It was difficult to credit that he

was an enemy or a wrecker of any kind. They couldn't make out why he'd
been arrested at such a busy time, leaving the collective without management. True, Avtukh, the third brigade foreman from Zagriazye, had taken
over as chairman, but oddly for a man who had always seen pretty much eye
to eye with Levon and never had a cross word with him, actually refused to
sign the petition for him ('But how do I know if he was a wrecker or not? If
the organs have taken him in, they must know something.') Stepanida didn't
waste much time persuading him; she lost her temper and before running
off through the forest to the district committee, called him a "wolf-hound",
which was what Avtukh was called sometimes in the village.

She was late getting back; the cows were being herded in from the fields
as Petroc toiled back with his scythe, dog-tired and in a foul temper with his
wife, his work and life in general. He cut himself a slice of bacon-fat from
the tub and broke off a piece of stale bread with corn husks in it - he was
extremely hungry and his legs were fairly buckling with weariness. Then he
caught sight of his wife in the yard. Stepanida was slowly hobbling in from
the gate, limping on one leg and he recalled her complaining about a pain
in her heel a couple of days ago. She must have picked up a splinter
somewhere - small wonder, running about barefoot since Easter in the fields,
the hay meadows and the forest, and now the villages if you please. Barely
reaching the parapet, Stepanida fell down and Petroc, after a moment's
pause, went over to her. Still chewing on the hard crust with his toothless
mouth, he asked her:

"Well, how did it go? What did they say?"

"Oh, nothing. Gave me it back," she said, throwing the paper, folded in
four, to the ground at her feet.

"Dear oh dear! What's to be done then?"

"How should I know?"

Stepanida tried to rise only to slump back on the parapet again immediately; her heel was already blistered and she couldn't walk across to the hut
without the aid of a stick. That evening, Petroc and his daughter managed
to milk the cow somehow and then he found a big dock leaf by the fence
and tied it round the sole of Stepanida's foot, by now swollen and hot to
the touch. Stepanida had become unusually irritable, nothing could please
her and she flew out at both him and Fenya; Petroc understood how she felt
and took no offense, knowing that misery made nobody feel better. He saw
to the hens himself, fed the pig and fetched water from the well. He had
scarcely lain himself down on the bench in the passage where he slept these
nights when Stepanida called to him from behind the stove:

"Petroc, come here!"

Mastering his tiredness, he got up reluctantly and trailed over to her in his underwear.

"Petroc, you'll have to go to Minsk," she said, quietly but firmly.

"Minsk?"

"Aha. To comrade Chervyakov."

Petroc was stunned into silence, realizing at once what she had in mind. Minsk was a serious matter, especially for a man who'd only been to Polotsk three times, two of them as a young man when the Tsar had been on the throne. Still, she couldn't go, not with a foot like that, and he was concerned about Levon himself. He had to help the man but how was he to do it?

"You'll go tomorrow. I borrowed twenty off Kornila. I wanted to go myself, but there. . ."

"But where do I find Chervyakov? Don't suppose it's that easy, a town and all!"

"They've got a Government House there. It was in the papers - they've built a Government House. That means Chervyakov's there as well."

"Hmm. . . but where will I go? What if. . . I've never been there in my life!"

"Well, now you will. What of it? Just ask and people will show you. Otherwise the man's going to be done for isn't he?"

Petroc made no reply. It was a bad business when a good man was done down and he felt sorry for him. He felt sorry for himself as well though - where the hell was that Minsk with its Government House and how was he going to get there? He'd heard the peasants say you had to go to Orsha and change, you had to buy a ticket. If he only knew how much it cost. Quite a bit, most likely. Petroc was simply overwhelmed by what his wife had unleashed on him that evening. Still, he knew if she'd once made up her mind about anything, she would stick to it. He would have to go.

"And don't tell anybody! If anything's said, I'll tell the foreman you've gone to the doctor's. Because you're not well."

"But. . ."

"Well, what 'but'? He's someone we know, sort of, Chervyakov. He might step in. You see him and remind him when he dropped in for a warm last winter, at Epiphany. And loaned us ten roubles. And you're returning it."

"That's all very well. Just the same. . ."

Petroc was very loath to go off on this unfamiliar journey to the end of the world, Minsk, the chairman of the Central Executive Committee. He was seized with terror as he tried to imagine what it would involve.

24

Two days later, however, Petroc was descending the precipitous steps of a railway carriage onto the crowded morning platform in Minsk.

With one hand he kept a tight grip on the slippery iron handrail while with the other he held on no less tightly to his carefully wrapped linen bag of provisions: a crumbling lump of bread, a slice of bacon-fat, an onion and two hard-boiled eggs. There was also a twist of salt and, lying at the bottom, an old tarnished knife with the blade snapped off at the tip. Petroc was dressed in his best for the occasion: woollen trousers, not new but clean; a satin shirt washed through by Stepanida, a little patched behind the collar at the back. The patch couldn't be seen, however, as he was wearing a rusty-colored jacket of homespun cloth over it. This had a pocket containing Stepanida's petition of twenty-seven signatures and a ten-rouble note. The other note he had changed in Lepel when he was buying his ticket; he had to keep the change for the return trip.

He slowly made his way along the crowded platform, amid the unaccustomed chatter and bustle, starting at every locomotive hoot and unexpected jet of steam from under the greased carriage wheels. His head felt as if he were drunk, giddy and full of buzzing noises, either because of his sleepless night in the overcrowded carriage or simply this city hurly-burly. He had no real idea which way to go from the station; it was a good thing he'd bumped into a fellow countryman from Holopenich in the carriage, who gave him approximate directions. Petroc headed along a narrow little pavement through a side alley, sticking close to the house walls and at times knocking into the ends of metal pipes sticking out at the corners. He was afraid of going near the edge because of the thunderous trams clanging along the roadway one after another - woe betide you if one of those hit you, that would be your finish! So he clung to the buildings with their endless succession of doors and windows: there were goods displayed in some of them, but he didn't look at them. A savory smell drifted out of a doorway and he stopped to stare. It seemed to be a diner with tables for four and white plates. Then people started coming towards him with fresh loaves of bread in their hands; some broke bits off on the sly and chewed them as they walked. Alongside a low dilapidated building stretched a lengthy chattering line, whose beginning was lost in a pair of open doors with the word BREAD in huge letters on the signboard. Petroc marvelled at seeing so many people in one line and hurried past along the roadway. A minute later, before he had got to the intersection where the Holopenich man had told him to turn right, he realized he'd made a mistake in wearing the boots which had been drying out since spring; they were pinching his toes unmercifully and made further progress impossible. He knew he should have travelled barefoot, but there was nobody barefoot here; all were shod, not like in the country. And Stepanida had nagged him: wear boots, you can't go barefoot in town. So he'd put them on and it was torture.

He soon forgot about the boots, however, either because he'd got used to the discomfort or because of the astonished admiration which over-whelmed him at the intersection; from here he could see a vast gray building of goodness knows how many stories, with a majestic towering facade, hundreds of windows, a great square courtyard in the middle and a broad white flag the size of a tablecloth waving over the roof. Just below on the wall was the White Russian coat of arms in stone. Petroc realized that he had reached the object of his journey - the chief building of Minsk, the seat of government.

He slowed down here so as to collect himself. This was no village soviet, not even the district exec, where a couple of steps from the street and you were in the door. But here? Try and guess which one of a multitude of doors opening onto the court was the one for you - not to mention the security; would they let him in without a pass? He would have to ask permission. As he got more and more anxious and his resolve, small at best, drained away, Petroc edged along the palatial building, glancing at the doors - which one should he try? He reasoned that if anybody turned in there off the street, he would follow them, but nobody did go in, they all passed by on the pavement. He didn't know how the time was getting along either; no doubt the sun had risen somewhere but who could tell with these buildings shutting off half the sky. Everywhere cool dense shadows lay along the ground, it was like morning in the pine forest.

And so Petroc walked past the three-sided square courtyard with no decision made or courage displayed. As he passed on a little further, he saw off to one side a pretty red brick church. Another time he would have stopped to admire it, but not now. Agitation rising, he fingered Stepanida's papers; he felt like taking out his tobacco pouch and lighting up but changed his mind and headed for Government House again.

This time he didn't spend any time admiring the facade and choosing a door. He turned the corner and made straight for the nearest entrance beyond its broad flight of stone steps. There seemed to be no one about either on the stairs or round the door, but as he peered more closely, Petroc noticed something white behind the door, something which stirred briefly before becoming watchfully still. It was a policeman. Petroc recognized him by the white shirt with the black holster-belt slung across it and the white cap and star on his head. It soon became clear that the policeman had begun keeping an eye on Petroc from behind the glass; the latter was out in the middle of the square by now, walking ever more slowly. He was willing himself to go on, though his feet were reluctant to obey him, stubbornly trying to turn off towards where there were lots of people - out of sight of the policeman. And his feet overcame his intentions; they turned away from the square and out into the street where Petroc found himself back on the pavement again, filled with joy and relief.

Here he relaxed and sighed as he realized he was soaked in sweat like at the mowing in Sheep Valley. For a while he walked on, not knowing where himself. He chided himself for his lack of resolution and for getting into this business in the first place, scolded himself for feebleness of character and kept trying not to get so worked up and scared. So what if there was a policeman? He hadn't come with foul intent had he? Just ask how to get to comrade Chervyakov or at least get the papers to him. It wasn't his initiative and he wasn't getting anything out of it, was he? It was for the common good, see, a commission from the collective farmers. He had nothing to do with it, he was practically a neutral. Hand it in and go back home, no reason to get excited. Despite all this, Petroc simply wasn't capable of subduing his stupid anxiety and might have wandered anywhere in this strange city and lost Government House altogether. Realizing this, Petroc came to a halt and relaxed his right foot a bit, probably totally skinned by now anyway, and wiped the sweat from his brow with his sleeve. No, he'd go to the policeman and just ask and that was all. What was there to be afraid of?

Petroc turned round in the street once more, trying to ignore his boots. As ill luck would have it, a natural human need now made itself felt and became ever more insistent, but there was no time for that and he put up with it. He slowed down at the corner of the monstrous building, just for a preliminary glance, so as not to appear in front of the door all of a sudden. Seeing nothing untoward, he passed the flower beds and, beside himself with nerves, turned towards the steps, fearing even to look where he was going. As he did so, he almost stumbled again - now there were two policemen in white by the tall doorway, gazing at him in silence as if it were he they were waiting for. Like a hare in a cornfield, he described a sharp loop and returned to the street almost at a run. While he was going past

Government House, he tried to give the impression of a man much preoccupied, definitely uninterested in anything round here.

This time he went a long way past the red church and did not stop.
Stopping would have meant turning back to that intimidating building again
and he just hadn't the strength to do that any more. Again nature was
prompting him to find a certain place, but he had no notion where that
might be. He did permit himself to get his tobacco pouch out and roll himself
a cigar. The first few puffs served to calm him down somewhat and Petroc
wondered, not for the first time but now with a special poignancy, just why
he had come here. When Stepanida's foot healed, she could have come
herself. She was bold, she wouldn't have got flustered in front of two
policemen. It was she who had accepted the ten roubles he didn't know
how to return and she'd collected the signatures he didn't know what to do
with.

Allowing himself this short breathing space, he smoked his cigar and
abandoned his recent awkward timidity as he strolled along the busy street,
gazing about him. All around loomed buildings of all shapes and sizes, with
countless windows, balconies and signs. Packed tramcars thundered
towards both ends of the street. Somewhere up above one of them, a dense
drift of sparks came down from the wires and Petroc thought that a fire was
breaking out. But nothing caught fire and no one in the street seemed to
pay any attention as they hurried about their business. Meanwhile, morning
imperceptibly turned into day and a hot sun rose above the corrugated iron
roofs as pavement shadows shortened and it began to bake unbearably.
Petroc tried to put up with it as best he could, though it was stifling inside
his woolen garments; he didn't take his jacket off though, fearing for his
papers and money. Limping slightly, he dragged himself along the pavement,
parallel with the tramlines for a considerable distance, constantly hoping to
find some bushes, a little gully or patch of waste ground which would come
in exceedingly handy. But the street continued on and on, buildings
stretched endlessly by on both sides, high and low, occasionally one-story,
like in the township, but hemmed in by great brick edifices. And everywhere
windows and doors, windows and doors. You could leave the pavement and
enter some of these doors, things were on sale there, but Petroc merely gave
them a preoccupied glance and passed on. The pain in his foot had inten-
sified; he was placing the side of the sole on the ground now and cursing
himself for not greasing his boots at home, making them softer maybe and
avoiding chafing. He'd been in a hurry to catch the Lepel train, however, so
he had to endure his present torment. His agitation mounted as he realized
time was passing and he'd accomplished nothing yet. There was no sign of
what he was looking for either. Once he did glance into an evil-smelling alley

with crumbling walls, but there were women and children in the yard; one was hanging out washing on the line and turned to give him a hard stare. He hurried back to the street in embarrassed silence. Good job she hadn't asked him anything - what would he have said to her?

Up ahead on the other side of the road loomed the green tops of tall trees and Petroc increased his pace, much cheered, but soon slowed again: there were lots of people here too, some taking their ease on benches, others reading as children played about their feet, others still were simply strolling along the shady walks. A young woman came towards him along the street with a shaggy dog on a lead and carrying an open umbrella. Petroc marvelled: why? It was sunny, not a cloud in the sky. He stood there for a while, looking about him and grimacing painfully before wandering on to where the street forked on rising ground. Beyond a finely decorated house with rows of bay windows, rose an enormous grey building very similar to Government House. A high wooden fence ran along this side of the street, behind which lay a peaceful little courtyard, with chestnuts at the very end at the foot of the hill. The courtyard gates were open wide, though there was no one to be seen; from somewhere came the sound of running water. Petroc peered inside timidly. Tucked away in the dense shade of the chestnuts was a metal water fountain and nearby a barelegged little girl in a brief, flowered, summer dress was playing. Further off were some small sheds, lilac bushes and elders set among long grass and weeds. It looked as if what he was looking for might be in there.

When he entered, the girl recoiled in fright from the copper bowl in which she was washing something for her dolls. Her sharp little eyes stared at him expectantly and Petroc said the first thing that came into his head:

"Can I have a drink?"

"Yes," she responded readily and lifted her thin little shoulders as she dashed for the other side of the fountain.

Petroc thought she was going to run off into the house for a mug, but she was already holding it in her hands. She pushed hard on the lever and a limpid stream of water quickly filled the mug. Petroc drank hastily as his eyes searched feverishly through the bushes near the shed. He had been right, it seemed: there was a wooden toilet tucked away in a corner of the courtyard.

The little girl asked him something but he no longer had the patience to reply. Striving to stay unruffled, he made off almost at a run along the overgrown path.

When he came back the little girl had disappeared; her copper bowl lay near the fountain and water was flowing across the grass-covered stones. Petroc was glad of her absence, he had felt awkward in front of the urban toddler and felt almost happy to be out in the street. Then he confronted the main problem again: what to do next. He was still very uneasy about the task he had undertaken. Surely he couldn't go home empty-handed? What would he say to Stepanida? He could well imagine what Stepanida would say to him.

With renewed determination, Petroc went back to Government House. This time his intentions were definite: come what may he would go up to the policeman and inquire. They couldn't arrest him for that and might not even tell him off, though they would have reason enough. He'd ask politely how he could see comrade Chervyakov: if not now, then some time later, he could wait. And if it was absolutely impossible to see him, could the comrade policeman hand over a peasant petition on behalf of their chairman to the President of the Central Executive Committee. He had been a good chairman, in the party sense and as a farmer, why had he been arrested? The local admin men were a clique but comrade Chervyakov could sort it out, he was a man of principle and held a powerful position. He'd punish them likely. Then again the debt was preying on his mind, it had to be returned. Petroc wasn't the sort of man to sponge off another, never had been. Stepanida neither. Whatever she might be in other matters, as regards money she was always scrupulous. She'd do anything to repay a debt.

Limping heavily as before and sweating profusely under his thick woollen jacket, Petroc walked past the red church, linen bag in hand and approached the angle of the familiar building. Two cars emerged from the courtyard, driving across his path; he had barely time to leap out of the way as he glanced over them. No, Chervyakov wasn't there. In the first car sat a bespectacled man with a grave expression, while the second was occupied by military personnel in caps, tunics and shoulder belts. They went off swiftly along the street, overtaking the tramcars. The wide expanse of the courtyard was empty as before; there wasn't a soul to be seen near the doors nor behind the glass. Petroc was disconcerted - did this mean he would have to go inside the building? Of course he should have inquired this morning, at least there had been someone to ask. Now what was he to do? Stand where he was? Knock or open the door himself?

Treading indecisively, as if testing each step with the sole of his boot, he ascended to the broad stone porch and approached the nearest door. He chanced to peer through the glass and shuddered with alarm - a hunted visage was looking at him from the other side. The face was covered in gray stubble, the lips were twisted in suffering, forehead damp with perspiration and a dim droplet hung from the tip of its sunburned nose. Petroc wiped his face and paused before timidly touching the broad handle and giving it a strong tug. The door held firm. He pushed it away from him, no use either.

Then something flickered behind the glass and he heard a muffled incoherent voice - the policeman, of course, in his white shirt, white cap with
the star on the peak. He was saying something but Petroc couldn't hear and
kept trying to open the door. Then the policeman took a pace to one side
and the adjoining door opened with no bother.

"What do you want, citizen?"

It was probably a different policeman from this morning, a pleasant young
black-browed face, pistol slung on his smartly taut wide cross-belt. Some
sort of badge tinkled on his left breast as he held the heavy door open in an
inviting gesture. Petroc didn't want to go in, he placed his bag by his feet
and undid his sweat-soaked pocket with shaking fingers, drawing out the
crumpled sheets of the petition.

"I would like to see comrade Chervyakov. See, it's written here. . ."

The policeman came outside, apparently interested, took the papers and
ran his eye over Stepanida's rather uneven lines.

"You're too late, uncle."

"Maybe I could wait."

"It'd be a long wait."

"I see," said Petroc despondently, still pretty much in the dark. It seemed
the policeman was having a joke at his expense. But if he wasn't what was
he to do? "And there's a debt as well. Ten roubles, see, give it back. . ."

"What ten roubles? Who to?"

"Well, comrade Chervyakov. He lent it to us, see?"

The policeman's handsome face was strained and anguished like a man
with a bellyache; he was probably having difficulty understanding as well.

"Hmm. A loan. . . What a time to remember! He was buried yesterday."*

"What, he's died? I see. . ."

The policeman was summoned inside the building and Petroc was left
standing in front of the door. It appeared his business was actually finished
and he should go home. He conscientiously stowed Stepanida's ill-fated
papers in his pocket and picked up his bag. It was so hot out in the courtyard
that he felt unwell and all of a sudden forgot the turning for the station. A
hot haze filled his head and persisted all the way to the station, while he
stood in the ticket line and all the time he was sitting on a bench by the wall
waiting for the Orsha train. Everything happening around him seemed alien
and hateful, and he very much wanted to get home. To his wretched
farmstead on the edge of Golgotha, to the gully, the swamps and hummocks,
his own little corner in this vast inhospitable world. . .

*   *   *

---

*The historical Chervyakov committed suicide to avoid being arrested during the purges.

25

Stepanida got almost no sleep that night, merely dozing off from time to time; her head was filled with thoughts of all kinds, but most of all with anger and a sense of outrage: what had they done, the swine! For some reason she wasn't afraid of them. She had feared the German aliens, yes, but these were her own people, she'd known them since childhood and though she knew what they were capable of, she couldn't bring herself to be afraid of them. Even Guzh seemed more inclined to shout and threaten than actually do anything terrible. Even those who'd nearly done for her, even though they were strangers wandered in from somewhere, they were still her own sort and spoke her own language, or Russian. There was war on of course but why had people altered so much?

She could hear them beating up Petroc in the yard and Guzh losing his temper; she tried to get up but was so dizzy she lay down again behind the stove. She stared dry-eyed at the smoke begrimed ceiling, listening to the shouting in the yard and thought no, this is unforgivable. She would never forgive them for this. No one had a right to forgiveness for such a thing.

She felt bad. The right side of her head ached severely and she couldn't even touch her hair without pain. It was all swollen probably. 'They can't have fractured the skull, can they?' Stepanida thought anxiously, but her thoughts sped at once to Petroc. Where had they taken him? If they hadn't killed him they would put him in the cellar under the church, that was where they were herding all the prisoners now. Petroc must be there. And what had he done to be put under lock and key? Hadn't he given them vodka? Or was it instead of her? When he started interceding for her? They'd have taken both of them in that case. Still, they'd have taken her first, probably.

It seemed as if she had endured her lot in full measure and lived out her destiny. Though in a way she hadn't lived at all in this harsh world of God's making. She had always been planning, putting things off till later; long years had merely been a preparation for a better future. The individual farmer had been rooted out, collectivization brought in, no time for joy or pleasure then: they'd thought, never mind, later when everything was organized, then they'd be in clover. But then came the five-year plans and the struggle against the class enemy - it was all shortages, anxieties, troubles. There was always the worry about getting enough to eat, economizing on bread and surviving till the new potatoes. There were no clothes for the children, nowhere to get shoes. Life was hard and the thought was: just get the children on their feet. And the children had grown up and now this war had come along.

How long would the war last? How could they survive to see the children? Probably they couldn't manage either one or the other. Not within the bounds of possibility. What could she accomplish then? What was within the bounds of her capacity?

For good or ill, she knew what she had abundant reserves of, something she would never abandon, even on the very edge of destruction. In the course of her hard life she had learned what truth was and had developed, inch by inch, a human dignity of her own. Anyone who has once felt themselves to be human can never turn into an animal. Much in her life, especially grief and trouble, had taught her that you must live kindly towards your neighbor if you wanted them to treat you as a human being. Man was made, likely, to repay good for good and could hardly repay evil with good. Evil could give rise to nothing but evil, it could do nothing else. The only trouble was that human good was powerless in the face of evil; evil took account only of power and its only fear was punishment. Only the inevitability of retribution could subdue its rapacious temper and compel it to take thought. Without that, chaos would reign on the earth, much like that mentioned in the Bible.

Sometimes she had heard tell of the Germans: a cultured nation. Maybe it was in some ways, but how could a cultured person allow himself to resort to open brigandage, as these Germans did? She hadn't read their books and knew nothing of their high-level politics. She was used to judging great things through small, the world by her own village. And she was right. She knew that good people do not behave basely either of their own accord or under duress. Baseness is the weapon of the base. It was one thing for the Germans to come to her land bearing arms, it meant that right was not on their side. Whoever is in the right has no need of weapons. Again, you had only to see who was working in with them to understand what sort of people they were themselves. She wouldn't knuckle under to them till her dying breath because she was a human being and they were brutes.

Stepanida lost consciousness from the pain and perhaps even dozed off, but she was soon awake and trembling at the barking of a dog close at hand; she realized it was Rudka going mad outside. He was barking in the yard, by the woodpile seemingly. But who was he barking at, who could be walking round the hut at this hour? In some alarm, she raised her head and peered out from behind the stove. It was completely dark inside the hut; the window opposite barely glowed. It was from that window that the quiet insistent knocking came.

Her heart began hammering as she attempted to rise; gripping the stove with both hands, she came out from behind it, her eyes fixed on the window. The quiet knocking on the lower pane was repeated, insistent as before.

"Who's there?" she quavered, then froze.

"Open up, Ma. Friends."

"What do you want?"

"Open up now!"

"No, I won't. I'm on my own here and not well, I'm not opening up."

Probably on hearing his mistress' voice, Rudka began barking more boldly and skipped nearer the doorstep. She wanted to add that Petroc wasn't here and there was no vodka, nor was it right to knock up an old sick woman at night, but she reflected that words wouldn't stop them. They could kick the door down or the window and there would be a repeat of what happened the previous night. To her surprise, however, they left off knocking; after a brief conversation they apparently went away, since Rudka could be heard farther off, over by the fence and the gates under the limes. She stood for a while, listening and thinking that perhaps it hadn't been the police. In that case, who? Not from hereabouts, probably, as they had spoken in Russian. Who could it have been? Had the Red Army turned up? Or partisans maybe? She had heard a week ago that a considerable partisan force was gathering in the Zaberedin forest. Once in the small hours, something had lit up half the sky over there, followed by a crash that reverberated over the entire forest. They weren't sleeping then, the partisans or Red Army men, party people anyway, they were cooking something up. No indeed, the party wouldn't let the Germans pass. Maybe Fyodor was with them and they could have told her something. Oh what a fool she was, not letting them into the hut.

The small nocturnal incident had completely unsettled Stepanida; she went over to the window and through the streaming glass peered out into the murk of the autumn night, listening intently. But there was no one anywhere about. Rudka had settled down and the intruders must have been far away by now.

Stepanida couldn't sleep and made no effort to do so. For what remained of the hours of darkness she sat on by the window, absorbing the hushed, watchful silence of the night. Her head still ached but she had come to terms with the pain to some extent. When the windows grew gray at the approach of dawn, Stepanida got up. She now realized that she couldn't just remain on the farm, just suffering in ignorance. She'd had enough of the unknown which had swallowed up Fedka, Fenya and now Petroc. No, it was time to go somewhere and get something done.

Rudka was quiet out in the yard, or maybe he'd just run off somewhere; meanwhile the piglet was stirring uneasily in the shed. She could hear him through the wall and remembered he hadn't been fed for two days. Concern for the pig gave her an influx of strength and she betook herself out of the hut into the passage, finding the old iron pot by feel and pouring in the husks from the millstones. She opened the outer door with timid irresolution; it turned out to be unlocked and at once she recalled the nocturnal knocking at the window. They hadn't even tried to open the door. Not the polizei then. It had been some group of strangers, passers-by. Again she felt a pang of regret. Why on earth hadn't she let them in? It might have been her only chance to learn something about Fedka.

She placed the feed in with the pig and found a lump of bread for Rudka; then she sat down on a bench to think: what should she do next? First and foremost she had to find out about Petroc, if he was still alive. To do that she had to go to the township; nobody could tell her anything hereabouts.

After a time, she rose and went into the boiler-house. In the bottom of the tub among the salt, there were still two lumps of bacon-fat left; she picked one out. Then there were half a dozen eggs under a broken jug by the stove recess and a dusty bottle of cherry brandy on the shelf, left over from last summer. She placed all these items in the little light basket she used to take to the township before the war and went into the yard.

Outside it was cold and windy as it had been for days, but it wasn't raining; it had probably ceased at dawn, though the yard and track were deep in mud. Her head still ached and she found it hard to stoop; she donned a warm kerchief and buttoned up her quilted jacket. She had nothing to put on her feet; she habitually went barefoot till the frosts and then wore some old battered shoes or the felt boots dried out over the summer lying about behind the stove somewhere. She couldn't wear them in this mud so she just walked to the road barefoot. She didn't lock the hut - the lock had got lost somewhere; she just dropped the hook in the ring and that was that. There was nothing to steal in there and locks were no use against the polizei.

She walked along the verge, sometimes through the mud, sometimes in the wet grass, skirting the yellow pond by the main road, and clambered up onto the low embankment. She hadn't been here since the day when dumb Yanka had spotted the Germans beyond the pine wood; a good deal seemed to have changed. The wires stretched taut, high on the telegraph poles, were humming just as they had before the war, before they had been cut down during the retreat. So the lines had been restored for the new German order to speak along. The highroad was covered in fresh tire marks from carts and motor vehicles, hoof marks and footprints. That meant the bridge was in operation. Not far in front, a cart with a frisky white horse between the shafts was entering the pines, its driver waving his whip urging his horse on. She thought she'd been behindhand in reaching the road, otherwise she might have ridden with him. She glanced back to see if anyone was going in her direction.

No one was behind her on the road, but up ahead a vehicle sped out from the pine wood bend, followed by another, then another. These vehicles were somewhat smaller than the one which had been at the farmstead, but were heavy and ponderous enough, loaded as they were from top to bottom. Stepanida got down into the ditch to keep clear of them and stared at the windscreen of the first, trying to make out the faces inside. The glinting glass made it hard to see anything, but she realized there were Germans sitting there: dark collars with buttonholes, bright epaulette edges, peaked cap tipped backwards on the one next to the driver. The first truck roared past, enveloping her in the stench of petrol, then came the second. She saw three young Germans sitting in the back of the third and pleasant music was coming from the mouth organ one of them was playing. When this lorry drew level with her, the young chap on the end, his cheery face flushed from the wind, called out:

"Mama, gip eggi!"

"Mama, speck!" the second joined in and flung a lump of white fat at her; it slapped into the roadside mud without reaching her.

She said nothing to them, just stared as the cheerful, cheeky young men roared by her, an old worn-out country wife, a foreign mother nearly murdered two nights before; not a muscle twitched on her face. Oddly enough, she felt no fear of them now and wouldn't have said a word to them if they had addressed her. In her mind they had ceased to be people. They were monsters and talking to them would have been absurd. She even regretted that she hadn't thrown anything else down the well that night, hadn't set the hut on fire, say, burn the lot of them along with their officer. She'd been far too cautious and timid. And why? Fear was no guide. Look at Petroc, so terrified he did everything they wanted just to escape worse. And what had he got for his pains? Arrested for no reason at all. And they'd murder him or hang him too.

She'd been through a lot of misery with this Petroc and there'd been a lot of harsh words, but she was so sorry for the man now she could cry. And what harm had he ever done them? Who had he bothered? If he hadn't helped anybody either, it was because he couldn't, that's how he was. But he was incapable of doing anything bad. He was really too kindhearted for these times - or former times either, come to that. That was the way he was, sooner give than take. Step aside rather than go for what he wanted. He hated quarrels, all for the quiet life. What did you get in this life if you kept quiet? And so he'd got nothing.

She remembered chasing him to Minsk to see Chervyakov and felt a stab of conscience for the hundredth time: Petroc wasn't up to things like that at all. Still, she couldn't have gone, hobbling about the yard for all of ten days.

She'd been suspicious of Petroc for a long time after that: had he given the petition in? Had he not found the place, not done the job, been too frightened? She'd worn him down with questions, but Petroc stood firm: he'd given it to the policeman. It was alright, all they had to do was wait.

Waiting, of course, was foreign to her temperament and as soon as her foot began to heal, she trotted off to the township on a crutch and had a blazing row with the district administrators. They even threatened to send her after Levon, but she was fearless. She also interceded on behalf of the teacher, the same one who later became headmaster and who had recently been hanged by the Germans. A month later the teacher had come to the township from Polotsk. They'd let him out. Whether this had anything to do with her intervention was an open question. Maybe just the least little bit; when a man's drowning even a straw can help.

True, Levon never came back; evidently he was done for. Now there were more urgent matters on hand.

If the Germans didn't look on them as human beings and treated them like animals, then that was how they should behave towards the Germans. Total contempt, hatred and resistance wherever possible. Especially as any other sort of attitude held little promise. The business with Petroc had convinced her of that.

She passed through the pine grove on the road, glancing at the deeply excavated pit in the sand at the bend, and at length glimpsed the first township huts in the distance, the fire station tower and the bare poplars along the main street. The wind was swirling clouds of gray smoke above a few chimneys; it was morning in the township and stoves were being stoked up. After the Jews had been driven out, a lot of the huts were empty and others were occupied by squatters and the police. Outwardly, little had changed in the township where day-to-day life was probably going on much as it had done before the war. On the other hand, a good deal had altered on the road - the embankment had been renewed and the bridge shone yellow with its new planking. That had been missing half the summer and the embankment itself had been ripped up by bombs, as if pigs had been rooting there. And now they'd gone and rebuilt it all. So they could drive across it, push their trucks on East to the front, transporting everything their army needed. Evidently that was a great deal if they needed an insignificant road like this with its twenty-yard bridge over a swampy little river. They couldn't manage without it, clearly.

She approached the bridge slowly until, with a kind of inner turmoil, she ventured onto the new white boards and fingered the planed handrail. Everything was of wood, rough-cut wood tightly fitted together and fastened with heavy-duty nuts and bolts, designed for protracted use, very likely. So then, the Germans would be using it and the polizei would be grabbing folk and driving them over this bridge to the township to hang them on telegraph poles or stick them in the church crypt, or bury them in the quarry on the other side of town. A very necessary bridge, no denying that. There'd be no life because of it.

It had been fine those few months when there had been only naked posts here and yawning craters scarred the embankment; not every traveller had been intrepid enough to cross the river on two shaky slats. Life had been peaceful for a time, nobody had come breaking your door down; the Germans were nowhere to be seen in the Settlement, never mind the farm. The new order didn't reach as far as them.

Stepanida traversed the bridge then halted, struck by an idea: how about burning the thing down? It was made of wood after all, maybe it would catch and burn; then life would be as free as it had been before. Yes, if she were to pour kerosene on the planking, the stuff Petroc had got in the settlement. . .

Stepanida went back to the bridge again, feeling the boards in different places with her bare feet: no, blast it, the stuff wouldn't burn. If it had been summer now. . . but it was all wet and made of fresh timber, what's more; no, it wouldn't catch hold. If she could have got a bomb here!. . . Stepanida was so stunned by the suddenness of the idea that she ceased to notice she was on the road at all, forgot where she was going and why. She recalled Petroc's recent words and it dawned full upon her - that's the way it had been! Stepanida knew Kornila of the Settlement well enough to be certain he was connected with this business of the bomb. But Kornila. . . maybe he'd listen to her now? She would beg him!

And Stepanida turned back along the road, away from the river and towards the pines, beyond which lay the turnoff in the other direction, onto the hill and the Settlement.

She encountered nobody on the road; far behind, someone was trailing leisurely along, probably from the township. On the Settlement road, however, she at once caught sight of Alexandrina, a woman of her own age, alongside whom she had got married once upon a time; she remembered them both going through the church ceremony in winter, at Epiphany. She also recalled the black stallion belonging to Alexandrina's father breaking its leg that day on this very same bridge, plunging a hoof through a hole in the planking; that was the sort of useless bridge it had been. Alexandrina was walking slowly, the corners of her kerchief tucked under her armpits and leading by the hand a thin, sickly little boy, very warmly wrapped. The women greeted one another.

"Haven't seen you in ages, Stepanida, where are you off to? How're you getting on?"

"So-so, you know. . . These days everything's so. . ." Stepanida was somewhat flustered, caught unawares by the question. She simply didn't know how to reply, so she hurriedly inquired: "What about you?"

"Oh dear, Stepanida, troubles pile up. I'm taking my little boy here to the doctor; he's eaten something bad and can't get rid of it, five days now," Alexandrina babbled away, forgetting her own question. "Just what I didn't need, dropping on me now," she glanced round cautiously at the road and added quietly: "You know, my officer Vitya's come back, he had a real job to get out. . ."

"Victor! You mean from the war?" Stepanida was astonished.

"Dear lord, what a war! He was badly shell-shocked, he gets headaches, his hands are shaking. . . oh it was awful there at the front he says. . ."

"Tough was it?"

"You're telling me! He says they were run over by tanks and our lads only had rifles and they. . . anyway they scattered in the forest. Some got taken prisoner and some got home, those who lived near. . ."

"I see."

Stepanida listened but felt an instinctive mistrust towards this woman, her former friend, there was something she didn't like here and she thought: Victor's come home, so where's my Fedka? Fedka wouldn't run home and he wouldn't give himself up either; if there was no news then. . . probably Fedka had returned to the earth.

She felt angry on her son's behalf and envied Alexandrina: he might be shell-shocked but he'd come back. And she had five at home without the eldest, a hutful of boys. Hers was empty. There had been two and now. . . no one left.

Mulling over these gloomy reflections, Stepanida reached the Settlement, but instead of going along the main street, she turned off where the kitchen gardens began and headed along a path to where a grain shed stood under a maple, a stone's throw from Kornila's hut. She hadn't been to his place for almost ten years, since the collectivization in fact, and she noticed that in the interval his farmstead had by no means gone downhill - in fact rather the contrary. A chain clinked behind a tall, well-maintained fence, accompanied by a dog's savage barking. Stepanida halted, fearing to open the newly fitted wicket gate all the way. She reckoned somebody would be bound to come out. She didn't want it to be Vandzia, Kornila's tall, lean wife; she'd never got on with her since the day of the wedding. Although they hadn't actually quarrelled, they had never spoken to each other and if they chanced to meet on the road or in the township, they acted as strangers and exchanged no word.

She looked over the gate for a minute at the hut, with its fine porch and veranda, glassed in with small panes under a new thatched roof. Scattered about were an assortment of yard outhouses, sheds, sties and storehouses. Quite the kulak's spread, thought Stepanida to herself. Although Kornila was only a fireman in the township, he had spare time, that was the main thing. He'd always put his back into things, always willing to put in the effort.

Kornila stuck his head out somewhere round the side of a shed and regarded her from a distance. She scarcely recognized him in the heavy-shouldered, black-bearded man who slowly drew back two or three heavy metal bolts.

"You're. . . like in a fortress," she joked, keeping her face straight. He probably sensed the strain behind the light remark and let her into the yard without responding. Whereupon he locked it again, just as carefully. "I'm here on business," she said, "but I don't want anyone to. . ."

"Alright, let's go into the shed. Actually I was in there when. . ."

He conducted her slowly past the black, snarling dog, then past the angle of the passage, then on into the yard via the manure heap against the wall of the sty, turned again past a kind of partition and found themselves at last by the half-open door of a shed piled high with an immense amount of wood and metal scrap, wheels, planks, some oak offcuts, blocks, tools and bits of iron festooning the walls. There was a carpenter's bench by the door. Nearby, a quilted jacket lay on a low wooden block and next to it, a cart wheel on which Kornila had obviously been working. As soon as they entered, the master at once seated himself on the block and took his hammer to the wheel. He asked no questions and she stood in the doorway, not knowing where to begin.

"Making something?"

"Yes. What else can you do. . ."

"Everything alright at home?"

"Yes, more or less."

"They arrested my Petroc. Yesterday."

"That's bad if so," he said, his voice still cold, not even raising his head from the wheel; he may have struck the wheel rim more forcibly with his hammer. "He must have done something."

"But he didn't."

"People don't get arrested for nothing."

She didn't particularly want to argue with him, having long acquaintance with his difficult, reclusive ways, but she couldn't help thinking: if he won't sympathize a bit, he might at least be surprised. But he showed no signs of that, he had withdrawn himself, either that or he was concentrating on his work. Had he really become as thick-skinned as that?

"I have a favor to ask," she said simply, reflecting that perhaps this was best - no wasted words, straight to business.

"And what's that?" he brought out, still cool and indifferent, pulling the iron tire onto the wheel rim, his neck flushed with effort above the collar of his woolen jacket.

"Give me the bomb."

For the first time, perhaps, he glanced at her suspiciously from beneath his bushy eyebrows and hemmed into his beard.

"I know you've taken the bomb. The one lying beside the bridge. Give it to me."

"You know a lot," was all Kornila said.

"Go on. What do you want with it anyway? Times like these, it'll just be on your mind all the time."

"So why do you want it?"

"I need it."

"Who says I've got it?"

"Nobody. I just guessed. I know you very well, don't I, Kornilka?"

She paused and almost ceased to breath as she watched him, following the movements of his broad rough hands bending a white wooden rim onto which the metal tire was disinclined to slip. Kornila levered it away with his chisel, then settled it properly with a few deft blows of his hammer. He heaved a heavy sigh.

"So what do you want: something for nothing?"

"Nothing?" she was astonished. She'd never really considered paying Kornila, and what could she pay him anyway for a thing of that nature these days?

"Killing a flea costs you something these days," rumbled Kornila. "Times like these. There's a war on!"

"Well, you know, money. . ."

"Heh! What money? What good's that now?"

"Well, I've got about two pounds of bacon-fat. Half a dozen eggs. . ."

"Eggs, she says! I can get eggs - for an omelet."

'The old skinflint', Stepanida began to get annoyed with herself. She recognized the old Kornila, the one who wouldn't give you snow in winter, they used to say. Still, it was a good sign he wasn't arguing about having the bomb. She'd hit the spot there and rejoiced quietly at it. The rest was just a matter of negotiation.

Yes, but how?

"I believe you're not on the Germans' side, are you. You're still a human being I hope."

"Always was. Not on one side or the other. I'm for myself."

"So you took the bomb. Obviously you knew it would come in useful."

"Knew? Course I did! And so it has. For somebody."

"Me, Kornila."

"I don't care, you then."

They both fell silent. Kornila kept revolving the wheel in his hands, though there was no more work to be done on it now.

"So what can I give you then?. . . I've got no cash, the Germans have eaten the cow and shot the hens; I've only got half a dozen left. Guzh has arrested my man and taken him into the township. What else have I got?" Stepanida was at her wits end.

"What about the little pig?" Kornila asked suddenly and gave her a short piercing stare, "Or have you not got that either?"

"I've still got that, aha. For spring." Stepanida stopped, flustered. He didn't want that, did he?

"Good thing you have," said Kornila, apparently indifferent as he got up and made for a corner and rummaged about among the scrap metal. At last he drew out a curving length of wire, which he proceeded to chop into nails.

"So it is, aha. But. . . alright, take the pig. I'll give it to you."

"Around twenty pounds, would it be?"

"Around that. He's a good fattened piglet," Stepanida boasted, her voice faltering and was surprised at her own offer: could she really give it up? What would she be left with then?

"Well, if it's for a pig," Kornila had livened up somewhat. "I mean this. . . it's some article for these times! But what do you want it for exactly?"

"That's my business now. I need it!"

"Alright, I know. Maybe for somebody in the forest? Good trade article that."

Kornila pondered for a moment, then peered outside and shouted at the dog; he waved his arm silently for Stepanida to follow him. In the yard, they slipped through the small gate at the rear of the farmstead, overgrown with blackcurrant, gooseberries and young cherries. Down by the fence among the docks and nettles, Kornila raised a layer of pea stalks, from behind which peeped the end of something long and rounded, like a pestle with a metal box welded onto the end. It was the bomb.

"There!" he said with restrained pride, before swiftly covering it up again. "Hundred pounder. A whopper."

Stepanida felt a tremor of excitement, sensing perhaps for the first time the danger she was inviting. But it was too late to draw back - let him have the pig.

"I'll harness up the horse. . . night, though. Soon as it's dark, I'll fetch it over."

"Well, naturally, soon as it's dark," she agreed softly.

26

Even before it got dark, Stepanida went anxiously out into the yard and peered through the gates, then stood beyond the palings and gazed out at the Settlement track. She knew it was rather too early and that Kornila wouldn't come till it was completely dark; he'd said that himself and as a man of his word, he had meant what he said. But she couldn't just wait in the hut; she hadn't even eaten that day, hadn't made up the stove, so impatient was she to see Kornila because - God forbid! - the police might swoop and then what could become of the two of them?

She had already run across the polizei that day in the township; she had gone there immediately after Kornila and finally reached the prison in the church crypt. Since she'd last been in the township, the polizei had got themselves securely settled in. They had erected a construction of planks against the ruined shell of the church and hung up some heavy gates, before which stood a sentry with a rifle. She was pleased to see the sentry was Nedoseka, Antos and thought she was in luck. Skirting a considerable pool of rainwater, she turned off the square towards these gates, intending to inquire about Petroc as sweetly as she could and hand over the basket if possible. Nedoseka, however, stopped her some way off with a harsh cry:

"Back! No further!"

"It's me, Bogatka from Yakimovschina," said Stepanida, thinking he hadn't recognized her. But after she had spoken, Nedoseka's swarthy gipsy face was unchanged, severe and unapproachable.

"Back, I said! No nearer!"

"I only wanted to ask if Petroc was here."

"Not allowed, I tell you, back!"

'Damn and blast you!' thought Stepanida and switched her basket from one arm to the other in frustration. 'What now?'

"Just tell me where they've put him" she asked, getting angry herself. But Nedoseka looked as forbidding as she had ever seen him. It was as if some changeling had taken over. After standing there for a while, she tried to edge nearer without being noticed.

"No nearer! I'll open fire!" The polizei was in a frenzy and unslung the familiar rifle with the split and riveted stock.

She stood there in silence before going back to the other side of the muddy unpaved square, where the polizei directorate was now housed in a neatly whitewashed stone building with a balcony. She thought she might come across somebody she knew and ask them, but from some way off she saw some thug on the steps, complete with greatcoat and rifle, doubtless another sentry. Undecided, she crossed the square again and stood by a telegraph pole, placed her basket on a patch of dry ground and waited for Guzh or Kolondenok to show up, so she could make inquiries of them. As ill luck would have it, nobody emerged from the building; either they were busy or there was no one in there. She stood there in the wind and penetrating drizzle; her kerchief was wet through and her arms were freezing cold, but she waited patiently, keeping her eyes fixed on the police station doors. She did not at first pick up the sound of steps in the mud but as she spun round, she saw the teacher, Sventkovsky, striding towards the police station. True, he pretended not to see her or recognize her, even snuggling his head down into his greatcoat to avoid greeting her. She went towards him, however, as a last resort, recalling that he was a kindly man and might spare her a couple of words.

"Good day to you. . ."

"Good day," replied Sventkovsky coldly, without stopping, however. At this, she seized her basket from behind the pole and ran after him through the mud.

"Maybe you could give that to Bogatka, Petroc, he's here isn't he?"

"Yes, he's here," said Sventkovsky, glancing warily at the directorate building, barely slowing down. She feared he might get away and she'd never catch him.

"Maybe you'd give him this. . . there's eggs in there and bacon-fat. . ."

Sventkovsky took the basket without a word; the narrow little eyes in his haggard, pinched face flickered nervously about the square.

"And get out of here, straightaway! Now, quick!" he whispered urgently.

Stepanida's joy was tempered by the disconcerting realization of the concealed anxiety in the former teacher's words; she stared at his retreating back for a moment, hunched in the black woolen overcoat he had worn for nigh on ten years. He walked up to the porch, pausing to scrape his mud-spattered boots and with a last look back at her from beneath his hat brim, disappeared through the door. Only then did the menacing significance of what he had said dawn upon her, and she realized that he had spoken out of sympathy for her, rather than ill will. Probably something had happened and they'd found out about it and disaster hung over her head as well.

She certainly had no desire for that; she couldn't jeopardize her grand desperate plan by risking anything here in the township under the noses of the polizei. Starting off slowly, she steadily increased her pace until she was running along the street towards the high road. She needed to hurry, since time was surely getting short and there were vast numbers of things to do and anxieties to go with them. As she trotted along the high road she ruminated about what might possibly have happened and where. At home maybe or at Kornila's? Or had Petroc blurted out something he shouldn't? What did he know anyway? She had long ago dropped the wretched old wives' habit of talking over everything with her man, maybe because Petroc didn't share her ideas and clearly mistrusted her intentions. She'd done a great many hair-raising and risky things as and when she saw fit and Petroc had grumbled to begin with, then got used to her independence as the years went by, and to her primacy indeed, something which seemed to suit them both. God forbid he should ever find out about the rifle, he'd die of fright. A good thing Stepanida had kept it all from him. She'd long been convinced that the only things that stayed secret were what you and no one else knew, such was the world today and the people in it.

Stepanida slowed down only when she reached her own yard, where she sighed with relief on seeing that all was as it had been and the wood splinter still in the latch. She wondered if Sventkovsky had just wanted to scare her or chase her away from the police station. But his hushed voice had been conspiratorial almost and held a warning for her. Something was wrong here surely. Something else was going to happen.

After a moment in the hut, Stepanida went outside into the yard to wait for Kornila. She stared intently at the gray shadows thickening over the wide expanse of the fields, beyond which the Settlement huts, the hill and the high road telegraph poles were merging into the creeping murk. The near end of the track to the farm was more clearly visible, but even that was fading and drowning in the darkness before disappearing completely from sight.

Close by in the yard, the orphaned stray Rudka ran hither and thither; when she paused and stared into the distance, he also froze by her feet, staring and listening for something doggy of his own. And all at once she was amazed, as if seeing herself from outside: what had she embarked on? This was no rifle to be thrown down a well and all consequences with it. A bomb couldn't be hidden away like that and she must make sure she didn't get into a serious mess over it. The main thing was to keep out of the way of those swine now and maybe she would bring it off. Later on, that is, after a while. If need be she would delay matters, be patient and wait for the most favorable opportunity. Just let the bridge go up and she would abide the outcome. She was not afraid.

All the same, she did feel scared, even jumped, when Rudka gave a sudden yelp into the darkness, then stiffened, all snarling attention. Stepanida hissed at him softly and prodded him with her foot; Rudka quieted down and she knew exactly who was out there as she moved towards the gate. She could pick out the quiet knock of a wheel in a pothole and a horse's weary snort. Soon, against the glimmering sky, appeared the vague outline of a horses's head under a shaft bow, while squat Kornila waddled alongside holding the reins.

"I've been waiting," said Stepanida quietly, as she met the cart.

"What on earth for? I harnessed up as soon as it was dark and came on over. It's not far."

"I know, but. . ."

She wanted to say that any moment now they could get into serious trouble even on a short journey - bump into the Germans or the polizei who were scouring everywhere for their prize. Or some ill-intentioned person could be following, later to inform; disaster might strike at any moment. But she held her peace, rather than abrade the nerves of both of them. Things had gone well, be thankful.

"Where d'you want it?" growled Kornila as he passed under the limes and tugged on the reins.

"Where?"

Indeed where could she conceal it? The hut was no good surely, they'd find it there straightaway. She had to think of another suitable place, near the farmstead so she could keep an eye on it. She suddenly remembered the hollow behind the cowshed, heavily overgrown with raspberry bushes. There were pits there, half full of brushwood; that would do to cover it up and hide it away till needed.

"Let's put it behind the cowshed. In the ditch."

"The ditch it is. Makes no difference to me."

Kornila turned the front of the cart and gradually led the horse along the palings towards the gully. Stepanida, walking ahead in the blackness, pointed out the best route.

"Bit back from the fence here, tree stump over here. Now keep directly behind me."

She strode on confidently and lightly through the dark, familiar as she was with every blade of grass and every obstacle; Kornila slowly trailed along behind, clinking the bridle and quietly urging on his horse. Thus, in pitch darkness, they reached the thicket which rose like a dark wall on the lip of the gully.

"The pits are round here somewhere," Stepanida bent over, scrabbling with her hands among the grass. "I'll get the brushwood out first."

"Let's get it off first," said Kornila. "I'll take it and you give a hand. It's a weight. . ."

They went over to the cart and Kornila dragged the bomb with both hands from under the hay. Stepanida tucked its cold metal tail under her arm.

"It's blasted heavy!"

"What d'you expect! It's pretty powerful, you know! Not just a shell or anything. Boom!"

Very gingerly they lowered the long casing, slippery with rain, down onto the wet grass by their feet. Kornila, dropping down into the pit, pulled the bomb towards him.

"It's, you know, a little bit. . . There's something a bit wrong with it," he announced with difficulty as he straightened up, breathing heavily.

"Something wrong? Really?" Stepanida was on her guard.

"Just some little thing honest. One of the army men can sort it out. Just a minor fault," he hastily assured her.

"Why didn't you mention it before?"

"Why should you care? Does it matter? You're not going to use it yourself are you? A specialist can do it. An army man."

"So where do I find one of them now. . ."

She said no more, afraid she might blurt something out in front of Kornila. No outsider could know anything of her plans. Though Kornila wasn't an outsider, of course. She was also aware that she could hardly manage on her own; she would need assistants. Still, she could find them. There could be no problem there. If not now, then later. The bomb would be there.

"Does it matter if it's wet? Won't it rust?" asked Stepanida.

"Doesn't matter. The charge is inside the casing," Kornila said confidently. Stepanida thought he probably knew: he'd been in the army, served in the Polish campaign even. People said he'd nearly got to Warsaw.

They hauled the dry brushwood by the pit down onto the bomb. The previous summer, Petroc had cut back round the edge of the gully here to stop the bushes spreading and growing tall enough to shade the garden. His efforts now seemed absurd to her; the time had come to worry about other matters. Still the brushwood had come in handy.

"Well, let it lie there," said Kornila wearily, clambering out of the pit. "So, where's the piglet?"

"He's back in the shed. We have to go round in a circle so the tracks. . ."

"Well, of course, the tracks. . ." He tugged at the horse's bridle again, as Stepanida, almost by touch in the drizzling dark, led him to the path across the garden and pulled out a fence post, so that he could get through to the boiler-house. The empty cart swayed across the furrows without a jolt, in silence; the horse trod softly on the soft earth. By the woodpile they came to a standstill.

"Just here. I won't be a minute."

In among the wet dock leaves and nettles, she felt for the lower door of the shed, then knocked away the support and out of the darkness rolled a light-colored bouncing ball of a creature, grunting joyously and thrusting its rough snout against her wet insteps. She began to feel sorry for the little pig, all the grief she had shared with him and now she had to give him up to a stranger. She subdued this surge of pity by force of will; now that everything round her had crumbled to ashes, there was no time to pity a foolish animal, she had more important things on her mind.

"Come on, come here. . ."

The piglet came trustingly into her arms. As she lifted him, she pressed his warm, heavy body to her and took him over to the cart.

"Where d'you want him?"

"In the sack here. I've got a sack. . ."

Well, of course he would have a sack, how else can you carry a pig in a cart? How to get him in though, Stepanida wondered. In the pitch darkness she made clumsy work of thrusting him head first into the proffered sack, but the piglet, doubtless divining what was in store for him, stuck his legs out and convulsed his whole body, so that she could barely hold him in her arms.

"Now then, what's the matter? Quiet you silly thing!"

Kornila, however, deftly wrapped him in the sack, threw him into the back of the cart and covered him with hay. The piglet began squealing piercingly in the dark.

"Quiet, you! Blast it, he's little but he can sure. . ."

"Not so little!" Stepanida was prepared to take offense. "He's a nice spring piglet, that."

"So I thought. Otherwise. . ."

It looked as if Kornila was annoyed, seemingly the piglet was too small. He was no full-grown boar, that was true, but the bomb wasn't in working order either. It had to be mended, thought Stepanida, irritated. Who could do that round here?

"He's a well-fattened, well-behaved, lovely piglet. If it wasn't for. . . I wouldn't give him up in a hundred years."

"Alright," said Kornila, putting an end to the conversation.

The cart wheels squeaked as he turned it and Stepanida indicated the way out of the yard; Kornila pointed the horse towards the gates and stopped.

"And you keep quiet, eh? If anything happens I haven't seen you and I know nothing."

"What am I, a bairn?" Stepanida responded, thinking with dislike, no stupider than you, don't worry.

Kornila quietly drove off along the dark track. At first she could hear the pig struggling under the hay, trying to give voice, but gradually all became quiet. Rudka, hiding round a corner up till now, ran up to his mistress and yelped in the dark.

"Now then!" she said to the dog. "What do we do now?"

Only now did Stepanida realize how the piercing cold had got to her and how wet she was, especially her skirt, but an obscure excitement had laid hold of her and she couldn't sit still for a minute. She felt like setting off somewhere while it was quiet, doing something to bring nearer the hour when thunder would rock the high road and that damned bridge would be blown to smithereens. Let them repair it then, let them send their team to force people to labor. While they were engaged in doing it, time would pass, winter would be here and our lads would give them what for. She'd heard it from the men several times that our boys always waited for the winter, like against the Finns or in the war with the French before that. Winter always helped our side and she wanted to do her share of helping too, not just sit and do nothing. The point was, she now had something besides her bare hands. Down in the pit was a powerful force capable of reducing the bridge to matchwood. How could she get it under there though?

She recalled that there had been shelving ground under the roadway of the former bridge. Boys had sometimes crawled under there and frightened horses by snarling like wolves. It would be handy to put the bomb under there. The problem was - how? On her visits to the township, she'd only once stopped on the bridge and had never examined anything there at all closely. What if they'd filled it all in and levelled everything off? You couldn't put a bomb on the walkway, with people walking and riding by, could you?

She was getting thoroughly anxious about this and after going into the hut for a while, she ran out into the yard again and went down towards the high road. It was completely dark, with an intermittent drizzle and nagging wind. Before she reached the bend, Stepanida turned off into the fields and took the direct shortcut, running where she could to economize on time. At first she felt the rough stubble of the cornfield under her feet, then came the soft wet grass beyond the pines, which she had skirted on the field side. She traversed a small boggy area, then a sedge grown ditch and clambered up the sandy embankment not far from the bridge.

Here she paused to listen, shifting her wet kerchief back for the purpose. The walk had warmed her up but she felt extremely nervous, though the road was nocturnally empty and quiet. She was a little frightened in case anyone came across her here, especially someone she knew - how could she explain her presence? But everything was alright, it seemed. Down below the river water glinted dully by the embankment and Stepanida went down the freshly constructed incline towards it. She halted, staring into the impenetrable murk under the bridge, where the row of new piles stood pale under the broad, looming block of the span. She guessed rather than saw, that from the shape of the embankment a sizeable space remained between her and the bridge itself. The bomb could fit in there, it wasn't as big as all that.

Now satisfied, Stepanida climbed up onto the main road and walked towards the pines. For the moment all was going well and this gave her heart. The nocturnal excursion, however, had exhausted her and she was soaked with sweat under her jacket as she wandered quietly along the road. Once past the pines, she turned into her own fields, repeating in her mind: just don't let it fail, just let it come off. She hadn't the strength to refuse the task and she desperately wanted it to succeed. Nevertheless, she knew there was plenty of work ahead; she had to find accomplices, above all a specialist, an army man, to put the bomb right.

Tomorrow she'd have to run over to Alexandrina in the Settlement, she thought; Victor was an officer, he must know how to do it. If need be there were still five hens left in the henhouse, she could pay. He was sick, shell-shocked, he'd need chicken soup and such. She would beg him. . .

27

At first light, Stepanida emerged from behind the stove, set her kerchief right and wrapped her quilted jacket round her. Night, with its reflections, nocturnal visions and loneliness was over; day had begun, a day in which she had much to do, unusual things, terrifying if you stopped to think about it. . . She was wholly given over to her anxieties; she had even lived through a dream connected with the bomb. In it she was climbing a steep hill, carrying a heavy burden which was dragging her back down. Her legs were slipping, as if on a muddy track and her fingers found no purchase, but still she went on climbing and climbing. The summit was so close now, the edge of some sort of abyss; she had to summon up some kind of effort, just two steps more. Then, however, her mind clouded over and the vision changed. . .

Stepanida opened her eyes and realized that dawn was breaking. She hadn't made much sense of the riddling message of her dream and reality quickly pushed aside the visions of the night. Her anxieties drove her on as she went into the passage and from the trunk took out an old bag, ripped in one corner; in the boiler-house she put two handfuls of grain in her pocket from the jug which Petroc had never got round to grinding after all and flung the door open. It was a damp autumnal morning outside and ragged clouds fled before the wind over the limes, but it wasn't raining and the blue forests beyond Golgotha were sharp against the horizon; it was always like this before a cold snap or on the eve of the winter frosts. Stepanida went behind the woodpile and tugged at the loosely secured henhouse door. The hens were sitting in a little row on the perch, three facing the door and three the wall. On the straw in the corner, next to an old yellow egg were two fresh ones and the mistress of the farm thought affectionately: poor silly things, still laying! Their mistress hadn't fed them for long enough and they'd had to live on what they could find for themselves in the yard or the garden. Feeling guilty towards them, Stepanida sprinkled some seed from her pocket and the hens, fluttering and clucking, flew down together from the perch to the doorway.

She continued feeding them and as they jostled one another, competing for the grain, she wondered which of them she should take. She'd known them all since they were chicks and could distinguish them by the way they walked and their individual markings; she knew which one had laid and when. The speckled one with the black head laid the best eggs, she wouldn't take her. The worst layer was the short-tailed, young one with the shaggy legs; it was the scrawniest and most timid. Even now it was being pecked from both sides and resigned to picking up seeds behind the others. Still what meat was there on a skinny thing like that? So Stepanida selected a placid yellow hen, not the thinnest but not the best either. She calmly grabbed it by the wings from the rear and the hen gave itself trustingly into the arms of its mistress without resistance, Stepanida trussed its legs and put it in her bag. Then she returned to the passage and took an old cotton kerchief from a hook above the trunk and wrapped the bag in it.

Before leaving, she looked round the bare walls of the passage, all the corners and the green trunk with the red-flower pattern, but she could find nothing else suitable as a gift in the whole, war-plundered dwelling. If Victor wouldn't do it for one hen, she wouldn't grudge the lot, let him eat them all, just as long as she got that one thing, the thing that monopolized her thoughts, drained her energies and might well claim her life too. In her hands was an opportunity which fell to few; it had become her chief end in life and she would strive to bring it to fruition. It was a pity she couldn't do it all herself, but people would help her. They had to. All she had to do was find suitable accomplices - no brutes, no cowards. Then Petroc would yet hear what happened on the high road. If only she could bring it off.

Of course she realized that people would be the problem. It would have been fine if she could have fixed on one of the men, if Fedka had been home, or Petroc even. Once again she cursed herself remembering her refusal to admit those mysterious night-walkers - maybe they would have given her a hand? Still, who can foresee things which only might happen? How could she have known who they were? Even now she was only guessing. Supposition was easy, but so rarely confirmed.

The mud on the track which had frozen overnight chilled her bare feet and she tried to choose places where it was drier and grassless. The grass was soaking wet with icy morning dew and even colder to her feet than the mud. It was an overcast morning, with the sky gradually clearing and a cold windy day setting in. However, she noticed neither the morning nor the cold; she was considering the best way of approaching Victor and talking him into agreeing. At one time he had been a fine easygoing sort of lad, a pal of Fedka's, forever running across to the farm. Once she had told them both off for playing with matches: they'd crushed about eight boxes of match heads to use in a homemade gun and she'd been afraid they might scorch their eyes and cripple themselves. Of course, as they grew up they went their different ways. Victor had joined up a year earlier and become an officer before the war, with three triangles in his collar-tabs. He could cope with a bomb surely, Kornila had said it was only a minor fault, a specialist could mend it easily.

Stepanida ran across the main road, empty at this hour and went along the familiar dirt track into the Settlement. The outer huts were already visible; the Amelyanov boys were harnessing the cart in the end yard; passing the garden Stepanida could hear masculine bad language carried on the wind. The track grew somewhat drier as it climbed the hill but there was a pit with a broad pool of standing water, rippled by the wind; she gave it a wide berth and when she came out on the track again and glanced up ahead, she froze for a second. Three men were coming towards her from the Settlement street. Two she recognized at once, the polizei Guzh and Kolon-denok, but the third. . . The third was walking between them, head down and hands behind his back; one glance was enough to confirm he had been arrested. Her heart palpitated unpleasantly, when it seemed. . . but even in her own mind she dared not pronounce his name while the least doubt remained. Stepanida wanted to be mistaken and thought: let it be someone I know, a neighbor or a relation, only not him. Dragging her steps uncharac-teristically she went on towards the men and the familiar outline grew ever clearer before her eyes: squat figure in gray jacket, wide-set shoulders, heavy measured tread. Both he and the polizei were pacing leisurely along through the mud - Guzh in front, Kolondenok behind - as Stepanida wished for the earth to swallow her up to prevent their meeting. But they had noticed her and regarded her from a distance with keen awareness. As he got nearer, the prisoner also raised his eyes. It was Kornila.

Nonetheless, she walked on as if not recognizing any of them, though her legs were trembling so much it required an effort of will to place one in front of the other. Stepanida would have passed them by without a word had it not been for Kornila's look. His bearded face, outwardly calm, expressed such misery and concealed anxiety that Stepanida stopped in spite of herself. Guzh at once did the same.

"Where are you off to, activist?"

"The village, can't you see?" she said, looking askance at him and thinking: Well, I'm done for. They'll take us both in. But Guzh first nodded at the bag.

"What've you got there?"

"A chicken!"

"Let's see!" the senior polizei thrust a demanding hand out and she passed over the bag. Just like ten years before, it was all being re-enacted, on a more frightening level. "Right, Potap, take it. When we get back you can wring its neck. Come in nicely," he said, almost calmly, however, as he handed the bag to Kolondenok. Thereupon he turned to her and pierced her with his menacing stare. "Still wandering about, eh?"

"That's it. Am I not allowed?" she asked, calling on all her strength to withstand that brazen stare. She thought he would place her next to Kornila in a minute and take them both off to the township. That would be terrible. It was noticeable that he hesitated for some seconds deciding what to do.

"Alright, wander away!" he said, mysteriously sarcastic and turned to Kornila. But Kornila was no longer looking at her; he was staring sadly across the overcast expanse of wet fields. "Quick 'arch!"

Off they went down to the main road, while she wandered into the Settlement, weak and irresolute. Kornila's arrest had been a bitter blow and threatened destruction to her entire plan. Surely it wouldn't all collapse, all that effort go for nothing? But why hadn't they arrested her? Were they leaving her till later? Maybe they didn't know about the bomb? Or had they been searching for it and arrested Kornila? And he hadn't told them where the bomb was. And he wouldn't either. Or maybe he would? Once they started the torture, giving you the works, who could stand up to that? What on earth was she to do?

It didn't immediately dawn on her that there was no point in going to Alexandrina's; there was no reason to go to the Settlement at all. She had to save herself by her own efforts. But how - and where?

Near the first Settlement huts, she peered about fearfully. The polizei and Kornila were already approaching the pine wood along the road. She stopped, paused for a moment, then swiftly ran back the way she had come. Now she had to get home, to her own walls, as if they still held some sort of certainty, some kind of assurance.

The polizei and Kornila had disappeared into the pine woods meanwhile as she ran panting across the road and, alternately running and walking fast, reached the farmyard. Passing the hut and the boiler-house, she ran on by the woodpile and beyond the sheds to the gully's edge. Rudka bounded out from somewhere, whining joyfully; he was hungry but there was no time for him now - she had to hide the bomb somewhere else. While still in the garden she became nervous on seeing that the cart had cut prominent tracks across the beds and led away to the gully in a distinct curve. She nearly collapsed in terror when she peered into the pit - the yellow iron tail of the bomb was sticking out sideways from under the pile of brushwood they had thrown in. Did they really have to make such a mess of hiding it - the first person to come along would have seen at once what lay under the branches.

Of course they'd been working in the dark, at night and it was easy to make mistakes then.

Stepanida ran swiftly towards the hut and got the old shovel by the woodpile, thinking it would be better to bury the bomb this time. But where? In the garden? Behind the cowshed? By the gully? Probably on the gully edge, the soil was soft there and grassless, she could throw lots of rubbish in, dead leaves and such. They'd hardly look there. Let it stay there. Apart from her nobody could find it. It would be secure.

She began digging among the alders not far from the first pit. The new one was three paces long and narrow, like a child's grave. At first the work was easy, the mold yielded easily to the spade; after taking off the first layer, she straightened up. Further down, tree roots began to hamper progress; they penetrated the soil in all directions, tough and tangled. She chopped them off with her spade and pulled them out by hand. Some she tried to snap but they just bent into white knots, spraying her head, face and shoulders with earth. Wet through with sweat, she scrabbled in the pit for two hours or so until it was knee deep. She hastily cleaned out the white, root fragments, but didn't throw the earth far away, knowing she would soon be needing it. When the pit was ready, Stepanida rested for a while on the edge of the hole and put the spade aside. Now to fetch the bomb.

It was about twenty paces to the previous pit. Once there, she began tossing out the brushwood and got to work on the long, heavy metal roundness of the bomb itself. Rudka leapt around her hands, sniffed the yellow casing and sneezed. Stepanida tensed herself to roll the bomb out of the pit and felt a pang of fear - it had moved the merest fraction, then rolled back again! This was terrible - she simply didn't have the strength! She rose and wiped the sweat from her brow with her sleeve. It had been all very well rolling the bomb into the hole, how was it to be got out? By herself too. Thoroughly on edge by now and refusing to allow herself to relax, she seized the bomb and with an immense effort shifted it a bit higher. Then she started at the other end and raised the nose. As soon as it lifted, the tail stubbornly slid back to its former position in the pit. Stepanida almost wept with frustration - what on earth was she to do?

After pausing to consider the matter and calm herself down, she got out of the pit and started looking for stones round the edge of the garden. There were plenty of them but too small so she wandered farther afield and found two more sizeable ones which she brought to the pit. Now, placing these in turn under the nose and tail of the bomb, she had to roll it out onto a level spot. She toiled long and hard, pushing and rotating, working with her hands while bracing her knees in the damp earth. Her skirt and jacket were completely covered in mud and she was soaked in sweat before she finally freed the bomb from the pit and fell exhausted alongside. Damned bomb! Stepanida wondered if she would collapse before finishing the job, but somehow she endured. Now the bomb had to be dragged over to the other pit. All the time she was afraid that someone would come wandering along and catch sight of her in the bushes. She was visible both from the yard and the track through the sparse shield of alders - if she could only hide it while no one else was around.

The bomb was easy to roll along the gully rim, crushing the grass with its yellow, mud-spattered flanks. Further on, among the alders, this was no longer possible and Stepanida took hold of the rounded iron tail-fin. If she raised it slightly, it was possible to tow it along but it took time and was an enormous drain on her already much depleted reserves of strength. She dragged the bomb about five paces, then let it slip as she herself fell backwards into the grass and gulped air for several gasping minutes. Somewhat recovered, she again hooked her fingers in the wet tail-fin. This time she managed an even shorter distance before dropping again. Her subsequent efforts jerked it a step at a time, no more, to the edge of the gully; her back was racked with pain and her wet hands and knees had been raked raw by the twigs and roots. And she hurried. All this time she kept looking about her through the almost naked thicket in the direction of the farmstead - God forbid that anyone should come by and see her. Then she would be done for along with the bomb. And after all her efforts!

When at length she had dragged the bomb to the pit, it seemed that her strength had gone completely; she couldn't roll the thing over the mound of excavated earth and fell face down across it. She kept driving herself: that's enough, get up, and she kept promising: I will, in a minute, I will. But she did not. Then she made an effort to rise and all went dark before her eyes, as her heart seemed to burst from her chest.

She lay like that for a long time, clasping the bomb's filthy casing, she herself being caked with mud from head to foot. When her breathing had settled down somewhat, she remained prone and bracing her heels against some gnarled alder roots, strained for the last time and moved first the tail, then the nose. Crushing its way through the crumbly soil, the thing at last fell into the pit. Stepanida lay on the mud for a while, then got up and took her spade.

Covering the bomb up was easier; she shovelled earth into the pit and trampled it down on top. Then she raked the surplus soil together and spilled it all around. After that she swept the earth from the alder bole and shook the saplings and the lower branches of the trees, so that no trace remained to indicate anyone had ever dug here. Some way off among the alders she collected an armful of blackening leaves and strewed them over the digging site, the gully edge and all about, so that no trace of fresh earth was visible.

Finally she fetched brushwood from the first pit and flung it about as though the foot of man had never trodden here.

Leaning on her spade, she barely made it back to the yard, where the starving Rudka met her with a quizzically attentive look. But now she couldn't even give him a kind word; she stopped him as he tried to keep after her into the passage, a dog's place was in the yard after all. She put the passage door on the hook and hauled herself to the sleeping shelf behind the stove and fell into it just as she was, in kerchief and quilted jacket.

She lay like that, in the freezing hut, numb with exhaustion, listening to noises near and far and musing that the main job was done now. The rest was secondary. She just hoped for a few days more of freedom, to see Victor, call in at the township, talk things over with one or two people. If you were in trouble, you always went to people - who else could you help you? It was people who destroyed you, but they were the ones to help as well, weren't they? Even when there was a damned war going on.

After lying there for a while she felt somewhat rested; her arms and legs continued to ache but her mind was at peace. The chill began to get to her. She hadn't lit the stove for several days and the hut was bitterly cold. No doubt she should get it going overnight otherwise her teeth would be chattering come morning. And boil up some potatoes too. She was very hungry and there wasn't a crust of bread in the place.

Stepanida swung her feet down and slowly slid to the floor. Evening was already drawing in outside, but it was still light; a fresh wind moaned round the walls and the lime twigs tossed in agitation as they bent before its ceaseless assault. The stove was already laid, she had only to put a match to it. She took a pine splinter from the bundle and stuck her hand down between the stove and the wall, where she had hidden the matches from Petroc. She had just retrieved the box when Rudka began a sharp barking from the yard. Her heart sank in foreboding as she sprang to the window, matches in hand. Rudka was racing round the yard and barking frenziedly as four men with rifles came along the track from the road, marching fast. Even from a distance she could recognize most of them "Well, this is the finish!" she said to herself.

To her own surprise she was not particularly afraid and didn't try to run away anywhere; it was as if she had been expecting this ending, realizing its inevitability. She merely racked her troubled memory for things she should do but nothing came to her. Perhaps she had already accomplished everything? She sneaked a glance through the window behind the stove, then ran out into the passage, probably to get as far away as possible from the windows. Rudka was still barking at the gate when the first shot rang out. Rudka gave a piercing squeal and fell silent - for ever was it? She knew her turn would be next.

Her powers of thought had returned, however, and she rushed into the boiler-house and hooked the door. No, they weren't going to take her that easily. She was no Rudka. Or Petroc either. Not even Kornila. She'd keep fighting. Let them kill her! If they did, well. . . that would be their victory. But they hadn't killed her yet and she wouldn't surrender.

Three blows of a heel against the door echoed round the passage.

"Open up!"

She squatted down in the boiler-house behind the thick oak doorpost and kept quiet.

"Stepanida, open up! We'll break the door down!"

'Break it down!' she thought savagely to herself.

But it was no easy matter, likely, breaking down an ancient oak door three inches thick, a forged iron hook driven into the wood and the ends deeply embedded. Break it down then!

From the conversation outside she could distinguish Guzh's growling and the thin murmurings of Kolondenok and Nedoseka.

"Hey, activist! Open up nicely now, or it'll be the worse for you! You know me!"

"Shut your foul mouth!" she yelled, unable to contain herself and regretted it at once: why did she have to respond to them? Let them wonder where she was, keep knocking. Beating their heads against a wall.

She thought they were going to start breaking down the door, but they hammered at the window instead and there came a tinkle of breaking glass, then a crack as the frame fell in. This was worse; at this rate they'd soon be in the passage. Good job the boiler-house window was tiny. But they'd find a way. . .

"Bogatka, come out, don't be afraid!" came Sventkovsky's reasonable tones, almost unruffled. 'That one's there as well!' thought Stepanida grimly. 'The nice man.' "Just show us where the bomb is. You hear. We won't touch you."

'Is that all they want?' thought Stepanida and crawled from the door to the millstones. They were out there apparently, she could hear footsteps in the passage. One of them had crawled in through the window and opened the door for the others. But they wouldn't open the boiler-house door. . .

No sooner had the thought crossed her mind than the door was thunderously shaken and dust rained down from the walls. More crashing thuds ensued; they were obviously using an axe. This was even worse of course;

it altered matters, narrowing her safety zone and with it hope of any sort. But she had no hope in any case; she had a clear vision of her fate, she was merely putting off the final moments by all means she could contrive. Her deep regret was that her great enterprise had not materialized, her plans had collapsed. This made it imperative that theirs shouldn't succeed either.

They could probably have shot her through the door - there was no concealment from bullets here. But they held their fire. It seemed they wanted her alive. To tell them the whereabouts of the bomb, was that it? That meant they hadn't got what they wanted out of Kornila. Well that would be doubly true of her.

All four of them seemed to be hacking at the door, which rocked on its frame; only the heavy forged hook and iron hinges prevented it from falling to pieces. Still, they'd smash it all the same, sooner or later. Stepanida already knew what she had to do and her only fear was that she might be too late to effect it. She scraped about under the millstones and with trembling hands rolled out the heavy bottle of kerosene. The door was shaking and cracking under the assault. Stepanida tugged the wooden stopper from the narrow neck and splashed the liquid onto the door, then to either side of her onto the walls and in the corner. In the process she was plentifully splashed, arms, legs, skirt - everything stank of kerosene, but it didn't matter now. Hurling the bottle to the ground, she took the matches from her small jacket pocket. She never had got round to lighting the stove. Kneeling, she struck a match on the box.

The first attempt was a failure, the door didn't catch and the match went out. Then she pulled off her kerchief and soaked it in what remained of the kerosene. When she struck the second match, the scarf caught at once and burned with a crimson flame; as it scorched her hands, she threw it on the doorstep.

Stepanida fell face down on the hard earth floor, trodden over the years by Polish squires, nobility, farm laborers, Petroc her husband, and her children and watched the fire as she choked on the stinking fumes. The flames from the kerchief had leapt across to the door at once, twisted up under the roof and licked along the wall logs; some clothing by the door was alight; the writhing red tongues of fire swirled and twined round amid the leaden gray and black smoke, reaching up for the resinous beams of the boiler-house roof. She was already suffocating from the smoke and pressed herself closer to the cool, earthen floor.

Somebody shouted threateningly from the passage; she couldn't make out what exactly, but the assaults on the door ceased. Then came the echoing report of a rifle shot and something struck the bin behind her. A bullet! Let them shoot, she was afraid of nothing now. Then came a shot from the other side, from the yard, and a second bullet clicked off the millstones and flew into the corner, which was already a mass of curling roaring flame. The boiler-house was blanketed in layers of black smoke which the busy tongues of flame could scarcely penetrate. Breathing was getting more difficult and she lay curled and motionless on the floor, legs drawn up. She knew she would soon be consumed when the roof fell in, or suffocated even sooner, if she hadn't been shot by then. But by now she was indifferent, she had done all she had to do and had no hope for any kind of salvation.

Outside they were shouting anxiously and fired several more shots through the wall, but inside the boiler-house she could hear almost nothing. The devouring fire was gaining strength; the corners and walls crackled, whistled and roared; the roof, the storage bins, domestic utensils - everything wooden, old and dry was ablaze. Unbearable waves of heat and sparks lapped round her; her head and feet were baking and the hair on her neck was already on fire. She buried her face in the sleeve of her quilted jacket and slowly, agonizingly suffocated. She didn't know which would happen sooner, the burning or the suffocation in the smoke, and which was better now. For a while her mind dimmed and she became oblivious; then she suddenly felt the cotton wadding on her back come apart as her jacket burned. It was the end now and she thought incongruously: why on earth hadn't anyone seen her with the bomb? One of the locals - a shepherd, man or woman - to remember the place and leave a sign marking the spot.

Meanwhile, breathing became impossible; she was finally suffocating as the hair glowed on her head and the jacket poured out its choking stench. The elbows with which she had despairingly covered her face were on fire. And again came the startling thought: maybe it was for the best that no one - good or bad - had seen her, and it would remain a mystery. It would make no difference to a decent person, but at least these here could go mad. Let them puzzle, search, rack their brains - where? And not sleep day or night, be frightened till their last breath.

This unexpected thought brought consolation with it and was the last flicker of her tortured mind before final oblivion.

She did not hear the polizei rushing out of the passage as the fire reached them, could not see the entire roof of the hut and boiler-house wrapped in flame with the wind sweeping it powerfully towards the cowsheds and grain shed, or the vast sea of fire raging across the whole farmstead, howling, crackling and roaring as it went; buildings, wood, trees near the walls, the fence, all were consumed in turn, burying the yard in ash and sparks.

Dense clouds of sparks and burning bundles of straw were borne in the smoky night sky across the gully to the pine woods and the high road with the bridge she hated across the swampy river Derevyanka.

Nobody tried to put out the fire and the farm burned without hindrance all night and smoldered all the next day. The polizei wouldn't let anyone near it and kept well away themselves - fearing the tremendous explosion of the bomb.

But the bomb was awaiting its hour.

Typography and binding design by Mark Frnka